THE BIDDEFORD SPIES

Jim Haskin

THE BIDDEFORD SPIES

A Novel by
Jim Haskin

Strategic Book Publishing and Rights Co.

Strategic Book Publishing & Rights Co., LLC
USA | Singapore
www.sbpra.com

For information about special discounts for bulk purchases, please contact Strategic Book Publishing and Rights Co. Special Sales, at bookorder@sbpra.net.

ISBN: 978-1-946540-48-5

Books by Jim Haskin

Jimmy and the Big Turtle

Jimmy and the Secret Letter

DEDICATION

To my wife Alice, our five daughters, five sons-in-law,
and thirteen grandchildren.

ACKNOWLEDGEMENTS

Advice and support of Las Plumas Writers' Group, King County, Washington was essential to completion of this novel. Special thanks are due Doris and Wayne Littlefield, Barbara Brown, Barbara Boyle, Skip Buchanan, Kathie Arcide, James Fletcher, Bill Oaks, Ariana Miklowitz, Margie Hussey, Gina Simpson, Lora Hein, Sue Meyers, Don Ulmer and the late Dave Bartholomew and June Goehler.

Many thanks to Doris Littlefield for editing this book.

Cover artwork provided by local artist, Tim Burns, Carnation, Washington.

This is a work of fiction. Names, characters, places, and incidents

Book One

Gestapo Headquarters, Nazi Germany

Biddeford-Saco, Maine

Boston, Massachusetts

New York City

PROLOGUE

Gestapo Headquarters, Nazi Germany

March 24, 1942

When Germany invaded Poland in 1939, Admiral Wilhelm Canaris commanded Abwehr, the group responsible for military intelligence. In 1941, not satisfied with Abwehr's progress in the United States, Hitler ordered a second group be formed to spy on Americans. Colonel Kurt Falk, a college professor and Hitler favorite, commanded "Covert Operations".

, The group trained at Gestapo Headquarters and Falk reported to SS Commander Heinrich Himmler. Hitler demanded the two agencies be separate with "Covert Operations" providing information on American convoys and troop movements. The Abwehr, with thousands of employees, would continue to be Germany's primary source of intelligence.

Not used to losing battles, the high command had concluded American convoys supplying the British made a difference in the "Battle of Britain." Hitler planned to break the stalemate on the Eastern front with a new campaign the middle of May 1942. Generals planning the campaign feared American convoys supplying Russia would change the balance of power. Short of operational tanks, Hitler delayed the attack until the middle of June. Loss of the Battleship Bismarck, March 1941, left the *Kriegsmarine* with only U-boats to sink American convoys.

Under constant pressure from Hitler, Abwehr planned "Operation Pastorius" to appease him. The plan had four agents landing on Long Island beaches in June 1942 and four agents landing on the Florida coast the same month. "Operation Pastorius" was a two-year plan funded with $172,000 in small bills, equal to several million in 2018. The agents were trained to terrorize America by destroying power plants, factories, airports, bus terminals, and New York City's water supply.

Colonel Falk, working with a Nazi sympathizer, developed plans to land agents at Biddeford, Maine, in April 1942 to gather information from the waterfront of New York City (NYC). Canaris was not informed of Falk's plan nor was Falk aware of Abwehr's plan to land agents in North Carolina the same week.

Falk took a sip of coffee before giving final instructions to the agents traveling to America and the *Kapitan* of U-boat 101 transporting them. "We have covered the details; are there any questions?"

Kapitan Schmidt replied, "The crew is anxious to sail, Colonel."

Falk looked at Otto Langer and Bernhard Wellenhofer. "Remember, gentlemen, if you're caught, you'll be tortured for information and shot as spies. Cyanide is less painful and has the same outcome. We've trained you for six months; I know you can do the job."

Team leader Langer replied, "NYC was my home for fourteen years; we're not going to fail if we use our training. If that's all, Herr Falk, we'll finish packing."

"You're excused."

In unison, Langer and Wellenhofer rose from their chairs to execute a perfect "Heil Hitler" with heels clicking before they left.

Kapitan Schmidt looked at Falk. "I know the mission is important or you wouldn't have asked for me. I'll be out of combat for a month. I prefer sinking convoys."

"I'd rather be home with my family readying to pick tulips, but the Fuehrer wants me here. Not all officers serving in the *Kriegsmarine* are dedicated party members, I chose you because of your loyalty to the party. If Langer is successful, you'll know when convoys sail and you can sink them."

"I am willing to attack convoys before they reach the middle of the Atlantic where they're difficult to locate and rough seas protect them. The closer U-boats are to enemy shores, the more successful we are. I've been sinking ships for two years, I know of what I speak."

"High command is aware of your effectiveness, and you'll be back in action in July."

"Yah, may I go now?"

"Good luck, *Kapitan*, Heil Hitler."

"Heil Hitler!"

With a fresh cup of coffee, Falk wondered why Hitler approved "Operation Pastorius." Eight agents with $172,000 to spend seemed ridiculous. His plan to land two agents in Biddeford, Maine, was a trial run to test the safe house concept developed by Brown, the Biddeford contact. If successful, they could use the site again. Personally, he thought the safe house was a good idea with some risk of detection.

After a phone call from Gestapo Commander Heinrich Himmler, Falk paced the floor. With the British still in the war, the Third Reich needed a decisive victory on the Eastern Front. Otherwise Germany would be fighting on two major fronts when allied forces invaded France. He knew it, the generals knew it, but Hitler had his own plans.

Minutes later, Himmler walked in. "Good morning, Colonel Falk. Normally I wouldn't barge in like this, but something has bothered me all morning."

"Good morning, Herr Himmler. You're a busy man. My time is your time."

"Let me be candid, what is your assessment of Operation Pastorius?"

"I'll be frank, but you may not like my answer."

"Speak out, man, there's nothing either one of us can do to stop it."

"It's overly ambitious, poorly planned, and an invitation for agents to defect. I'd say there's a ten percent chance the agents will accomplish any part of the plan."

"Thank you for being candid; your assessment is the same as mine. Buying $172,000 American dollars isn't cheap. The Reich is paying a premium in gold for every dollar purchased in the underground economy."

"Yah, but we have plenty of gold if the Reich decides to spend it."

"That's a different issue. What are the odds on your plan?"

"I could be prejudiced, maybe seventy percent. The plan you approved has two agents landing in Maine with a local contact and safe house. Their objective is the NYC waterfront where they'll gather information U-boats need to sink convoys. If all goes well, the plan could work. The downside is the Biddeford contact being discovered, or someone accidentally walking into the safe house. There's a chance Langer could be recognized by someone he worked with. He went to college in NYC and lived there for years working as a reporter. Each of these rated a ten to the downside, hence, a seventy percent success rate."

"I approved $8,000, is that enough?"

"Yah, that's enough to get established. To gather information, Wellenhofer needs a job working on the waterfront. Employment will provide an income and an easy source for intelligence gathering. Langer can work the restaurants and bars and send information. They'll be living near the docks in cheap rooming houses. Agents need to mix with the people, you can't have them living in fine hotels."

"Canaris thinks opposite."

"It seems so, but he could be right, only time will tell. We have effective agents in England providing valuable information, but they have been there for years. So far, we haven't been able to duplicate that effort in America. Hopefully, Langer can connect with Germans on our side to establish a network. If the plan works, we'll have information the rest of the year."

Himmler asked, "And if he can't connect?"

"There is Plan B that sends additional agents to Maine; there's no Plan C." Falk spread his hands. "We could land agents in Georgia or North Carolina, but the coast is heavily patrolled. So far, our U-boats are doing a good job intercepting convoys from South America. Having another U-boat off the southern coast could upset Doenitz's plan."

"I agree. You're relying solely on Brown to move the agents to NYC?"

"The alternative to Biddeford is landing tired agents with suitcases on Long Island, not knowing what faces them on the beach. The New York and Massachusetts coastlines are patrolled by destroyers, the Maine coastline isn't. No plan is without risk, but the safe house concept is the best one."

Hitler had great expectations for both plans, having ordered regular progress reports. Falk knew that was troubling Himmler.

"I'm not part of the establishment; do you want me to talk with the Fuehrer?"

"Nein, I'll cross that bridge when I come to it."

CHAPTER 1

Biddeford, Maine

Midnight – Thursday, April 9, 1942

As the clock struck midnight, *Kapitan* Schmidt, commanding German U-boat 101, signaled for a course correction, steering southwest to Biddeford, Maine. Moving slowly through choppy waters, the U-boat encountered rolling fog three kilometers from shore. The navigator signaled for a course correction heading south toward Fortune Rocks. At 1:00 a.m., one kilometer from the shore, U-boat 101 dropped anchor, waiting for a signal from the beach while two sailors dressed in black wet suits inflated a rubber raft. Two men dressed in overalls with dark jackets and stocking caps joined them on deck. A light from the beach penetrated the moving fog, sending three short flashes. *Kapitan* Schmidt said in English, "Good luck, Langer. It's time to make shore."

"Thank you for the voyage, *Kapitan*. We are ready."

Schmidt said to the sailors, "The man on the beach is Brown. Speak English only. If you're captured, use cyanide capsules or be tortured for information and shot as spies. Germany is depending on you."

The sailors responded, "Yes sir," and headed to the raft carrying three suitcases.

Langer and Bernhard made their way to the raft to join the sailors. Once they were secured, the U-boat submerged leaving them afloat. Clear of the U-boat, Bernhard manned an oar while a sailor corrected their course. Langer leaned over the side to throw up. U-boats traveled underwater in daylight and on the surface at night. Not used to rough seas, he still suffered from seasickness experienced on the trip. A sailor asked, "Are you all right, sir?"

"I'll feel better on land."

The sailor giving course corrections said, "I see a light from the beach, row to port."

It seemed forever before Langer saw a man's outline at the water's edge. He blinked the light again as the raft navigated choppy seas. Wearing boots, Brown pulled the raft to the beach. "Welcome, I'm Brown! You're the first Germans to set foot on American soil since the war began."

The sailors jumped into shallow water to stabilize the raft as Langer struggled to get over the side. A sailor went to his aid, placing a shoulder under his arm to assist him.

After a minute, Langer said, "Thank you, I'm all right now."

Brown shook his hand. "Many are seasick, Green, after crossing the Atlantic, I was. I'll carry two suitcases; Red can bring the other one." He turned addressing the sailors, "Heil Hitler, you may return to the submarine."

They responded in unison, "Heil Hitler."

One sailor said, "May God be with you."

On the return trip to the U-boat he remarked, "Brown used German. Doesn't he know the rules?"

His comrade shrugged. "He wanted to show his party loyalty. You said, 'May God be with you.' What's that about?"

"I want them to succeed, and so does God."

"I don't believe in God, but with or without him millions will be killed. I guess you can pray you're not one of them."

After loading the car, Langer asked, "How far is the safe house?"

"Ten minutes from here. There's no electricity or water, the house has been closed since fall. The bedrooms are upstairs where you'll find clean clothes, the kind typically worn in this part of the country. There are liverwurst sandwiches for tonight and food for two meals tomorrow." Brown hesitated. "Speak only English and don't leave the house during the day. No military time, the correct day is Friday, April 10th, 1942, and the correct time is 1:55 a.m. Eastern Standard Time. I'll be returning for the trip to Portland, Maine, at 2:00 a.m. Eastern Standard Time, Saturday morning. Set your watches accordingly. The extra day will give you proper rest for the trip to NYC."

Langer responded, "I agree, chances are we'll feel much better tomorrow than today."

Brown said, "There it is," as he followed a driveway to a stately two-story house painted white with green shutters. The secluded house sat on a small hill with a front porch and two steps. A chimney above the roofline interrupted straight exterior lines.

Bernhard said, "It's very plain. There's no architecture. All lines are straight."

Langer replied, "The early settlers were farmers. They cleared the land and built homes and barns with the lumber. Most early buildings were rectangular boxes with a pitched roof and fireplace."

Brown stopped the car a good distance from the house on new gravel. The ground in front of the car looked muddy. "Here we are! With any luck, you two will be drinking beer in NYC Saturday night."

Bernhard asked, "Is the beer good in America?"

"It's okay. Try Schlitz, Miller, or Budweiser, they're the best. The brew masters are still German, Americans can't make good beer." Turning to Langer, Brown said, "Making all these arrangements is expensive. Do you have my money, Green?"

"I was instructed to give you five hundred dollars. The second group will have more."

Brown said, "We don't want to be seen unloading the car. Grab the suitcases and I'll bring the food. You'll find candles and kerosene lanterns on the fireplace mantel. Burn the candles in the bag and clean the holders; don't use the lanterns."

Brown took Langer to the side, "You and I can talk while Red brings in the water. There are four gallons in the trunk." Brown handed Langer a sheet of paper. "There are two men in NYC that will help, but you need to contact them in person and pay for their service. One is good with a radio but doesn't have one. The man walks with crutches and he's located a radio he can buy with four hundred dollars. Your name is Green. His name is White. Give him a thousand dollars so he can buy the radio, the extra cash is a down payment on his service. The second man wants to be in the fight. He's an unemployed actor named Gray. Give him four hundred and you can use him when needed. Trust White with the code book and concentrate on your orders. There's no reason for Red to meet these men in the immediate future." He stopped to think. "That's it for now. I'll be back at two Saturday morning. Get some rest. You'll need it."

~ ~ ~

The house had an eerie feeling, cold and damp from the long winter. Langer shone the flashlight along the walls looking for the kitchen. He found a remodeled kitchen with a gas-fired oven and range. He twisted the lever mounted on the back wall that read "Gas" and lit the pilot light. Slowly he turned on the four burners to warm the kitchen. He reached into the bag for candles and handed two to Bernhard. "Get the candle holders from the mantel, it's time to eat."

Bernhard turned his flashlight to the fireplace mantel where he found two candle holders.

The bag of food had four liverwurst sandwiches and four bottles of beer. Langer took the first bite, exclaiming, "Yah, lots of mustard," chasing it down with a swig of beer.

When they finished eating, Langer said, "We'll take two gallons of water upstairs to wash. Grab a glass from the cupboard and bring the candles, time for some well-deserved sleep. So far, so good, everything has gone as planned."

~ ~ ~

Portland, Maine

Clarence Aldrich received a phone call Friday afternoon from the Stiles' family attorney. He wanted the house opened three weeks early with the utilities checked. His wife was planning a birthday party for their son. "I don't want to upset your schedule, Aldrich, but if you open the house this weekend we'll know everything is working. Keep this on the hush, it has to be a surprise, or I'll never hear the end of it."

"I can adjust my schedule. If I run into problems, I'll call."

Aldrich was employed as a caretaker for several homes in the Biddeford-Saco community, opening and closing them on a schedule and maintaining the properties during summer months. The Radke family watched over the Stiles' house during winter months and Rolf Radke had a key to the front door.

Aldrich called the Radke residence and spoke with David Radke who happened to be celebrating his twelfth birthday. "I would love to come to your party, David, but something unexpected came up. I'm having dinner with friends, their son is leaving for active duty, it will be close to nine when I get to Biddeford. If by chance, there's an extra piece of cake, I'll take it off your hands."

"I'm sure Mom will bake a chocolate cake, she always does."

"I have a tight schedule. Can you help on Saturday?"

"I sure can, tell me what needs to be done when I bring the cake."

"Sounds good, David, see you about nine."

~ ~ ~

Sleeping all day Friday, Langer and Bernhard woke hungry as the sun set behind the trees. Free from the nighttime rocking of the U-boat, both were feeling better. Langer lit a candle and went to the kitchen to prepare dinner while Bernhard rested on the couch.

As Aldrich pulled up the driveway, he noticed the front door was ajar with a glimmer of light shining through the crack. He looked at his watch, almost nine, David was on time. He fetched his suitcase from the back seat and headed to the house, expecting David to greet him. He opened the door to find a man standing in the front room.

Moving toward the man, he asked, "What are you doing here?"

Startled, the man stepped back swinging his arm toward the voice. The large flashlight struck Aldrich on the head, knocking him to the floor face down, bleeding profusely from the right temple.

Langer had food on the plates when he heard a voice followed by a loud thud. "Are you all right?"

"Yah, but I need you right now."

He headed to the front of the house. To his surprise, Bernhard was standing over a man face down on the floor in a pool of blood.

"What happened?"

"I got off the sofa to join you in the kitchen when I heard a man say, 'What are you doing here?'" He surprised me. I accidentally struck him with the flashlight. I didn't mean to hurt him."

Langer checked the body for a pulse. "He's dead!" He took his time getting up. "This changes our plans; we can't stay here waiting for Brown." Langer paused to think. "The man must have driven here, let's inspect the car."

A black Ford sedan was parked in the driveway. Other than a jacket and birthday present in the back seat, the car was empty. Bernhard turned toward the house to discover a boy walking in the front door. He ran toward the house, shouting, "There's a kid in the house."

A stunned Langer shouted, "Get the kid!" as he followed Bernhard.

When David Radke entered the house, he saw a figure lying on floor in the dim candlelight. After several steps, he realized it was Mr. Aldrich. "Oh my God!" he uttered.

He heard a man yell, "There's a kid in the house."

A second voice shouted, "Get the kid."

Instinctively, David ran to the hallway and jammed himself into the corner under the staircase. The hallway was pitch-black, but a crack in the door painted a narrow stream of light on the floor. *Please, God, make them go away.*

The hallway door flew open causing David to hold his breath, body crouched, motionless. Footsteps on the stairs above brought a temporary sigh of relief. A pause followed before a second set of footsteps pounded up the staircase; the man was taking stairs two at a time. A voice rang out, "Take the rooms on the right; I'll get the ones on the left. Find the kid and we'll teach him to mind his own business. Don't kill him up here; I want him next to the old man when we burn the house to destroy the evidence."

A frightened David heard their plans to kill him. *I was only bringing Mr. Aldrich a piece of cake and now they want to kill me.* His grandfather or Uncle Joe wouldn't save him; he hadn't been gone long enough for anyone to miss him. He sat motionless, biting his lower lip so hard he could taste the salty flavor of his own blood while sorting out his options. Tick, tick, tick went the seconds before he realized the value of time, every second counted.

The murderers would search downstairs if they didn't find him on the second floor. Screwed shut for the winter, the backdoor offered no escape, and the front yard had insufficient cover. Stumbling from the corner, David ran to the sewing room at the rear of the house. He ripped curtains from the window which failed to open despite his best efforts. *What to do?* Scanning the room, he smashed the glass and wooden dividers with a nearby stool.

Six feet to the ground looked like ten and there wasn't time to remove broken glass from the window frame. Fear gripped his senses; *I can't sprain an ankle jumping to the ground.* With shaking hands, David grabbed the seat cushion from a rocker and placed it on the windowsill. Sitting on the cushion he swung his legs to the outside before dropping to the ground. The fall seemed to take forever, but he hadn't broken a leg or sprained an ankle. Rising quickly, he headed for the trees bordering the property.

A man shouted, "He's downstairs, I heard a window break."

His partner replied, "The kid has a head start, we'll never catch him in the dark."

In the woods, David prayed, "Thank you, God, thank you so much." He turned left searching for the path home. The fear he felt minutes ago had been replaced with a sense of euphoria not previously felt in his young life. *This is my woods, try to catch me now.*

Running full speed with head down, he changed direction to avoid a large root and crashed headfirst into the trunk of a large maple tree. Only ten feet from the homeward path, David lay still on the ground with blood gushing from a cut forehead and broken nose.

After rushing down the stairs, Langer turned to Bernhard, "We have fifteen minutes to get out of here. Do as you're told, and we'll be all right."

"Yes sir, like you say."

"Gather anything of value, the mantel clock, paintings, silver set, and place them in the car... it must look like we robbed the house. I'll put the old man in the kitchen and open the gas burners. Take kerosene from the lanterns to soak the curtains. They'll make a fuse to ignite an explosion. We'll use the car to get to Boston; we can't wait for Brown. Get with it, the sooner we leave, the better."

Langer placed the body in front of the stove. He removed Aldrich's wallet, pocket change, rings, and watch before turning on the gas. Pausing, he made sure all bases were covered. In the front room, Bernhard had spread the curtains from the front room to the kitchen.

"Good work!" Langer took matches from his pocket to light the curtains. "That does it; let's hit the road."

On their way to the car, a fireball followed by a huge explosion startled the men. Unknown to them, the propane tank had been filled earlier in the week. Stunned by the magnitude of the blast, they watched flames consume the kitchen and rear of the house. Smoke, fire, and debris filled the surrounding air. Langer had succeeded in eliminating the evidence; most of the house would be destroyed before help arrived.

"Why did we take things from house and burn it down? I don't understand."

Langer patted his partner's shoulder. "When the police find the car, they'll think we robbed the house and abandoned the car when it broke down."

"The car is going to break down?"

"After I remove the oil plug and cross thread it; the car will stop when the engine runs out of oil. Tonight we sleep in the car. Remind me to wipe the car clean of fingerprints in the morning." When the car started, he remarked, "Look at the gas gauge, almost full."

Langer handed Bernhard Aldrich's wallet and personal things. "Count the money."

A minute later Bernhard replied, "There's forty-seven dollars."

"That will help before we start spending our own funds. If they fit, put his watch and ring on and split the money. You'll be living on your own for the first week, we can't be seen together. What's the height and weight on the driver's license?"

Bernhard used a flashlight to study the license. "It fits you, 5'8" and 160 pounds. He's sixty, but you could gray your hair and add glasses. The watch and ring are too small for me, they're more your size."

"The police will think the explosion destroyed him and everything else. Their only witness is the kid. He paused. "It won't take authorities long to figure out it wasn't someone in the community who burned the house."

Bernhard asked, "What does that mean for us?"

"If the Federal Bureau of Investigation (FBI) suspects they're dealing with spies, NYC will be on alert for weeks. If they make one of us, we're in trouble. Pray God will be with us, Bernhard, we need all the help we can get."

"It's my fault."

"What's done is done, there's no going back. Concentrate on the mission and staying out of sight; that will serve you well."

On the drive to Boston, Langer contemplated while his partner dozed off. Under normal circumstances his plan would work, the cops would be looking for burglars, and they would be free in NYC. *War changes everything, the FBI and NYPD (New York Police Department) will be relentless in their efforts to catch us. The car has to stay in Boston, and I have to follow my orders to terrorize NYC.*

Not familiar with the two-lane road, Langer drove with caution, pulling off the road to rest for several hours at the halfway point. He wanted to reach Boston before morning traffic, but not in the middle of the night. For miles, they were the only car on the road.

CHAPTER 2

Biddeford, Maine

Friday Night, April 10, 1942

The Radke family had lived in Biddeford, Maine, since 1880, the year four-year-old Rolf migrated with his parents from Busum, a small German fishing village on the North Sea. Like his father, young Rolf had saltwater in his veins and joined his dad on the lobster boat when he turned eight. He grew up speaking German at home and English in school. His father suffered a heart attack the year Rolf graduated from high school, leaving his son an old boat to support the family. The father passed away when Rolf was twenty, and his mother died a year later. At age twenty-two, Rolf married a high school sweetheart. Three years later, the couple was blessed with a son they named William Rolf Radke. Seven years passed before his wife died giving birth to a stillborn daughter.

Like his father, son Bill joined Rolf on the lobster boat at eight. He gave up fishing at sixteen to work at the local Ford dealership. A quick learner, he earned a mechanic's wage at nineteen.

Sylvia Radke met her husband in 1924 when the family car broke down in Biddeford. On vacation with her family, the car was towed to the Ford dealership where Bill worked. The tall, good-looking mechanic in blue coveralls needed an extra day for Portland to deliver a new clutch. She accepted his invitation for dinner that night. It was love at first sight for both of them. Her banker father didn't approve, but her mother said, 'If you don't follow your heart, you'll have reservations the rest of your life.'

The couple was married in Boston, witnessed by family and friends. They rented a home in Biddeford and welcomed their daughter a year later. Marilyn Agnes Radke was named after her two grandmothers. A son David was born in 1930.

When Rolf's cousin migrated in 1938, the family purchased a five-bedroom, two bath home to accommodate Joe Radke. With multiple incomes, the Radkes were considered to be upper middle-class, a distinction few Maine families achieved.

World War II separated many families, including the Radkes. The man who could fix anything, Bill Radke, went to work at the shipyard in Portland, Maine. Old machinery from the 1800s broke down daily, requiring the two millwrights to work six and seven days a week. Too tired to commute, Bill rented a room in Portland, spending few weekends with his family.

In Boston, Sylvia's sister, Clara, was caring for their bedridden mother. At Christmas time, Sylvia sent her daughter, Marilyn, to help her Aunt Clara care for Marilyn's grandmother.

~ ~ ~

Friday night, without his father and sister present, the Radke family celebrated David's twelfth birthday. His mother smiled. "I have a surprise; close your eyes, David." She left the kitchen to fetch a large chocolate cake with twelve candles.

Grandfather Rolf said, "You can open your eyes, son, after we sing Happy Birthday."

"Wow, chocolate cake!" David took a deep breath, blowing the candles out on the first try. "Papa gets the first slice, Mom the second, and then Uncle Joe. The bigger piece is for me. We haven't had chocolate cake since my last birthday."

David took an old white plate from the cupboard. "I'm going to take a piece to Mr. Aldrich."

His grandfather said, "If you wait till the dishes are done, I'll drive you there. It's getting dark and a black bear sighting was reported yesterday."

"If a bear shows up, he can have the cake."

Sylvia said, "He knows the path like the back of his hand. Be back in an hour, David."

"The dishes will be done in a few minutes, he can wait for me."

"Thanks, Papa, I'll take the path, but you can pick me up in an hour."

While David's grandfather and mother washed dishes, Joe went to the porch for a breath of air. Darkness had settled in to reveal a starless night. He had given David ten dollars for his birthday to buy a new baseball and glove. Suddenly the sky lit up followed by an explosion which looked to be coming from the Stiles' house where David had taken the cake.

David's mother and Rolf rushed to the porch.

"My God, David is there." She grabbed Joe, "Go find David and Mr. Aldrich, they're in trouble. I'll call the fire department."

Joe turned to Rolf, "Take the truck and I'll take the path. We'll probably get there at the same time, but we'll know if David is on the path."

Joe went to the kitchen for a flashlight and headed toward the fire. The Stiles' house was a quarter of a mile walk. A heavy smoker, he ran less than a block before slowing to a walk, breathing heavily. When he reached the end of the path, the house was engulfed in flames with sparks showering outbuildings at the rear of the property. Shaken by what was taking place, he didn't hear a muffled sound from the woods. After several deep breaths, Joe trotted across the lawn toward the front of the house as Rolf pulled up.

Joe said, "Bob filled the propane tank last week. It must have exploded—the rear of the house is gone." His voice shaking with emotion, he said, "David wasn't on the path. The outside water is on the back of the house, there's nothing we can do."

"I know," Rolf responded with tears in his eyes, "maybe David got out."

With sirens screaming, the volunteer fire truck came up the driveway with Chief Charlie Jones at the wheel. He quickly assessed the situation saying, "The others will be here in a minute. My job is to save whatever we can, meet me at the outbuildings to help with the hose." The chief steered the fire truck toward the back of house. As he drove off, a car came skidding to a halt with a neighbor that lived north of the fire.

Rolf said, "You and Ed can help Jones with the hose, I'll look for David."

After extinguishing the fires on the outbuildings, the three men turned to watch the walls of the house cave in.

Jones shook his head, "This is the worst fire I've seen in my thirty years of fighting fires. Propane is safe; I've never seen a tank explode."

Rolf walked the perimeter of the property for ten minutes yelling, "David, are you here? David, we can't find you. David! David, are you here?"

Hearing his name woke a bleeding David from a bad dream. He felt woozy looking at the burning house through blurred eyes. *This can't be a dream; my head hurts and there's something in my eyes.* Reaching for his eyes, he felt blood running down his face. He struggled to his feet to answer Rolf's call. David shouted, "Over here," before fainting.

Rolf ran to his aid, shouting, "David's alive; he's back in the trees." His grandson lay in a heap, his eyes rolled back in his head.

Chief Jones, a trained medic, said, "It could be a concussion. John will be here with the ambulance any minute. David needs to go to the Portland hospital. They have the equipment to treat head injuries."

They turned to see the ambulance approaching, followed by a volunteer fireman. By then, people were on the lawn wanting to help. The volunteer looked to Chief Jones who crossed his arms over his head, the sign to send them home.

John, the ambulance driver, asked, "Is anyone hurt?"

Jones replied, "David is out cold from a head injury and injured nose, he could have a concussion. Hold his head still while I apply bandages to stem the bleeding. From the look of his clothing, he could have fallen and skidded into a tree. What's this? Something must have scared him, he peed his pants." Jones stopped to think, "There's a good chance David was running from someone, he was clear of the fire."

Rolf agreed, "I think you're right, Charlie. He wouldn't be running out of control this far from the fire."

Jones said, "Go with the ambulance, Rolf, to watch over David. Joe and I will wait for Chief Dunsmore. The four of us can lift him on the stretcher, two on each side."

As the ambulance disappeared into the night, Police Chief Emmit Dunsmore pulled up. "That's a big house to burn in twenty minutes. Did the propane tank explode?"

Joe spoke slowly, "We celebrated David's birthday and he left after the party to take Aldrich a piece of birthday cake. I went to the porch for fresh air and saw the fireball followed by the explosion. By the time I got here, flames engulfed the house, and debris had started fires on the outbuildings."

Jones replied, "The place was blazing when I got here and the rear of the house had already burned. Rolf found David on the edge of the woods. From the looks of his clothing, he was running full speed when he hit his head. Something scared him, he peed his pants."

Chief Dunsmore took off his cap and scratched his bald head. "We can interview David tomorrow. Was Aldrich here? I don't see him."

Joe said, "Aldrich must have been expected or already here. David wouldn't be bringing cake to an empty house. You'll learn more tomorrow if there's a heavy fog to cool things down."

Dunsmore said, "I need help to mark off the area." He paused, "Please don't discuss this with anyone until the investigation is completed."

On his way back to the office, Chief Dunsmore sorted through information he had. *David was bringing Aldrich a piece of cake, but Aldrich and his car are gone. David was running from something or someone to bang his head that hard and pee his pants. I need his statement to determine what happened.*

Jones walked into Dunsmore's office and threw himself in a chair. "We both know time is of the essence, and our key witness is in a coma."

"I know, Charlie, but we need to talk with David before I call for help. The evidence is questionable."

"With all the cover-up, it's not a local yokel looking for booze money. Locals don't steal cars and burn houses. This is the worst thing that's happened on our watch; it makes me sick to my stomach. Do you have Aldrich's first name?"

"Everyone used his last name. You can't assume a cover-up until we talk with David. Maybe Aldrich didn't show and David was running from the explosion." Dunsmore speculated. "The Stiles' daughter gave me a letter regarding the house. It's in the file." He removed a document from the filing cabinet. "The name is Clarence Aldrich, and he lives at 104 Elm Street in Portland. Three years ago, he drove a 1937 black Ford sedan, License 60-467."

Jones replied, "The license might still be valid, but Portland has hundreds of black Ford sedans. The 1937/38 models look the same. Send the information to the State Patrol and the Portland police, we might get lucky." He took time to think. "I'm assuming Portland, but Boston is only ninety miles and a much larger city to hide in."

"I'll include the license plate with a maybe. On Saturday Boston has frequent trains to NYC, Portland has one. I'll call Aldrich, could be he's still in Portland."

The phone rang for a minute with no answer. "He's not home."

"And he's not here as promised. If I were you, Emmit, I'd call the FBI. We both know the young, well-trained detectives at the State Patrol have joined the military or the FBI. If we're looking for German spies, we can't expect any help from the State Patrol."

"Be serious, Charlie, German spies? You're overreacting to the story in the paper about German submarines reported by fishermen."

"Emmit, you and I could destroy more evidence than we find by stomping around in the fire debris. We can't let someone burn a historic house and get away with it. The FBI will be here at daybreak if spies are involved. If you're certain there are no German spies, save the call."

Dunsmore sat for a minute. "You always were a better detective than me, and you're right. Missing person, missing car, and a house destroyed by an exploding propane tank aren't a coincidence. I have the number for the FBI right here." He spoke with Agent Andrews at the Portland office. "The good news is they'll be here at daybreak."

"What's the bad news?"

"They want a guard posted at the site, and I'm scheduled to work tonight. I'll need a backup, and you're deputized. I'll get the sleeping bags while you're making a fresh pot of coffee."

After Jones left, Dunsmore called the police chief in Saco, the town across the river. The volunteer said Chief Robinson would be back on Monday afternoon.

~ ~ ~

At the hospital David was taken into X-ray while Sylvia and Rolf waited in the lobby for David's father. Bill walked in before the doctor arrived.

"The police brought me here. Why is David in emergency?"

Rolf replied, "It's a long story. We're not sure if others are involved, or David was careless running through the trees. Nevertheless, he has a bloody nose with cuts on his forehead, could be a concussion. The X-rays will help with the diagnosis."

A shaken Bill asked, "How can I be a good father when I work sixty hours a week? If I'd been there to celebrate his birthday, this wouldn't have happened."

"It's not your fault, Bill. We can't be with David every minute."

Rolf said, "Sit down, son, and relax, I'll fetch some coffee."

When Rolf returned with coffee, Bill sat up, with shoulders squared. "Thanks, Dad, I haven't had a cup of coffee this good in months."

"Don't be thanking me, the coffee is free."

A doctor entered the waiting room and stepped up to Bill. "I'm Dr. Phillips, David's specialist. He has a concussion, and I'm sorry to say, a broken nose. Dr. Reed will do his best to straighten it, but his nose might have a bump on it, like a boxer. I've arranged a room for you and Mrs. Radke, courtesy of the hospital. There are blankets in the lounge and Mr. Radke senior can sleep on the sofa."

Bill asked, "When can we see David?"

"Not tonight. If all goes well, tomorrow morning between eleven and twelve. The young heal quickly with proper rest."

Sylvia said, "Thank you so much, Dr. Phillips, you've thought of everything."

Phillips replied, "You'll find clean underclothes in the room provided by the volunteers. You can use the facilities at will." His eyes twinkled as he added, "The room comes with a 'Do Not Disturb' sign."

CHAPTER 3

Boston, Massachusetts

Saturday, April 11, 1942

The German agents approached Boston with several challenges to overcome. Langer selected a residential street with a vacant lot several miles from the train station to park the car. A box in the trunk had the necessary tools: a wrench, gloves, coveralls and a piece of cardboard. After donning coveralls, he used the cardboard to slide under the car. With the drain plug removed, several quarts of oil flowed into the sewer before he jammed a rag into the hole to stop the flow. Langer rubbed the oil plug in some loose debris and cross threaded it back into the pan. Using a clean rag, he wiped oil from the grate and worked his way out from under the car. "If the engine doesn't quit on the way to the train station, we'll let it run until it does."

"I have learned much from you the last two days." Bernhard reached down to help his accomplice to his feet. "I'm sorry about the old man, he surprised me."

"Forget that; what's done is done, there's no going back. Wipe the car down while I change clothes and clean up."

When the engine started to knock, Langer pulled over on a hill overlooking the train station. He turned to Bernhard. "Let's review your plan. Tell me step by step what is going to happen this morning and next week."

"I'm going to walk to the train station and purchase a round-trip ticket on the morning train to New York City. After breakfast in the train station I will pick up a newspaper to read on the train. In New York, I will board the C subway train to the Bronx and get off at 68th Street station." He stopped to catch his breath.

Langer smiled. "So far, so good partner."

"I need to rent a room for less than ten dollars a week. Pay in advance, but only a week. Take Sunday to study subway and bus routes. Take different trains each day when I go out. Never eat in same restaurant a second time and go to a different theater every day. Monday take subway to Brooklyn and spend the day. Tuesday take subway to Manhattan and spend the day. Go to a different place each day and keep myself busy. Always leave the room at seven and never return before seven. If anyone is watching, they must believe I'm working. Sunday, take the subway to Yankee Stadium and wait where they sell tickets. You will meet me there before the one o'clock game with the Boston Red Sox."

Langer slapped his partner on the back. "If you stick to our plan, I'll see you Sunday. Think positive thoughts, but more important, think like the police and act like a spy."

~ ~ ~

Saturday morning found David sleeping peacefully with normal breathing. The doctor assured Rolf and David's parents he would wake before noon with a good appetite. "Youngsters recover faster than adults."

Sylvia replied, "Thank you so much for the room. My husband slept through the alarm."

"I'll convey your gratitude to the administration."

"If I can get a hotel room, we'll spend the night there. If I can't, we'll spend the night in your room." She kissed Bill goodbye.

~ ~ ~

At the Stiles' property, the FBI agents arrived at daybreak. Agents Andrews and Warner introduced themselves. Warner asked, "Before we enter the site, is there anything in particular we're searching for?"

Dunsmore responded, "The boy in the Portland hospital, David Radke, had a piece of birthday cake on a white dinner plate for the caretaker, Clarence Aldrich. We've searched the path and lawn for the plate and didn't find it. If the plate is in the ashes, we'll know David entered the house before it burned. The back of the house was destroyed by the blast, but the dinner plate could be in front of the house."

Andrews answered, "You two have been here all night; get some breakfast, we'll see you later."

Andrews suggested as he threw pants to his partner, "Let's don our gear and go in from the porch. I'll go left, and you go right. We're investigating a historic wooden house ignited by propane gas."

Warner replied, "The house was accessible to the ocean. It could be spies bedding down for the night."

Warner saw the remains of a sofa with smoldering cushions. Rummaging through the debris, he felt something solid that turned out to be a dinner plate with a sticky substance. He held it up for his partner to see. "This could be the plate we're looking for."

Andrews replied, "If that's the plate, David was in the house." He continued to sort through debris finding remains of a kerosene lantern he placed in the evidence bag. Minutes later, he found pieces of glass and a second lantern in the same area. "I've got two kerosene lanterns from the center of the room. They're broken, but they didn't explode."

Warner said, "They should be next to the fireplace unless someone emptied them to ignite a fire. I read someplace that curtains were soaked in kerosene to make a fuse."

"It must have been a training manual; I read the same thing. They soaked the curtains, opened the gas burners, and lit the curtains on way out the door. Germans probably have the same manual."

"We've found what we were looking for; let's check the rear of the house."

Andrews said, "I would put a dead body in the kitchen."

Warner agreed saying, "You start left, I'll start right, and we'll meet in the middle."

After an hour of searching through charred remains, Andrews said, "I've found remnants of a denture, looks like the lower jaw."

Warner exclaimed, "That's almost as good as a body, a dentist can identify the owner. Bingo! Here's part of a belt. What's left of the leather has a western look."

Andrews said, "We'll ask Chief Dunsmore to cordon off the area if the boss wants experts to finish the job. We have enough evidence to prove someone was in the kitchen when the propane tank exploded. The boy can fill in the details."

~ ~ ~

At eleven, Dunsmore and Jones returned. "Did you find anything of interest?"

Warner said, "I found a dinner plate, with a gooey substance, next to a sofa, and Andrews found two kerosene lanterns in the middle of the room. Lanterns and plate survived, they're made to resist heat. Unfortunately, we found a denture and part of a belt in the kitchen. They'll be sent to the lab for analysis."

"David is awake and hungry. After breakfast they'll clean him up and we can talk with him after one."

Andrews said, "You made the right call, Chief, what happened here wasn't the work of an amateur. The evidence points to a professional, but we'll need more to confirm it. Other than the items mentioned, we found nothing else of interest. We're heading to Portland to start our report, see you at the hospital at one."

CHAPTER 4

Portland Hospital

Saturday, April 11, 1942

Warner and Andrews met Dunsmore and Jones at the hospital. They found David on the edge of the bed chatting with his mother and doctor. Andrews asked, "Is this a good time for David to spend a few minutes with us?"

The doctor smiled. "He feels better now than last night. I think he can handle it."

David said, "It's okay with me."

"I'm FBI Agent Andrews."

"And I'm Agent Warner. Take all the time you need, David, but please start at the beginning."

After several deep breaths, David said, "Yesterday was my twelfth birthday and Mom made a chocolate cake. I wanted Mr. Aldrich to have a piece, and I left after dinner while Mom was doing the dishes. It was getting dark, and the path was the quickest way there. When I got to the house, Mr. Aldrich's car was in the driveway and the door was open. When I walked in, a man shouted, "A kid just went in the house!" Then another man yelled, "Get the kid!" The voices sounded harsh, like they wanted to hurt me. Mr. Aldrich lay face down on the floor in a puddle of blood." David paused to take a deep breath.

Warner said, "Take your time, we're in no hurry."

David continued, "I was so scared, I peed my pants." He hesitated; admitting you pissed your pants was embarrassing. "When I was small, Mr. Aldrich played Hide and Go Seek with me and his grandson Russell. We would hide under the staircase, that's where I went."

Warner asked, "What happened to the plate and cake?"

"It wasn't with me under the stairs, I don't know. The men were in the house in seconds and went upstairs. The one who seemed to be the boss said, "Don't kill the kid upstairs; I want him next to the old man when we burn the house." Seconds passed before I figured it out; if they found me, I was dead." He paused to wipe his eyes and spit into a tissue. "Excuse me, I can't blow my nose, it hurts too much."

His mother consoled her son. "We know, David, it wasn't bad manners. You can continue if you want."

Almost sobbing, he said, "Please catch those men. Mr. Aldrich was like a grandpa to me, I'm going to miss him."

Agent Warner said, "We'll do our best, David, we'll do our best."

"The only way out of the house was the front door, but there's no place to hide on the lawn. Mr. Aldrich used long screws on the back door to fasten it shut for the winter. I ran to the sewing room in the back, but the window wouldn't open. I grabbed a footstool and smashed the glass. I couldn't dive out the window or sit on the broken glass to jump, so I took the cushion from the rocker to sit on while I got my legs through the window. I closed my eyes and jumped on the broken glass. My hands were cut, but I got up and ran to the woods. I heard a man shout, "He's downstairs, I heard a window break." The other man said, "The kid has a head start, we'll never catch him in the dark. Let's get out of here."

"In the trees, I changed course toward the path home, and from what they tell me, I hit a tree headfirst. When I woke up, someone was calling my name. The next thing I remember is my mother holding my hand in the hospital. It seems like a bad dream and I'll wake up with Mr. Aldrich standing there, saying, 'God has given us another day, David; let us make the most of it.' I pray he's with God; Mr. Aldrich was a good man."

Agent Andrews and the others took handkerchiefs from their pockets to wipe their eyes, remaining silent for a minute. "I'm sorry for your loss, David; we all share in the grief. Your concern for a good friend will strengthen our resolve to catch these men. I need to clarify a couple of things. We found a white plate at the front of the house. We also found part of a western belt with a large buckle and some carving on the leather."

"I've seen that belt many times. Mr. Aldrich wore it with a pair of western pants."

Andrews gently continued. "Think back, David, was the front door or the door jamb damaged in any way, had it been forced open?"

"The door was open when I got there, it wasn't damaged."

Warner made a sketch. "If this is the front door, was Mr. Aldrich facing the front or the rear of the house?"

"The rear, he was facing the kitchen."

"You said it sounded like the men's voices came from the car. How far was the car from the house?"

"It was parked at the end of the driveway, maybe one hundred feet."

Warner looked to the others. "It's early in the year to open a summer home and Mr. Aldrich had missed your birthday party. What was his reason to come Friday night?"

"Mr. Aldrich called Friday afternoon and said he couldn't come to my birthday party. He mentioned a tight schedule and needed my help on Saturday. The Stiles' house was scheduled to be opened the first week of May. I think he wanted to start the old mower and clean up the lawn. We had trouble with the mower last year when we cut the grass in October." David stopped for a moment, "I think Mr. Aldrich thought it was me in the house when he walked in. Papa has a key. He wouldn't leave the door open. The fields around the house are full of raccoons and skunks."

Warner asked, "Did you see what the men were doing at the car?"

"I didn't see them when I walked across the lawn. It was getting dark—they must have been on the other side of the car."

"*Mainahs* don't pronounce R's; did the *killahs* sound like locals?"

"I don't think they're from here, the men didn't have an accent."

Andrews said, "Thank you, David, you've been most helpful. I'm asking you not to discuss this with your neighbors or classmates while we're investigating the fire. We know the killers can't identify you, and I want to keep it that way. If someone presses you for information, tell them the FBI will keep the community informed and change the conversation. Can you handle that?"

"I'll do whatever you ask if it helps catch those men."

"Good! We'll get to work and you can go back to sleep."

Dunsmore, Jones and the agents stopped at the coffee shop.

Jones spoke first, "I'm sure Aldrich surprised the killers. If that's the case, how did they get into the house without a key? David said the rear door was screwed shut and there were no signs of forced entry to the front door or door jamb."

Dunsmore speculated, "Maybe someone else provided a key. Some of our summer residents leave a key at my office. Some leave keys with long-time residents they've known for years. The Radke family had a key to the Stiles' house. The evidence points to someone other than Aldrich opening the door."

Warner said, "The elitists in the agency tend to discount local law enforcement. You fellas would have figured it out on your own without help. We do, however, have more assets at our disposal to solve the case. You find the house key while we find the car. My gut tells me the car is in Boston and the criminals are in NYC. He paused to gather his thoughts. "Let's shake hands and get to work. David's grief for the loss of his mentor broke my heart."

Dunsmore replied, "I think you speak for all of us."

~ ~ ~

Saturday Afternoon, NYC

Langer decided to seek a room in Brooklyn's Bayridge neighborhood. Bayridge had a substantial Norwegian population, his mother was Norwegian and he grew up speaking the language. He knocked on the door of a large house with a sign: Room for Rent.

A plump Norwegian woman answered his knock.

"I need a room for a couple of nights, can you accommodate me?"

The woman frowned at his request.

He smiled, asking, "Do you speak Norski?"

"Oh, of course… welcome; you can stay as long as you want. Temporary rent is two dollars a night, eleven if you decide to stay a week. There are two rooms sharing a bath, you'll like it."

"Is the room on the first floor? I have a bad knee."

"It's at the end of the hall on the right. You look tired. This is a quiet neighborhood; you can catch up on your sleep."

"You're very observant, Mrs…"

"Christensen, you can call me Astrid."

"Remarkable, my name is Arnold Christensen. You can call me Arnie."

"Come on in, Arnie, I'll show you the room."

After he paid for the room, Astrid said, "If you'd like, you can join Thor and me for breakfast Sunday morning; we would like to hear about your mother."

"I would love to, but I plan to go to an early church service and meet with a friend in Manhattan. I haven't been in NYC for years."

"You can go to the Lutheran Church with us; they have an eight o'clock service."

"Thank you, Astrid, but I'm Catholic. Is there a Catholic church nearby?"

"Three blocks from here. Turn right when you leave, walk two blocks, turn right, you can't miss it."

Langer took her hand, "Thank you for your hospitality, you remind me of my mother. Like you said, now is a good time to catch up on my sleep."

~ ~ ~

Bernhard thought the train station in Boston looked similar to the one in Berlin. Two large boards had departures and arrivals. After picking the next train to NYC, he approached the ticket window with a churning stomach. *Calm down, you can do this.* The ticket agent rudely demanded, "State your destination."

He wasn't ready for the harsh attitude. "New York."

"New York's a big state, where in New York?"

"NYC, please, train one eleven. I'll carry my luggage if that's possible?"

"Round trip is nine dollars. You can board with two pieces of luggage fifteen minutes before the train leaves."

Bernhard handed the man ten dollars. As he reached for the change, he asked, "What track does it use?"

"Check the Departure Board."

After a breakfast of oatmeal and raisins with milk, Bernhard's stomach settled down. He managed to sleep on the trip, waking when the train braked at Grand Central Station. Without asking for help, he found the subway to the Bronx. He boarded with his suitcase, ignored by everyone except one man. "Keep the luggage to yourself, buddy."

Bernhard exited the train station to find a bustling residential neighborhood of two story brick homes with shops and markets on every corner. The contrast between the big buildings of Manhattan that he saw in pictures and where he was standing surprised him. NYC looked similar to Berlin, very crowded with everyone ignoring one another while tending to business.

Looking around, something struck him. *Where are the posters, pictures of Roosevelt, and party flags? All I see are American flags, what do these people believe in?* It would take time to understand Americans.

Born in Hamburg, Germany, in 1907, Bernhard had experienced only chaos in his life. The Great War, the Weimar inflation that followed, and the lack of jobs had haunted him at every turn. Not married, he finally found hope and opportunity after joining the Nazi Party in 1933. Fluent in English, he ended up in Covert Operations a year ago, teaming with an older agent who attended college in America and worked for a New York newspaper. They roomed together for months speaking only English in the room.

Needing a place to stay, Bernhard checked the addresses he had circled in the want ads. Not willing to ask for directions, he walked east. Three blocks passed before he spotted a large wooden structure with a Room for Rent sign. The dilapidated porch slanted toward the steps bare of paint. He used the door knocker and waited several minutes. A disheveled man opened the door. "What do you want?"

"I need a room, please."

"What's your name?"

"Martin Tweitmeyer."

"Do you have ten dollars, tweetie?"

"I have money, but only nine dollars, please."

The man stopped to think, he was out of bourbon and it was late. "Okay, you can have the room for nine, tweetie."

"May I see it, please, and the bathroom?"

"You better take it; it's getting late to be looking for a room."

"Like you say, I'm sure it will do."

"Come in, the room is the second one on the right. The bathroom is across the hall, you share it with three other guys. You needn't worry; they're all outstanding citizens with good references."

"Like you say, I'll go to the room."

Bernhard opened the door to the stench of tobacco smoke. A nonsmoker, he couldn't get used to the odor. He removed a pack of matches from his pocket and lit several to change the smell. The double bed had a threadbare spread covering a worn-out blanket. A dresser with a missing lower drawer supported a lamp and two ashtrays. A broken chair in front of the window hid the lower half of a dirty shade. "There's no towel in the room."

"You'll get one when I get the nine dollars."

Bernhard handed the man a ten-dollar bill.

"I haven't change, tweetie."

Tired of being insulted, Bernhard placed his hand on the man's arm, gripping it firmly. "You'll have it before I leave, won't you?" He applied pressure.

Surprised at his strength, the man stuttered, "Shu-sure, friend, I'll have your dollar."

Bernhard grabbed the towel from his arm. "I thought you were an honest man."

CHAPTER 5

Biddeford, Maine

Sunday, April 12, 1942

The coffee hour at the Biddeford Lutheran church attracted a noisy crowd Sunday morning. Everyone wanted to know what the other person knew about Friday night's fire? Those who witnessed the blaze were thoroughly questioned by friends. Chief Dunsmore wanted to leave but couldn't get to the door. A female friend, showing some anger, responded to his denials saying, "I've known you for years, Emmit, you know how to speak the truth. Saturday you promised to inform the community and you've said nothing."

"Patience, my dear, there's no substitute for patience. The department has sought help from the State Patrol and they asked me not to comment until all the facts are known. We'll meet tomorrow morning and, with their permission, release a statement in the afternoon."

Another man said, "Jack Tough said he saw a black car coming and going from the direction of the Stiles' place. He said a car passed him right after the explosion."

The comment piqued Dunsmore's interest. *Jack Tough saw a car leaving the scene? One car means the intruders walked or were driven to the site and used Aldrich's car to escape.* "If you'll excuse me, I'm going home to have breakfast."

~ ~ ~

Jones phoned Dunsmore. "Good afternoon, Emmit. Have you heard the rumor about Jack Tough seeing a car?"

"I have, and I'm headed that way."

"Pick me up. I can't get away from this case."

As he got in the car, Jones related, "The guy I heard it from said Jack saw a car coming and going, not two cars."

A limping Jack Tough answered Dunsmore's knock. "Welcome to my humble abode. There must be something important going on to get a visit from you two. What have I done to upset the hypocrites this time?"

Dunsmore said, "Friendly visit, Jack, we need your help. Rumor has it you saw cars on the road Friday night."

"I was walking my dog as the sun went down, or maybe the dog was walking me. Neither one of us can walk very far, but we got down to the mailbox. A black car going toward the Stiles' place honked the horn. Not many cars this time of year and I figured it must be Aldrich, he does that sometimes. On the way back I saw the fireball, followed by an explosion. As I was watching the fire, a dark car coming from that direction passed me at a pretty good speed with the lights on. I'm not sure if it was the same car, no honk this time. The fire truck went by before I got to my cabin and lots of other cars, including the ambulance."

Dunsmore asked, "You're sure there was only one car from the direction of the fire?"

"Like I said, there was one car going north, twenty minutes later one car coming south. The car looked black, but it could have been any dark color. I know nothing about cars, never owned one."

Jones said, "You've been a great help clarifying the number of cars. If your knees won't support you, come to town and live at the parish house for the elderly."

"You and Emmit are good men, Charlie, I can talk to you. Live in town, no thanks. I would rather light my hair on fire and beat it out with a hammer than live with hypocrites."

Dunsmore said, "Hypocrites are flawed people just like the three of us."

"My time is near; when God is ready, I'll be gone."

Jones said, "I thought you were an atheist."

"I fought in the first war, oldest private in the battalion. From personal experience, there are no atheists in the trenches. All the privates, corporals, sergeants, and officers are praying that the next incoming shell doesn't have their name on it."

Dunsmore asked, "You lied about your age?"

"Yeah, said I was thirty-five. The recruiting sergeant winked, and the doctor laughed, but they took me. If you guys happen to be passing by, take a quick look-see."

"I know we can't change your mind so we'll look in on you. The friend you had breakfast with on Saturdays, is he around to help?"

"That fellow is a writer, the book is finished. He wanted stories from my days as a guide. The story about my tussle with the black bear is the best part of the book. The bear wrecked my right knee and left shoulder. That's why it's a good yarn, the bear is dead and I'm telling the story." Tough coughed to clear his throat. "I liked Aldrich, he was a decent fellow. He'd bring me donuts and hot coffee from Portland. When you catch those guys, you can hang them from the oak tree in front of my cabin."

Dunsmore chuckled. "You've been reading too many Westerns, Jack. Criminals in Biddeford get tried by the hypocrites, but it's a fair trial."

Concerned, Jones said, "You've limited mobility, Jack. What about food and medical care?"

"Willie Snyder's son picks up things I need from the store. The hypocrites can't take my property; I have money for taxes. That writer fellow gave me two hundred dollars for my stories, and I still have money from trapping in the winter. I have food in the root cellar, and a deer will wander across the property to provide fresh meat. Don't worry about me starving, God will provide, he always has."

Dunsmore said, "If you recall something that might help with the investigation, please contact me or Chief Jones."

"Like I said, check on me if you're passing by."

On the way back to town, Dunsmore said, "I'll call the Stiles' daughter when we get back. The guys who did this were driven to the house by an accomplice; we're looking for three men." He looked to Jones. "You arrived at the scene shortly after the explosion, did you pass a car?"

"I've been racking my brain, and I can't be sure. It's a big truck with the siren blaring on a narrow road. There are several spots where a car could pull over."

"I thought you'd have mentioned a car if you'd seen one."

Back at the office, the phone rang shortly after Jones left. "Good afternoon, Chief Dunsmore speaking."

"Good afternoon, my name is John Hornbrook; I'm the Stiles' family attorney."

"Do you have information regarding the investigation, Mr. Hornbrook?"

"Not really, but there is something you should know. My wife planned a birthday party at the Stiles' home for our son the first

Saturday in May. Aldrich was early to open the house at my request. I doubt he shared this with anyone else. Ms. Stiles hadn't been informed; I planned to call this week to invite her to the party."

"I wondered why Aldrich was early, there's still snow on the ground." Dunsmore paused. "Don't beat yourself up over the timing. Opening the house early is normal; many residents open their homes before the season, depending on the weather or a special occasion."

"That's what I would tell a friend, but it still hurts. The community has lost a good man."

~ ~ ~

Andrews was reviewing the evidence when Dunsmore called. "Your boss said you were in Boston to check out a car. I thought you might be at the office."

"Yeah, sitting here reviewing the evidence a second time. Do you have something?"

"There's an old guy who lives on the exit road from the Stiles' house. He was walking his dog and saw a black car going north that honked the horn. He said Aldrich honked on occasion. Twenty minutes later, after the explosion, a car passed him going south. He thought the car was black but couldn't identify the model. He was certain there weren't two cars going south after the explosion. Neither Jones or the ambulance driver saw the car."

"Good work, Chief, put that in your report. The Boston Police picked up a 1937 black Ford sedan with two large paintings in the back seat. I'm headed to the pound to talk with the mechanic and check out the car. The only thing missing from the scene is the key."

"It may take time, but I'll find it. I called the Stiles' daughter and she's mailing an extra key for comparison. She took Aldrich's death really hard. We need to wrap this up quickly, so the loved ones can have closure."

"There's a good chance German spies, working with a local contact, are loose on the East Coast. The director has assigned Warner and me to the case. You'll have our full support."

~ ~ ~

Andrews arrived at the city pound accompanied by a Boston police officer. The mechanic had the trunk and doors open. He said, "When they found the car, there were drops of oil leaking from the oil pan. I put the car on the hoist to check the oil plug, it was cross threaded. I've repaired the damage and added oil, the car should start."

Andrews said, "Let me check the contents before starting the car."

The trunk revealed the mantel clock, knife set, silver set, and a jewelry box. There were two original paintings in the back seat. The jewelry box contained several pairs of diamond earrings and a gold chain with a large cross. The other items were costume jewelry with little street value. *The earrings and gold chain are easy to pawn, why leave them behind?* When they finished checking the contents, Andrews said, "Let's see if the car runs."

The mechanic had a master key and the car started with a slight knock that disappeared as oil circulated through the engine. He commented, "Whoever did this wanted you to think they robbed a house and abandoned the car when the engine broke down."

Andrews replied, "A good cover-up, but the car breaking down doesn't match with the facts. Hold the car as evidence and make a list of stolen goods."

"I'm familiar with the protocol. Stolen goods are sent to the property section."

On the drive to the hotel, Andrews speculated, *The Stiles' daughter will be happy to have her jewelry box back. Burglars would have pocketed the earrings and gold chain and left the costume jewelry. A spy couldn't risk pawning jewelry.*

CHAPTER 6

New York City

Sunday, April 12, 1942

Sunday morning found Bernhard attending the nine o'clock service at the Lutheran church. Arriving early, he spent fifteen minutes praying for Germany and his mission.

After church, he had breakfast in a small restaurant where he sat with a second cup of coffee to read the paper. The Japanese occupied most of the islands in the Pacific Theater, putting the Americans back on their heels. After breakfast, he spent the rest of the day reading about NYC while riding the subway system and bus routes.

~ ~ ~

After sleeping fourteen hours, Langer woke early to launch a busy day. While eating breakfast, he looked at the list Brown had furnished. The list provided addresses and apartment numbers but no names. The radio operator lived in a tenement district in the Bronx, known to be a tough neighborhood. Sunday was probably the best day to knock on his door. The trip would take an hour using public transportation, but the route left him two blocks short of the address.

He bought a New York Post newspaper to read on the journey. After reading the lead stories dealing with the war he turned to the local section he had covered for years when he worked for the Post. The lead story was written by Joe Murphy, a colleague he despised. *The no talent son-of-a-bitch Murphy had replaced him.* The bus stopping brought him back to reality. *Living in the past is a dead-end street. Stay alert and get off at the next stop.* The street had several abandoned cars stripped to the frame, ground floor windows were broken on several buildings and trash lay everywhere. Looking ahead, there was a group of teenagers standing on the corner. The bus hadn't left yet, and the driver shouted, "You're not safe here, friend, get back on the bus."

"Thanks for your concern, but the man I'm seeing needs my help."

"Have it your way. Good luck, you'll need it."

Langer took a deep breath; the address was in the middle of the next block. He walked toward the boys confident they were no match for a man trained in martial arts. As he neared the group of six, the leader stepped out saying, "This is our street, man, and no one passes without paying his dues." He took out a large switchblade knife to emphasize his point.

"I'm a social worker. The man I'm helping lives in the next block. Would you please walk with me for protection?"

The leader looked at the group shaking his head. "This dude wants us to protect him from bad guys, like the gang that's waiting for him in the next block. That's not our turf, man, but to get there you need to pay the toll."

Another youth stepped forward. "The toll is twenty bucks, man; you're not getting outta here if you don't pay the toll."

Langer glared at the teens. "If you don't get out of my way, I'm going to kick your ass. Use that knife, and I'll cut your balls off with it."

The younger members looked scared, and the two that challenged him looked at one another waiting for the other to speak. The leader said, "We don't want to cut you up, man, give us the money and you can go."

"I'm counting to ten and if you're not out of my way we'll see who the better man is. One, two, three, four, five, six, seven, eight, nine, and ten." Langer had his hand in his coat pocket and took out a set of brass knuckles he put on his left hand. "Now it's a fair fight," he said, waving his hand for the leaders to step forward.

The leader knew he might be overmatched but needed to save face. He charged Langer, brandishing the knife. Langer thought... *this kid has no training*. He bent low and moved to his right swinging out his left leg to upend his attacker. The youth cut his left arm with the knife as he fell awkwardly on his side. Langer moved quickly striking him at the base of the skull with brass knuckles leaving the boy unconscious. He sprang to his feet shouting, "Who's next?" to an empty corner. The group scattered to avoid him. The confrontation lasted less than a minute before he became boss of the corner. He left his attacker on the ground.

Langer searched the surrounding area before continuing his walk. The man lived in a basement apartment on a side street. Following instructions Brown gave him, he knocked three times and waited thirty seconds before knocking twice more. He heard a shuffling sound followed by the release of the dead bolt. The door swung open revealing a disheveled bearded man on crutches.

"Sunday is the best day to be in the neighborhood; I was expecting you."

"I met six of your neighbors on the corner."

"The young gangs roam the streets during the day. You must have kicked the shit out of the leader and the others ran."

"That's what happened."

"The young teens come out in the daytime; the older gangs rule the streets at night. They both know I haven't any money so I come and go as I please."

"Brown said you want to join the fight."

"That's right, the Bolsheviks killed my parents in 1918; I hate those bastards. My radio quit last week so I'm off the air at present. I can get a new one for four hundred dollars, with no questions asked."

To communicate, I'm Green, you're White. I have a thousand dollars for you and the code book."

"Good. Here are a dozen addressed envelopes you can use. Mail the information to me, there's no reason to come here again. Meet me at the Rathskellar at one o'clock Sunday morning, and I'll bring you up-to-date. I don't attract attention using a cab, but you might."

"I like the Rathskellar on Saturday nights, but wandering the streets after midnight won't work. The Sandwich Shoppe off-Broadway is busy on Saturdays. Come after eleven, I'll be there early to reserve a table."

"I understand you need to come and go without attracting attention. The Sandwich Shoppe at eleven will be fine."

"Should I use the same route back to the bus?"

"It's the shortest way."

"I have ten minutes to catch it, see you on Saturday."

Langer checked both ways when he reached the street. The gang had left. As he walked briskly toward the bus stop, glancing over his shoulder he noted three youths in hot pursuit. Halfway there, a NYPD patrol car turned the corner and stopped. The patrol car waited as he started running to catch the bus. Satisfied of his intentions, the officers headed toward the boys who'd been following him. He skidded to a halt as the bus pulled up.

The other contact lived near the Brooklyn Bridge in a middle-class neighborhood Langer had written about in 1934. Wanting to protect his identity, he put on a baseball cap, mustache, and sunglasses. The building had a speaker system to announce callers and a buzzer to open the door. The apartment was on the second floor at the rear of the building. The man was standing in the hallway when he exited the elevator.

"I thought you'd be here Sunday. Come in and have a cup of coffee and a donut, they're fresh this morning."

Langer entered a clean living room with tasteful furnishings, similar to the apartment he had in Manhattan. "No proper names, please. I'm Green and you're Gray."

"Good disguise, I wouldn't recognize you if we met on the street. I've lived here for ten years—share the place with my ex. You can afford to be divorced in the city, but you can't afford to move out on your own. We've been divorced for three years—she has boyfriends, I have girlfriends, no problems. We get along better now than when we were married. I'm auditioning for a new role. My ex has a small part in an off-Broadway play."

"What you'll be doing has risk, can you handle that?"

"The Russians and the Jews are the scum of the earth. If it takes sinking American convoys to beat the Russians, I'm a player." After a short silence, he said, "Germany has to find a way to bring the war to America."

"If you're caught, you'll be executed; if I'm caught, I'll use a cyanide capsule. I'm trained to avoid detection; the risk is higher for you with no training."

"I read military novels; they're realistic in defining disguises and stealth tactics. I also can play an Englishman or Negro with appropriate dress. The risk is high, but so is the reward. Germany needs to cut the supply lines to win the war." Gray smiled. "I graduated from Columbia in 1921."

"From what I've heard, Columbia is a good school. The Reich appreciates your help; men with your courage can change history. I need you for the next two or three weeks. Our discussion leads me to believe you'll have no trouble with your assignment. Can I phone you?"

"Call in the evening when my ex is working. Do you have money for me?"

"I have five hundred dollars. I'll give you one hundred dollars a week for the next five weeks. If we're still operational after that, there'll be more." He handed Gray the money." Give me your phone number. I'll call Tuesday night with instructions. Most of the work will be between eight and midnight, the same hours your ex-wife works."

"Will I be a full-time player the next two weeks?"

"Most certainly, but I need to arrange the schedule. Your first assignment is Wednesday night. It's important you observe what happens and leave with the crowd when they rush the door. Disappear into the night with a prearranged plan to get home in the shortest time possible. Regardless of circumstances, ignore me. If you recognize me and I walk west when I leave the building, you'll walk east. I'll call Tuesday night with a time and place. Wear casual clothing or dress as a merchant seaman."

"That's it?"

"That's it, nothing more. You're in training, bide your time. Thanks for the coffee, you'll hear from me."

The ride back gave Langer time to think. *We started with three players and now there are five. Brown must have spent time in NYC and met both men at a party rally before the war. The radio man seems reliable with a good reason to take part in the war. The Bolsheviks killed his parents. Somehow, he escaped and came to America. The self-addressed envelopes go to a PO Box, no risk of detection.*

His instructions to use the devices sooner rather than later presented a challenge along with the added risk of being caught. Gray seemed perfect for the part to place the devices—master of disguise, acting skills, and knowledge of the city. He'll get his wish to bring the war to America.

Langer decided to have dinner at an Italian restaurant to help gain back the seven pounds he lost crossing the Atlantic. The skirmish in the Bronx had tested his endurance. He enjoyed a large order of spaghetti and meatballs with cake for dessert.

CHAPTER 7

Biddeford, Maine

Monday, April 13, 1942

Chief Jones organized the evidence to tell a story others could understand. Monday morning, he went to Dunsmore's office.

"Good morning, Emmit. If you have time, this could be important."

Dunsmore smiled. "I have time. You mentioned German spies the other day, so tell me how you arrived at that conclusion."

"Consider this. The killers had been in the house all day Friday when Aldrich showed up. He surprised one of them when he walked in expecting to see David. The killer had access to a heavy object, maybe a large flashlight that he swung in self-defense. If someone surprises you from the rear, you react. Regardless of how it happened, killing Aldrich wasn't part of the plan. Needing a new plan, the killers went to the car to see what they could use when David unexpectedly showed up. With their cover blown, the Germans reacted to the situation."

"What you're saying makes sense."

"The normal protocol has spies working in pairs. The one in charge used the oldest scheme in the playbook. I haven't read a German 'whodunit' book, but burning the house is common in American novels. Jack Tough is a reliable witness—one car going north, one car coming south. The evidence points to a twenty-five-minute timeline and one dark car.

"I think the spies were met by a local contact that drove them to the Stiles' house to rest early Friday morning. The plan was to drive them to Portland Saturday morning to catch an early train to Boston. Killing Aldrich changed everything. With David Radke on the loose, they couldn't wait for Saturday and took Aldrich's car to Boston. We know one thing for certain; someone had a key to the Stiles' house. We'll find the accomplice when we find the key."

"You're assuming he still has the key. There's no lock for a key, the house is gone."

"You're right, the key is incriminating evidence; it's probably at the bottom of Biddeford Bay. Why didn't I think of that?"

Dunsmore replied, "Agent Warner hadn't considered it." He paused to think, "The risk of being caught goes up if they arrived Thursday night."

"A German U-boat travels underwater in daylight and on the surface at night. On a U-boat sleeping is done in shifts. The noise, diesel smell, and constant rocking at night make for a strenuous two-week trip. It's well known that fatigue leads to poor decision making. The risk goes down with proper rest. The man making decisions Friday night wasn't tired, he probably slept all day Friday in a comfortable bed."

"I think you're onto something. If you're planning a network of spies, you need a safe house to care for them. A day's rest after a long voyage would be part of the plan. The Stiles' house was perfect, well off the main road and closed for winter. The contact we're looking for has local knowledge. He might have known Aldrich with access to his schedule."

Jones added, "Spies would need a shower, shave, some food and clean American clothes. I'm sure they're headed to NYC as we talk."

"We need to catch the contact, that's what Warner meant when he said to find the key. There are two German families with boats, the Radkes and the Klingers. Billy Klinger had his appendix removed Friday afternoon and his parents were at the Medical Center. Both families were close to Aldrich. David expected Aldrich to be at the Stiles' home, he didn't have Rolf's key. I'm not sure if the Klingers had a key."

~ ~ ~

At the Portland office of the FBI, agent Warner was discussing the case with his superior. After presenting the evidence, Special Agent Hurley concurred, "I agree with you, the caretaker and boy disrupted a plan to put spies on the East Coast. I've contacted Special Agent Pennoyer in NYC, the spies are probably there. Our job is to find the Biddeford contact. I'll prepare a Press Release for Chief Dunsmore, placing the blame on a ring of burglars robbing summer homes before the season. With stolen goods showing up in three states, the FBI has been asked to help with the case."

Warner cautioned, "Dunsmore needs to announce something before he's accused of a cover-up."

"Dunsmore can handle his end until he calls for help. Please convey to him the need to limit the story to burglars. We don't want Biddeford folks thinking spies are amongst them." Hurley paused. "The records are sketchy but check with INS (Immigration and Naturalization Service) for Germans migrating or applying for visas in the last six years. Also check with Columbia University and City College of New York for

German students. There's a possibility that one of them spent time in the states."

~ ~ ~

Hans Klinger left Fritz with the cleanup and headed home for a fresh bandage to cover the scrape on the back of his hand. He also needed some tender loving care to help heal the loss of his close friend, Aldrich.

Many times, after dinner together, he and Aldrich would sip brandy and smoke their pipes while commiserating over the news. Aldrich had been a good listener with carefully crafted answers to Hans's rants about President Roosevelt's lend-lease program to help the British fight Germany. In his heart he knew Aldrich had been right, but the British were bombing his relatives and childhood friends. *Why does life have to be so complicated? War isn't like baseball where one roots for one team, not both.*

Heidi greeted him at the door with open arms. "Did you have a good catch?"

"We got a good start, but the nets fouled up and we lost an hour. I need a bandage for my hand." He held up his right hand for her to see.

After sympathizing over his hand, she said, "Chief Dunsmore called and wants to talk with you."

~ ~ ~

Dunsmore asked, "Is Fritz joining us? I need to chat with him too."

Hans answered quickly, "The nets fouled up. Fritz stayed at the docks to mend them. You need nets to fish, and tomorrow we need to make up lost time."

"You and Aldrich were close. Do you have a key to the Stiles' house?"

"I had a key, but it went to the bottom weeks ago. Fritz had the keys when the chain broke at the dock. We found most of them, but not the key to the Stiles' house. I wanted to tell Aldrich Saturday." He used his sleeve to wipe at his eyes. "I really miss him."

"I'm sorry you lost a close friend; the community shares in your grief. The key you had is at the bottom of the bay?"

"We got cold after a few minutes searching the shallows. The key went out with the tide."

"For the record, did anyone else have a key?"

"I do not know."

"I forgot to ask, how is Billy doing?"

Heidi smiled. "He's coming home tomorrow. An appendectomy is no big deal at age twelve. Billy is chafing at the bit to talk with David, but so is everybody else in Biddeford."

On the way to the Radke home, Dunsmore thought, *another twist to the missing key.*

Rolf and Joe were home; the truck sat in the driveway.

Joe opened the door. "It's Chief Dunsmore, Rolf. Come on in, Emmit."

"Thanks, Joe, I won't be staying long." Rolf was sitting at the table reading the paper.

"Rolf, do you have a key to the Stiles' house?"

"I *had* a key to the Stiles' house; I lost it three weeks ago."

Two lost keys, seems impossible, ran through Emmit's mind. "Do you have any idea where the key was lost?"

"My second set of keys had the Stiles' key. I lost the keys in early March, but they showed up in the church lost and found the next week. The Stiles' key was missing from the ring. I planned to tell Aldrich the next time I saw him."

"Do you know who found your keys?"

"No idea. Pastor Alex said ushers place stuff in the lost and found most Sundays."

"I used to usher—don't remember any keys, but gloves and bibles were common. Do you remember who ushered that Sunday?"

"Probably Don, we went to the early service."

Dunsmore said, "He has breakfast with his prayer group Wednesday mornings; I'll catch him at the diner." Heading out, he turned at the door with one more question. "Had you marked the keys to identify them?"

"The key was marked with an S. I used red boat paint."

"If either of you remember something else, please give me a call."

On the return trip, Dunsmore decided to stop at Willie Snyder's cabin. Willie greeted him as he stepped from the car. "Hi, Chief, this must be about Friday's fire."

"Good guess. How well did you know Aldrich?"

"I really didn't know him. Might have seen him on occasion, but we seldom talked. I mind my own business; spend most of my time here or fishing for striped bass. I rely on Wolf to do my shopping and drive me if I have someplace to go."

"You and Aldrich weren't close?"

"I'm not close to anyone, ask Wolf."

"Does he still work at Maine Outdoors?"

"Yes, he still works there and lives in Westport. Comes by twice a month to do shopping for Tough and me. Jack fills his head with stories from his past, Wolf loves it. Now *there* are two guys who are close. Did you know Tough's real name is John Murphy? Jack said his father beat him when he came home drunk. He changed his name to Jack Tough when he ran away from home. He got the name from a Western, but it didn't work. The older guys would beat him up saying, "You're not that tough."

Dunsmore chuckled. "Maine stories never cease to amaze me." He looked Willie in the eyes. "Do you have a boat or access to one?"

"Can't afford a boat, Chief, I use my waders when I fish," Willie said sarcastically.

"I need to ask the routine questions, no offense please."

"No offense taken. I want those killers caught and hanged from that oak tree."

"Jack Tough has first bid on the hanging tree—you must share the same Westerns."

"Wolf buys books at the secondhand store in Brunswick. Most of them are Westerns that we share."

"If you think of anything else that might help, let me know."

Dunsmore drove slowly on the way back to the office. *I find two men who had a key, but both lost it. Jack saw a car Friday night, but he can't identify the car. I've found nothing solid—every piece of evidence is a maybe.*

~ ~ ~

New York City – Monday

Unbeknownst to Langer, Abwehr's plan to land German agents on the coast of North Carolina on Sunday, April 12, failed. German U-boat 85 delivering the agents was sunk Saturday at midnight with no survivors. Several recovered bodies were wearing civilian clothes and carrying wallets with U.S. currency, draft cards and local driver's licenses. Not wanting to frighten the public, the FBI did not release the story.

Monday morning Langer put his luggage into two lockers at the subway station and spent the rest of the day checking out former party members with no success. Most had moved and the one he talked to suggested he defect. After dinner, a dejected Langer picked up his luggage planning to check into an old hotel in Bayridge. Before transferring to the last bus, he used a phone booth to add a mustache and glasses, with a baseball cap. The booth had a needed Bayridge phone book fastened with a chain that he cut with wire cutters. At the hotel, he paid one week's rent on a second floor room without checking it out. The room smelled of smoke and contained a single bed, old knee-hole dresser, a cloudy mirror on the wall, a lamp, and small closet.

A dirty bathroom across the hall was shared with two other tenants. Tattered towels sat on the worn-out bedspread covering a blanket with holes. He spent the balance of the day matching addresses with a map of Bayridge, circling likely spots to place the devices. After dinner, he walked the neighborhood to check street lighting looking for obstacles that could interfere with his plans.

Bayridge had a "dime a dance" hall six blocks from the hotel where women danced for ten cents a dance. Before the war, middle-aged men frequented the dance hall looking for companionship. The war had added soldiers, sailors, marines, and merchant seamen to the clientele. The way the women dressed intrigued Langer. The younger hostesses wore short skirts with blouses made of cotton or silk. They would be easy targets for darts the device fires. He needed only ten minutes to check the floor plan and exits. The main entrance was a three-foot-wide door, perfect to create panic when frightened dancers rush the exit to escape.

~ ~ ~

Satisfied with his plan, Langer stopped at a pay phone to call Gray.

"I have instructions for Wednesday night, no notes please." He proceeded to give the address and time for Gray to be there. "Stay on the bar side and be prepared to leave around nine. Get there early to set up your escape route. Do you have any questions?"

"Not that I can think of. This sounds exciting; I'm finally involved in the war."

"You won't be for long if they question you. After the explosion, get out and get away. Meet me in Manhattan, Thursday, for lunch at McCormick's Pub after one. You're meeting Mr. Green for lunch."

~ ~ ~

Bernhard spent the day in Manhattan, marveling at the neon lights that 42nd Street offered. On his second walk past the theaters, several aggressive panhandlers swore at him when he declined to give them money. All these bums begging on every corner, it doesn't make sense. In Germany they would be rounded up and sent to work camps. I wonder if the government allows them to reproduce more degenerates.

Where are the posters and party flags? Have Americans any sense of pride in their leader? What are these people proud of? On the other hand, maybe they have a sense of independence that I've never experienced. I need to learn more about them to be effective. He returned to his room to make notes and plan the next day.

CHAPTER 8

Biddeford, Maine

Wednesday, April 15, 1942

Wednesday morning found Dunsmore drinking coffee with Jones.

Saco Police Chief Robinson walked in. "Good morning, Charlie, good morning, Emmit."

"Good morning, Ralph. I need to call Hurley; the FBI is releasing a false narrative to hold the reporters at bay. Have a cup of coffee; this will only take five minutes."

When Dunsmore returned, Robinson said, "I talked to the mayor this morning. He's praying the contact doesn't live in Saco."

"I'll give you the rest of the story while you finish your coffee."

"The press release sounds like a cover-up. Can you tell me what's really going on?"

"I can share it with *you*, not the mayor, not your wife and family, or your mistress, if you have one."

"I get the gist, Emmit. I'll investigate the German families living in Saco and those living north of Saco. You can investigate Biddeford and south. If the guy's smart, he's thrown the key away. My plan would have spies landing at Fortune Rocks and using the Stiles' house to rest before going to Boston to catch a train to NYC."

Dunsmore said, "We reached the same conclusion. There's a rumor that Civilian Defense is planning a shore watch with a large tower at the Biddeford Pool. The artillery battery will be staffed by June; the Germans won't be using any location close to Biddeford."

Robinson agreed. "Sounds like a good plan. After the investigation we can work with Civilian Defense to help with the shore watch. Good meetin', the mayor will be pleased; he wants to be part of this."

~ ~ ~

Early Wednesday morning, U-boat 101 approached Biddeford Bay to receive a transmission from the local contact. Wind and waves caused static on the radio. The message was delivered in code:

> Agents discovered by safe house caretaker.
> Caretaker killed, house burned.
> Agents fled Friday night in caretaker's car.
> No contact since drop.
> Cancel 2nd team plans till further notice.
> Message received?
> Message received. Will stay till Monday for next contact.

~ ~ ~

Portland, Maine

Sylvia Radke said, "Thank you for the good care you and the other nurses gave my son, our family is deeply appreciative."

"David is a good patient who tries to care for himself. He's very mature for twelve."

David felt embarrassed by all the fuss, he wanted to go home.

"Thank you, Nurse Flynn."

"You're welcome, David, have a safe trip home. Remember, young man, no sports or hard work for the next ten days."

On the bus David fell asleep while his mother read the paper. The FBI had a press release placing blame on a ring of burglars robbing homes before the season. She looked at her sleeping son, thinking, *This episode has wiped out part of our savings and put my son at risk. I hope they find the killers before they do any more harm.*

NYC – Wednesday Evening

Langer stepped back from the mirror to check his appearance after gluing on a false mustache. He selected the old man's disguise to place the first device. *This will work.*

Sitting down to finish a beer, he checked his plan. The first of its kind, the disc-shaped device fit in the right pocket of his raincoat with the trigger mechanism in the left pocket. The apparatus contained one hundred metal darts powered by an inflammable gas. It could be triggered on the way out the door. He recalled the first time it was fired.

~ ~ ~

Germany

SS Agent Gunther Engel spent 1931–32 teaching the German language at Columbia University in NYC. Assigned to Covert Operations, he was training Gestapo agents for espionage work in America. Behind bulletproof glass, technicians were demonstrating a new device that fired a pattern of tiny darts followed by a flash fire.

Engel explained, "The trigger to fire the device will be effective up to fifty feet. The bottom of the disc has two strips of tape to fasten it to a horizontal surface. The disc needs to be secured to be effective. If you forget that, you'll only be scaring people."

Langer assured Engel, "I won't forget."

Engel added, "The darts will harm anything within a twenty-foot radius while spreading less of the area with a flash fire. With the chaos caused by fire, you won't be noticed leaving the building. Remember to get out of the building before people stampede the door. On a small scale, this is the ultimate terror weapon. You have room for six, use them wisely."

"Can they accidentally explode?"

"The trigger requires a battery, install it the day you fire the device. There's a safety after the trigger is armed. It could take two weeks to get to NYC, so I would use them in the next thirty days, sooner if possible. I have no idea how long the gas will be effective."

"Yah, I plan to use them in restaurants, subway stations, and automats."

"NYC has many dance halls. Dancing exposes the female body, ideal for this device. The heavier side of the device has the darts, the lighter side the gas. The darts will fire in an arc from the weighted side."

"If I use two devices at the same time, will I need to reset the trigger?"

"I'm not sure, hadn't considered it. If the trigger doesn't explode both, it will only take seconds to reset it. Placed on a dance hall table, the device will do maximum damage to the dancers. Under those conditions, two would be very effective. Think of it, exploding gas and two hundred darts in a twenty-foot radius." Engel stopped to think. "The devices are numbered on the protective strips, use lowest numbers first. Pocket the protective strips. Authorities needn't know the number built."

Langer gloated, "Germany has the best engineers in the world, no one can stop the Third Reich."

"If the plan works, I'll join you at Yankee Stadium on the Fourth of July. I wanted to be the first agent in America, but they said no. Stay alive and we'll make a good team."

~ ~ ~

Langer flipped up the collar on his raincoat before leaving the hotel. The "dime a dance" hall was a short walk in the crisp April air. Unlike other dance halls, the dancers were singles, no couples or neighborhood groups.

Langer purchased a beer from a pretty girl with a tray full of bottles. He stood on the edge of the dance floor to observe couples jitterbugging to a swing tune he hadn't heard before. A middle-aged woman on a small stage viewed the dancers as she changed records. The next song played was a popular Glenn Miller tune, *Chattanooga Choo Choo*. The jitterbug looked difficult with the couples dancing apart with arms extended. A slow tune followed, allowing the men to hold the girls close, far more rewarding. He fidgeted with the disc in his coat pocket while checking the trigger device in the other pocket. He looked toward the bar; *Gray's disguise must be clever.* Langer couldn't spot him.

A hostess approached with a suggestive smile. "Would you like to dance? There's a slow tune next."

"No thank you, I'll watch for a few more minutes to get into the swing of things."

The woman on the stage announced, "This is the last song before the break, it's the one you've all been waiting for, Tommy Dorsey's *Manhattan Serenade*."

As the couples joined together on the dance floor, the woman on the stage dimmed the lights. Langer sat at an empty table bordering the dance floor. Most patrons were dancing with no interest in an old man. He wiped the table surface dry with a handkerchief before removing the protective strips covering the tape. He looked both ways while securing the device to the tabletop. The woman changing records was talking to a couple on the dance floor as he moved toward the front door. Ten feet from the door, he removed the trigger, unlocked the safety and pushed the button. The small explosion followed by screaming women didn't stop him as he walked out the door into the cool air of spring. A sense of guilt gripped his conscience; he had injured or maimed innocent strangers, but wait, some were soldiers. Feelings didn't slow his walk, but people running to the scene did. A man grabbed him by the arm. "What happened in the dance hall?"

He shook his head. "I don't know."

"Oh my God, that girl is on fire. She needs help!"

Langer turned to see the man running while pulling off his coat to smother the flames. Those anxious to get out rushed the three-foot door, trampling the unfortunate that had fallen. He flattened himself against a building to stay clear of onlookers. As the crowd swelled, people slowed allowing him to move along the building past the swarm. Sweat soaked his clothing and two blocks from the hotel he stopped to throw up.

The death of the caretaker Friday night hadn't bothered Langer. Bernhard had killed the man accidentally. If the device killed people, the story will be covered on the front page of the morning papers. Retching up dinner had taken a toll. Feeling wobbly in the knees, he took deep breaths to recover. He hadn't seen Gray and wondered if he got out.

A man across the street, walking a dog, came to his aid. "What happened at the dancehall? Are you all right?"

What to answer? "The flu... I think it's the flu. I live in the next block, better not get close."

"Okay, you'll probably get home on your own."

"Yes, thank you." Back on his feet, he walked on shaky legs to the hotel, removing the disguise before staggering into the lobby. *Thank God*, the clerk was sleeping. Sitting on the bed, he started to convulse, shivers came and went while stripping off his wet clothes. He left his underwear on the bed and wrapped a worn-out bath towel around his waist for the trip to the bathroom. His heart sank as shivers came more frequently as he reached for the locked door.

"Please hurry, I need to use the bathroom."

"So do I, you'll have to wait your turn. Use the toilet on the first floor."

A dejected Langer walked back to his room. Almost dry, he dressed in a flannel shirt and pants before getting into bed. The smelly blanket warmed his body as nausea returned, but there was nothing left to retch up. Exhausted from the ordeal, he fell asleep. He dreamt of the burning girl needing help while he walked away. *Help me, why won't you help me?*

He rushed to the bathroom to retch. The man in the next room asked, "Do you want me to call a doctor?"

"No! I think it's the flu, rest will cure me."

"I need to use the toilet." He handed Langer a towel and bucket. "Clean up your mess."

~ ~ ~

Hands of several male dancers were hit by darts, but the darts couldn't penetrate their winter clothes. Female dancers wearing cotton and silk dresses or short-sleeved blouses took direct hits from the darts. Those near the table were scorched by the flash fire burning their hair and clothing. Dancers across the room rushed to help, but others ran to the door, knocking down several girls trying to escape with burning hair or clothing. Screaming girls rolled on the floor to extinguish the flames, driving the darts further into their bodies as they rolled.

An Army medic, Star Booth, witnessed the explosion from the other side of the dance floor. He removed his jacket to help smother flames while shouting for a first-aid kit. A naval firefighter did the same. The sailor noticed the crying women had multiple wounds on their arms and bodies where little darts had embedded their skin. He yelled, "Get the women off the floor, they need to be standing."

The woman from the stage brought a first-aid kit with a container of Vaseline. "Put this on the burns until the ambulance gets here. I'll help the girls at the front door."

The sailor said to the girl he'd been dancing with, "You have fingernails, pull those darts from their arms and apply iodine."

When the police showed up, Booth said, "Close the entrance until the ambulance arrives. We don't need thrill seekers unless they have medical training."

The officer replied, "Who the hell are you to be giving orders?"

"I'm an Army medic. There is no fire, tell those outside to come inside for proper treatment. The others are witnesses needed for questioning. Don't argue with me, do your job."

The officer talked with his partner before they left the building to handle the crowd.

Two ambulances arrived with sirens blaring, carrying nurses and a doctor. After talking with the medic, the doctor helped the burn victims first while nurses assisted others. More ambulances and police cars arrived simultaneously, followed by Captain Frank Moran of the NYPD, who would take charge.

After the wounded were treated, Moran asked, "What happened here?"

Booth replied, "I saw the explosion."

"Tell me what you witnessed."

"I don't know what went on before the explosion. I was on the other side of the floor with a good view when something exploded with a flash fire, like gas burning. The girls surrounding the area were hit by darts, and several suffered burns from the flash fire. The guys had burns and cuts on their hands, but their clothing stopped the darts. Chaos followed and the sailor and I were able to help the wounded."

A police officer handed a disc to Moran. "I found this on the floor, it's still warm."

"Thank you, officer." He placed the device in a canvas bag.

"The woman working the stage stepped forward. "I'm Ellen Jensen, I own this place. Keeping an eye on the dance floor is my job. An old guy, wearing a raincoat with the collar turned up, sat down at the table where the explosion happened. I was busy scolding a soldier for putting his hand on a girl's butt. When I looked back at the table, the guy was gone. Then came the explosion and all hell broke out."

The waitress that sold Langer a beer said, "He bought a beer off the tray when he came in and stood near the dance floor."

"Could you identify him?"

"He had glasses and a cap... his collar was turned up, I didn't get a good look at his face. He seemed old, I'm not sure."

A second hostess said, "I asked him if he wanted to dance. He said no, and the next time I saw him he was near the door. He pointed something in his hand at the table. I don't know how old he is, but he's not young."

The officer that found the disc said, "There's a sticky substance on the table, and the device had something sticky on it."

The sailor said, "That thing is military. Only the military puts darts and gas in a tin can to hurt people."

Booth remarked, "When it exploded, the man was gone."

His comment started a murmur in the group. Detective Moran held up his hands. "Please, I need silence, unless someone else has something to add." He waited a minute while the crowd looked at one another.

"If you witnessed the man setting the device, please talk with Officer Powell so he can take your statement. Before you leave, the rest of you, give your name, address and phone number to the officers at the other table. Do not discuss what happened here tonight with family, friends, your priest, pastor or rabbi. The investigation could take several weeks. During that time silence is your best defense from the perpetrators. We can't protect all of you. In short, keep your mouth shut and go about your business. Hold up your hand if we've missed something."

The hall remained silent.

In the squad car, Captain Moran called the FBI and the NYPD lieutenant in charge of cases involving explosives. "Get here as soon as possible. This guy could do considerable damage if we don't catch him."

CHAPTER 9

Bayridge

Wednesday Night, April 15, 1942

Dressed as a merchant seaman, Gray arrived before nine. He purchased five tickets to dance and selected an older hostess to dance with. It was the first slow tune of the set and she snuggled up close. After a second dance, he excused himself and headed to the restroom.

Ten minutes later, he purchased a beer and watched couples jitterbug. At fifteen minutes past nine, the woman changing records announced, "This is the last song before intermission. It's the one you've all been waiting for, Tommy Dorsey's *Manhattan Serenade*."

Couples filled the dance floor. Across the room he noted an older man move to a table next to the dance floor, sit for a short time then walk toward the door. The waitress asked, "Do you need a refill?" Gray shook his head no as something exploded on the other side of the dance floor with a flash fire. The dancers closest to the explosion were screaming. Girls were beating on their heads to extinguish burning hair.

Gray froze for several seconds before heading to the door, ignoring two injured girls lying on the floor. Outside the hall, a soldier was using his jacket to extinguish flames on burning heads. Some girls were tearing open their blouses and dresses to remove something he couldn't see. The spectacle of women tearing off their clothing and exposing their breasts excited him. He wanted to fondle them but left the scene before help arrived.

After boarding a bus for the ride home, he realized his wishes were coming true. Langer had him there to witness the devastation, on-the-job training. The man at the table before the explosion could have been Langer. German scientists had developed a fantastic weapon that caused grave damage and created chaos while the one activating it walks out the door. *He's training me to place more devices, maybe this week.*

Armed with these devices, he alone could bring the war to America. *Dance halls are a good venue, but not for me. The NYPD will have every dance hall under surveillance, they're not dumb.*

The thought of girls tearing off their clothes excited him beyond his wildest dreams. *Wait a minute, all dance halls aren't in white neighborhoods, Harlem has a slew of them. Tomorrow I'll dress as a Negro and check out the Harlem neighborhood. Many clubs are bases for prostitutes who wear as little as possible, and the other girls wear sexy clothing.*

The NYPD cares little about Harlem; there'll be no cops at the door. The thought of helping a big busted Negro babe take little darts from her breasts aroused him. He hoped his ex-wife would satisfy his lust as she occasionally did between affairs.

At the apartment his ex-wife stood waiting in the front room. "We need to talk, Harvey."

"I thought you were working."

"I developed a headache thinking of my state of affairs." She handed him an old-fashioned. "Sit down and enjoy the cocktail, this will take awhile."

Harvey sat down knowing the conversation would be about him and their arrangement. "I got a part-time gig today that pays me enough to handle my share of the expenses for the next three months. I should be working full-time by next month."

"It's more than that, Harvey. I'm ready to move on with my life and you're not part of the plan. I have a contract for the next year doing soap commercials; I can pay my own way. No man will be interested in me if you're part of the scene. I want you out of here by the end of the month, no argument, please, I want to part as friends."

"I only have a part-time job with no place to live."

"Use your spare time to find a roommate; living with me isn't an option. Sleep on the couch or set up the cot. I'm going to bed."

"You're not being fair, I need more time."

"Most would say three years is a reasonable time frame to start over. I'm paying the bills and providing occasional sex; you have the better of two worlds. Neither of us will change under current arrangements. It's time to move on, Harvey."

He sipped his drink thinking of the situation. *She won't change her mind this time, we're through.* Setting up the cot, he started to develop a headache. Better to deal with this tomorrow.

Readying for bed, he started to think of popular Harlem clubs where he could place the devices. He needed to succeed to receive the balance of the money Green offered. The High Heel Club would be a perfect spot, plenty of action and a lot of bare legs and scanty tops. I'll go there tomorrow night as a black reporter to case the joint. If the dancers act the same as the ones in Bayridge, he could move to a table on the edge of the floor when the dance started and be on his way out when he fired the device. I can grab one of those Negro babes when she tears her blouse off. With his ex-wife in the next room unwilling to meet his needs, he tossed and turned his way to a troubled sleep.

CHAPTER 10

New York City

Early Thursday Morning, April 16, 1942

FBI Special Agent Larry Pennoyer was in his office when Captain Moran walked in. "Sorry to keep you up, but we needed a lab report on the evidence. The lab says the device is German or Italian. It's designed to fire metal darts in a semi-circular pattern. The darts are propelled by gun powder ignited by a flammable gas."

Pennoyer studied the device. "The Italians didn't build it. I'd bet the farm it's German. Makes sense the spy used it in a dance hall. The girls are wearing dresses and blouses, nothing to stop the darts. Terror devices were discussed during training, and this thing fits the description. It's compact, creates a flash fire, and shoots darts at unsuspecting people. It also creates chaos and fear. The report said four women suffered bruises and broken bones exiting the building."

Moran said, "We need to catch this guy today or tomorrow before he strikes again. The NYPD will be policing dance halls for the next week. The guy who placed it was wearing an old raincoat with turned up collar, hat, and glasses. Informants say he's less than six feet with a medium build. No one got a good look."

"Still watching the waterfront?"

"Costello, added another guy last night; we're tracking two suspects."

"If you were the spy, Moran, where would you strike?"

"The darts can't penetrate heavy clothing, that's why he chose a dance hall where outer wraps are removed. A roller rink could be next, girls with bare arms and legs. I'd have cops watch the rinks."

"Witnesses said the guy didn't hang around to see the damage, but no one saw him leave." Moran stopped to think. "I doubt if this device is a one of a kind, he probably has more with orders to use them."

Pennoyer got up from his chair. "Imagine a crowded theater lobby at intermission, people milling about. Set at five feet, the darts will hit people in the face and the flash fire will cause a panic. I'd set two devices on top of a cigarette machine."

Moran shook his head. "We can only cover dance halls and roller rinks, there are too many theaters. God help us if this guy has your imagination. I have five detectives working the cheap hotels and boarding houses around the dance hall. Surely someone saw the guy on the street, we have to find him."

Captain Moran raised his voice. "The NYPD is hands off our investigations to a fault. We're helping the FBI on the waterfront, and I'm asking for your help to catch the spies before they hurt someone else. I want a coordinated effort, not the FBI and NYPD going in different directions."

"We'll follow your plan, Moran. My job is to assist the NYPD, not run the investigation."

"Thanks Larry, you're making my job a lot easier."

~ ~ ~

At six in the morning the phone rang in the Hurley residence.

"Pennoyer here, I'm sorry to wake you."

"Good morning, Larry, give me a minute to wake up; the coffee is still in the can."

"You suspected the crime in Biddeford was connected to German agents."

"Yes, our information takes the case that way. You're calling to tell me you caught them?"

"Not yet, but last night someone exploded a device built by military intelligence at a dance hall in Bayridge. The thing isn't big enough to hold explosives, but powerful enough to trigger a flash fire and shoot small darts. Women dancers suffered cuts and severe burns, no fatalities at this time. We're assuming the perpetrator was a German spy with orders to terrorize the city. At present, newspapers are in the dark, but that will change if he strikes again. Do you have anything on your end?"

"Terrorizing civilians is part of war, always has been. We're helping the local police by providing assets they don't have. It may take time, but we'll catch the contact. Thanks for the call, Larry."

~ ~ ~

An exhausted Langer slept until a bad dream woke him at eight. He rushed to the bathroom for a cold shower to revive his senses. The hotel served oatmeal, coffee and a piece of toast for breakfast between seven and nine. He glanced through the New York Post for a story on the dance hall, nothing reported. The silence angered him. With a renewed spirit, he gobbled down the rest of breakfast. *I'll use two devices tonight.*

Langer checked out of the hotel before ten, wearing glasses, a mustache, and NY Giants cap. On the way to the subway, he stopped several times looking for a tail. After fifteen minutes, he boarded a train to the Bronx.

~ ~ ~

Two NYPD detectives were going door-to-door on the street Langer traveled the night before. A woman being interviewed said, "See the man with the dog across the street, he walks the dog every night, talk with him."

Detective Tracy crossed the street, showing his badge to the middle-aged man. "Excuse me, sir; did you walk your dog last night?"

"I walk him every night after he eats."

"Did you see anything unusual last night?"

"I saw lots of people milling about at the dance hall." He stopped talking to think. "Wait a minute, there was a guy throwing up in the next block. I crossed the street to check on him. His back was to me, and he mumbled something about the flu. Said he lived close by and refused help. We went in opposite directions; I have no idea where he lives. When I got to the dance hall the ambulance was there. The cops told me to turn around and go home. What happened?"

"A small fire, some panic, no serious injuries. Can you describe the man you saw?"

"He was on his knees with his back toward me; I didn't see his face. He was wearing a raincoat with the collar turned up and an old cap. Check the hotel two blocks down, he might be there."

"You've been very helpful, thank you."

At a dead run, Detective Tracy headed to the hotel. The building had seen better days. A wooden structure with peeling paint, a sagging roof, and stairs in need of repair did little to welcome guests. The desk clerk wasn't impressed when he showed his badge.

"Will you guys ever stop harassing me? What the guests do is none of my business. For a dollar and a quarter, they get a room."

"I don't care what goes on here. I'm looking for an older man, raincoat with collar turned up, mustache, and cap," the detective replied.

"He might have checked out an hour ago. Been here a couple days, never got a good look at his face."

"No forwarding address?"

"Are you kidding?"

"Did you see him last night?"

"I don't work nights, I own this flea trap. The night guy sleeps most of the time, but you could ask him, he'll be here at eight." He stopped to think. "There's something going on with the guy you're asking about. The mustache and glasses might be part of a disguise." He stopped to check the ledger. "No surprise, he signed in as Chester Smith. Chester had the middle room on the second floor. You might ask the guy across from the bathroom if he saw him."

Tracy located the bathroom and knocked on the door across the hall.

A burly man with a partial beard and tattooed arms answered. "Get outta here, I'm not buyin' what you're sellin'."

Tracy showed his badge. "Just a couple questions, sir."

"Make it short, I'm clean."

"Did you know the guy living next door, the man with the mustache and glasses?"

"If he had the room next door, he's the one throwin' up in the bathroom last night. Made a mess, but I made him clean it up. He didn't have glasses or a mustache."

84

"Can you describe him?"

"A little green around the gills, said he had the flu. The man was on his knees over the bowl. I don't know how tall, but the guy was medium build, short brown hair, looked to be in his forties. Not the usual bum you see around here."

"We should have a likeness later on; would you take a look at it?"

"I work the afternoon shift. I'll be free after lunch."

"If we come up with something, I'll be back, Mr— "

"Buck, the name is Buck."

~ ~ ~

In the Bronx, Langer selected a rooming house two blocks from the subway. The owner wouldn't rent by the day, and Langer started to walk out when the man asked for fifteen bucks a week. He stopped walking at ten. He had one of the three rooms on the third floor that shared a grimy bathroom with tub and shower. Living in filth was the downside of living in NYC on a tight budget.

After unpacking, he needed to get ready to meet Gray for lunch in Manhattan. On the way to the subway, the sun shone brightly, but a cold wind from the north went through his raincoat, chilling his body. *I need a sweater to wear under this coat.*

CHAPTER 11

New York City

Thursday Afternoon, April 16, 1942

Langer arrived at McCormick's Pub to find Gray sitting at a table in the rear, a good choice for privacy. "Good afternoon, Gray, it's a nice day out there."

"Good weather for this time a year. Have a seat."

"Years ago I liked their steak sandwich; what are you having?"

"They make the best Reuben sandwich in the city. That was a good show last night, well cast with a surprise ending. The writer had a good script."

"One never knows if the conclusion will satisfy the audience. I plan another showing tomorrow night in a different theater."

"All I need is the proper costume and I'll feature it tomorrow night."

"Good, the sooner the better."

After ordering, Langer removed a device from his coat pocket. "Place this on a table next to the dance floor. Tell the waitress you want a better view of the dancers' feet so you can learn the steps. Promise her you'll leave when the dancers return. Make sure the table surface is dry, remove the protective strips, secure the device to the tabletop, and put the protective strips in your pocket. This is the front, the darts fire in a semi-circular pattern." Langer looked Gray in the eyes, "Do you have any questions?"

"Not really, your explanation was good."

"Put this in your pocket. I'll show you the trigger when I get back from the restroom."

Gray smiled; he was joining the fight to help his beloved Germany.

Langer observed Gray for five minutes to make sure he was working alone. He tried flirting with two younger women with no success. He watched the waitress serve their lunch convinced Gray hadn't been followed.

"Sorry to take so long." Removing the trigger from his pocket, he explained, "The trigger requires a battery. Install the battery and set the safety while you're placing the device. Release the safety and push the button on your way out the door. Listen carefully, Gray, don't hang around to watch people scream and run, get the hell out of there. If you're caught, they'll surely torture you for information before they shoot you."

"I understand the consequences. It looks easy to use; I shouldn't have any trouble."

"Don't abuse or lose the trigger, I only have two."

"I understand."

"Do you know this neighborhood?"

"Yes, I have a friend that lives two blocks from here."

"Is there a secondhand store nearby?"

"There's one in the next block around the corner. What about Saturday night?"

"If you're successful Friday, meet me at ten Saturday morning on 42nd street in the theater district, I'll be walking east. If you're not there, I'll assume you've been picked up or have a good reason not to come. Don't wear a disguise, I'll find you."

"My ex-wife wants me to move out in the next two weeks. I could use another two hundred to help with expenses."

Langer thought it over as he sorted out the information Gray had provided. *He's living with his ex-wife. She's met another guy and wants him out of the apartment. With Gray setting the devices, I can concentrate on convoys. Two hundred is a reasonable request.*

"I can do that." Reaching for his wallet, he said, "Good luck tomorrow night, Gray. Remember, fire the device and get the hell out of there."

"Thanks for the money, I won't let you down. See you Saturday at ten. Good luck, Green."

Langer walked to the corner to check in both directions, things looked normal. The secondhand store was halfway down the block on the right. A freshly cleaned wool cardigan sweater fit well under his raincoat. On the way out, he spotted a skirt and blouse combination displayed on an old mannequin. That might be helpful, but I can't try it on. He asked a woman passing by, "My wife and I are the same size, will that skirt and blouse fit her?"

"Hold the blouse up next to your chest; I think the skirt is fine."

Langer held up the blouse. "It fits you. The outfit may be a bit young for your wife."

"We're attending our silver class reunion. The invitation said to wear something unusual that makes us look eighteen."

"That will do it, but you'll need a sweater. Is she full figured?" The woman held her hands to shape a large bust size.

"Some men would say larger than average."

She threw Langer a sweater after checking her wrist watch. "I'm running behind, you're on your own." On the way out she commented, "A matching shoulder bag would be nice."

"Thank you so much, you've been very helpful."

I'll need shoes, those I can try on. The women's shoe section had a large selection but nothing that fit. The men's shoes had several pairs of tennis shoes, including a blue pair that looked perfect with the skirt. *It's a baseball game; many women will wear comfortable footwear.* He tried on the shoes, they fit. On a nearby table sat a brown wig matching his sandy-brown hair. On the way to the cash register, there were several brassieres displayed on mannequins. A large-sized one with substantial padding hanging on the end of a rack looked perfect.

Makeup proved to be no problem; a clerk at the counter selected the needed items: lipstick, rouge, powder, and cheap cologne. The clerk suggested several mustaches and a black wig to make him look younger if he decided to dress as a comedian. Paying for the items, he noticed some Macy's bags. "Please pack my things in a Macy's bag, I'll wear the cardigan."

Heading to the door, he realized having another outfit would be beneficial. A white silk shirt and black pants were on a mannequin with a black leather jacket and red scarf. The outfit was twenty-five dollars, a reasonable price to change one's identity. For three more dollars he could get the black shoes with raised heels, popular with Puerto Rican men. He went to the counter. "I'll take that outfit and the shoes if they fit."

"They're size ten."

"That's my size; please put them in a Macy's bag too."

~ ~ ~

Back in the Bronx, the sweater warmed Langer's body as he walked the neighborhoods. Try as he may to put last night's attack at the dance hall in the back of his mind, it still occupied his thoughts. *It will be in tonight's paper, I'll get my credit.* He shook his head. *That kind of childish thinking will get me killed.*

War is war, there's no credit, and the medals are meaningless if you lose. Nevertheless, he would check the paper for a story.

He passed a theater where the marquee read: Premier Showing Friday night, *Yankee Doodle Dandy* at 8:00, *Ghost of Frankenstein* at 6:00. An iconic actor, James Cagney, would insure a sell out. *If I can place a device between shows, there'll be panic.*

Langer purchased a ticket to check out the lobby. One wall had several glass shelves with autographed pictures of well-known actors. A shelf about five feet from the floor looked perfect, the darts would fire face high and the flash fire would cause chaos. The glass shelf would resist the adhesive, but the device placed against the wall would be as effective.

Convenient for Langer, the patrons jammed the small lobby at the end of the first feature, waiting for the second show. Smoking in theaters was permissible in NYC, creating a blue haze that produced an eerie almost surreal atmosphere. No one noticed when he picked up a picture and placed it back on the shelf.

A seat in the rear of the theater would do. He slept through the picture but woke when others leaving stepped on his feet. The lobby was filled with people coming and going. He walked to the wall with the shelves where three women were admiring the pictures. He smiled, squeezing his way between two of them. Neither flinched, but both corrected him when he picked up a picture. One said, "Look, but don't touch."

What am I doing calling attention to myself? He spun away, disappearing into the crowd.

He sorted through his options on what disguise to use on the walk back. *Yankee Doodle Dandy* would be playing at several neighborhood theaters. *I'll find the one best suited for the device.*

~ ~ ~

Left to his own, Bernhard felt comfortable mixing with the many foreigners working on the docks. Some spoke their native tongue, others mixed their native tongue with English, but few spoke English as well as he did. He moved from the bar to share a table with a middle-aged man that appeared slightly drunk. "My name is Martin; can I join you in a drink?"

"Yeah, sure, I could use a beer."

Bernhard returned carrying two glasses of beer. "I didn't catch your name?"

The man slurred his speech, "What are you, German or Hungarian?"

"German-Pole, did I miss your name?"

"Fleming, I'm Danish." He swigged down some beer. "Work on the docks?"

"Yah, sick this month, haven't worked in weeks."

"Get back soon, lots of guys not showing up. We got two more ships to load before the convoy sails."

"Are those the ones leaving on Tuesday?"

"I don't know why should you know? Load the ships and keep your mouth shut. My foreman said spies hang around the docks trying to gather information. Maybe you're a spy?"

"Nein, nein, I'm not a spy. The Germans are killing my people."

Fleming said. "Six comes early, got to go. Thanks for the beer. Sorry to correct you, but we need to watch what we say. Loose lips sink ships."

"When you meet someone new, you are not sure of what to say. I was making conversation. I will try to be more careful."

"Hope you get back to work soon, we're short of help."

When Fleming left, Bernhard moved to another table where two older men were arguing which baseball team was better, the Giants or the Yankees. Both seemed to have good points, but

Bernhard knew little about baseball. *I'll buy a drink and learn about the game.*

"I'm new to the city, may I join you?"

"Are you a dock worker?"

"Yah, I came here for better pay."

"Sit down friend, our glasses are getting empty."

"I'll buy a round, be right back."

The two continued their argument, ignoring Bernhard who was thoroughly confused by the statistics they used to make their case. He ignored them while listening to other conversations hoping to pick up useful information. He learned nothing about convoys, but he knew his conversational tone was too polite for the waterfront. *I need to use some of the same expressions and slang I've heard tonight to be effective.*

Bernhard downed his beer, saying, "Sore neck, I need some sleep."

With newfound confidence, he forgot to check the other side of the street before walking to the subway. Fleming stood in the shadows across the street with a fellow detective, watching the bar.

"That's Martin. Follow him until Sunday night. If I'm right, he'll take you to his contact. Good luck, Tom."

The newly formed FBI, with little experience in undercover work, relied on the NYPD to police the waterfront. Detective Costello with ten years' experience worked the waterfront bars five nights a week. Bernhard was the second suspect since Tuesday who responded "Nein, nein" when asked if he's a German spy. Costello looked at his watch, time for one more bar.

CHAPTER 12

Biddeford, Maine

Thursday, April 16, 1942

Thursday morning found Heidi Klinger up early making coffee for Hans and Fritz. Hans came into the kitchen to greet her with a kiss. "Good morning, hon, coffee smells good."

"I haven't seen Fritz since Tuesday, is there something wrong?"

"He's busy with tackle."

"I sense there's something wrong, Fritz hasn't been himself this week. He seems distant, detached from the family. Maybe he's ill and not sharing it with us."

"I think not. He bought a radio at auction weeks ago. He spent the last two weeks trying to get the thing to work. He's never been—what word I look for?"

"Talkative, is the word? He's never been very talkative."

"Yah, talkative, that is it. Since war began, all he talks about are gosh darn Russians and Jews, and he not say gosh darn. I do not like Russians, but not spend all time hating them, Fritz is all hate."

"What kind of radio did he buy?"

"Old ship to shore radio. When it works, he takes time listening to ships." Hans finished his coffee and headed to the door. "It five, time for work. Please have lunch about one. I will ask Fritz, he may not come."

~ ~ ~

Portland, Maine

Thursday morning, Agents Warner and Andrews were reviewing a list of German students that attended college in New York City and Boston. NYC graduates far outnumbered those from Boston with several catching their attention. Otto Langer, born in Germany, fought for Germany in World War I. He graduated in 1926 from Columbia University with a degree in journalism and went to work as a reporter for the New York Post the same year.

Andrews called the Post editor for information.

The editor confirmed Langer worked there for ten years. He mentioned Langer's affiliation with the American Nazi Party. "In 1935 he wrote several articles praising the Third Reich and was furious when the Post refused to publish them. Seeking recognition for his work, and in violation of his contract, he sold the articles to a weekly paper published in German."

Andrews said, "I talked with a reporter that said Langer was sent to Germany in 1936 to cover the Olympic Games and never returned."

"Yes, that's correct. Langer was looking for a free trip home, that's why he asked to cover the Games. It didn't surprise me or bother his colleagues that he didn't come back."

The Post editor promised to mail several photographs of Langer, including a copy of his 1936 driver's license.

Before hanging up, the editor cleared his throat saying, "I heard through the grapevine that a historic house in Biddeford burned

Friday night. There's no one in Germany better equipped to spy on America than Otto Langer. To me, Biddeford would be the perfect landing site this time of year. The man is more American than German, and he's an amateur actor, knows makeup and the art of disguise. He might be the man you're looking for."

Andrews said, "It doesn't make sense to mail me the information. Can you deliver it to the NYPD?"

"That will save time. I've worked with their artist, Leon Lawrence, on past suspects." He paused, "Knowing the NYPD, you better work through channels. I can deliver the file to them in thirty minutes, but Lawrence will need authorization to work on it."

"Special Agent Pennoyer will contact the NYPD, they're working together. Please don't mention this to anyone. The less the spies know works to our advantage; we need to catch them before they get organized."

"I understand; this involves National Security."

Andrews hung up the phone turning to Warner. "My gut tells me the older of the two is Otto Langer."

Warner said, "I agree, he lived in NYC for fourteen years and speaks perfect English. I've never read German books, but the cover-up suggests we're looking for a guy that reads American novels."

"I think you're right. Let's take this to Hurley for a second opinion."

After hearing their report, Hurley said, "Good work, guys, I'll contact Pennoyer."

~ ~ ~

When they finished talking, Pennoyer said, "Your guys uncovered the first suspect, good work, Hurley. Anything going on in Biddeford I should know?"

"Chief Dunsmore is more than competent as are the people assisting him. They're working on a list of possible suspects, but there's nothing new at this time."

Pennoyer added, "Until we learn something new, we're assuming the device fired Wednesday night was placed by German spies. The NYPD wants a 24/7 alert if a second device is fired. The first one severely injured nine and harmed twenty-two more. You'll have a full report by tomorrow."

Hurley sighed. "Sorry to hear that. We're operating on the premise the agents were sent here to establish a network to gather intelligence on our convoys. Planning an attack on civilians is against the Geneva Convention."

Pennoyer countered, "We can prosecute terrorists using the Geneva Convention, but we can't enforce it. Captain Moran is in charge, I'll get the information to him ASAP. Keep me informed."

Hurley offered, "Andrews and Warner have been working with Dunsmore, can you use them?"

"Yes, tomorrow will be fine. FBI Headquarters won't send help unless the NYPD requests it."

"They'll be on the first train."

When Pennoyer hung up, he was already deciding how to use Andrews and Warner. *Their involvement in the investigation since the beginning will help the NYPD. I'll call Moran.*

Moran quickly accepted his offer and agreed to send someone to meet the agents at the train station. "Thanks, Larry, they'll be working with Tracy until we catch the bastards."

~ ~ ~

Biddeford, Maine

Dunsmore and Police Chief Robinson were discussing possible suspects.

Robinson said, "I've checked out four German families. Karl and Marlene Amsel came in 1935; they drive a 1936 black Chevrolet. Both work the afternoon shift at Maine Outdoors. They have expressed their dislike of Russians, Jews, and Poles. They're in their early fifties with no children or church affiliation, and they speak German in the home."

"Worth checking on," said Dunsmore. "See if you can determine where they were Thursday night."

"There's a single guy, Raymond Martz, living north of Saco in a small cabin. He fought for Germany in the first war, hates Russians and Jews. He migrated in thirty-six or thirty-seven and wants to go back. Appears to be in his middle fifties and works on fishing boats as a day laborer. The captains say he works hard, but not the day after he's paid, so they pay him weekly. It appears Martz has a drinking problem. There's electricity in that part of the woods, but the cabin doesn't have it, nor does it have running water. Captain Larsen said you can barely stand his smell on open water; he seldom bathes."

"Stop there, Ralph, Martz isn't your man. I think he's the same guy I see wandering the streets drunk."

Robinson continued. "Then there's Franz and Karen Richter, they came here in thirty-five. He fought in the first war as a corporal, claims he was shot three times. Like the others, he hates Russians, Poles and Jews. They both work at Maine Outdoors and carpool to work with the Amsels in a thirty-six black Ford sedan. They sometimes attend the Biddeford Lutheran Church.

"Edgar Metz migrated in thirty-six with his wife, no children. He works at Maine Outdoors and carpools with a friend from Biddeford." Robinson paused, "I walked their properties, no radio antennas."

"We can't search their homes without a warrant, so do the best you can without violating their rights. Do you have pictures? Maine Outdoors has security."

"Right here," Robinson said, handing the photos to Dunsmore.

~ ~ ~

Thursday night, a man walking through the park stopped where the paths intersected to look both ways. Other than birds and squirrels, the park looked empty. He removed an envelope from under a rock and walked briskly toward his car. At home, he opened the envelope. "Today, I heard a man say his brother was sailing from Philadelphia at 5:00 a.m. Sunday, May 3rd. His friend told him to shut up; he had a cousin in the same convoy."

CHAPTER 13

Gestapo Headquarters, Nazi Germany

Friday Morning, April 17, 1942

An anxious Engel walked into his boss's office, head of Covert Operations. "Good morning, Colonel Falk, you wanted to see me?"

"Good morning, Engel. Would you like some coffee and a roll?"

"Yes please, if you will join me."

"I plan to, missed breakfast." He spoke to his secretary. "Coffee and rolls will be here in ten minutes."

Engel watched as Falk picked up the device Langer used in America. "I understand from the lab, Langer has several of these."

Engel replied, "That's right, he has six. The device works well in crowded places."

"In a crowd of civilians, I'm sure it's useful, but it wouldn't be effective in combat. Our engineers should be devoting their time to developing weapons that can win the war. The report from Biddeford isn't good. Our agents killed the caretaker at the safe house, burned the house to cover their tracks and escaped in the caretaker's car. We'll assume they took the train from Boston to NYC Saturday morning before authorities could piece together the information." Falk stared at Engel. "Local thieves don't kill and burn houses in Biddeford, Maine. The authorities could be looking for Langer and Bernhard." Falk continued to stare at Engel as his secretary came in with a tray.

"Be careful, gentlemen, the coffee is hot. Enjoy!"

Falk nodded. "Thank you, Julie." After a bite of his roll, he sipped his coffee all the while staring at Engel. For the first time, the cool and collected Falk showed anger. Slamming his hand on the desk, he asked, "Why wasn't I informed about these devices before Langer left?"

A shocked Engel answered, "I didn't think it necessary. Langer can't spend all his time on the waterfront. American and British bombers are killing German civilians, why can't we hurt American civilians? We bomb England."

"We can hurt American civilians, you're right on that point, but you're wrong about Langer being the one to do it. Langer is in America to set up a network to provide intelligence on convoys, information our U-boats need. You have him hurting forty or fifty civilians, while American convoys supply the British and Russians with fuel and planes that kill thousands of Germans every week."

Falk continued, "If he's using this thing, the mission is in jeopardy. The device has military written all over it, and the police will find it during a routine investigation. The Americans are not incompetent fools, they'll pick up Langer and six months of planning and executions are wasted. Brown hasn't heard from him."

Engel replied, "Brown assured us the house was closed for the winter." He paused before confessing, "I didn't think it through. If Langer uses the device, the NYPD will be livid; it will strengthen their resolve to catch him. Once the police have a likeness of either one, the game is over. We need to move them to Philadelphia or Boston as soon as possible."

"Yah, where neither one is familiar with the city. I'll give the order, but it may take another week or two for all this to play out. Cancel plans to send a second team." He shook his head still staring at Engel. "The Fuehrer is following this, you fool. When he hears the plan may fail, he'll be furious. I'll take the blame, but you made the decision to use the device without my permission. I cannot protect you."

Engel looked at the floor, responding with choked words. "Does it have to be that way?"

"Yah, there's no room for failure. We no longer shoot inept agents; they're sent to the Russian front. You've heard the rumors."

"I'm an SS Officer with no combat training."

"You were in the first war."

"That was twenty years ago, everything has changed."

"The Russian front has enough officers; you'll be a foot soldier." He rose from his desk looking Engel in the eyes. "Stay close to someone you trust and pray for the best. If given the chance, risk your life and win an Iron Cross."

Falk walked to the window admiring the early blossoms of spring. Realizing his own fate may have been sealed by Engel's decision, he deliberated for a time. "Who knows? If I've already stepped on someone's toes without knowing, I'll be joining you on the Russian front." The thought renewed his anger. "Get out of my sight."

~ ~ ~

Shortly after Engel left his office a lieutenant handed Falk a message transmitted early Friday morning from Biddeford.

Falk read the message and sent for Engel.

Engel returned to Falk's office looking like a whipped puppy.

A relieved Falk said, "I just heard from Biddeford, the contact wants a second team sent to arrive April 30. You're getting a second chance; select someone to partner with. The message also said there's a convoy sailing from Philadelphia early Sunday morning, May 3, but no mention of Langer furnishing the information. Regardless of the source, we know when the convoy is sailing and there's enough time to plan an attack. You've gone from goat to hero in just a few hours."

"Thank you, Colonel Falk. I won't let you down."

"Bring me your plan with a list of needed supplies, and forget about hurting civilians, that's not the mission."

"I understand. Focus on convoys regardless of the danger."

"You're dismissed, Engel."

Engel clicked his heels. "Heil Hitler!"

~ ~ ~

An hour later Engel returned to Falk's office.

Falk jumped up, "You should be getting ready to sail, what are you doing here?"

"I know it's been a long day with many challenges, but I want you to reconsider sending two men. I would be better off on my own. Meier is sick, and there's no one else with adequate English. Some of the younger men are promising, but their presence could compromise the mission. I've no time for on-the-job training, let me go alone."

Falk sat down to think. "On your own you might contact Langer. We still haven't heard from him."

Engel said, "We train agents to work in teams. Americans probably think the same way. No man won a war dying for his country, but I promise to do my best."

"Himmler wants our agents to work in pairs, I can't change that." Falk looked at a roster of the available agents, "Take the Italian, he's bright and speaks good English. The mafia controls the NYC waterfront, Tesoro speaks Italian, and he could be helpful."

"Tesoro only been with us a couple of months, I hadn't considered him. Someone who speaks Italian makes sense. Left to my own devices, I wouldn't have chosen him."

Falk smiled, "Meier getting sick could be a blessing. Take the day to get ready and be back in my office at six tomorrow morning. You're dismissed."

"Heil Hitler!"

"Heil Hitler!"

CHAPTER 14

New York City

Friday Morning, April 17, 1942

At seven o'clock Friday morning, Special Agent Larry Pennoyer sipped coffee waiting for the phone to ring.

World War II expanded the role of FBI from fighting interstate crime to National Security, coordinating efforts with the military and local police departments. With spies in NYC, Director Hoover had taken an interest in the investigation. Pennoyer's secretary announced, "Director Hoover on line one."

"Good morning, Director, how can I be of help?"

"Good morning, Pennoyer, those spies have created a stir here in Washington. I need an update for a meeting at ten."

"I thought you might call. As we suspected, there are two active spies in the city. The NYPD says the device used Wednesday night is German. I've sent it to our lab for confirmation."

"Good work. Do you have a positive identification on the guy who did it?"

"Several people saw him, but the man was wearing an old man's disguise and no one saw his face. The evidence points to someone with knowledge of the city and staying in cheap boarding houses. Hurley's agents have identified Otto Langer as a suspect. He graduated from Columbia University in 1926 with a major in journalism. The New York Post hired him the same year; he worked there for ten years. At his request, the paper sent Langer to cover the 1936 Olympic Games; he never returned or contacted the Post."

"If Langer is the leader, you'll catch both of them when they meet to exchange information."

"Detective Costello from the NYPD works the waterfront and he has identified two suspects they're following until Sunday night. We think Langer will meet his partner Sunday at the Yankee/Red Sox game. From past experience, we know Langer used his press pass to attend Yankee games in the thirties. If he meets with one of the men Costello is tracking, we could solve the case."

"Is there a picture of Langer we can use to identify him?"

"The Post had two pictures from thirty-six. The NYPD will have copies for every patrolman by the afternoon shift with orders to follow Langer if he's identified. In a perfect world, one leads us to the other."

"What's going on in Biddeford?"

"The local police are competent. The Radke boy said he heard two voices, but he didn't see the men. A witness saw a car coming and going but didn't see the driver. Local German residents are being questioned, but nothing solid at this time."

"The NYPD has the assets and experience to catch these spies. If German agents follow training they'll have cyanide capsules with orders to use them when challenged. Good luck, Pennoyer, you're going to need it to catch these men alive."

~ ~ ~

Friday morning, Warner and Andrews boarded the early train to NYC. Stopping at every small town, the trip seemed to take forever. Warner thought ... *If our assumptions are correct, we could catch Langer by Sunday.* A remarkable feat for law enforcement involving several jurisdictions, something they all could be proud of.

On the train platform in NYC, Warner held up a card with his name. Detective Tracy could spot another detective without a sign and greeted him with exuberance, hand extended. "Welcome to NYC."

"Good afternoon, thanks for picking us up. I'm Warner, my partner is Andrews."

"I'm Richard Tracy, not Dick Tracy. My friends call me Rich."

Andrews chuckled, "There's no reason to think you're Dick Tracy, Rich."

Tracy laughed, "I could see you snickering, Andrews. We're woefully short of detectives, and Pennoyer volunteered your service. It helps to have someone who's familiar with the case."

On the drive to police headquarters, Andrews asked, "Did you have any luck making the guy from the dance hall?"

"I missed him by twenty minutes. He knows how to use the buses and subway. The guy is cautious, moving every couple of nights. Moran and I agree with you, Langer is the number one suspect. You guys do good work."

Warner replied, "We'll take credit after we catch them. Have you any other clues?"

"No activity last night, but tonight could be a different story. We're covering the popular dance halls, night clubs, and roller rinks, but there's no way we can police every venue that features dancing. The theaters are releasing *Yankee Doodle Dandy* tonight. They'll be packed, Cagney is a NYC icon. Most theaters are in old buildings with small lobbies, they're very vulnerable."

Andrews asked, "Do you have a plan at this time?"

"My men are checking the Bronx and Queens theaters this afternoon to figure out likely targets. There could be two hundred or more possibilities in the city, but only thirty or forty would make sense. The NYPD can cover up to fifty theaters, but we can't cover them all. The back-alley theaters in Greenwich Village and downtown Manhattan will be hit and miss, not to mention the amateur groups that produce plays on weekends. The ticket sellers at the major theaters will have a sketch of Langer, but little time in the crush to sell tickets before curtain call. Langer is an amateur actor, he probably has several disguises."

Warner asked, "If this device causes a flash fire, does it have an expiration date?"

"The Navy says it takes two weeks for U-boats to cross the Atlantic. You can't build a device the day you sail, but the gas used could limit their effectiveness to four or five weeks. The lab said the device took a team of engineers months to build."

Andrews said, "With that kind of effort, you know the Germans built more than one. If there's ten or more, Langer could be anxious to get the job done. Knowing the device works, two agents could fire two a night this weekend, twice the bang for the buck."

"The device is shaped like a giant clamshell, fully loaded with darts, it could weigh several pounds." Tracy added, "Put yourself in Langer's shoes. Wednesday night was his first experience as a terrorist. Screaming women with burning hair rushing the door bothered him. The man didn't return to Germany in 1936 to attack Americans. He's obeying orders like a good Nazi should."

Tracy sighed, "The NYPD seldom asks for help, we're like male bears, no room for outsiders. We need your help to catch these guys before they harm more New Yorkers."

Warner replied, "Catching the spies is priority one, two and three at the FBI, that's why we're here. The NYPD has many assets, but the FBI has more, and we know how to access them."

~ ~ ~

At NYPD Headquarters, Captain Moran was looking through Langer's personnel file while Lawrence was working on the sketch. Lawrence said, "It's a good thing we have a graduation picture from Columbia along with the driver's license. It gives me a good picture of how he aged. I'll add six years and we'll have a likeness of how he looks today."

Andrews asked, "Can you do a second sketch adding a mustache, sunglasses, and a Yankees cap, and then a third sketch of him with mustache, beard, and wire glasses?"

"I can do that. I'll have three profiles finished by two this afternoon. How many copies of each are needed?"

Moran looked at Andrews, "Five hundred will do. I need them on the heaviest stock available."

"I'll have them reproduced on 53 lb. photo paper."

On the way to the garage, Moran said, "The device took time to develop; the Germans probably made a dozen. The agents could place two devices a night this weekend, but the mayor and commissioner won't go 24/7 unless there's another attack."

Andrews offered, "Do you want me to talk with them?"

"Nah, forget that, we'll probably be on a 24/7 Saturday after Langer fires a second one tonight."

"I can understand their reluctance, it's a big city and a 24/7 might drive the spies underground, making them harder to catch."

Moran said, "I haven't the manpower to police the city day-to-day. Let's hope the bad guys we're chasing everyday take the weekend off. Tracy has the Bronx and Queens. We'll develop a plan for the rest of the city."

~ ~ ~

Bernhard felt disquieted Friday morning as he shaved. He had paid rent through Saturday but could leave today. The basement where he stored his second suitcase had a door opening to the alley. *Today is garbage day. I'll leave when the truck comes.* He packed quickly, wiping the room clean of fingerprints. A book of matches from a Manhattan restaurant sat on the nightstand alongside a newspaper with several circled addresses in the rooms for rent section of the want ads.

With light from a small flashlight he retrieved the suitcase. The sounds of a garbage truck broke the silence. The truck was rolling slowly to the next stop, blocking the view from the east, perfect cover to leave the building.

Walking the other way, he looked over his shoulder to see if anyone was following. The detective at the rear of the building lost sight long enough for Bernhard to clear the alley. At the corner he boarded a bus to Queens where he had checked several boarding houses yesterday.

At the front of the building, a detective dressed as a street cleaner waited patiently for Bernhard to exit the building.

Bernhard got off the bus at the next stop and checked the best route to Brooklyn. He chose a Flatbush Avenue neighborhood, finding a boarding house near Ebbets Field, a block from the bus line. After paying rent, he headed for the docks to have lunch and listen in on the surrounding conversations, confident his disguise would protect his identity.

An hour later, the detective at the rear of the boarding house went to the front to join his partner. After checking with the owner, the detectives knew for certain Martin (Bernhard) had given them the slip.

After following him for a day, both had a good idea what he looked like. With Costello's help, the artist could create a likeness. They called Moran to report Martin's getaway.

~ ~ ~

At NYPD headquarters, Lawrence and Costello were already working on the sketch when the detectives arrived. The artist had several basic profiles; to those he added hair, nose, mouth, and ears. Once the three detectives agreed on a look, the artist would go to the next step. An hour later he had a basic portrait drawn in pen and ink. "That's the best I can do fellas." Lawrence stretched. "Do we have a likeness?"

Costello replied, "You hit a homerun. That's the guy I drank beer with."

The other detectives agreed. "Let's go to lunch; I'll drop this in the photo room for reproduction. The guys on the afternoon shift will have copies of Langer and Martin when we return. You're not aware of this. I had just completed a sketch for Moran when Costello walked in. If the one I sketched this morning and this one work together, you might catch them this weekend."

Costello commented, "Good work, Leon, I need results to get through the long nights in those cheap waterfront bars drinking beer with dockworkers and trying to stay sober."

~ ~ ~

Later that afternoon, the precinct captains were briefing the afternoon shift of NYPD officers. "You have the basic stuff now for something that's top priority." Several officers woke their partners. The captain held up sketches of Bernhard and Langer. "We need to catch these guys ASAP before they do more damage. I want each of you to take time to study the photos; you can't do your job with your head down.

"If you identify one of the suspects, follow from the opposite side of the street, do not arrest him. When you reach a phone, use the code word 'zero' and the dispatcher will ask for the location. Give the information and get back to the suspect. You'll be joined by two detectives who will continue the tail. Pick up a packet and catch these guys."

~ ~ ~

Joined by two other detectives at the Bronx police station, Tracy, Warner and Andrews were planning their afternoon search with a map and phone book. Tracy said, "We'll cover more ground if we split up, about ten theaters per man. On a scale from one to five, rate each of the theaters. This isn't exact science; we're playing the law of averages. Good luck, men, see you back here at six."

Tracy said to Warner and Andrews, "I'm headed to Bayridge to show the photos to a witness. He's our best bet. I'll take the theaters in Bayridge."

Tracy made good time in the afternoon traffic, making the trip in twenty minutes. The owner of the hotel recognized him.

"Chester Smith hasn't returned," he said sarcastically.

"I have some sketches for you to look at."

"Glad to, we're all detectives at heart."

He studied the sketches. "This is your man, same build and facial features. I've never seen the other guy." He handed Langer's photo to Tracy.

"Is Buck upstairs?"

"Should be, I haven't seen him go out."

"I'll knock on his door."

"Step back after you knock, he's got an angry side to him."

"Thanks, sounds like good advice."

Buck was quick to answer. "I thought it might be you."

"The lighting in the hall is poor, can I come in?"

"Sure, there's nothing to hide in here. You have some pictures for me?"

"Yeah, there are two different sets."

Buck took the first set. "This isn't the guy." Tracy handed him a second set. "I can't be sure, but this looks like the guy that was barfing in the bathroom."

Both the owner and Buck identified Otto Langer. "Thanks, Buck, you've been a big help."

CHAPTER 15

New York City

Friday, April 17, 1942

Friday afternoon, Langer had lunch at a restaurant in Greenwich Village. There were many off-Broadway theaters in the village, but few fit the profile for his device. *Yankee Doodle Dandy* was featured at the Village Theater, the largest movie theater in Greenwich Village. Like several others, the theater featured a wall for autographed pictures in the lobby. The busy streets outside the theater would lose him in the hustle and bustle of activity that made Greenwich Village famous. *Yankee Doodle Dandy* played at 8:45. Brimming with confidence, he smiled as he exited the theater. *This time I'll get a good look before I leave.*

~ ~ ~

The detectives working the Bronx and Queens joined Tracy, Andrews, and Warner for dinner. There were eight theaters with open display shelves that held pictures of stars.

Tracy said, "We'll cover these eight theaters; uniformed cops can cover the rest. I'd place the device at five feet where it would do the most damage."

Warner added, "We want Langer alive, but we can't let him explode that thing. Arrest him on the spot with hands held high. DO NOT let him fumble in his pockets. Langer could have a cyanide capsule in his mouth. If he bites it he'll collapse in seconds, and there's nothing we can do to keep him alive. Let's change clothes, no suits or hats."

Warner dressed in a leather jacket and jeans to stand outside the theater Langer visited on Thursday. *If it were me, I'd set the device here.* With the large seating capacity and small lobby, the theater offered a perfect setting.

~ ~ ~

Langer chose the mustache, beard and glasses disguise. His black raincoat carried the device and trigger. With time to kill, he decided to walk the mile to the subway station in a light drizzle. The breeze felt good as he walked briskly to stay warm while reviewing his plan to cause mayhem.

After triggering the device, he would join others rushing the main doors to get out.

A bar several blocks from the theater seemed opportune for a drink to reinforce his courage. A shot of whiskey followed by a beer had the desired effect.

At the box office, he waited patiently in line for a ticket, not knowing the large man in a black raincoat standing at the ticket window was a firefighter from Greenwich Village. An Army firefighter, anxious to see *Yankee Doodle Dandy,* stood ten feet behind him.

The theater lobby featured spring colors with a vase of tulips at the end of the concession counter. The shelves with pictures had forsythia sitting on green maple leaves. Langer had attached several leaves to the device, to match the décor.

Wanting to be one of the first in the lobby between pictures, he sat next to the door in the back for the first feature. During credits, he slipped out to work his way to the picture shelves. He moved two sprigs of flowers, replacing them with the device. It looked like a decorated rock.

Minutes later, moviegoers jammed the lobby making it difficult to leave or enter.

He worked his way toward the main doors while fumbling with the trigger. The large firefighter in the black raincoat had forged a path along the wall, trying to get to the concession stand. Fifteen feet from the doors, Langer switched off the safety while removing the trigger from his coat. He raised his arm to trigger the device and saw the large man in the dark raincoat step in front of it with his back turned.

The flash fire followed by the explosion struck the firefighter in the shoulders with the raincoat taking the punishment. Fire ignited his hair and the hair of others standing on either side. The perimeter radius of darts hit people in the neck and face. Their screams silenced all conversation.

What he witnessed in ten seconds was enough, time to get out. Knowing the outcome gave Langer an advantage as stunned onlookers stared in shock.

"Fire, Fire," someone yelled.

Langer realized if he stayed on his feet, the crowd would push him out the door. He screamed, "Keep moving, keep moving." Those in front responded and he was on the sidewalk in seconds. People behind him were stumbling over bodies of women and children knocked to the floor trying to leave the theater. Men who went to assist others were pushed to the floor. Langer couldn't believe the chaos the device caused in a crowded lobby. The crush to get out was causing more injuries than the flash fire and darts.

A block from the theater, he slowed to a normal walk with several stops to make sure no one was following. He boarded the train with a sense of accomplishment. *I've done it, I've done it, and they haven't caught me.*

Inside the theater, chaos had replaced reason. Patrons were jammed so tight they couldn't help themselves, and those wanting to help the injured couldn't reach them. The Army firefighter removed his jacket and threw it to a man with burning hair. The man buried his head in the jacket extinguishing the flames, and then had the rationale to help those around him. The large firefighter pulled his coat up to extinguish flames on his head and used his bare hands to help others.

Darts had struck people in the face and neck. The theater manager appeared on the stairs trying to restore order. He shouted through a megaphone, "STAND STILL, STAND STILL. THERE IS NO FIRE. If you're injured, help is on the way. Do not rush the door, please stand still. You can use the theater's side exit doors, the ushers will help. Those in the lobby stay put, there is no fire, help is on the way."

Outside the theater, a veteran cop grabbed a screaming woman. "What happened in there?"

"A fire broke out from nowhere; there are people with their hair on fire."

"Are you all right?"

"I think so!"

"Go to the corner and call the emergency number on the box. Tell them Officer O'Malley said to send ambulances and doctors to the Village Theater in Greenwich Village. Can you handle that?"

"Yes. Is there anything else I can do?"

"Not really, please hurry."

O'Malley worked his way through the crowd on the sidewalk; none of them had any visible injuries. Reaching the doors, there

116

were men shoving people to the side to protect those lying on the floor. O'Malley blew his whistle for twenty seconds as the crowd slowly calmed down. He grabbed a sailor and several other men. "Help me move the injured to a safe area. The rest of you stay where you're at, help is on the way."

The sailor replied, "Yes sir," as he helped an older woman to her feet.

Adding assurance, the sailor said, "We'll stay here, officer, until help arrives."

In minutes, O'Malley had restored order at the main doors with help from other officers. As the crowd moved back into the theater, he moved to where the firefighters had things under control. The manager kept repeating, HELP IS HERE—HELP IS HERE.

The big fireman sat examining his coat while his wife put ice on his head to soothe his burns. He recognized O'Malley. "Good to see you, Mike. Why are you working evenings?"

"The department suspected something like this was going to happen. How did you get burned, Howard?"

"Something exploded behind me and fire blasted out igniting my hair, and these little darts struck my back."

Sirens filled the air as ambulances and police cars arrived at the scene.

O'Malley looked to the floor, noting the device under the shelving. Still warm but stepped on. "This caused the damage."

Howard surmised, "The only reason to use that thing is to hurt innocent people. We're at war, Mike. Only a spy or an enemy of the people would use such a weapon."

A man and woman approached O'Malley. The woman said, "We saw the man that did this. He was standing behind the usher when he pointed something toward the picture wall. I saw a sudden flash and heard a muffled explosion. Fire burst from the wall and small objects hit people on both sides of the man in the black coat. The man who did this left with the crowd."

The woman's husband said, "There was nothing we could do to stop him."

"If you don't mind, please stay here until Detective Tracy shows up. I need to question others for information."

~ ~ ~

Tracy knew he selected the wrong target when a patrol car pulled up outside the Paramount Theater. He met the officer at the car door. "They hit the Village Theater, Lieutenant."

"Greenwich Village, he outsmarted us."

"That's O'Malley's beat, he knows the ropes."

On Tracy's arrival at the Village Theater, a precinct sergeant greeted him at the curb. The medics and firemen were loading the injured while others waiting to make statements were seated on the lobby staircase. O'Malley had taken several eyewitness reports; they all sounded the same. The man triggering the device looked to be in his forties with wire-rimmed glasses, mustache and beard. The man had a turned-up collar; no one had a good look at his face.

Tracy addressed the people on the stairs. "I'm sorry to detain you, but we need your statements. The theater has set up three tables to expedite the process; it shouldn't take more than an hour. One quick question, can anyone identify the man from a likeness?" No one raised their hand. "We'll pass the photos around to refresh your memory."

He went to the theater manager. "How many were hurt?"

"I'd say thirty, more or less. Eleven were taken by ambulance to emergency; the others were treated here by doctors and medics. Those little darts hit some in the face and neck. Thank God no one was hit in the eye."

"Do you have names and addresses of the injured?"

"I do, Lieutenant. The theater has a form they filled out."

~ ~ ~

Langer walked slowly from the subway station to the boarding house. The remorse he felt Wednesday had been replaced by a sense of euphoria. The theater attack was successful, but the big guy in the black coat had taken some of the darts and redirected the flash fire. Langer sat in his room contemplating his next move, wishing he knew the outcome of Gray's effort.

Reviewing information Gray had provided, Langer recalled Gray saying, "I can play a Negro." Harlem with its dance halls and swing clubs was the perfect place to use the terror device, but it would take guts to terrorize Harlem. If caught, they would devise a painful death after beating him senseless.

A flashback from Engel's training came to mind. *You need to think like the police and act like a spy.* He checked the subway schedules for an escape route if he set a device Saturday morning. *I'm meeting Gray between ten and eleven and the radio operator for lunch at noon. I have more than enough time to set a device.*

A busy restaurant he frequented in the thirties would be perfect. A corner cabinet housed pictures of family celebrations and autographed pictures of celebrities. With proper timing, he could trigger the device and be gone in seconds. The subway station was on the same side of the street with a train running every thirty minutes to Grand Central Station. The NYPD would be focused on preventing a Saturday night attack. *Think like the police and act as a spy.* Tired from his efforts, he went to bed.

CHAPTER 16

Harlem, NYC

Friday Night, April 17, 1942

An anxious Gray, dressed in a fashionable striped suit, left his apartment at nine for the trip to the High Heel Club in Harlem. He wore dark glasses and a black raincoat with the collar turned up. He would need more money from Langer to be effective, the suit cost forty dollars. Deciding to walk to the bus stop, he opened his umbrella to shield his new hat from the rain and protect his black makeup. He knew the part well after rehearsing all day but playing a Negro presented a challenge. Under close scrutiny the makeup was a dead giveaway.

Thursday night he wore a black leather jacket and cap, with horn-rimmed glasses to play the reporter role. Sitting in the corner on a quiet night, he attracted little attention while developing a plan to place the device. He was sure the bouncers at the front door would react to the fire, allowing him to slip away as they rush to help. His fantasy of groping a Negro babe would have to wait another day. On the ride to Harlem he went over the role for the umpteenth time, making sure every detail was correct.

Exiting the bus, Gray took several deep breaths and a swig from his flask to calm his nerves. In his early years as an actor, he would get nervous and sweat profusely if he blew a line or missed a cue. Sweating wouldn't work with black makeup and he would get his ass kicked by the bouncers for playing a Negro. *This is it, Harvey, you're in big time show business with one chance to get it right.*

At the door, the bouncers were collecting a fifty-cent cover charge and checking for identification. The bouncer glanced at him. "I need fifty cents."

Gray handed him two quarters and walked in to a swinging scene of dancers doing the jitterbug. The girls were scantily clad and several male dancers had their coats off as they lifted their partners, twirling their way around the jammed dance floor. He signaled the waitress from the same table he used Thursday night.

"How can I help you, sweetie, you look lonely. Where's your girl, man? You need the right girl to have fun."

"Later, right now I need a beer and a shot of whiskey to get started. Bring your friend in half an hour darlin', I'll be here."

"You can stay here for now, but the place will be packed shortly. The drink with tip is a dollar."

Gray handed her the money, saying, "When the dancin' starts after the break, can I move to a table next to the dance floor so I can see the footwork? I'll leave when they come back."

"Of course, you can, sweetie. Maybe you'll be ready for a partner by then."

"I'm sure of that. One with a good-sized rack would do."

"That can be arranged. Move to the bar, darlin', I need this table."

The band stopped playing as Gray moved to the end of the bar, standing in the shadows along the wall. The band would be back in fifteen minutes. The cleaning crew had rearranged the tables; the one he'd selected was forty feet from the door. He caught the bartender's eye. "Another beer, man, I need to get in the mood."

"Yeah, thirty-five cents will get you a beer. You must be new, haven't seen you before."

"Checkin' out the action, I'm new in town."

The leader of the band announced, "I have three requests for *Moonlight Serenade*. Snuggle up guys, this is a slow one."

The couples at the table Gray had picked left their seats quickly to get a spot on the dance floor. *Now's my time, don't panic, Harvey.*

As he walked to the table, a waitress said to the club manager, "The dude in dark glasses was here last night. He didn't dance or take off his coat, could be the law."

"I'll keep my eye on him."

Gray had his handkerchief out when he reached the table wiping a corner dry as he sat down. Taking the device from his pocket, he removed the protective strips to secure it to the tabletop. He downed half his beer while checking the door. One of the bouncers was gone and the other was talking to a waitress. With trigger set, Gray walked toward the door thinking, *now is the time to fire the device.*

Heading to Gray's table, the manager saw him walk away, happy to see Gray leaving. Still watching, he saw Gray turn and point his hand toward the table. The manager used to shootings and fights wasn't prepared for what followed. An inferno erupted from the table, causing dancers to use their hands to extinguish flames while young girls tore at their blouses and dresses. Some of the men looked at their hands while others stood staring in a state of shock. Racing to the door to catch Gray, the manager yelled, "That son-of-a-bitch set off a fire."

Gray froze watching a young girl tear her flaming blouse off. She screamed when her partner tried to help and fell to her knees as others aware of the fire rushed for the door. In the excitement, Gray didn't see the large tuxedo clad negro headed for him. The delay would change his life forever.

The manager shouted aloud as he neared Gray, "You're a dead man."

Screams emanating from wounded girls muffled the threat as Gray moved toward the door, fighting his way out with a group closest to the door. He gulped several breaths of fresh air to clear his lungs and headed towards a bus stop three blocks from the club.

The club manager, a former football player, was helped out the door by a bouncer. He sprinted to catch Gray, crushing him with a hard tackle to the middle of his back. Gray saw stars and passed out as his assailant turned him over, punching him in the face. Discovering Gray was white, he shouted, "He's a white honkey."

He threw Gray over his shoulder quickly moving away from the crowd. Nearing the corner, he used the side street and alley to enter the club through the rear door. After throwing Gray in his office, the manager saw the chaos on the dance floor and people stacked up trying to get out.

He ran to the stage to announce, "There is no fire, return to the club. Clear the door bouncers, there is no fire. Get those people outside back in the building so we can care for them."

The bartenders looked confused. "Don't stand there; get the first-aid kits, clean towels and plenty of whiskey to cleanse wounds. Did you call the fuzz?"

Answering no they broke into action.

A passing patrol car, noticing the confusion, stopped to help those outside. Bouncers had cleared the door and were coaxing people to go inside as others fled the scene when they saw a police car in front of the building.

An older Negro officer asked a bouncer, "What happened here?"

The bouncer said, "I didn't see anythin'. A girl said somethin' exploded causin' a fire. The dancers were hit by these little metal things."

The officer turned to his partner, "Call for doctors and ambulances. I'll take care of the street until help arrives." He could hear screams inside the building and asked the bouncer. "How many are hurt?"

"Twenty or thirty—can't be sure. Some have burnt hair and the girls are screamin' tryin' to get those darts out. There's lots of blood."

The manager approached the officer. "Tom, we need doctors to remove those darts, they have jagged edges. One of the working girls said they hurt like a bee sting."

"Help is on the way, Jess. This wasn't the mob or an unhappy customer; someone was trying to hurt as many folks as possible."

"There was a guy who left before the explosion. He was wearing dark glasses with a black raincoat. The waitress said he was here last night, didn't dance or leave with a girl. I had my back turned when he walked out."

A bouncer handed the officer the device. "This was found on the floor, it's still warm."

Sergeant William Cassidy from the Harlem precinct got out of a patrol car to take charge of the investigation. Ten to fifteen young girls were on the floor, many with torn blouses and several men with darts in their hands and arms were standing next to their women.

Sergeant Cassidy asked, "Is there any hard evidence?"

"This thing was found on the dance floor a few minutes ago, it was warm."

Cassidy examined the device and stressed, "What happens in Harlem stays in Harlem. It's important you not mention this thing to anyone, and answer 'no comment' if reporters poke around. If they won't take that for an answer, blame it on the mob."

Two ambulances arrived simultaneously with a young Negro doctor who took charge. After examining two women, he said, "Sedate the people on the floor before they go to emergency, more ambulances are on the way." He turned to Cassidy. "How did these people get hurt?"

"Forget the cause, doctor, get the injured to the hospital, we'll question them in the morning. You and your staff will not mention this to anyone; the perpetrators are still on the loose."

The manager stated, "The club will give those who are left some brandy to calm their nerves, or a drink of their choice. Don't worry about my people, Sergeant; they'll keep their mouths shut."

"Good!" Cassidy turned to the Negro officer. "Help is on the way, Tom, get statements from everyone. I'll be back after I report this to headquarters."

~ ~ ~

After the smoke cleared and everyone had left the premises, the manager and two bouncers went to his office to check on Gray. He lay on his side moaning. The manager kicked him in the groin. "This honkey bastard did this. Take him uptown. Slice his tongue out, and bring his balls back to me as a souvenir. Put his wallet under the body, the cops will find it."

Gray moaned through his broken jaw, "Please."

"Shut up, honkey, you're a dead man. Get him outta my sight." He kicked Gray in the stomach. "That won't hurt in a few minutes."

When the bouncers returned, the manager had reservations on how he handled the killing. The way Cassidy talked, it appeared there had been more attacks and the fuzz hadn't caught the guilty guys. He looked at Gray's testicles sitting on his desk and said, "On your way home, call the Harlem precinct and tell them where the body is. I don't want to know the details, do it and keep your mouths shut."

~ ~ ~

At half past ten, Sergeant Cassidy phoned Moran's office. "Someone hit the High Heel Club around ten; it looks like a terror attack. People had burning hair and girls and guys were shot full of metal darts. I wanted you to know ASAP, I'll file a report in the morning."

"Son-of-a-bitch, we also had an attack at Greenwich Village. Was the guy Negro?"

"Yes. The waitress said he wore dark glasses and a black raincoat with the collar turned up. She didn't get a good look at his face."

"In Harlem they have their own set of laws. Talk to the manager again, and make sure he knows it's a matter of national security. If they've killed the bastard, we need to know who he was and how he's connected to Langer. We're spread thin around the city, I can't send a detective."

"I understand, Moran, but we both know what happens in Harlem stays in Harlem. See you shortly."

Moran, Tracy, and Pennoyer were meeting in Moran's office. Larry said, "We did all we could, they outfoxed us."

Moran replied, "We're not up against a typical spy. Langer fits the profile of a domestic terrorist—his knowledge of the city makes him unique. A second terrorist on the loose will spread our resources to the limit. We can't stay on a twenty-four seven alert for more than two days."

Shaking his head, Tracy said, "Thank God for Howard Baker; his raincoat took a majority of the darts. We can't cover every venue, they'll strike again."

Moran said, "Langer knows the devices have a shelf life for the gas to be effective. I'm convinced he'll hit tomorrow."

Pennoyer informed them, "I've asked for additional agents, we'll have them by tomorrow afternoon. My men are preparing a list of possible targets, and I suggest the NYPD do the same. We can compare lists and use our assets accordingly. After they finish the first list of commercial targets, we'll work on a list of boarding houses and cheap hotels where Langer could stay. We might get lucky."

Moran assured, "The NYPD will do our part. I'm putting every cop in the city on Langer's tail. This guy is hurting New Yorkers, we'll get him."

Pennoyer offered, "My guess is Langer will strike tomorrow morning before heading to a different city."

Moran looked at Pennoyer. "The issue is ... where will Langer strike?"

"Subway stations, restaurants, department stores, delis and Grand Central Station have morning activity. Those are off the top of my head, there must be more." Pennoyer stopped to think. "If he ends up doing the opposite of what we're thinking, we're the ones in trouble. It takes a minimum of twenty men to cover Grand Central, we can only spare five. I'll take Grand Central Station, and the remaining agents can cover the major subway stations."

Tracy agreed, "I think Pennoyer is onto something; a morning attack makes sense. We have four hours to compile a list by precincts and communicate with the precinct captains. Local officers can add to our lists, the odds are in our favor."

Moran commented, "The guy in Harlem was Negro, I doubt if there are any Negroes in the Nazi Party. He might be an actor wearing black makeup in a poorly lit venue. It has to be a New Yorker; a German spy is not going to hit Harlem."

As they were talking, the phone rang.

"It's Cassidy, Frank, with more information from Harlem. I just received an anonymous call. The informant said there's a dead body behind the Smokehouse Grill. I'm on my way to check it out; you'll hear from me within the hour."

"When you finish, get some sleep and finish the investigation tomorrow." Moran looked tired when he hung up the phone. "That was Cassidy; he's checking a body found behind the Smokehouse Grill. We'll hear from him within the hour."

"We'll stay until he calls." Then Pennoyer asked, "What time does the precinct captains report for duty?"

Moran responded, "They start at five and spend fifteen minutes with the desk sergeant from the night shift. The officers report at five fifteen for briefing. The day shift starts at six. Precinct captains need to redo assignments to cover the five percent that don't show up. Some of the officers that volunteered to come back are overweight retirees with drinking problems. It's no way to police a large city, but the war has taken twenty-five percent of the force." He stopped to think. "Yesterday, the plan for Saturday morning was to have the NYPD check a list of boarding houses and cheap hotels. I haven't the manpower to add restaurants and department stores to the list."

"Neither does the FBI," Pennoyer confirmed.

Tracy spoke. "The NYPD will search the flophouses, cheap hotels, and check the secondhand stores. Officers not assigned can help with the subway stations and restaurants. I will alert

128

the department stores; they have their own security, mostly retired cops."

Pennoyer said, "I agree with Tracy. Remember, gentlemen, our task is to apprehend Langer tomorrow or Sunday. He'll lead us to the accomplices."

~ ~ ~

Cassidy headed to the Smokehouse Grill. "It's been a long day, Tom, not the time to be picking up a dead body."

"My gut tells me it's the guy who set the fire. I didn't believe Jess had his back turned when the guy walked out. What happens in Harlem stays in Harlem. It's the eleventh commandment for most."

As they turned into the alley, two dogs were chewing on the dead body. Both men accustomed to heinous crimes of retribution in Harlem were horrified at the spectacle. They put on face masks, surgical caps, goggles, rubber aprons and rubber gloves to examine the body. Cassidy found the wallet as his partner opened a body bag for the trip to the morgue. He hadn't worked the streets for several years and turned to throw up after placing the body in the wagon.

"Sorry, Tom; I've been away from the beat too long. I've never seen anything like this in my twenty years on the force."

"This is the guy we're looking for. Too bad there are no witnesses, but then there's never a witness in killings like this. When in doubt, blame it on the mob."

A green-gilled Cassidy replied, "I agree, take me back to the precinct. Take the body to the morgue and do the paperwork, please. I pity the poor guy who has to do the autopsy."

~ ~ ~

When Moran hung up the phone, he took a deep breath. "The dead guy is Harvey Earl, a forty-five-year-old actor wearing black makeup. Earl must be left over from the Nazi Party. His death appears to be retribution. Cassidy will investigate tomorrow, and we'll have a full report tomorrow afternoon."

Tracy said, "This could be our first break. If Earl had escaped, he would have struck again." Tracy looked to Pennoyer. "We'll need your help to keep a lid on this for a couple of days. Someone in Harlem will contact the press and twenty bucks will buy the story."

"I'll have the bureau contact the papers and radio stations, they can enforce the war powers act, but that won't stop a leaked story. We have two days to catch Langer before the story makes the Monday news."

Moran yawned, "I think we've done all we can do tonight, let's get some sleep, five o'clock is four hours from now."

CHAPTER 17

Biddeford, Maine

Saturday, April 18, 1942

Jones sat in Dunsmore's office reading the teletype of Friday night's attack at the Village Theater. Dunsmore said, "Langer must enjoy maiming innocent people. I hope he didn't learn that at Columbia or the NY Post. This little device goes off, spraying darts and flames, the unimaginable terror weapon."

Jones replied, "Germany has good engineers. They're way ahead of us in rocket technology and devices like the one used in NYC. We don't target civilians—start doing that and you'll lose your humanity."

Special Agent Hurley walked in interrupting their conversation. "After all those phone calls, we finally get a chance to meet. Don't tell me. You're Dunsmore, and you must be Jones."

Dunsmore chuckled. "That's right. Charlie doesn't carry a revolver. Good to meet you, Hurley, where are Warner and Andrews?"

"They took the early train Friday morning to NYC. The bureau has every available man looking for Langer and his accomplice. Finding them is the number one priority on the East Coast. I see you've read the report on last night's episode. Langer could strike tonight if he has another device."

"I hope you're not passing through, we need a press conference this afternoon. Charlie and I aren't held in the same esteem as the FBI. Someone needs to feed the reporters that are hungering for a story." Dunsmore handed Hurley a sheet of paper. "Saco Mayor Henry Lowell will introduce you. Here are the names you need to mention."

Hurley said, "That's a short press release, leaves time for questions. The two of you will join me, one on each side of the podium. Be prepared to answer questions. Now let's get some breakfast; all I've had is a cup of coffee and a stale donut."

Returning from breakfast they noted Biddeford-Saco residents lining up at the school gymnasium well before the doors would open.

Arriving forty-five minutes early, Dunsmore allowed those waiting to be seated then headed to the rear door where he met Hurley and Jones.

At the end of Hurley's presentation, a reporter sitting near the stage stated, "This sounds like a cover-up to me. What you said I already knew."

Dunsmore stepped forward, "Our only witness is twelve-year-old David Radke. He was taking a piece of his birthday cake to Mr. Aldrich. Unbeknownst to David, the killers were loading the car when he walked into the house. He heard their shouted threats but did not see the men. David escaped through a rear window and ran into the woods. Running hard he tripped on a branch and crashed into a tree. David has recovered, he's back in school, and the perpetrators are on the run. They're interested in saving themselves, not in harming David."

With no more questions, Dunsmore closed the meeting with, "Thank you for your interest. As the investigation proceeds, we'll keep you informed. Now go out and enjoy this beautiful sunny afternoon."

CHAPTER 18

New York City

Saturday Morning, April 18, 1942

Bernhard, dressed in longshoremen clothing, sat sipping coffee at a restaurant near the docks. With Langer's approval, he would risk getting a job on the docks. His false papers contained identification with a mustache and wire-framed glasses.

A man sitting at the counter was conversing with a fellow worker. "Those ships we're loading are heading to Boston for the rest of the cargo before they sail next Thursday."

"Keep your voice down, you damn fool. You could be leaking valuable information. Loose lips sink ships."

"All right, I forgot."

"Let's go, if I sit here any longer, I'll skip work."

Their conversation piqued his interest. He wrote the information on a napkin. "Convoy sailing from Boston next Thursday." *I have my first piece of information on the enemy from a meaningless conversation in a restaurant.* He paid the check and walked to the corner where a police officer stood confronting a confused man. He approached the officer with a smile. "Could you direct me to the Union Hall? I'm new to the city."

"Two blocks east, one block north," the officer replied without turning around. He was examining a photo while comparing it to the man standing in front of him. "You're going to the precinct, friend; you look like the guy we're looking for."

"Turn around, dummy, so does the guy behind you."

Bernhard, looking over the officer's shoulder saw a sketch of himself. "Thank you, officer." With sweat beading on his brow, he joined the crowd crossing the street. *They've made me; every officer in NYC has a picture.*

He walked quickly to the subway station to board a train to Brooklyn. His sense of accomplishment had been replaced with a fear sending shivers down his spine. He sat motionless on the train with his face buried in a newspaper, trying to cope with his anxiety. Unable to develop a clear plan, Bernhard decided to get off at the first stop near his room and wait for Langer's advice on Sunday.

The angry officer couldn't chase two suspects at the same time. Ignoring the man's cutting remark, he said, "I'm not going to cuff you, but one false move and I'll use the nightstick."

~ ~ ~

Langer spent half the night tossing and turning, mulling over his options. Three or four times he remembered Engel's last words. 'Use those devices sooner than later, they won't keep forever.' *I'm here to report on convoys not to maim innocent people. Placing these things is a dangerous game that might jeopardize the mission. What to do with the remaining three?*

He rose early to shower and clear his head. Once more he recalled Engel's remark concerning the device. 'Sooner than later' rang in his ears. I'll place one at the Morning Café. The café has a clientele of loyal Saturday customers, different from the weekly regulars. He chose the mustache and glasses disguise, adding a beard.

In Manhattan, he crossed the street to check on a tail. Looking back, he bumped into a man he'd met at a Nazi Party rally in New Jersey, Tommy Schulze. Six years later, with a different look, Schulze didn't recognize him.

Langer said, "Excuse me please; I had my eye on a pretty girl. Wait a minute, we might be acquainted, aren't you from New Jersey?"

"I was, moved to the city in thirty-eight." Schulze eyed him. "You're Otto Langer, the Post reporter. A friend said you went to Germany to cover the Olympics and decided to stay. I didn't recognize you with the beard and glasses."

"Are you still in the party?"

"The FBI deported Herr Stewart in thirty-nine and the party dissolved without his leadership. What are you doing here?"

"Can we go someplace to talk in private?"

"We're both headed toward the café, we can talk there. I have a wife and two-year-old son, so I can't use my apartment."

"Some place private would be better."

"On Saturday morning, you can't hear yourself in that place. We'll wait outside for a corner table." He looked to Langer for a reaction. "Are you hiding from the police?"

"Only you know I'm here."

As they headed to the café, Schulze figured it out. "You must be an agent with a disguise like that. How in God's name did you get here?"

"How I got here isn't important; we can talk about it later. Are you willing to help me?"

"I'll help if it doesn't jeopardize my family." Schulze pondered as they waited for the light to change. "Are you here to blow things up?"

"I'm here to collect information on convoys. America is supplying the British with new equipment, food and petrol. If we can stop the convoys, the war will be over in a year."

"And if you don't stop the convoys?"

"No one talks about that, it isn't an option."

They crossed the street to the café, joining a small group outside waiting for tables. "Wait here, I need to use the restroom then I'll get a table."

Schulze walked toward the restroom in the back hallway and left through the rear door. Langer had put him in a difficult situation. He didn't care who won the war, he could live with Germany running the government. But to win the war, Germany would need to capture NYC. Living in a war zone was out of the question. *I can't turn him in, and I can't help him. Forget what happened and go home.*

Ten minutes later Langer entered the restaurant to check on his table. He wasn't surprised when Schulze's name wasn't on the list. *He left the restaurant through the back door.*

A dejected Langer walked two blocks to a small coffee shop to ponder his next move. If Schulze wanted to turn him in, he would have come back with the police. I'll decide after talking with Gray. If he survived his first experience, there's a good chance to place the rest of the devices. It was time to meet Gray on 42nd Street.

~ ~ ~

Langer got to 42nd Street before ten walking slowly on the north side of the street checking the marquees. He stopped several times to read the posters before crossing to the other side of the street. After stopping several times on each side of 42nd Street to read the paper there was no sign of Gray. The NYPD and FBI had squelched the story; the paper hadn't reported either attack. No Gray and no credit for his work, what else could go wrong? Looking at a clock in the window he murmured, "It's ten forty-five, time to meet the radio guy."

~ ~ ~

The Sandwich Shoppe was already filling up when he got there after eleven to grab a table in the rear of the restaurant. Good for privacy but hard on White who used crutches. Arriving ten minutes later, White sat down with a troubled look.

"I'm a bearer of bad news; it's hard to say good morning."

"Tell me now; I've had a rough day."

The waitress interrupted, "We're really busy on Saturday, and I need your order now."

"Egg salad with a sweet pickle, potato chips and coffee for me," said White.

Langer asked, "Can I get an omelet, toast and coffee?"

"Breakfast is over, soup and sandwiches please."

"Then I'll have tuna fish, coleslaw and milk."

"Be back in ten minutes."

White said, "The radio was delivered Thursday, it doesn't work. It was probably stolen and reported to the police. I can't get it repaired by a shop; they'll check the serial number."

"If it's a tube you can fix it."

"Not that easy, I don't know which tube to replace. I considered replacing all the tubes, but they're in short supply, some will be out of stock for a month. The government is taking all the tubes."

"Get a repairman that will take a bribe."

"Too risky, he could take the money and report me the next day. If I wait until September–October, it will be safe to fix the radio."

"I don't have the time, we need a radio now. How much does a tube checker cost?"

"I have no idea, only the best radio clubs have a tube checker. I'm not fooling with those guys; a lot of them are veterans."

"Join a group and check the tubes at a weekly meeting. You can't participate without a working radio. You're a cripple, play on their sympathies."

"Most of the clubs don't meet on a regular basis, they talk on the radio. I can't join without a working radio. I've only had a day to figure out options, there must be a way to get the radio fixed. If you get information mail it to me."

The waitress delivered their meals and Langer wolfed down his sandwich. "Meet me here next Saturday at the same time." He reached into his money belt for four hundred dollars. "Get the radio fixed or buy a new one, I can't operate without a radio." He left five dollars on the table.

CHAPTER 19

New York City

Saturday Morning, April 18, 1942

Early Saturday morning, a NYPD precinct captain was talking with his officers in the briefing room. "Listen up, this is important. I know protocol says we work in teams while searching for suspects, but today you'll be working solo. We're going to check boarding houses, cheap hotels, anyplace that rents rooms on your beat. You'll have pictures of both suspects." He held up the packet containing the pictures. "The men we're looking for are German spies that might be armed. Feet spread with hands behind the back before cuffing them. If they're fumbling in their pockets for something, assume a gun and act accordingly. Shoot for the knees; a dead man can't tell tales. The commissioner wants them picked up today before they hurt your friends and family. Are there any questions?"

"If they give me trouble, can I kick the crap out of them?"

"We think they've split up to avoid detection, but you can't be sure. German agents have martial arts training; use force only when necessary."

"If I find the guy, do I call for backup?"

"Of course, you can, but no heroics. German agents carry cyanide capsules; they won't chance being taken alive."

The captain left the podium and walked among the officers. "Other than the sketches, we know the men are of medium height and build. The older of the two graduated from Columbia and lived here for fourteen years working as a reporter for the Post. The man knows his way around the city. If you catch one of these guys, it won't make headlines; the FBI will take credit and thank NYPD. No more talk, hit the streets and do your job."

~ ~ ~

Andrews and Warner, working with three other agents, provided pictures of the spies to the ticket window clerks and porters at Grand Central Station. They were interested in the Boston and Philadelphia trains, but made sure the less traveled trains were also checked. The protocol would be repeated before and after Sunday's Yankee/Red Sox game.

Working the Bronx, Detective Tracy checked the cheap hotels while a dozen officers worked the flophouses and rooms for rent. He left pictures and his card at hotels with multiple shifts. None could identify the German spies.

~ ~ ~

August Funk, a sixty-two-year-old retired officer, complained to the desk sergeant at the Brooklyn Precinct, "I won't work without a partner. What happens if I find one of these guys? I haven't fired a gun in three years and I sure as hell can't chase them."

"I can't help it, Gus, four guys didn't show. I have a cruiser with a radio, you can drive between stops."

"What good is a cruiser if I find the guy in a room? Forget it, I'm calling in sick."

"The guys we're chasing aren't run-of-the-mill punks, they're German spies. The chances of you finding one are a hundred to one. I've known you for thirty years, you've never shirked duty."

"That was before a pint a day and fifteen pounds." Funk stood motionless, staring at his friend. "I'm a patriot, I'll do it. If the son-of-a-bitch gives me any trouble, he's dead."

"Gus, you heard the captain, don't confront the suspect."

"Uh-huh, I'll use my usual good charm."

After two hours on the job, Officer Funk parked in front of a well-maintained boarding house near Ebbets Field. The gray-haired owner smiled. "Are you a rookie cop working alone?"

"Yeah, smart-ass, it's my second week on the job. Have you seen these guys?"

The owner looked at the sketches. "Yeah, this guy is here, upstairs in the first room on the right." He identified Martin (Bernhard).

Funk asked, "Does the door have a lock?"

"Of course," the owner replied, "I'm not running a flophouse."

"No offense, friend, I'm asking a needed question. Is he here this moment?"

"I don't know, go up and knock."

Funk started to sweat. "Come with me, I'll need you to open the door if it's locked."

"Give me a break … I don't get involved with these guys. What they do is none of my business. If you want in the room, wait for him to show up."

"Let's cut the crap. This is very important, I'm not hassling you. You getting involved could save lives. Give me a break; I'm just doing my job."

The man eyed Funk, he seemed sincere. He removed a set of keys from the drawer. "Okay, follow me."

"Is there an elevator?"

He rolled his eyes. "Yeah, at the top of the stairs, it goes to the penthouse." Climbing the stairs, he turned to check on Funk. He was grasping the rail and breathing hard.

The owner knocked on the door several times before opening it. "He's not here, see for yourself."

Funk waited a minute to catch his breath. Without a warrant he couldn't search the room. "I'm gonna call for backup. Is there another staircase he can use?"

"There's a back door but only the front stairs. I can handle myself; this guy isn't the first bad apple to rent a room."

"Don't shoot the guy, we want him alive." Funk took time for several deep breaths before heading downstairs to the front door.

An exhausted Bernhard left the bus two blocks from his rooming house. He walked east to approach it from the opposite direction. He had broken the rules by renting a room on the second floor with only one staircase, it wasn't possible to enter or leave without being noticed. He looked over his shoulder before turning the corner for the half-block walk to his room.

After catching his breath, Officer Funk opened the front door. A man climbing the entry steps looked like Martin (Bernhard). At the same moment Martin saw Funk and decided to turn tail and run.

Fumbling for his gun, Funk yelled, "Stop or I'll shoot."

Bernhard was halfway to Flatbush Avenue before Funk had his weapon drawn. Reaching the bottom of the stairs, Funk yelled again, "Stop or I'll shoot." Aiming his .38 with shaking hands, he realized there was no chance of hitting the man.

The son-of-a-bitch got away.

Bernhard reached Flatbush Avenue to board a Manhattan bus. A paper from the seat covered his face. Five minutes later, he departed the bus to join the Saturday crowd shopping at a busy market. He spent the rest of the day crisscrossing the city before stopping at a secondhand store in the Bronx to purchase an old suitcase, a gray fedora hat and blue overcoat.

He hadn't worn a dress hat and overcoat in Germany, but they were common attire for many men. The frequent moves and being on the run were draining his cash. There were two clerks in the store; he waited for a young girl with too much makeup and chewing bubble gum to check him out.

Walking out the door wearing the overcoat with hat renewed his confidence. He was sure the risk taken to change his appearance would pay off. The police officer assigned to the store had left to back up his partner at a flophouse in the next block. Returning, he asked the young girl, "Anything happen I should know about?"

The girl seeking attention blinked her eyes as she said, "Not that I know of, officer, but I feel much safer when you're in the store."

The officer smiled thinking, *She's too young for me.*

~ ~ ~

As twilight came, Bernhard found a delicatessen. He needed sandwiches with something to drink before boarding a train for an all-night ride. Standing in line waiting to be served, a man asked, "Don't I know you from somewhere?"

Bernhard stuttered, "I-I don't think so, I live in Queens, came here to visit my mother."

The man shook his head, "Your face looks familiar, sorry to have bothered you."

While waiting, Bernhard looked in his wallet; he had two fifty-dollar bills and three singles.

"That will be two seventy-eight, friend."

Bernhard placed three-dollar bills on the counter. As he was pocketing the change, a woman, accompanied by a small boy crying hysterically, walked in. The boy broke loose from her hand, falling at Bernhard's feet. Reaching down to help the boy up, a flustered Bernhard missed the rear pocket with his wallet. Handing the boy to his mother, he inadvertently kicked the wallet under the counter.

A man at the rear of the line grouched, "Get moving, I haven't got all day, the joint closes in fifteen minutes."

The woman snapped, "Can't you see he's trying to help?"

"Yeah, yeah, give me your ticket lady, I'll punch it."

A scene was the last thing Bernhard wanted. Gathering his bag, he mumbled, "Sorry to have troubled you."

On the train, Bernhard reached for his wallet. *Oh my God, I left it on the counter at the delicatessen.* His heart raced as he counted change in both pockets, $1.27 was left. The wallet had a driver's license, Social Security card, and one hundred dollars. He looked at his watch, the place was closed. Langer had money, and the next team of agents coming would have a fresh supply of U.S. dollars if he could survive till then.

I'll go back in the morning, it's my only chance. He moved to the corner of the car to huddle up hoping to get some sleep as the cold night air settled in.

At the delicatessen, the owner-operator found a wallet under the counter while cleaning up. He didn't recognize the name on the driver's license as a regular customer. He placed the wallet in the drawer under the cash register before leaving for the night.

~ ~ ~

Officer Funk was apologetic explaining how Martin got away. "I'm sorry, Sergeant, I did my best. The guy saw me and ran;

there wasn't time to use my thirty-eight and the cruiser flooded when I tried to start it. He was gone a good five minutes before I could call for help."

The desk sergeant replied, "If you'd confronted him, Gus, he might have taken your weapon and shot you. They've killed one person and wounded another hundred. For spies it's life or death, they won't hesitate to kill you. I'll get a warrant for you to search the room."

Funk found a few clothes in the dresser and more clothes in a large suitcase. The suitcase had a small portfolio containing forged documents, including a longshoreman's union card. *I'll be damned; he planned to get a job on the waterfront. I might have screwed up the arrest, but I stopped the son-of-a-bitch before he got started.*

As Funk was leaving, the rooming house owner asked sarcastically, "Did you catch him, Officer Flunk?"

"By the back of the neck, genius, I'm calling for backup to pick up the belongings. While we're waiting, you can prepare a refund on the rent paid in advance. You do keep books, don't you?"

CHAPTER 20

New York City

Saturday Afternoon, April 18, 1942

On the way back to his room, Langer thought, *so much for accomplices, one is probably dead and the other is inoperative.* With good luck, Gray was killed by the Negroes he hurt and not picked up by the police. He didn't want to consider the bad luck options. The police will be checking boarding houses and cheap hotels by now, it's time to move.

He took time to cut his hair down to the scalp and shave his head. The new look offered several options. He could travel bald-headed or use a wig with black sideburns and mustache. He decided to dress like a Puerto Rican, selecting the black wig and black mustache. He darkened his face and hands with makeup to cover his light complexion.

When he finished dressing, the mirror revealed a man dressed in creased black pants, white shirt, red scarf, and black leather jacket. He looked Puerto Rican, considerably different than the old man disguise of raincoat with turned up collar.

After packing his belongings, he wiped down the room with a dirty shirt. *The boarding house has a back staircase and the rent's paid through Sunday night.* Just after one p.m. he was exiting through the back door as a police officer entered the front door.

The owner came to the door. "Sorry to make you wait, what can I do for you, officer?"

"I'm Officer Puich." He held two drawings out to the boarding house owner. "We're looking for a couple suspects; have you seen either of these guys?"

"Not this one." He looked closely at Langer's picture, "This could be the guy that came yesterday, he has the last room on the left."

"Is the room locked?"

"No, he wanted a locked room, but I removed the locks years ago. Too many keys to track and guests were always walking off with them."

"I'll check to see if he's in the room, but I need you to go with me. If something happens, get out of the way and call this emergency number."

"I can do that, officer."

Finding the room vacant, Officer Puich called the precinct for a search warrant and backup.

While waiting for help, he checked the back yard. A man repairing a gate across the alley smiled. "Hello, officer, can I help you?"

"You can! Have you seen anyone leaving the boarding house?"

"A man left about fifteen minutes ago with a suitcase. I saw him from the corner of my eye, didn't see which direction he went."

"Do you recognize him in these pictures?"

"The men in these pictures have light hair; the guy I saw had dark black hair with a big black mustache. I said hello, but he didn't respond."

"Was he the only one?"

"The only one I saw. That door is rarely used by guests."

"Thanks, neighbor, I'll let you get back to work."

Puich returned to the front porch to greet his backup. Armed with a search warrant, they checked the room. Langer had done a good job sweeping up the hair and wiping away fingerprints. On the way out, the backup officer found a lock of hair in the hallway. "This looks like something from a barbershop. You said the guy had black hair?"

"That's what the informant said, dark black hair and a big black mustache."

"Maybe he cut his hair and used a wig. I'll go to the precinct and file a report. Are there more places to check?"

"Six more, but I think this is the guy. He wiped the room clean, cut his hair and added a black wig and mustache to look Puerto Rican."

~ ~ ~

Moran and Tracy were in Precinct 16 making plans to cover the city for another attack. Tracy spoke, "The odds are in our favor if he shows his face."

Moran agreed, "But no one knows the odds. Suppose he has more disguises, spies have been known to dress as women. Odds favor us if he fits the sketch but favor him if he uses a different disguise."

A ringing phone interrupted their conversation.

"Tracy speaking."

"I'm on my way, sir, with new information."

"What's your name, officer?"

"Officer Puich, sir, be there in ten minutes."

Puich filled them in on what took place at the boarding house.

Moran said, "We need to get an updated likeness. Go to the special unit and meet with the artist. He can start with your information. Stay with the artist until Detective Tracy shows up with the informant. I'll make the necessary calls."

Puich replied, "Yes sir, I'll call if there are any problems."

Moran directed Tracy. "Pick up the informant across from the boarding house and take him to the artist. We need to get a likeness ASAP."

No one answered when Tracy knocked on the door of widower Arthur Tremaine. He went to the rear of the house to check the garage. The gate wasn't locked, but the garage was empty. *He's probably gone out for the afternoon. With no description of what he looks like, I can't check nearby stores.* A disgusted Tracy headed to the special unit to meet with the artist.

When Tracy entered the office, Lawrence was talking with Officer Puich. "Sounds like a basic disguise, black wig and black mustache to look Puerto Rican."

While talking, the artist was putting overlays on a dark-skinned face with black hair. In minutes he had created a resemblance of Langer's disguise. "Do I have a likeness, Officer?"

"The informant said he looked like that. I didn't see the guy."

Lawrence said, "It's a disguise used by a lot of criminals in NYC. If you went to the Westside you could find a hundred guys fitting this description." He photographed the image before adding glasses to the picture then took another photo. After adding a beard to accompany the mustache and glasses, a third photo was taken. "It's one thirty. Give us an hour and we'll have a thousand of these, is that enough?"

Tracy replied, "Five hundred of each would be better."

"You got it, come back in an hour."

Tracy said, "Outstanding work, Puich, you can go back to your beat now."

~ ~ ~

Moran was coordinating the search while making plans to protect the city. Tracy walked in behind Officer Funk, accompanied by a younger officer carrying the contents of Martin's room.

Tracy asked, "What have we here?"

"I just missed him, Rich. The owner of a Brooklyn boarding house identified Martin and I ran into him on the porch steps. The son-of-a-bitch ran before I could cuff him. By the time I got ready to shoot, he was out of range. I'm sorry, Rich, I'm too old to work alone, the guy got the best of me."

Tracy put his hand on Funk's shoulder. "Don't beat yourself up, Gus. Considering the circumstances, you did your best. Without your help, we couldn't identify the neighborhood or be sure of what he looks like, not to mention the evidence. I'd say good work, wouldn't you, Moran?"

"It's outstanding for a retired officer working alone. I'm going to put you in for an accommodation, you've earned it."

Funk felt relieved, but still not satisfied with his performance. "Thanks, Moran, but I should have gotten the bastard."

~ ~ ~

After reviewing the evidence brought in by Puich, Moran said, "I think he cut his hair and shaved his head. Now we're chasing a bald-headed guy between forty and sixty, a Puerto Rican man in his forties, or a man between forty and sixty with a variety of disguises. The law of averages says we have a better chance of catching Martin than Langer.

"I suggest the force only look for Martin on Sunday. The rest of us, knowing the nuances, can look for both. We'll work in teams, one guy with the pictures, his partner ready to react. Unless he chances renting another room, Martin has no place to hide or sleep. What would you do, Tracy?"

"It's forty degrees out there with frost forecast for tonight. That eliminates the parks. Funk said he was running with just the clothes on his back. The man needs a warm coat to make it through the night. We're policing the secondhand stores, but we can't cover every store in the city."

Moran added, "His best bet is riding the subways. He can change trains frequently and use restrooms in larger stations. The trains operate all night on weekends."

Tracy said, "I hadn't thought of that. We haven't the manpower, but the Transit Authority could help. They have additional officers on weekends. Make the call; we'll need all the help we can get."

Moran hung up the phone and took a deep breath. He, with Tracy's help, was pressed to finalize plans to use the unassigned detectives and twenty-seven retired officers that responded to their call for help, some as old as sixty-five.

Moran said, "The retired officers can work the theaters in their neighborhood or their old beat. They can wear civvies; their old uniforms may not fit."

Tracy chuckled. "Funk looked like a stuffed sausage in his blues, civvies are better. If I were Langer, I'd avoid anyone in uniform with paper in his hand."

Moran smiled. "The law of averages is amazing. We had two thousand officers on the streets, and a retiree catches the spy. No reader would believe it if you wrote that kind of stuff in a novel. Is there a good comparison?"

Tracy laughed. "You could have your seventy-year-old grandmother working the streets, or your grandfather playing for the Yankees."

Grinning, Moran said, "Farfetched but good analogy. Now, where are we going to spend our time Saturday night?"

Tracy said, "I know you want in on the action, Moran, but we need someone to coordinate the effort. Langer will probably go someplace we don't anticipate. My gut says no more devices after tonight. Harming civilians won't win the war, sinking convoys will. They'll have cyanide capsules in their mouth if they even suspect they've been made. We won't take them alive."

Moran sighed, "That's what Pennoyer thinks too. His agents are covering the larger subway stations, airports, and Grand Central Station. We can't be sure these guys will be at Yankee Stadium on Sunday. Scared rabbits run for cover.

"Pennoyer will have five agents overnight at Grand Central. On Sunday, all his available manpower will be at Yankee Stadium. It's less paperwork for us if the FBI arrests these guys and charges them with espionage. The case would go directly to the Feds and our prosecutors wouldn't make a name for themselves. Let's have an early dinner before the action starts."

While they were enjoying coffee, Tracy contemplated. "What if Langer and his partner are here to create a diversion and there's another team of agents already on the water? Dunsmore hasn't caught the Biddeford contact and he doesn't have a good suspect. The Germans may have a second landing spot or use Biddeford again. Germany is losing thousands of lives every week to our bombers. Risking the lives of a couple spies makes little difference in the big picture."

Moran agreed. "Your analysis makes sense. We can't be on a twenty-four seven alert, week after week. The politicians in

Washington are getting briefed on Monday. If we don't get results, soon, Director Hoover will take over. That information came from the police commissioner."

Tracy grimaced. "God help us. The average cop on the street has no respect for federal agents."

~ ~ ~

Langer grabbed the first taxi to the upper Westside, a neighborhood dominated by Puerto Rican gangs. In the past week, he learned Puerto Ricans are patriotic with thousands of their young men enlisting in the armed forces.

Langer checked into a medium-priced hotel, registering as Juan Perez and paid a dollar extra for a room on the ground floor. After a hot bath and nap, Langer applied dark makeup before adding the wig and mustache. The black pants with white shirt and red bandana provided the final touch. Unknown to him, police had checked the hotel two hours earlier.

While eating, Langer came to grips with the situation. Engel was wrong to use a weapon that harmed civilians; it intensified a search for the perpetrator. *I'm in control and I'm here to report on convoys.* On the way back to the room, a sense of guilt overwhelmed him. *What am I thinking? Engel was following orders and I'm questioning those orders.* "Sooner than later" rang in his ears. In the room, he put two devices on the bed while considering his options.

Years ago, this neighborhood was famous for dance halls featuring Latin dances. In 1936 the police did little to enforce law on the Westside; gangs had their own set of rules.

He remembered a dance hall with subdued lighting featuring the rumba and tango. The owners had little regard for fire laws and packed the hall on Saturday nights. He picked up the devices hoping they'd still be effective. *The action starts at nine, I'll set these things around ten.*

~ ~ ~

Saturday afternoon, every cop on the street had a pocketful of pictures; it seemed too much information was worse than too little. Constantly switching pictures and dropping them on damp sidewalks did little to help the situation. Coffee breaks to get out of the cold were forbidden; the city was on high alert with tension filling the air.

Anxious theater managers delayed entry for some moviegoers while confirming their identification. A man purchasing tickets at a Bronx theater resembled Langer. Unfortunately, the man had a tin replica of a large clamshell in his pocket that his son had made for a school project. He and his family missed the early show.

CHAPTER 21

New York City

Saturday Night, April 18, 1942

Langer selected the black leather jacket; the old raincoat wouldn't do for tonight. He placed two devices and trigger in the pockets. Wanting to check dance halls first, he walked four blocks to the closest one. The cool night air made him alert and ready for action. The dance hall had a line of dancers waiting to be ID'd by a large man checking everyone. Regardless of where he placed the devices, there would be several bouncers blocking his escape.

Moving on, he turned at the corner and headed north. Passing a bar with loud Latin music, he paused. There wasn't a cover charge and no one was checking identification. The building looked packed, maybe two hundred people. A low ceiling trapped a haze of blue smoke over the dance floor full of couples doing the rumba.

A small stage with a band sat at the back of the room. To the right a trio of busy bartenders was preparing drinks for several waitresses. To the left was a vacant table next to the door, the farthest table from the dance floor. He held up an empty Genesee beer bottle and a waitress nodded her head. As she served the beer, Langer remarked, "Looks like a busy night."

"About the same, do you dance?"

A smiling Langer handed the waitress a dollar, "I'd probably step on your toes, haven't danced in years and I don't know the rumba."

"Beer is fifty cents on Saturday with a quarter tip," she left a quarter on the table. "I have some good-looking friends that will teach you to dance, if you know what I mean."

"Let me drink a couple of beers first to get in a party mood."

He observed the dancers as the band played another rumba. The women were scantily clad and the younger girls weren't wearing brassieres. The men wore tight pants and silk shirts with small scarves around their necks. The dancers were very sensual as they whirled and clicked their heels. Near the end of the music, a twirling girl melted into her partner's arms, ending the dance with a passionate kiss.

The whole scene aroused his passion as pretty teenage girls with inviting smiles walked past him on the way to the restroom during the break. After a swig of beer, his thoughts returned to the job at hand, where to set the devices. The aisle leading to the restroom offered a clear path to the dancers, but the distance from his table to the dance floor would neutralize the devices. He had to get to the edge of the dance floor.

He went outside to get familiar with the area and figure out the shortest route back to the hotel. *When the band comes back from a break is the best time.* He returned to the club to observe tables fronting the dance floor. There were two couples at a table left of the aisle. The waitress approached. "You need another beer? I'll bring it on my next trip."

"Another beer will be fine. Can I move closer and sit at one of the tables near the dance floor when the music starts? It's difficult to see the moves from back here."

"You will have to leave the table when the dancers come back."

"If I can see their feet and connect the steps to the music, I could dance with one of your friends." He handed her a dollar. "Keep the change."

"Thanks. What's your name?"

"My name is Jesus, and yours?"

"Maria, many Puerto Rican girls are named Maria, but you know that."

When the music started, dancers left their seats to claim space on the dance floor. Langer headed down the aisle, removing a device on the way. The surrounding tables were emptying as he wiped the surface dry with a handkerchief before placing the devices on each corner of the table. After checking to see if they were anchored, he turned the table five degrees and moved it closer to the dancers. Satisfied with his effort he walked toward the entrance. After several deep breaths, he unlocked the safety on the trigger. Turning around near the door he fired the first device, reset the trigger and fired the second one.

Instant indescribable pain and fear assaulted the dancers within the firing pattern. Reeling from the first volley, a second spray of darts pierced their tender skin moments later. Flash fires set hair and clothing afire on dancers near the devices, creating mass hysteria and chaos as they swatted at their heads and clothes trying to extinguish flames. Several girls fell to the floor holding their eyes; the scene reminded him of a horror movie. Fearing fire, several dancers bolted to the door, Langer's cue to get the hell out of there.

Moving quickly, he rushed outside and down the street, turning the corner seconds later. He knew the terrorized dancers would stampede to the exit, jam the three-foot-wide doorway, and trample those who fell in their panic to escape. Others would pound the darts deeper into their arms and backs before they knew what to do. Engel was right; the device was the perfect terror weapon.

Needing to avoid road blocks, Langer walked at a brisk pace toward the hotel. *I'll use the last device on Sunday night and put this behind me.* Pilots dropping bombs on civilians didn't witness the suffering firsthand; they remained distant from the butchery. These harmless looking devices were separating him from humanity.

Inside the club, the busy bartenders looked up to see dancers charging the door with their hair ablaze and others rolling on the floor. One bartender grabbed several towels and yelled at his partners, "Call the police and find the first-aid kits. I'll help the dancers."

Not the first fire experienced by the band leader, he commanded, "Get off your asses and help. Use your coats to put out the fires and help those people on the floor."

The male dancers closest to the devices had grease on their hair and suffered burns. Their female partners with hair blazing were helped by the band members, using their coats to smother flames. Several young girls not wearing brassieres had multiple cuts on their breasts and torso.

After covering a young girl with his coat, the band leader discovered small metal objects embedded in her arms and chest. Using his fingernails, he tried to remove a dart, but the girl screamed, slapping at him. The dart had ragged edges that tore at her flesh. He yelled at the bartender, "Bring whiskey and clean towels."

The bartender responded, "Got it. We called the police."

Women cried as they watched their friends scream in pain. Unbeknownst to Langer, the scientists had adjusted the firing pattern up, and added ragged edges to the darts with a slow-acting poison to the tips. The poison was activated by moisture, producing pain similar to hornet stings. Unlike Bayridge, several girls were hit in the face.

Dancers pounding their arms inflicted more pain as the poison reacted to their moist flesh. Other dancers trying to remove the darts screamed as the ragged edges opened soft tissue to the poison.

At the door, several girls had been knocked down by people trying to get out. A large man shouted, "There is no fire, stay where you are." He grabbed a man that was pushing people out of the way. The man took a swing and found himself thrown across the floor.

Outside the door, several dancers were crying for help. A man placed his coat on a young girl and saw a dart in her neck. She screamed when he tried to remove it. People not injured had moved a safe distance from the door waiting to find out what happened to their friends. Without coats they shivered in the night air.

Retired NYPD officers Sergeant Hugo Fernandez and Officer Jose Cruz were in car 264. They turned the corner to find screaming people in front of a popular club. Other patrons were trying to help as people streamed from the narrow door.

Knife fights on Saturday nights were common, but this wasn't a knife fight. Something terrible had gone wrong inside the building. Fernandez said, "Put the lights on and call for backup. This looks serious; make sure they send doctors and ambulances. Ask those on the sidewalk to stay; we'll need statements from everyone. I'm going inside."

He approached a man trying to assist a young woman and asked, "What happened?"

The man replied, "I don't know. There are people inside with burnt hair. Someone said they saw a flash fire, I didn't see it. This girl has small metal things in her arms and chest, but she screams when I try to remove them."

"Wait for the doctors; they'll be here in minutes. Don't leave and ask the others to stay until you hear from me."

Inside the building, Fernandez realized the mixed cries of the injured dancers caused the frightening sounds he heard. The dance floor was covered with people beating on their arms and backs while others sat stunned with burns on their heads and neck. Some girls had torn their dresses open exposing breasts covered in blood. Two men were pouring whiskey on wounds, and waitresses were giving people whiskey for their pain. A dancer with a bucket of ice and towels was helping those with burns.

The band leader approached Fernandez with a small metal object that looked like a carefully crafted dart designed to hurt people. "I took this from a girl's arm, but the ragged edge tore the wound. You can't remove them without causing damage."

Fernandez placed the dart in a brown lunch bag that many NYPD officers used for evidence. Now he knew what others on the force knew and feared. A terrorist was loose in the city with something that fired penetrating darts designed to hurt civilians. A second man approached him with two clamshell looking objects. "I found these near the dance floor, they're still hot."

Fernandez smelled the gas and gun powder used to explode them. He placed the devices in the bag as he heard the sound of sirens. He spoke to the bartender and those helping the injured, "Stay here and wait for the medics. Don't move people with facial injuries."

He headed to the door where the large man had restored order. Outside, he addressed the dancers that left the building. "The medics will be here in minutes, it's safe in the club. Please go inside, we need your statements. Gather to the right next to the bar, they'll give you a free drink. If you're here as a spectator, please go home. The NYPD will close the street in minutes." Sirens screamed as onlookers left the scene.

Fernandez met the doctor outside the door. "This was a terror attack. The perpetrator placed devices that exploded with flames, burning those close by and fired little darts." Fernandez showed the doctor a dart. "The darts are coated with something that creates a stinging sensation."

"Thank you, Sergeant. The doctor examined the dart. "We'll need to sedate the injured before treatment. How many ambulances are needed?"

"At least fifteen, I counted thirty with serious wounds."

"I'll get fifteen, but it will take time. Block off all the streets leading back to the hospital, I want a clear path. The initial call is sending six ambulances. In the meantime, we can sedate the injured."

"They're all badly hurt, but none are in a crisis state."

"Sedation will help with pain until we can treat them at the hospital."

Two medics approached with a gurney. "Call for ten more ambulances and sedatives for fifty people."

As the medic left, five more ambulances arrived at the scene. "Will you instruct them, Sergeant, so we don't waste time?"

"Gotcha, doc, I'll get them in as quick as possible."

Officer Cruz was directing traffic as cruisers and ambulances came down the street. A wrecker showed up to tow an abandoned car. He ruled the street with an iron hand.

Doctor Tower couldn't believe his eyes as he entered the building. The crying and screaming was loud, but people scratching their arms and backs and the blood that accompanied it was gruesome. A nurse came to his side. "Get blankets and cover the girls with exposed breasts before they go into shock. I'll start sedating the ones on this side of the room. When additional doctors arrive, we can finish quickly."

~ ~ ~

At headquarters, Captain Moran sat at the hotline hoping the phone wouldn't ring. The NYPD and FBI had done their best to avoid another attack. Shortly before 10:00 p.m. the phone rang. Officer Cruz said, "There's been a terror attack on the Westside in a Latin bar. I have a cruiser waiting for you."

"How many were injured?"

"Forty to fifty and the injuries are serious. We have six ambulances with ten more on the way. I've got the street, Fernandez is inside the building."

"Be right there." As he left the office, he directed, "Get Tracy there ASAP and have the communications people briefed. They'll alert the commissioner, mayor, and FBI."

On the way to the cruiser, he said, "I'll kill that son-of-a-bitch with my bare hands when I catch him." Ranting took off some of the edge, but he could feel his heart beating and blood pressure rising. Ten feet from the cruiser, he grabbed at his heart and sank to his knees on the sidewalk. The officer in the cruiser was looking the other way, but a second officer leaving the building ran to his side. His pulse was faint and color had drained from Moran's face.

Running to the cruiser, the officer yelled, "Call emergency! Moran is down, probably a heart attack. I'll stay with him. Call and alert the desk."

On the way to the hospital, efforts to revive Moran failed, he was pronounced dead in the emergency room. For the past year, he had kept secret his doctor's warning that stress and lack of sleep could cause a heart attack. He was due for a physical in May, a requirement of his request to serve beyond his thirty years with the department.

At headquarters, officers were shocked to learn of Moran's death. Many wiped tears from their eyes while others sat motionless. The desk sergeant wiped his eyes and blew his nose, time to restore order. The phone rang and the switchboard operator pressed the button. "Front desk, can I help you?"

"Maybe I can help you. A clerk in my secondhand store told me a man purchasing clothes today acted odd."

"Was it something he said or did?"

"I don't know, she just said he acted odd."

"What did he buy?"

"He bought a dark blue overcoat and a gray fedora hat. The cop assigned here was gone for some reason, and she forgot to tell him when he got back."

"Thanks, neighbor, this could be important information. Criminals change clothes as part of a new disguise."

"Good, I'm glad I called."

The desk sergeant prepared an all-points alert bulletin: 'Stop anyone in a gray hat and dark blue overcoat.' Unfortunately, gray hats worn with dark overcoats were in style, causing many to be needlessly stopped.

CHAPTER 22

New York City

Saturday Night, April 18, 1942

Lieutenant Tracy, working Greenwich Village, took time to reflect after receiving the bad news. *Langer is always a step ahead of us.* With sirens screaming, the cruiser raced up the Westside Highway. They arrived at the scene as medics started moving the injured to ambulances. Officer Cruz greeted Tracy. "The disaster inside is horrific. There are more than thirty seriously injured and another twenty the doctors are treating."

Tracy asked, "Where's Moran, he should be here by now?"

To answer his question, an officer jumped from the cruiser and ran to Tracy; he had tears in his eyes. "I'm sorry, Lieutenant Tracy, Captain Moran died of a heart attack while leaving headquarters. The medics couldn't resuscitate him."

Tracy exploded. "Forget your orders. If Langer resists arrest, he's a dead man. Moran could have retired."

Fernandez took Tracy by the arm and walked him from the scene. "We need to get statements from people inside; I can't do it without your help."

"I'm sorry for my behavior. Moran was like an older brother, kept me out of trouble my rookie year. I'm all right, I can do my job."

More detectives showed up as Tracy threw his shoulders back, ready to go to work.

Several witnesses saw a Latin man, fortyish and wearing a black leather jacket, walk to a table bordering the dance floor. Seconds later he walked toward the front door and shortly after, the devices fired and chaos followed. The waitress serving Langer said our picture looks just like him, but added, "Many men that come here look the same."

Tracy shook his head. "This time he used two, how many more could he have?"

Pennoyer and two FBI agents assisted in gathering statements, but no one offered anything new. At midnight, the road blocks hadn't reported any arrests. Langer had slipped through the net.

~ ~ ~

Back at police headquarters, the desk sergeant handed Tracy information from the secondhand store.

Tracy shared it with Pennoyer. "Martin needed a warm coat to survive the night, this could be him."

"I think you're right."

"He won't need an overcoat for Sunday's game; the temperature will be in the seventies."

Pennoyer said, "Martin can't hide forever, he'll need Langer's help to send information if he has any. Langer probably used the week to recruit others. We know of Earl, but it's likely he found someone with a radio to send information."

Tracy said, "The terror attacks make little sense if the mission is gathering information on convoys. Spies work undercover, behind the scene, they try to blend in."

"The Abwehr may want to bring the battle to America. The spies may be here to destroy the city's infrastructure." Pennoyer stopped to gather his thoughts. "Something in my gut tells me Langer will dress as a woman tomorrow. It's not necessary for Martin to recognize him. They'll meet and walk hand in hand into the stadium. If we get Martin, we get Langer."

Tracy nodded his head. "Both of them have managed to stay one step ahead of us. Martin could rent a subway locker for the coat and show up in shirt sleeves. Moran purchased twenty Red Sox jackets and caps. We removed the logos from the caps. Our detectives will look like Red Sox fans, but recognizable by their cap. He also planned to have three female detectives, wearing Yankee jackets, patrolling the front entrance. If these creeps show up, we'll get them."

"If we don't, Director Hoover is taking over Monday. There's a plane waiting on the runway."

A pensive Tracy remarked, "Let's pray Moran's plan works. If it fails, the commissioner and mayor plan to take charge Monday morning. That should be an interesting power struggle."

~ ~ ~

To stay out of sight on the way back to the hotel, Langer used alleys. Walking fast he got there before the road blocks were set up. At the top of the steps he stopped to light a cigarette when a voice said, "Please, allow me."

A pretty Latin gal had a cigarette lighter in her hand. "I was just going in for a drink before bedtime."

"Thank you, I was doing the same. May I treat you to a drink?"

"I'll accept your offer; I don't like to drink alone. My name is Carmen."

"It's good to meet you, Carmen, my name is Juan." A nonsmoker, Langer crushed out the cigarette. "Wait in the lobby; I'll only be a minute."

He went to the room to check his appearance and to leave the jacket and trigger on the bed. He wanted to be seen with someone close to the time the devices were used. Passing the front desk, he noticed a nervous acting clerk had just hung up the phone. Trained to observe, Langer knew it was bad news and could be connected to his terror attack.

He approached the desk. "You seem to be upset, may I help?"

"My sister was dancing at the Island Bar. Her companion just called to say she's on her way to the hospital with multiple cuts and singed hair. I told her not to dance in that place; it's full of bad people. She's only seventeen."

"I'm sorry for her misfortune. If there's anything I can do, I'm in room 150."

"Thanks, you are most kind."

Langer rejoined Carmen. "The desk clerk's seventeen-year-old sister was hurt while dancing at a bar and she's on her way to the hospital."

"It's probably the Island Bar; they don't check identification. My husband and I danced there before he left for the army." She squeezed Langer's arm. "Life goes on, a girl has needs."

They were sitting at a table for two when a waiter asked, "Are you having a drink or something to eat?"

"A drink please. What will you have, Carmen?"

"Rum and coke will do, and a bowl of peanuts, please."

The waiter seemed cool toward Carmen; Langer could feel the tension between them. *I've picked up a prostitute or a cheating wife who hangs around looking for a live one.*

"What will you have, senor?"

"I'll have a beer please. Do you two know each other?" His direct question stunned both of them.

Carmen said, "I come here frequently; we had a scrap a couple of weeks ago."

The waiter frowned, not challenging Carmen. "I'll get your drinks."

Carmen added, "He thinks I'm a bad woman because I go out with men after my husband deployed in February. I've had one letter since and have no idea where he's stationed or if he's alive. I receive forty dollars a month from the army; I can't afford to go out on my own."

"You don't pull any punches, do you?"

"And I don't sleep with every man that buys me a drink." She raised her eyebrows. "And I'm not going to sleep with you. I'll leave if you want me to."

"Of course not, I'm enjoying your company. I've never been married and most women have an artificial air that I can't stand. If you like me, you'll be receptive to a deeper relationship, now that you know I'm not looking for a wife."

"You're the first man I've met who thinks above the belt. What do you do during the day?"

The waiter returned with their drinks and handed Langer the bill. "It's the end of my shift, senor, you need to pay now."

Langer looked at the note on the bottom of the bill. 'She's trouble.'

He handed the waiter three dollars, saying, "Thank you and keep the change."

"Thank you, senor, have a good night."

Langer asked, "Where were we?"

"I asked you about your work."

"I can't say, my work is secretive, classified. The military doesn't want men with bad knees. I'm in intelligence, that's all I can say." He hadn't lied to his new friend. "And you, how do you spend your days?"

"I work in a sweat factory making uniforms for the navy; I've been there since I was fourteen. For several years I worked with my mother sewing dresses and getting raped by the foreman. Mother said it was part of the process, 'Puerto Rican girls can't complain; you'll be fired and put on the streets.' When I was eighteen, the foreman took me to the backroom like he always did. I stabbed him in the stomach when he tried to mount me. I rolled him to the side and ran to the office with blood on my clothes. An older white woman let me use the office restroom to clean up and I put on a fresh dress."

"After hearing my story, she said, 'Go back to work; what you did was self-defense'."

"What happened after that day?"

"The new foreman didn't rape me or the other young girls, and I never saw the ex-foreman again. I think he died."

Langer knew of the abuses in the garment industry. They were prevalent when he worked for the Post. Carmen's story played on his humanity, temporarily separating him from the war. He stuttered, "Y-you and your mother still work there?"

"My mother can't sew anymore; she has arthritis in both hands. The man that owned the company died. The woman in the office that helped me was his wife, the new owner. She stopped the men from abusing the young girls and encouraged me to get my high school diploma. The new foreman joined the navy in January and I replaced him. I lied to you; I can afford to buy my own drinks. I don't know why I said that."

Twenty minutes later they emptied their glasses and Langer rose. "I have a busy day tomorrow, a really tight schedule. I enjoyed your company, Carmen, but I need to get to bed." He shook her hand and with a smile said, "Good night and good luck on your promotion."

As he walked out, Carmen reflected. *He looked like a smart one, why didn't he go for the story? Elvis wrote something on the bill,*

I'll get even with him. The wall clock showed ten thirty. *I'll work the bars; it's the shank of the evening.*

Back in the room, Langer decided to wear the skirt, blouse and sweater to the game. Bernhard didn't need to identify him, it was probably better if he couldn't; the NYPD might have made him. *Get some sleep, tomorrow will have challenges.*

CHAPTER 23

New York City

Sunday, April 19, 1942

Sunday morning, a stiff and sore Bernhard woke to the squealing of the train's brakes. The only one in the car, he stepped from the train to an empty platform. Looking left and right for trouble, he spotted a transit officer boarding the last car. The officer hadn't noticed him. Feeling lucky, he climbed the stairs protected from the cold morning air by his blue overcoat and gray fedora hat. He purchased coffee and a Danish pastry for twenty-five cents.

Thirty minutes later he walked two blocks to catch a bus to the delicatessen. The ride gave him time to plan what to do if the owner wasn't there. He had two sets of identification and try as he may, he couldn't remember which one was in the wallet. One set read Walter Bruner, the other John Nesbitt. His thoughts returned to training. *Engel taught: If you're in trouble, act like a police officer and think like a spy.*

Bernhard arrived at the delicatessen at seven to find it didn't open until eight. The rattle of pots and pans from the kitchen combined with the smell of freshly baked bread ventilating to the cool morning meant someone was there. Taking a quarter from his pocket, he rapped on the window several times. Minutes later a full-figured woman wearing a baker's apron came to the door, shouting, "We open at eight, read the sign."

He yelled back, "I know. My wallet, I left my wallet here last night."

She walked back to the register and opened the drawer. After looking at the driver's license, she returned to the door shouting, "What's your name?"

"John Nesbitt." He had a fifty percent chance of being right.

"This isn't your wallet, mister."

"Please open the door, I can explain."

"Open the door, are you kidding? Get out of here before I call the cops."

"Call the police, I need my wallet."

"You want me to call the cops? What's with you?"

"Let me in so I can have breakfast. I'll explain everything."

She hesitated before taking the keys from her apron pocket. "You want breakfast?"

"Yes please. I'll tell you why when you let me in, otherwise, call the police and we can straighten this out."

The timer went off for the bread and she didn't want the cops on Sunday morning. The baker unlocked the door saying, "Sit here while I get the bread out of the oven. Then we'll talk."

Bernhard sat at the table thinking of what to say. *Every country has military intelligence, I'll try that.*

Holding the wallet, the woman said, "Walter Bruner's the name on this driver's license."

"Yes, and I can explain. My real name is Martin Tweitmeyer, I'm of German descent. I work for military intelligence. We're looking for two German spies hiding in your neighborhood. I've been on the subways all night trying to catch them; they're always on the move. I came here last night to buy sandwiches just before closing and left my wallet. I only carry identification provided by the agency. I couldn't remember which one was in the wallet. My contact won't be here until Thursday. I need money to survive."

The woman asked with an anxious voice, "Are you a double agent?"

"No! I'm assigned to NYC to catch German spies. If you called the police, I would have been arrested and held overnight, blowing my cover. How should I say it, the police can't be trusted. It was clumsy of me to drop the wallet, but lack of sleep leads to mistakes. I can serve our country better if you give me the wallet and make me sausage and eggs for breakfast with some of that warm bread. I'm sure you'll keep my secret. No one would believe the story."

A bewildered Marie Abel took her time trying to assess what the man was saying. She had no knowledge of intelligence and German spies walking the streets, but it all sounded so real. She handed him the wallet. "Will scrambled eggs with fried potatoes and sausage work?"

Bernhard took her hand, Thank you, so much, Miss—"

"Marie, my name is Marie. There's a pitcher of grapefruit juice next to the coffee, help yourself. Breakfast will take ten minutes. I'll have you out of here by eight."

"Please call me Martin. You remind me so much of my Aunt Jule."

After breakfast, Bernhard said, "Thank you, Marie, can I give you a hug?"

"Of course, I'm very proud of you, what you're doing sounds dangerous."

"It is, but we have our moments, like breakfast with you."

Bernhard handed her a fifty-dollar bill. "A dollar's worth of change, please."

"Breakfast is a dollar fifty with a quarter tip. My husband didn't go to the bank yesterday; otherwise I couldn't change a fifty."

"Lucky for me, couldn't cover breakfast without cashing a fifty and I need change for phone calls and subway tokens."

She handed Bernhard a few bills and a fistful of change. "God bless you, Martin."

"God bless you, Marie."

~ ~ ~

Bernhard had less than an hour to change his disguise. *Go back to the secondhand store, it wasn't policed yesterday. I'll show my identification if I'm challenged.* He prided himself for adapting to America so quickly by reading three papers a day, including the New York Times. Observing people in different situations and their responses helped. Cab drivers, stuck in a traffic jam, honked their horns incessantly. Pedestrians ignored traffic signals and swore at the driver if a car came too close. New Yorkers were abrasive by nature more interested in fighting government rules than respecting them. This behavior presented a striking difference between Germany's discipline and America's indifference.

The secondhand store had a policeman at the door checking IDs. He observed how the officer worked. Those he knew entered and left with a hello and goodbye. Others were compared to pictures he held in his left hand, or both hands on one occasion. He would be easy to overpower, but it would do little good. Bernhard approached the officer, "Good morning, sir, it's a beautiful day God has given us."

"If you call working on Sunday beautiful, I'll agree. You must be new to the neighborhood, haven't seen you before."

"I live in Bayridge, going to the game with my cousin from Boston. I need something cheap with Red Sox on it."

"You look like the guy in this picture."

"Is he German?"

"Yeah, he's about your age and build."

"We could be related, I have ten aunts and uncles, four living in New York. Do you have relatives in Europe that you've never met?"

The officer put the pictures in his pocket and stared at Bernhard.

Bernhard asked, "Don't you call for backup if you're not sure?"

"Don't tell me how to do my job, buddy."

A man and woman standing behind Bernhard said, "Let us in, you can check our papers on the way out."

"Go ahead." The officer waved them in.

"Let me see your identification, friend."

Bernhard handed the officer a driver's license and Social Security card. "I don't carry my birth certificate."

The officer handed the cards back to Bernhard. "You're going to the game?"

"Yes, with my cousin, the Red Sox fan. By the way, the two of us look like twins. He's from my father's side of the family. We're meeting for hotdogs and beer before the game."

"Go ahead, bring home a winner. I hate the Red Sox."

"I'll do my best."

The scene took valuable time. Bernhard headed to the men's clothing section. A Red Sox jacket and hat, *this is my lucky day.* The jacket and cap fit. *God is with me, it's a perfect disguise.* He also purchased a Red Sox umbrella for good measure. An older woman at the register said, "That will be three dollars, nobody wants Red Sox stuff."

"It's for my cousin; he lives and breathes the Red Sox."

He showed the jacket to the officer and headed to the subway. On the way, he stepped into an alley to change clothes then folded the dark coat to fit the bag, it might be needed again.

At a main subway station, he rented a locker for the topcoat and hat. The Red Sox logo on the cap was dirty and coming off. He took a knife from his pocket to remove the logo leaving a dark spot on the front of the cap. Brimming with confidence, he headed toward Yankee Stadium to join fellow Red Sox fans.

Ten minutes later, the secondhand store's owner came in to greet the cashier. She said with pride, "I got rid of that Red Sox stuff for three bucks."

"That's a good start; let's hope the warmer weather will sell some of those golf clubs I shouldn't have bought."

The woman didn't hear her boss, and blurted out, "The guy buying the Red Sox stuff was wearing a gray hat and blue overcoat. Did you sell those?"

"We sold them Saturday. No one comes here every day unless he's trying to change his identity. I'm calling the police."

The desk sergeant took the information and relayed it to Tracy in the meeting room. Tracy said, "This is Martin all right, with a perfect disguise."

Pennoyer said, "If Martin were going to Yankee Stadium to see the game, it would make our job difficult, but he's going there to meet Langer. He'll be alone on the corner eating a hotdog trying to look indifferent. There could be a thousand fans with Red Sox jackets this time of year, but it still narrows our search. The officers manning the bleacher entrances will have no trouble identifying him. If we don't get them before the game, we'll check everyone leaving the stadium, regardless of how long it takes."

Tracy replied, "The briefing is in an hour, the Red Sox jacket and cap will be included."

Pennoyer said, "Martin got through security at the secondhand store twice; he must be a convincing talker. I doubt if he'll have a ticket, so the suspects will dwindle as Red Sox fans enter the stadium. Martin will be easy to spot at the ticket window."

"Langer might meet Martin and grab a cab. There'll be plenty of empty ones leaving."

"We have all the options covered, Rich, if they show we'll get 'em."

Tracy briefed the precinct captains and answered their questions with help from Pennoyer. Tracy wanted officers dressed in civvies, with some wearing Yankee jackets and others wearing baseball caps of their favorite team. "Take the subway, bus, or carpool to the stadium. The scheduled officers to work the game will be uniformed. Langer probably went to Sunday games when he worked for the Post, no cops would make him suspicious. Some of your officers are Yankee fans. Catch these guys before the first pitch and they can enjoy the game. If the spies show, it's a home run."

"And if they don't?"

"We've struck out!"

~ ~ ~

Langer woke at eight with plenty of time to make the game. The old wooden hotel had a rear entrance leading to the parking lot. *I'll have breakfast near a train station and read the paper on the subway. Half past twelve is a good time to be at Yankee Stadium.* After showering, he took his time dressing, getting dressed as a woman wasn't easy. After applying lipstick, he added a shoulder bag that accompanied many women. He looked in the mirror. *I look better than most of the women I've seen on the streets.*

The last device and trigger were put in the shoulder bag. Satisfied with his preparations, he slipped out the back door. On the way to the subway, he passed a Catholic Church. Wanting something to eat, the coffee and cookies served after the service would be convenient.

Not spotting coffee on the way in, he asked an older gentleman, "I'm new, does the church offer coffee after the service?"

"We do, miss; it's down the hall to the left. Some of us don't drink the stuff, that's why we're out here. Father Thomas likes coffee but doesn't want food in the narthex."

"Thank you so much," Langer said, blinking his eyes.

"I didn't get your name, Miss—"

"Sarah, Sarah Martindale. I came to New York to care for my auntie, she's an atheist. I pray that she'll accept the Lord before passing."

"I'm sorry, Miss Martindale, we need to pray she'll get better and accept the Lord."

"That's what I pray for. She's all that's left on my mother's side of the family. Please call me Sarah."

"Have some coffee, Sarah, and we'll see you next week. My name is Edward."

"Thank you, Edward." Langer took his hand.

The room serving coffee offered homemade cookies and small sandwiches prepared by the ladies' guild. Langer filled his plate, smiling as he ate. A lady in her fifties approached. "I haven't seen you before, are you new?"

Langer smiled. "Yes, my name is Sarah Martindale. I came to the city to care for my auntie."

"It's good to meet you, Sarah, my name is Paula. My dad wanted a boy he could name Paul. Is your aunt here?"

"No, she's an atheist and has trouble getting around." He ate the last sandwich, waiting for a reply.

"I'm sorry to hear that. The church offers a special service for the disabled. You can check the schedule on the Announcement Board. I have to run, good to meet you, Sarah."

"I'm sure we'll meet again, Paula."

Langer left the church to board the subway to Grand Central Station. He bought a New York Post to read on the train. At Grand Central Station he waited in line to board a train to Yankee Stadium. If the disguise didn't hold up here, it wouldn't work at the game.

~ ~ ~

Bernhard boarded a train for Grand Central Station. He planned to exit before the station and catch a train at noon to Yankee Stadium. A train full of fans wearing Yankee and Red Sox jackets offered the best cover. He picked up a paper from the seat turning to the sports section.

The Red Sox won Saturday, much to the chagrin of the reporter covering the game. The story sounded like the man disliked the Yankees, and if he did, why cover them? There is much about Americans I don't understand. Reporters in Germany never criticized players. It was the referee's fault when the soccer team lost. On the other side, New Yorkers were easy to talk with and they had an opinion on every subject and ready to argue their side of the issue.

CHAPTER 24

NYC – Yankee Stadium

Sunday, April 19, 1942

Langer arrived at Grand Central Station before noon. Walking through the lobby area to the restaurant, he noticed a man wearing a Yankee sweatshirt looking at photographs and comparing them to passing people. The man was too tall to look over his shoulder, forcing Langer to circle to the right to advance from the side.

Five feet away, he saw a large photograph of himself taken in 1936 before he left to cover the Olympics. Seconds later, the man turned to a letter-sized artist's rendering of Bernhard. *They've made both of us!* Bernhard had only two disguises to avoid detection, and his money would run out in a few days.

With time to spare, he drank a cup of coffee while considering what to do. They needed to leave NYC, the sooner the better. Needing reassurance, he looked inside the bag, the cyanide capsules were there, but hard to access. He placed a capsule in a blouse pocket. *That's better.*

FBI Agent Warner turned to his right to see a woman walking toward the train to Yankee Stadium. Boredom got to most agents and officers doing surveillance. Lose concentration and a suspect could slip through the net.

Langer boarded the noon train to the stadium, taking a window seat in the first car. He buried his head in the paper, but at the first stop, his eyes were focused on strangers waiting to board the next train.

A man wearing a Red Sox jacket and cap looked up, it was Bernhard. Trains ran every ten minutes on game day to a small station across from the bleacher section. He would buy tickets and wait for him; they could go in as a couple. Safely in the stadium, he could share his plan with Bernhard.

With luck, both of them would be upstate tonight. With summer coming farmers with cows to milk and hay to store, would welcome them. After the game, we'll take a cab to Newark, New Jersey, and catch the train to Deposit, New York, boarding separately a day apart.

At Yankee Stadium, Langer purchased two bleacher seats for fifty cents. Still hungry, he bought a hotdog with sauerkraut and mustard. Standing next to a vendor selling Yankee paraphernalia, he had a good view of the area between the train station and stadium. He wanted a beer to wash down the hotdog, but beer was only sold in the stadium.

~ ~ ~

At the main entrance, Tracy walked continuously as time passed, waiting for the first pitch. The best of plans would fail if Langer was using a different meeting place.

Sensing Tracy's frustration, Pennoyer said, "It's early in the game, Rich, we'll get 'em. They might get bleacher seats if they rode the train. The agents inside are on the lookout for a couple fitting their physical description. Martin is taller; they'll be holding hands if Langer dresses as a woman. His hands are sure to be larger than the average woman, not to mention the shoe size. Few couples will fit those measurements, and we have a likeness of Martin."

"I wish I could, but there's no peace with that bastard on the loose."

"He's loose now, but not for long."

At Yankee Stadium, Bernhard stood in awe, taking in a magnificent structure you could admire, with architectural amenities not seen in other buildings. The stadium reminded him of the Roman Coliseum. The bleacher entrance looked busy with vendors selling hotdogs and drinks while others were hawking peanuts, pennants and Yankee paraphernalia. The triple deck main structure on either side dwarfed the bleacher seats in the middle. A twenty-five-cent sign hung above the ticket windows. No wonder the area looked different. The main entrance where he planned to meet Langer must be on the other side of the stadium. Most of the crowd had begun the trek around the north side of the stadium to the front entrance. Running to catch up seemed like a bad idea. He decided to wait for the next train and move with the crowd.

Langer spotted Bernhard walking toward the main entrance. Not wanting to draw attention by chasing him, he used his male voice to yell, "Wellenhofer!"

Bernhard recognized Langer's voice and turned back, but he wasn't there. Not sure of how to react, he stood motionless until a woman made a "come here" motion. He decided it was Langer in women's clothing. Langer took the last bite of the hotdog meeting him halfway. "We have twenty minutes before the game starts. The Red Sox jacket and cap are good, but we need to change the face. We'll use the men's room."

"You can do that?" Bernhard asked on the way to the men's room inside the station.

"Of course, I'm the master of disguise."

"I have many questions for you."

"Not the time or place for questions. Check the stalls to see if they're empty."

"Not a soul."

Langer pulled out a brown mustache, glasses and eye patch. "The mustache has to be fastened down, don't move. It looks good on you. Take off the cap, and I'll add an eye patch and glasses." He turned Bernhard toward the mirror. "Perfect, the closed eye will take time to get used to. You go first, and I'll join you when the coast is clear. We'll walk holding hands into the stadium. Here are the tickets."

Bernhard said, "We should make a good couple with our size differences." As he left the restroom, he swung the door wide open for Langer to get a good look.

People still on the pavement had their backs turned buying tickets or entering the stadium. Langer took Bernhard's hand saying, "Good luck, dear."

He responded, "May, God be with us."

At the gate, two plain clothes detectives were scrutinizing every male coming through the turnstiles. Smiling, Bernhard handed their tickets to the taker. He asked, "Am I safe in this jacket?"

Langer added, "We were at yesterday's game, but my husband didn't wear his jacket."

A voice in the back of the line yelled, "I'm here to see the game, move it, Alice."

The detective thought Bernhard fit the physical description, but the mustache, glasses and eye patch threw him a curve. The cap with the missing logo convinced him that Bernhard was one of the detectives dressed as a Red Sox fan.

Inside the stadium, Langer said, "Those two seats on the aisle are perfect."

The announcer said, "Please rise for the National Anthem and gentlemen remove your hats."

Langer poked Bernhard in the ribs, whispering, "Put your right hand over your heart," while surreptitiously placing a cyanide capsule in his mouth.

At the gate, a detective said, "The couple from Boston that just went through, there's something about them that doesn't fit. Our guys dressed as Red Sox fans are wearing new jackets and caps."

"Yeah, it was Moran's idea to remove the cap logos so they could easily be recognized."

"Yes, I get that, but this guy was wearing an old jacket and the cap had a dark spot where the logo had been, the rest of the cap was faded."

"I knew something wasn't Hoyle." He checked the pictures again. "This is the guy, the eye patch, glasses and mustache is a disguise. Stay here, I'll get help."

For Langer and Bernhard, it was old home week. Bernhard said, "I've been made and chased two times. The NYPD have my suitcase and personal belongings. I spent last night on the subway."

Langer said, "They've made me too. There are two pictures of me, one from 1936 and the other one with the old man disguise. We need to get out of the city this afternoon. We'll catch a cab to Newark and a train to Deposit, New York. We can find work there and lay low until fall."

"What will we do for money? I have less than a hundred."

"I have four thousand; we won't run out of money. Farm work includes room and board to compensate for the low pay. It's not necessary we work together; be much better if each of us finds a family we can relate to. I'll buy a car in the fall, and we'll go south to work in the citrus orchards. After a year, we can go to the west coast and we'll be free. The key is getting out of the stadium."

"What about sinking convoys?"

"We've been made, there's no city big enough for us to hide. If we don't escape, it's the cyanide capsule. I won't be taken alive. You should have one in your mouth."

As the Yankees were leaving the field in the first inning, Langer noticed two men in Red Sox jackets and caps ascending the stairs. They wore black leather gloves, carried newspapers and were focused on him. The FBI agents were briefed on the explosive device, but Langer could have a gun.

Langer had placed the shoulder bag between his knees for easy access and reacted to the threat immediately. "They've spotted me; you're on your own. Don't forget the cyanide capsule."

He pulled the device from the bag, removed the protective strips ready to place it against the back of the concrete step. The detective working the bleachers saw Langer take something from the bag and used a blackjack to knock him cold before he could secure and trigger the device. Bernhard heard the thud and saw Langer pitch forward on the fan sitting in front of him blocking his escape route. Bernhard bit the cyanide capsule and was dead in less than a minute.

The detective reaching over Langer to check Bernhard suspected cyanide when he couldn't get a pulse. He gave a thumbs-down to fellow detectives, saying, "It's over guys, one's dead and the other probably has a concussion, I hit him hard." Moran's plan had worked.

The detective said, "Get two stretchers and some help." He raised his arms, "Please stay in your seats, the men were fugitives on the city's most wanted list. We'll have them removed shortly, enjoy the game." As he was speaking, his partner put the device in Langer's bag and finished searching him. He also searched Bernhard, finding nothing unusual.

Tracy and Pennoyer arrived on the scene to witness the NYPD and FBI agents working as a team. The bodies were quickly removed and on their way to the hospital minutes after the encounter.

As they were leaving to file reports, Pennoyer remarked, "Let's make sure your officers and my agents share the credit."

Tracy agreed. "Amen to that. They were good soldiers, shouldering long hours and not sure who they were chasing until this morning. We both know the NYPD has little respect for other agencies that get involved in what they consider to be their jurisdiction. Working together, we eliminated two spies in a week, remarkable, outstanding police work."

"Your retired cops did a good job. I'll have Hoover write a letter to the commissioner. Let's go to headquarters and call Dunsmore, I have the home phone number."

Tracy had tears in his eyes as he patted the larger Pennoyer on the shoulder. "Moran didn't die in vain, he was with us today."

Pennoyer stopped. "The three of us will remain friends, okay with you, Rich?"

"I wouldn't have it any other way, Larry."

~ ~ ~

Pennoyer called the Dunsmore residence. It took fifteen minutes to explain the sequence of events leading up to the capture. "That's it, I'm playing golf tomorrow."

"I'm sorry to hear about Moran, from what I've heard, he was a good man. Give my condolences to Tracy."

"He was on the job when God took him. I know the force will miss him."

"We haven't been on the case that long, but it's nice to know we played a part in catching the spies." Dunsmore took a deep breath. "There aren't any new developments on this end; all we have are sympathetic Germans who are rooting for Germany."

"Do you want Andrews and Warner to help? I can ask Hurley."

"Not at this stage, too many poking around is as bad as too few. We're in the process of setting up a coast watch, but months away from implementing it. There are small bits of information we're trying to connect, but it takes time. I suppose the papers will be running stories and poking around Biddeford. Andrews and Warner have earned some time off. I'll call Hurley if I need them."

"Tracy sends his regards and wants to know if you'll take him fishing for striped bass."

"If he knew my record, he wouldn't want me as a guide. Willie Snyder is the best striped bass fisherman in town, I'll ask him to take us fishing. Tracy is welcome to stay with us if he promises not to catch more bass than Charlie and me."

"You can work that out. Good night, Chief."

"Good night, Pennoyer."

Book Two

Gestapo Headquarters, Nazi Germany

Biddeford-Saco, Maine

Hampton Beach, New Hampshire

New York City

Albany, New York

CHAPTER 25

Gestapo Headquarters, Nazi Germany

Saturday, April 18, 1942

Colonel Falk yawned trying to stay awake for an early morning meeting with Agent Engel and *Kapitan* Helmut Hruby to finalize plans to transport agents to America. Falk, in charge of Covert Operations at Gestapo Headquarters, planned to send two additional agents to Maine. The agents were making the trip with $8,000 and three sets of identification taken from obituary records. The funds were needed to establish a base of operations before seeking jobs on the New York City waterfront to gather information on convoys supplying Britain and Russia with gasoline, arms and food.

Kapitan Hruby's U-boat 74 had been completely overhauled with rebuilt engines, new battery packs, new bunks, and an updated galley. In two days of sea trials, the boat performed well. Whatever the mission, the boat and crew were ready to excel.

Not known to Hruby was Falk's request for a different *Kapitan*. Admiral Doenitz, head of U-boat operations insisted on Hruby, denying Falk's request for *Kapitan* Gruber. Gruber and Schmidt were two of the best at sinking allied convoys, and

Schmidt had a scheduled crossing in June, delivering "Operation Pastorius" agents to America.

Falk knew Hruby to be an able *Kapitan,* but he wanted a party member to deliver his agents. Hruby was a Christian. Doenitz sought information on the convoys, but he needed his best *Kapitans* to sink them. Hruby, assigned to training, hadn't seen battle in two years.

Engel, walking a block to attend the meeting, had serious reservations. If Langer hadn't established radio contact with Biddeford, the small radio he was carrying would be inadequate. Crossing the Atlantic took eleven to fourteen days and it could take a week to contact Langer.

The terror devices lingered in his subconscious. If Langer used them as ordered, he shuddered to think of the outcome if all six had been fired, or four, or even two. The NYPD and FBI would use every available man until they tracked him down. Bernhard couldn't survive without Langer; his funds would run out. If by chance he had survived, how would they find him? Thoughts of defecting flashed through his mind.

Falk and Hruby were setting the time table for the sailing. Falk asked, "Can you sail today with sufficient time to arrive on April 30?"

"I can sail in four hours. With rebuilt engines, eleven days is adequate with a small cushion for bad weather. If we run behind schedule, we'll spend more time on the surface. The boat has performed well in sea trials."

Agent Engel arrived, portfolio in hand. "Good morning, Herr Falk; good morning, *Kapitan* Hruby."

Falk responded, "Good morning, Engel, did you bring the checklist?"

Engel held up the sheet. "I have it right here. Let's see how it compares to Hruby's."

Falk put the checklists side to side on his desk. "I think you have everything covered. You have three sets of identification including a union card for the Italian. The funds are adequate for several months, but to be effective, you'll need jobs working on the waterfront. Communications must be transmitted in code."

Hruby said, "My trip plan is to Portland, Maine, with orders to open an envelope one hundred kilometers from shore for final destination."

"That's right, *Kapitan;* but there's a Plan A and a Plan B. Brown will contact you after nine Eastern Standard Time on what plan to use. The final destination is south of Portland."

Hruby added, "After the agents are delivered I'm to stay in the general area until I hear from Engel."

"You should hear from me in three days, but give me five before leaving. Let's hope we hear from Langer between now and then."

Falk reminded Engel, "Brown is confident he can get you to NYC, and *Kapitan* Hruby says the boat will be there on April 30. For your comfort and security, the boat will sail two crew members short. You and the Italian are listed as engineers. There's no need to interface with the crew."

Hruby said, "If that's all, Herr Falk, I'll ready the boat. Be prepared to board in three hours, Herr Engel. The Atlantic can be full of surprises this time of year."

Falk dismissed Hruby. "Good luck, *Kapitan*, you'll need it. Heil Hitler."

"Heil Hitler!"

Engel stayed to talk with Falk. Removing two Walther Pistols from his shoulder bag, Engel said, "I talked this over with Tesoro; these won't be needed. If we're stopped, they would be a liability, not an asset. We'll rely on our training to elude detection." He placed the weapons and two boxes of ammunition on Falk's desk.

"You're right, of course, if you start shooting your way around NYC, you'll never accomplish the mission. Work alone and meet every week to send messages."

"Thank you, Herr Falk. Heil Hitler!"

"Heil Hitler!"

On Engel's way back, Agent Mario Tesoro met him outside the building. "Did Falk insist on the pistols?"

"No, they're on his desk." Engel looked at his companion. "I've kept you in the dark on several issues. We haven't heard from Langer since he landed. That means he hasn't found an ally in NYC with a radio. He also had a device to terrorize civilians with orders to use it. If he followed orders to maim civilians, the NYPD and FBI will not give up until they catch him. Bernhard is very creative, but Langer has the money. They planned to meet Sunday at Yankee Stadium."

"You're saying that Langer and Bernhard could be captured by the time we reach NYC?"

"That's what I'm saying. We may need to start from scratch. The radio is adequate with a proper antenna placed on a tall building. Let's pray that everything goes well on the landing and the trip to NYC. Once there, we have sufficient funds to establish communications with Biddeford. If your identification gets you a job on the waterfront, the chances to gain information on convoys is endless. We're boarding in three hours. There's a car waiting, be ready in thirty minutes."

"I worked on the docks in London between semesters. Dock workers are the same in America as they are in Europe. I'm looking forward to drinking beer and making small talk. I have common people roots with a good education. I can go back to my roots."

"We'll make a good team, Mario, if we can get to NYC."

Alone in his room, Engel removed a box from the closet and placed four terror devices on the bed. Weapons development had made the device larger with one hundred fifty darts and a more explosive gas.

~ ~ ~

The scientist in charge of weapons development, Ernst Webber, stated, "The darts have ragged edges that tear the flesh when they're removed. The two marked with an 'S' carry the smallpox virus; the other two have an agent that produces pain like a hornet sting. Any contact with blood will produce smallpox or excruciating pain. Using the smallpox virus is not permitted under the Geneva Convention. In my opinion, if one's life is at stake, all is fair in war. Complete your mission, Engel, Germany needs to sink the American convoys to win the war."

"I'd prefer not to take the devices with the smallpox virus; do you have two more with just the pain agent?"

"I've been ordered by Himmler not to make anymore. You asked me six months ago to make a weapon to terrorize America. The devices with the smallpox virus are the ultimate terror weapon. Dance halls where women are scantily clad are good targets to use the devices. Imagine NYC dealing with a smallpox epidemic. It could take doctors a week to discover what they're dealing with if you set two devices, using one of each."

~ ~ ~

The terror devices looked harmless sitting on the bed. Did he have the courage to use one or more? *I can't shoot my way out of a tough spot, but a diversion could give me time to escape.* He wrapped the devices with underwear as he packed the suitcase he bought in America for his return trip to Germany in 1932.

CHAPTER 26

Biddeford, Maine

Sunday, April 19, 1942.

Sunday evening at the Amsel home, Raymond Martz wrestled with his next move. The Amsels often expressed their feelings regarding America's involvement in the war along with their hatred of Jews and Russians. Would they take the next step to help Germany win the war?

Martz visited the Amsel home routinely to get a good meal of knackwurst and kraut. He also needed a bath to scrub off the fish smell that protected his persona during the week. In return, he taught the Amsels English. Marlene learned quickly, but Karl struggled, agreeing to speak English when Martz was in his home.

Leaning back after the last bite, Martz cleared his throat. "Thank you for a wonderful meal and conversation about our homeland. We, like many others, are trying to forget that Americans will invade Europe to destroy Germany. The thought of that makes me angry, but I'm doing all I can to help Germany."

Karl asked, "How you help Germany, work on fish boat?"

"Working on fishing boats is better than making boots for the army." He looked at their faces to check the response.

Marlene Amsel looked on as her husband threw his arms up to express anger.

"What to do? We need eat, pay bills. How I help?"

"Easy, Karl, we're all friends. If I reveal my efforts to help Germany, can I count on the two of you not to expose me?"

Karl answered, "Yah, not stool pigeons."

Martz looked at Marlene. "And you?"

"Yah, I agree, not be stool pigeon. What we do to change war?"

"Good question. Suppose I told you there are two agents landing here on April 30 to spy on convoys that are supplying our enemies."

Marlene said, "If so, Raymond, how we help?"

"You can drive them to Boston where they'll catch a train to NYC."

Karl replied, "And if caught, they hang spies. Nein! We have life, Germany loses."

"Wait a minute, Karl, before saying nein. The British will give up in six months without American convoys. A couple driving a car with two men to attend a funeral is normal behavior."

"You'll be driving Thursday night, Marlene, to attend a funeral in Boston on Saturday. You will have the name of the deceased, the funeral home, obituary, and the church where the memorial service is being held. The four of you are making the trip together to save on fuel. They will find four suitcases if the trunk is checked, one for each of you.

"After delivering the agents to the train station in Boston, you can spend Saturday night in Portsmouth, New Hampshire. People from this part of Maine frequently go to Boston to attend funerals."

"Not think easy," Karl said shaking his head. "German spies kill Aldrich and burn house down." He looked at Martz. "Why

Robinson come with questions? You drove agents there?" A frown crossed his face. "You kill Aldrich?"

"Nein, the Stiles' house was a safe place for the agents to rest before leaving for NYC. Aldrich probably walked in and they were forced to kill him to protect their identity. The agents are now in NYC spying on convoys."

Marlene said, "The trip sounds exciting. Will police check cars?"

"No want drive at night. You can use car. Do you have license, Martz?"

"I don't drive, Karl, haven't driven in years."

"Nein, you need drive damn car."

Marlene said, "I drive damn car, you stay home."

"Crazy. Car stop, flat tire, police question—arrest Marlene."

"The agents speak English. Marlene is right, there's no need to be a married couple. The two of us could be brother and sister and the others cousins. I'm game if Marlene is."

"Karl, stay home. Two people enough."

"We married, not boyfriend."

"Act more like husband." She glared at Karl.

Caught in a family quarrel, Martz wanted to move on as if it were a done deal. "We need to look at the area and roads before the trip."

Marlene suggested a picnic next Sunday, April 26, to check out the back roads to Hampton Beach.

Martz said, "I'll map the route to Boston driving the back roads. Is that all right with you, Marlene?"

Marlene nodded her head. "What about gas? Boston long way, and we use car Sunday?"

"I have money." Martz took out his wallet to hand Marlene forty dollars. "That should cover the gas and food for picnic. Get some knackwurst and kraut with lots of onions and mustard."

"I make potato salad to eat with knackwurst. Karl likes potato salad." She crossed the room to sit on his lap and rub his back, wanting forgiveness for the way she acted in front of Martz.

Karl responded, "Right, Martz! Stop complaining and join team. Hampton Beach good spot, close to Boston, no police. I know route to Boston use other roads. We go Sunday morning, drive roads while light."

Martz smiled, "I'll come Saturday night to confirm things and bathe, otherwise plan accordingly. It's two hours to Hampton Beach, so I'll be here at eight on Sunday, there's no need to pick me up."

Marlene rubbed her hands together. "I read spy books as small girl. Boy stuff but not to me. I write my own book."

"We'll be successful. Last week's landing went well until Aldrich stumbled in."

Marlene said, "I want to understand … successful?"

"It means to do things right, Marlene. S u c c e s s f u l." He spelled it out for her.

Karl asked, "And David Radke, he get hurt?"

"He might have been with Aldrich or discovered the burning house and fell while running for help. Please remember, our agents are in NYC helping the cause."

Marlene asked, "You stay Saturday night?"

"That's a good idea, better if I spend the night."

~ ~ ~

Biddeford – Monday, April 20, 1942

Monday morning found a relaxed Dunsmore on the phone talking with Hurley while Charlie sipped coffee. Wanting to get back to their families, Andrews, Warner and Hurley had taken the last train from NYC to Portland, Maine, traveling most of the night.

Hurley said, "The three of us had Grand Central Station covered on Sunday; the NYPD did most of the work at Yankee Stadium. The pictures of Langer and Bernhard played a big part in their capture."

Dunsmore replied, "Bernhard chewed on a cyanide capsule— that takes guts. Did Langer use all of the devices before you picked him up?"

Hurley answered, "All but one. NYPD found a device on the steps ready to fire at detectives walking up the stairs. They were wearing leather gloves and holding newspapers in front of their faces for protection. Langer will be tried as a spy in NYC, found guilty, and get the electric chair. I know you have Langer on murder two, but it's better we try him here as a spy. The last thing Biddeford needs is the cost of a murder trial."

Dunsmore agreed, "Right, our budget can't handle a murder trial. *Mainahs* want justice; they don't care if someone else administers it."

Hurley closed with, "Keep me in the loop. I won't sleep well until the Biddeford contact is caught."

"Neither will we, let's hope it's sooner than later."

Ending the call, Dunsmore said, "That puts the spotlight on us, Charlie, what's the next move?"

"Punt to the FBI; we've learned nothing new since the fire and haven't the manpower to track suspicious individuals."

Dunsmore said, "You got that right, but there must be something in this folder we're missing."

Jones agreed, "Maybe we can't see the trees for the forest, but I lie awake going over details and there's nothing to lead me to any one suspect."

~ ~ ~

On the way home, Martz stopped at a payphone to make a call. A voice on the other end answered, "Hello."

"The arrangements are finalized, you needn't join us."

CHAPTER 27

Biddeford, Maine

Wednesday, April 22, 1942

New York papers Wednesday editions broke lengthy stories covering Sunday's FBI capture of German spies in Yankee Stadium. There was no mention of the terror attacks. Wire services forwarded the stories to local papers. Chief Dunsmore was mentioned in every story as a tireless chief of police dedicated to catching the spies. The coverage spoke of spies landing in Biddeford, Maine, killing Aldrich, and burning the Stiles' house.

At the diner, everyone was discussing the stories. One man boasted, "I knew the FBI agents and Dunsmore were holding back information."

Other diners were kinder to their local hero but knew from the stories that someone in Biddeford-Saco, or close by, helped the spies get from the beach to the Stiles' house.

One man pointed out, "If you read between the lines, there are traitors amongst us and they could be your next door neighbor. I don't think you need to load your shotgun; they're not going to bother anyone while trying to look harmless."

A woman said, "I don't feel safe with traitors running loose."

As she finished speaking, two more customers spotted Dunsmore and Jones entering the diner and walked in with them. The waitress drew a blank look, every table and all the counter seats were taken.

The owner came out of the kitchen to announce, "Be patient folks, my wife and neighbor are coming to help. I'm sure you have plenty to talk about while you're waiting. We'll make more coffee, still a nickel a cup, refills the same price. There's a tray of fresh cinnamon rolls next to the coffee, a dime as usual. Put your money in the bowl and help yourself. Hold your hand up if you're having breakfast." Fifteen people put their hand up. "Write your order on the pad with your name and put it on the spindle. Nancy will take care of the rest." He displayed a thumbs-up to Dunsmore.

Dunsmore smiled as Jones blocked the door, diner occupants exceeded the fire code.

Holding his hands up, Dunsmore said, "We thought you might have questions needing answers. Most of you read the paper, and there's nothing I can add to the story. What happened in our community bothers me, knowing that a neighbor might have helped the German spies. We can't be sure the traitor lives here as someone could drive a good distance to help. Similar cases have been solved with leads provided by the community. If you see any suspicious activity it should be reported to me or Chief Jones if I'm not available. I'll take questions now."

A lobsterman asked, "What really took place, Chief? The paper speaks in generalities."

Dunsmore said, "The evidence points to spies landing early Friday morning, probably at Fortune Rocks where the road is close to the beach. Their contact drove them to the Stiles' house to rest. It takes a German U-boat twelve to fourteen days to cross the Atlantic Ocean, depending on weather."

"This is purely speculation, but evidence leads to Mr. Aldrich coming several weeks early to open the house, surprising the spies. Whether they killed him accidentally or by intent makes no difference. Killing Mr. Aldrich changed their plans for the contact to drive them to Boston Saturday morning. The spies burned the house to cover their tracks and drove Aldrich's car to Boston where it was found two days later.

"From there the spies took a train to NYC. Their mission was to forward information on convoys to German submarines. The NYPD, with help from the FBI, captured the spies in eight days. Short of young officers, the NYPD asked retired officers to return to duty. One of the spies was discovered by a sixty-year-old retiree, Gus Funk." He paused, looking toward Jones. "Do you have anything to add, Chief Jones?"

Jones added, "For the record, the spy knocked out at Yankee Stadium hasn't regained consciousness. He'll be tried as a spy in New York State. That's good news for our community; the cost of a trial would be burdensome. Thank you for your support, and stay alert for any suspicious activity."

~ ~ ~

Early Wednesday morning, Martz went to a nearby stream for a pail of water. After bathing, he retrieved a chunk of bacon from the cellar to make breakfast. The smell of bacon and fresh coffee filled the room as he turned the omelet. Breakfast was his favorite meal, but the omelet and bacon took too much time to prepare on mornings he worked.

He poured a cup of coffee and sat back to savor his meal. He'd been playing the fool for three years, but it was worth the effort. I'll get those agents to New York City or die trying. Brown had done an exceptional job securing needed documents from his contact in Boston. The memorial service offered a perfect excuse for traveling.

Martz heard the bad news Wednesday afternoon at the docks from a jubilant group of fishermen. Much to his chagrin, he was forced to grin and bear it after learning the agents had been captured Sunday. He was sure they hadn't been taken alive; German agents were trained to use cyanide capsules. Would the news scare Karl Amsel? *I'm having dinner with them Saturday and we're going to Hampton Beach Sunday. I'll check the rock Thursday night. If there's no note from Brown, the landing is a go.*

~ ~ ~

Thursday morning, Brown wrapped a note in wax paper before placing it under the rock at the park. The note read, 'Nothing has changed; I still like our plans.'

Thursday night, Martz read the note and started preparing to deal with Karl Amsel. Karl would offer reasons to cancel the trip that needed to be answered one by one.

~ ~ ~

Biddeford-Saco – Friday, April 24, 1942

Saco Police Chief Robinson invited Dunsmore for breakfast to review their efforts. Robinson said, "If the German families I reported on are involved, we have no way of proving it. From my limited surveillance, they spend most of their time commuting to work or working. If they have a radio, it's well hidden."

Dunsmore nodded, "Same here. Other than Fritz, Heidi Klinger's cousin, there's no other suspect that owns a radio. The evidence points to a local contact with a radio, picking the spies up at the beach. But there could be two contacts, one operating the radio and one transporting. Fritz could be working with a Nazi sympathizer or vice versa."

Robinson said, "We need to call the FBI, we haven't the resources to track individuals or monitor radio messages."

Dunsmore countered, "Andrews and Warner will be here Monday."

Robinson smiled. "Good! We'll coordinate through your office. The FBI can handle the details."

~ ~ ~

On the way home from school, Billie Klinger stopped talking and turned to look David Radke in the eyes. "If you take that paper route, you'll mess up our plans for the summer. You'll be working all day and I won't have a buddy to hang out with."

"I need to save money for college; we'll be out of school in no time."

"I know that, but I wanted one more year of having fun, going places, chasing girls, you know what I mean."

"There's no Sunday paper, I can go trout fishing after church. There are creeks a mile from Biddeford."

"Okay, we'll go trout fishing on Sundays." Billie kicking at the gravel found a stone he picked up and threw across the road. "My Uncle Fritz has been acting strange since he got that radio. He spends most of his time in the shack talking on it."

"Who's he talking to?"

"I went to the shack to get him for dinner, and he was talking German. Why would he be talking German?"

"There are German families in the community. Some like the language they grew up with."

"All he talks about at dinner is the damn Russians and Jews. Mom shuts him up at the table, but he's always angry. He doesn't have any friends and he won't go to church with us."

"You can't be sure of that, he knows men on the docks and some have radios."

"I surprised him when I knocked on the door and he turned the radio off."

"What was he talking about, you understand some German?"

"You might understand German, but all I know is nein and yah. Someone helped the spies when they landed, I know that much." Billie started to cry as he walked in a circle. "Maybe Uncle Fritz helped those spies kill Mr. Aldrich."

David had never seen the brash and confident Billie cry, but tears welled in his eyes when Billie mentioned Mr. Aldrich. David couldn't accept that Fritz might have helped the spies. "You don't know what he says on the radio."

Billie was sobbing. "I had to tell someone." He quieted. "I can't squeal on my uncle, but a spy is different, he's hurting Americans to help Germany."

"Chief Dunsmore said to report anything suspicious; you need to talk with him. If Fritz isn't involved, they won't arrest him."

"Easy for you to say, he's not your uncle."

"I know, Billie. He's your mother's cousin, tell her."

Billie blew his nose trying to control his emotions. "I'll tell Chief Dunsmore, he'll know what to do."

~ ~ ~

Fighting back tears, Billie walked into the police station. "I need to talk with you, Chief, about my Uncle Fritz."

After Billie told his story, Dunsmore asked, "Can you tell me if your uncle went out the night of the fire?"

"I don't think so. The truck is parked at the shack, but he could go out after we're sleeping."

"I'll talk with your parents, Billie; I don't think your uncle is involved."

As Dunsmore was straightening up his desk, the phone rang. When he answered, a voice said, "Hello! I have a … what do you call it?"

"A lead, something of interest you witnessed?"

"Yes, that's it! I saw that Martz fellow using the payphone late at night. You know, the man that's always drunk and smells like old fish."

"He doesn't have a phone. There's nothing suspicious about that, other than the time."

"I've seen him twice, thought you should know."

"Thanks for calling. I didn't get your name."

"The name is Elaine Thompson, my family moved to Biddeford three years ago. I work at the A&P stocking shelves in the afternoon. We've never met."

"We'll follow up on your tip, Miss Thompson. Thanks for calling."

On the way home, he was pleased how the community was responding to his call for leads. He didn't think Fritz or Martz were involved, but time would tell.

CHAPTER 28

Biddeford, Maine

Sunday, April 26, 1942

The Biddeford Lutheran Church enjoyed a large turnout for the second service, and most had coffee and cookies in the fellowship hall after church. Dunsmore and his wife, Dorothy, were detained while he fielded questions regarding the fire and the spies caught in NYC. After answering the last question, he turned to Dorothy. "Let's have breakfast. I'll make scrambled eggs and sausage."

As they were leaving, Sam Griffiths approached them. "I don't think this is important, Emmit, but I've seen a new guy in town a couple of times and no one seems to know him. I was gassing up Friday and he pulled out of the station in a 1938 black Ford sedan, the same model Aldrich drove. May God be with our departed friend."

"What does he look like?"

"In his early fifties, medium build, full head of graying hair. He looks to be in good condition. Walter at the station said he hadn't seen him before. Not many visitors in Biddeford this time of year."

"Being in Biddeford isn't a crime; what they're doing here, might be." He grinned. "There's no shortage of black Ford sedans, the '37 and '38 models look the same with a subtle grill change. Did you happen to get a license number?"

"I'm sure it was a Maine license, but I had no reason to write it down."

Thank you, Sam. If you see the car again, follow it to its destination, record the license number and come to the station. Don't get involved, we'll handle the situation from there."

~ ~ ~

Raymond Martz had an uneasy feeling as he dressed Sunday morning at the Amsel home. He needed Marlene to transport the agents to Boston and last night she and Karl had reservations. He'd answered Karl's questions, but Karl might convince Marlene to back down. As he pulled his shoes on, he mumbled to himself, "Stay positive, Raymond, what's done is done." He put on a sweater and headed to the kitchen for breakfast.

Marlene greeted him, "Good morning, Raymond, oatmeal and raisins for breakfast. Karl will be here in minute."

"Good morning, the coffee sure smells good. A light breakfast will leave room for the knackwurst and potato salad."

"I learn English, but some words missing."

"You have a limited vocabulary; you don't know all the proper words."

"That is it, learned two this morning."

"Reading and listening to the radio will improve your English and vocabulary."

"I will get your coffee."

"Thank you, we have a flexible schedule."

Karl entered the kitchen. "Good morning, Martz, I see you ready. You like lunch? Marlene make potato salad and got dill pickles. Dill pickles good with knackwurst and mustard."

Marlene smiled, "Karl and me talked it over last night. Germany needs to win war, we help with plan."

Martz gave a sigh of relief. "Thank you so much. If we follow the plan, we'll be fine."

Once in the car, Martz said, "I have memorized the back roads to Hampton Beach. I will help Marlene find her way. That's what we need to do Thursday night."

Rain and brisk winds greeted them at Hampton Beach.

Marlene shook her head. "We go home. Only crazy people are outside."

"Marlene is right. Knackwurst tastes better hot."

"I agree, Karl, hot knackwurst tastes much better. Are you okay to drive home, Marlene? You've spent several hours driving on strange roads. There's no reason to be on the back roads now. Karl can take Route One back to Biddeford."

Marlene yawned. "I tired, need rest."

Karl insisted, "Sit in back, I drive home."

~ ~ ~

Kapitan Hruby, commanding U-boat 74, was discussing with *Korvettenkapitan* (Executive Officer) Merkel their position and schedule. "If the boat continues on the present schedule, we could miss the Thursday landing. We need more time on the surface."

"I agree, *Kapitan*, but rough seas have caused seasickness for the agents and new crew members. The men can't keep food down; they are losing weight. These damnable storms aren't going away in the next two days."

"If the boat doesn't arrive on time, the plan blows up. I'm going to surface early tomorrow and run until 8:00 a.m. The extra hours on the surface will get us there on time."

"You could be right, but I think we need to be on the surface longer. Three of the next four days would give us a cushion."

"We can't chance being late, better to be early than sorry."

"Years ago, I had a problem with seasickness, and the *Kapitan* put me and several others in the water. We used a tether rope and life jackets to float on the waves. I think we should try it tonight, it worked for me."

"I've heard of it, but never tried it. How many go into the water?"

"Eight! We can use two rafts and have a sailor in each raft." Merkel left the command post heading to the storage area where the rafts are stored.

Shortly after, *Oberbootsmann* (Chief Petty Officer) Bauer approached *Kapitan* Hruby. "There was a fight in the galley. The Italian agent and *Obertanrich* (Midshipman) Weber started a brawl that two sailors joined. Schafer suffered a broken nose. The men were no match for the Italian, he boxed as an amateur."

Bauer said, "We need to put the incident behind us, *Kapitan*. The current schedule has the crew cleaning twice a day with bleach, but the boat still smells of vomit. The veterans overreacted and took out their frustration on anyone they didn't like."

Hruby nodded, "This has been a difficult crossing, I understand their aggravation. We're going to put the seasick in the water to settle their stomachs."

"I was going to suggest that," said Bauer. "It's worked every time I've seen it tried."

"It has to work, we're falling behind schedule. You handle what went on in the galley, it's better not to involve the *Kapitan*."

"I'm a veteran and a little green on the edges myself. The men will try anything you suggest to get rid of the sickness. I'll talk with those that are suffering the most."

"All of us are. You're excused, Bauer, keep me informed."

Back in quarters, Tesoro was trying to explain to Engel what happened. Engel lay on his cot, weakened by seasickness and not eating in two days. *Oberbootsmann* Bauer pulled the curtain aside, "For those that are seasick, we're putting you in the water wearing wet suits. You'll have a life jacket attached to a tether to bring you back to the raft. The cold water and bobbing in the waves will help with the seasickness."

Engel said, "Whatever you say, I'll try anything that makes me feel better."

U-boat 74 surfaced with waves breaking over the bow. Wearing wet suits, four sailors carrying rafts made their way along the hull followed by six others in wet suits. The sailors placed one raft fore and the other aft. With the men in rafts, *Kapitan* Hruby submerged the U-boat allowing the rafts to float free. The seasick sailors and agents were shocked by the icy Atlantic before their wet suits warmed them. The waves looked high, but they had a pleasant effect on their stomachs. After thirty minutes, the sailors pulled the men back to the rafts. Out of the water the men felt stronger as they climbed aboard the boat using the foot holes to the rear of the conning tower. They hadn't eaten in days and headed to the galley for some hot soup and sandwiches.

The cook warned them, "Eat slowly, there's plenty of food."

Engel felt much better after consuming a bowl of soup with a sandwich and warm milk to wash it down. His legs were steady as he headed to his bunk with a sense of relief that no one was throwing up on the way.

Oberbootsmann Bauer watched as the combatants shook hands agreeing the Americans were the enemy and fighting amongst each other would do little for the war effort. He was pleased *Kapitan* Hruby had the wisdom to let the men involved work out their differences.

CHAPTER 29

Biddeford, Maine

Monday, April 27, 1942

Monday morning, Dunsmore welcomed agents Warner and Andrews. Shortly after, Chief Robinson walked in to discuss the lists of suspects. Dunsmore mentioned the unidentified man seen twice in town and Raymond Martz. He also mentioned Heidi Klinger's cousin, Fritz, who had access to a radio. He refilled his coffee cup saying, "That's it for Biddeford. Chief Robinson will explain what's going on in Saco."

"Several maybes," Robinson said, "but nothing concrete. The Rickerts are said to have a radio, which isn't a crime. The Amsels and Metz carpool with them. Informants state they share a common dislike of Jews, Russians, and everyone else at war with Germany. I would suggest one of you interview them at their convenience and catch Martz when he returns from the docks. Be prepared, the man smells like a ripe fish during the week. He bathes Saturday afternoon at the Amsels, so he won't smell quite as bad on Monday."

Dunsmore spoke up, "The unidentified guy might be the one we're looking for, but we needn't waste time on him. If I know Sam, he'll be searching the streets looking for the guy."

Andrews turned to Warner. "I'll take Fritz and Martz; you take the three German families."

Warner agreed. "We'll meet at the Biddeford Diner to go over our notes."

~ ~ ~

Sam Griffiths, with nothing to do on Monday morning, planned to spend the day looking for the black Ford sedan. He parked across the street from the post office, drifting off to sleep. Fifteen minutes later a black Ford sedan pulled into the parking lot. A short while later, a gray-haired man left the post office. The man would have gone unnoticed if he hadn't pulled in front of a car on the way out. The honking horn woke Sam as the car pulled away.

He started his car on the third try as the black sedan turned toward Kennebunk. When he reached the turn, there was no sign of the car. Five minutes passed before the black sedan came into view. Ten minutes out of town, the car turned onto a private drive partially blocked by overgrown bushes that took away any view of the property.

Griffiths drove past the drive and parked on a deserted driveway. With binoculars in hand, he decided to go through the woods to look for a cabin. Well off the main road sat a two-story log cabin with a black sedan parked at the front. Ignoring Dunsmore's instructions, he went to the rear of the property where a child's swing set and teeter-totter separated the cabin from the garage.

Looking up, he spotted a radio antenna attached to the top of a pine pole supported by the peak of the roof. Radios were preferred by many, they were cheaper than the phone and one could communicate with fishing boats.

With no sign of activity, Griffiths decided to look in the window. *If I'm caught, I'll tell them I'm looking for my dog.* With knees creaking, he bent low to the ground to approach the window. Using his shirtsleeve to wipe sweat from his brow, he rose slowly to get a good look at a large room with table and chairs to the right and the kitchen to the left. Across the room on a separate table sat a Halicrafter radio and several notebooks. The single pane window not only let in cold and heat, but it provided little privacy for those talking inside.

Ten minutes passed before the gray-haired man sat down at the radio. He fiddled with the controls for several minutes before contacting his party. From twenty feet away, the conversation was difficult to understand, but Sam knew when the man switched from English to German. "Nein," started the sentence. Nein meant no, but he couldn't understand the rest.

After a short time, the man shut the radio down and left the room. Minutes later, a car started. *Dammit to hell he's flown the coop.* He ran to the front of the property; the car was gone. As expected, the front and rear doors were locked. Suddenly, it hit him; he forgot to get the license plate number.

Griffiths worked his way through the Biddeford-Saco traffic, taking twenty minutes to reach City Hall. Joyce asked Griffiths to take a seat, Dunsmore was on the phone.

"This is really important, Joyce. Tell Emmit I'm here, he'll know why."

"He's talking to Portland. Sit down, Sam, before you have a heart attack. I'll get you a cup of coffee, cream or sugar?"

"Black, with one lump please."

As Sam sipped the coffee, Dunsmore walked in; Griffiths looked troubled. "Good morning, Sam, what can I do for you?"

"You can call me a big dummy, and you'd be right. I followed the stranger this morning, but forgot to get the damn license plate number."

"Let's go! You can tell me the rest on the way."

"I'm sorry, Emmit, but the thrill of the chase got to me. I parked across the street from the post office and fell asleep. Someone blew their horn and I saw a black Ford pull out of the parking lot and turn on the road to Kennebunk. I followed it to a private drive a couple of miles out of town. The guy didn't see me, but I ignored your advice and looked for the cabin. He's staying in a two-story log cabin with a Halicrafter radio."

"You're sure no one saw you?"

"If they did, they didn't let on. There's a large antenna mounted at the rear of cabin. I was there for five minutes before the guy used the radio to talk with someone in English before switching to German."

"Did he originate the call?"

"I think so. He talked for five minutes before turning the radio off. A couple minutes later I heard the car start. I ran to the front of the house, but the car was gone and the door was locked."

As they passed the post office, Sam said, "Turn on the road to Kennebunk."

"You couldn't follow because your car was parked blocks away?"

"That's right. He's probably been gone close to an hour. Slow down, the driveway is coming up."

Dunsmore missed the driveway on the first try. The black Ford was gone, but the chimney had a trace of smoke.

"He must be coming back—the fire is still going."

"The man left in a hurry, he wasn't concerned about the fire or closing the draft."

"We'll need a warrant to search the cabin."

"I can't help you. My wife and I play bridge Monday afternoon."

"That's all right, Sam, you've done enough."

While the judge was preparing the warrant, Dunsmore went to the clerk's office to check on the property. The clerk happened to be the same Joyce that did everything at City Hall. She started laughing when she found the property and saw the owner's name.

"You won't believe it, the property is owned by our beloved Mayor, Mason Fillmore."

"There's nothing easy about this investigation. Do you know who lives there?"

"Fillmore doesn't, he rents the property."

"I can't check with the neighbors; there aren't any."

"If I were you, I'd talk with Jack Tough and Willie Snyder. They know what goes on in *them thar hills*."

"You're right, what would I do without you?"

"A pay increase would be nice. Please recommend it to the council."

Dunsmore smiled, "I can do that."

"You might also check with Don Stevenson, he handles Fillmore's properties."

CHAPTER 30

Biddeford, Maine

Monday Afternoon, April 27, 1942

Dunsmore called Don Stevenson for details on the rental property. The cabin was rented by Mary Shiffman for April, May and June. She couldn't make April first and requested Stevenson mail two keys to Albany, New York.

"I visited the property last week; it was occupied but nobody was home. The woman claims to be a writer finishing a book. I had a writer for six months last year. There's a $150 security deposit, I'll meet her when she brings back the keys."

"Have you seen a stranger driving a black Ford sedan?"

"I saw a man with gray hair at the post office this morning. I'm at the post office three to four times a week. Today was the first time I've seen him."

"Was there anything peculiar about him?"

"He looked like an athlete, broad shoulders and good posture."

"Thanks, Don, you've been helpful."

Dunsmore stopped at the judge's office to pick up the search warrant before talking with Jack Tough. Jack knew of the cabin, but his bad knees kept him out of that part of the woods. "I think it's the same cabin that writer fellow, I sold my stories to, rented."

"Thanks, Jack; if you remember anything else, please leave a message in your mailbox."

Willie Snyder knew of the cabin but hadn't been in that neck of the woods in months. "There's no reason to go there, I have the same surroundings fifty feet from my cabin."

Protocol calls for two officers to search a property, but Jones was in Boston visiting a sick friend and wouldn't be back until Wednesday. It would be wise to have backup, but Dunsmore didn't want to waste time looking for Andrews and Warner. "Would you mind going with me, Willie? I need someone to man the radio while I'm in the cabin."

"Sounds exciting, should I bring my shotgun?"

"No need, you'll be staying in the car. If something happens, contact Joyce. The cabin is vacant so there's no reason for something out of the ordinary taking place. Do you know the way from here?"

"Yeah, we'll be there in minutes."

The cabin looked the same as it did an hour ago. After showing Willie how to operate the radio, he circled the cabin to check the rear door. It was locked with curtains drawn.

The garage looked unused, with weeds in front of the doors. At the front door, his knock went unanswered. After checking the locks manufacturer, Dunsmore removed a large ring of keys from his briefcase; the fourth key opened the door. The hallway led to a large multipurpose room and kitchen.

Dunsmore's call "Anyone home?" was followed by silence. A cold coffeepot sat next to the morning dishes stacked in the sink. The room felt chilly with only small embers remaining in the fireplace.

An opened notebook and instruction manual sat next to the radio. The notebook had a page dated April 8. The next page contained German and English words arranged in strange formations running down the page. The next three pages had more of the same. *Someone is either copying code or trying to translate it.*

Turning the pages, he found more of the same with dates at the top of every four or five pages. It seemed like gibberish, but it needed to be examined by an expert. Removing a small camera from his briefcase, he photographed each page before returning the notebook to its original position.

Wanting to leave before the man returned, Dunsmore wiped footprints from the floor on the way out. Willie was sleeping in the car.

Dunsmore dropped Willie at his cabin before heading to the diner. Andrews and Warner were getting in their cars when he arrived. Heading to the door, he waved for them to join him.

"Have another cup of coffee, I have something interesting." After going over the information between bites of a hotdog, he concluded with, "That's it, another suspect to track."

Warner said, "We'll send the film to the agency, but we shouldn't jump to conclusions. The stranger should be easy to follow."

Dunsmore confided, "I'm more concerned with what he says on the radio."

Andrews agreed. "And I just happen to have a listening device we can plant."

"There is a window by the radio."

Andrews added, "I think Martz should be home by now. He might be more cooperative with you than a stranger; you better join me, Chief."

Martz hadn't returned when Andrews and Dunsmore got to his cabin. Men living alone in the woods built small cabins by a creek. Martz's cabin was twelve by seventeen feet with a fireplace, window, front door, and a trap door at the rear, leading to a root cellar. The creek water was clean, but many boiled the water for cooking and drinking. An outhouse stood at the rear of the cabin with a small storehouse ten feet from the ground to protect food from bears and smaller animals looking for a meal.

"Well, lookee here, I got company, including the police chief." Today Martz wasn't playing the part of a drunk. He had been sober for months and the pressure had taken a toll. "You're welcome to come in, but there's only one chair."

"We can talk out here, Mr. Martz, if that's convenient."

"It may be convenient for you, Chief, but I need to get a fire started to make dinner." He wiped his mouth with the sleeve of a worn-out jacket before taking another drink from his bottle. "There's nothin' like the hair of the dog to settle a man's nerves. I'd offer you a drink, but I need the rest for myself, you understand."

"We can talk while you're starting the fire."

"Good idea. The door isn't locked, come on in."

"We'll let you get settled before we come in."

Martz left for five minutes. "It's okay to come in now."

Andrews looked at Dunsmore with skepticism; the look said. 'You ask the questions.'

"You've heard of the fire and stories of spies being in Biddeford?"

"I have. Too bad about Aldrich, I liked him, everybody liked him. I get most of the news from the guys I fish with."

"There's talk that you've been making late night phone calls."

"Could be, some nights I go to town and wander the streets. No one talks to me, so I call people in the phone book. Most of them are sleeping, so they won't talk. Once in a while someone invites me to church."

"So you call people you don't know at eleven at night?"

"That's early, sometimes it's after midnight. You should try it, Chief, sometimes they swear at me." Martz went to the stove to move the whistling tea kettle. "You two wanna stay for dinner? I'm havin' deer stew. Eat that most nights this time of year when I don't bring home a fish or lobster."

"No thanks, Mr. Martz. If you notice anything out of the usual, contact the office."

"Will do, you sure you won't stay for dinner?"

"No thank you."

~ ~ ~

Andrews said, "Stop at the cabin, we'll place a listening device."

"I understand they don't record. Someone needs to be listening that understands German."

"That's right! I don't speak German."

"Same goes for me. I can swing by the cabin, if you'd like to talk with the guy."

"It wouldn't hurt to interview him. If he's not there, I can place the listening device. If he's talking with U-boats, it's probably at night. Warner and I can take turns if you can provide someone that knows German."

"I trust the Radkes. Both Joe and Rolf were raised speaking German." Dunsmore squinted into the setting sun.

When they reached the cabin, a black Ford Sedan was parked in front.

Andrews wrote down the license plate number, Maine 60-748. "Let's say we're looking for poachers killing bears for their fur. You ask the questions, Chief. I'll talk if you hesitate. I can flash my badge if necessary and say I'm from the game department."

At their knock, a gray-haired man opened the door. "Good afternoon, not many visitors come here. Can I help you?"

"I hope so. I'm Police Chief Dunsmore and this is Andrews, a representative from the Fish and Game Department. We're looking into rumors of bear poaching and wonder if you've seen anyone around or heard any shooting?"

"I'm pleased to meet you, name's Max Schroeder. The answer is no, I haven't heard or seen any strange activity, but I've only been here a couple of weeks. A friend of mine rented the cabin for three months and couldn't be here on the first, so I accepted her offer to use it."

"Writers often rent the cabin. Are you a writer?"

"I am, but I'm starting a book, not finishing one. My friend, Mary Shiffman, rented the cabin to finish her first novel, but she can't get away from work."

"May we come in?"

"Sorry, of course you can."

As they entered the room, the radio stood out. Andrews said, "Being this far from town is a good reason to have a radio."

"It came with the cabin. Now that I've figured out how to use it, I spend my downtime listening to ship traffic. The radio's cheaper than the phone and very handy if you need medical help or the fire department. Yesterday at the post office, I heard about the awful fire Friday night two weeks ago. The man that told me about it said you suspect German spies. Hard to imagine they'd strike in a small town like Biddeford."

"Do you speak German, Mr. Schroeder?"

"I grew up speaking German. If it weren't for my age, I'd be fighting Japs in the Pacific. He pointed to a photo next to the radio, "That's the family, we live in Albany. My wife and Mary both work for the State of New York in records. The department is so understaffed they work six days a week. No vacation time for another three months."

Dunsmore said, "I stopped by earlier, saw smoke from the chimney but no one home. Was concerned something might be wrong."

"Dentist, Chief, I had a bad cavity that needed attention. My mouth is still numb."

"Well, we won't trouble you anymore, but if you see something strange, or hear any shooting, please contact the Biddeford police station."

He offered his hand to Dunsmore, nodding at Andrews. "Nice meeting you, Chief."

Schroeder paced the floor after Dunsmore and Andrews left. *What did they want? It sure as hell wasn't a poacher. I've been here a couple of weeks and the authorities come to the cabin. Maybe the agents spooked them, but that game warden guy had FBI written all over him.*

It's for certain I can't stay here any longer, but leaving tomorrow will draw less suspicion. He packed his clothes and the notebook before bed.

On the way back to the office, Andrews said, "If we start checking Max Schroeder and Mary Shiffman tonight, we could have something by noon tomorrow."

"We can't check the license plate until morning."

"Let's get the film on the way; we can still make the last pickup. Martz looked drunk, he wasn't acting."

Dunsmore agreed. "We'll stop at the phone company and talk with Gladys. Unless she knows his voice, once the nickel falls, Martz would be just another caller. She comes on at ten. I'll talk with her before she starts her shift."

Andrews remarked, "Even drunk, Martz sounds intelligent and he speaks with a good voice."

Dunsmore agreed. "I don't think his voice changes drunk or sober."

"We'll take our time going over the evidence and decide how to spend tomorrow. Are the dentists in the phone book?"

"Joyce will give you the addresses, there's only two. The special tonight at the diner is meatloaf with homemade chili sauce."

~ ~ ~

Monday morning David rode his bike to school to get an early start on the paper route. He packed his papers and headed toward the first subscriber. An hour later he was breezing along with only four more papers to deliver before his last delivery. At the Miller residence, he took time to pet the dog. Riding to his next customer, the bike was hard to steer. A hissing sound revealed a flat front tire. *Dangit, my first day and I get a flat tire.*

He shrugged his shoulders and walked the bike out of town. Adding to his predicament, he needed to don his rain gear when the rains came. *What else can go wrong?* The next two subscribers lived on a dirt road full of mud. The final gasps of winter frost left the ground a mess. He sloshed through the mud to the Couture home. *Only a block to go.*

Approaching the church, the rain was blown sideways by the high winds. Pastor Alex lived in a cottage at the rear of the property. Hoping he would drive him home, David walked up the front steps with thunder sounding behind him. Reaching for the door he heard Pastor Alex shouting at someone in German.

He knocked, but thunder roared even louder as Pastor Alex shouted, "Yah!"

David knocked harder; the door was finally opened. Looking flustered, Pastor Alex greeted David sharply. "What are you doing here?"

An astounded David answered, "I had a flat tire and saw your light; here's your paper."

Pastor Alex spoke more gently, "I'm sorry, David, with the thunder and rain I couldn't hear the radio, you surprised me. Come in out of the rain."

"Thank you, Pastor, I need a favor."

"Is it a ride home?"

"Yes sir, my bike has a flat tire and the roads are a mess. Walking home will take forever. I saw a pickup in the drive, otherwise I wouldn't ask. Grandpa Rolf will come for me if I call."

"I brought the pickup home from work for a test drive. Give me a minute to shut the radio down and I'll have you home in no time."

On the way home, David said, "I didn't know you speak German."

"I grew up speaking German. I'm from the Sudetenland, the second territory annexed by Germany in 1939, the first was Austria. I have a German father and a Czech mother. I use the radio to speak with my wife in Boston. It's far cheaper than the phone. I had to raise my voice over the thunder, it's not raining there."

"Here we are, David. I'm not going to come in, say hello to your family."

~ ~ ~

Dunsmore found Gladys drinking coffee before her shift began. "It must be important for you to be here after nine. I'm paid to work nights, that's why I'm here."

"It is important, or I'd be home getting ready for bed. I haven't seen Bob lately, is he well?"

"Your paths aren't crossing, he's working most days. Business is starting to slow with summer on the way, that's why I need to work."

"Are there many phone calls after ten?"

"More than you think. The rate for long distance calls goes down after eleven and many take advantage of the lower cost.

Since the war, people are making more calls out of our time zone to their sons and relatives serving in the military. I have people calling after eleven to Illinois and Missouri."

"I'm more concerned about local calls from the payphone."

"Once the nickel falls, I can't tell where the call originated. My job is to handle both incoming and outgoing calls. I haven't time to figure out who's making calls."

"That's what I thought. Do you know Raymond Martz?"

"Is he the man who smells like a ripe fish?"

"That's him."

"Most folks try to avoid him, including me."

"Could you recognize Martz's voice from mine if he made a call late at night?"

"Not a good question. I talk with you frequently, I know what you sound like and the conversation starts with a greeting. I've never heard Martz speak."

"Sorry to have bothered you, Gladys. For the record, Martz has done nothing wrong, he's not under investigation."

"I'm happy to hear that. Off the record, I'll make a record of late night calls for the next couple of weeks."

"That would be helpful, thank you."

"I'm willing to help if my effort helps catch someone breaking the law or helping the enemy."

Dunsmore went home to get his own car before staking out the payphone outside the drugstore. Maybe Martz would place a call tonight.

~ ~ ~

Martz put the gin bottle away and brewed a fresh pot of strong coffee. He needed all his wits to deal with Dunsmore and the FBI. He sipped hot coffee reflecting on what was said and how he reacted. Being drunk was an asset, he didn't have to act.

With a second cup of coffee, he sat down at the small desk built into the wall. He took pencil and paper from the drawer to write, 'Dunsmore and FBI agent poking around. Check Thursday before landing.' He wrapped the note in wax paper and placed it in an envelope.

He left the cabin to take a circuitous route to the park. The walk took ninety minutes, but no one had seen him. Clouds covered the moon as the envelope was placed under a large rock.

On the way back, Martz walked well past the business district before heading back to use the payphone. The hours of walking had a sobering effect. Needing to be drunk, he drank the rest of the gin in the park. With little tolerance for alcohol, the gin had an immediate effect on his speech.

Smiling, he walked slowly toward the payphone to make harassment calls, not aware of the car parked in the next block. Looking for a number to call, Martz used a flashlight. Not knowing the benefactor of the call, a nickel was inserted and the operator asked for the number. After his third attempt to speak, the number came out. Gladys laughed after placing the call, this had to be Martz.

Dunsmore watched him stagger from the phone booth and trip on the sidewalk. Under normal circumstances, the police would help a drunk, but in this case, Martz was on his own. Dunsmore thought the phone calls were part of a hoax Martz used to create a false image the community believed to be true.

Martz got up to start the walk home, having walked the distance many times. Tonight, he lurched left to right, tripping on a root. This time he stayed down to sleep it off. Dunsmore ignored him and went home.

Martz headed to the docks to go to work when the birds started singing in the morning. It usually took until Wednesday or Thursday before smelling bad. This week he accomplished it by Tuesday.

CHAPTER 31

Biddeford, Maine

Tuesday, April 28, 1942

Dunsmore rose at six, needing to check with Gladys regarding last night's calls. Gladys, as usual, had a quip. "You should get more sleep, Emmit; it would help with the bags under your eyes."

"Thanks, Gladys, I see you still find me irresistible, I won't tell Dorothy."

"Dream on, Emmit, one man is one too many."

"Speaking of one man, did a drunk make a call around midnight?"

"That's a silly question. You were probably watching the payphone. A drunk placed two calls around midnight. I can't give you the numbers without a warrant, but I'm going for coffee, be back in a minute."

Dunsmore leaned over the counter and copied the numbers. On her return, he bid Gladys farewell and greeted the next operator.

The FBI could match the numbers with the names by tomorrow. The diner offered two eggs with bacon, toast and coffee for thirty-five cents. He found Warner and Andrews at a rear table, waiting for their breakfast.

"This is great, two birds with one stone. Good morning, gentlemen, I hope you slept well."

Andrews replied, "I don't think either one of us will sleep well until we find the contact, local or not. Tell us what you learned after I left you yesterday?"

"After dinner I went back to town to stake out the payphone. Martz showed up drunk and made several calls. He used a flashlight to find numbers in the phonebook. Gladys said a drunk made two calls before midnight. I copied the numbers from her notepad while she fetched a cup of coffee. You have the technology to put a name to a number."

"When Martz left the phone booth, he circled the booth, tripped and fell on the sidewalk. Staggered to his feet and fell again. That time he stayed down to sleep it off."

Andrews asked, "I wonder what he did after we left the cabin till the time he made the calls?"

Dunsmore described, "Martz walks from the woods to the docks every day. The man has an abundance of energy. Walking another three miles to meet someone wouldn't begin to tax his stamina."

Warner asked, "Do you know of any change in his behavior?"

Dunsmore contemplated. "I've had several complaints about him. The most common are wandering the streets drunk and smelling like a ripe fish. Someone saw him using the payphone a couple of times and phoned the office. She identified herself, some don't. A man without a phone using a payphone isn't strange behavior, but waiting until midnight is."

Warner took over. "If there's a need to arrest him, the FBI will do it, we have a broader jurisdiction. I'll forward these numbers to the bureau and we should have information on Martz, Schroeder and Shiffman by noon with a complete picture by tomorrow." He stopped to think. "Martz isn't the guy we're looking for, but he might be a sympathizer helping the contact.

There's no way of knowing unless we watch him when he's not working. If he's involved, the payphone is the best way to leave coded messages. Unless we can connect a phone number to an address, we're chasing our tail."

Dunsmore said, "We'll search Fritz's cabin while he's at work. Last week his cousin seemed uncomfortable with my presence, she was trying to protect him."

Andrews sipped his coffee and put down the cup. "This is day two of the investigation and everything we find needs to be sent to the bureau for help or confirmation. It occurred to me last night, the investigation might last four or five weeks without any progress. The Germans aren't likely to send more agents while we're still investigating the first two." He took time to reflect. "However, if I were running the show, I'd have another submarine on the water while we're sitting here trying to figure out their next move." He paused again. "For the record, Schroeder had a tooth filled yesterday morning."

Dunsmore said, "I didn't think he'd lie. Schroeder hates Russians and Jews; but he's in a cast of thousands living in the northeast. We need to eliminate suspects like him, so we can focus on new leads." He handed the license plate number to Warner. "You'll get a quick response. It'd take me two days."

Warner replied, "I'll work with the state and bureau while you two do the field work. We'll meet at city hall for dinner, pick up hamburgers and chips."

Dunsmore looked to Andrews and said, "That'll work for us. There's beer and cokes in the fridge."

~ ~ ~

Dunsmore wasn't the only early bird Tuesday morning. Brown was up at six to make coffee. At the municipal park, he headed to the rock, walking slowly not wanting to attract attention. After looking both ways, he removed an envelope from under the rock. The envelope was soaked, but the wax paper protected the note. He shoved the envelope in his side pocket before heading back to the car.

With a second cup of coffee and some toast, he read the note. Dunsmore and the FBI asking questions were normal activity, but he never thought Martz would be the target of an investigation. If I don't hear from Schroeder soon, they may have discovered him. On his way out the door the phone rang.

~ ~ ~

David rose early Tuesday morning, wanting to talk with his grandfather before leaving for school. Rolf looked at his grandson, "It must be something important to get you out of bed an hour early to have breakfast with two men who rarely talk in the morning."

"It could be important, that's why I need to talk with you. I got to the church late with the paper. It thundered and lightning flashed while I was standing on the porch. I heard Pastor Alex talking on the radio in German, shouting *nein* and *yah* and a word that sounded like Thursday, but I'm not sure. He seemed irritated when he answered the door. 'What are you doing here?' he asked. I didn't know what to say, so I handed him the paper. Then he responded in a softer voice like he always sounds. Pastor said he was talking with his wife in Boston and the storm caused him to raise his voice. I'm confused, Papa, why would he be speaking German?"

"Pastor Alex grew up speaking German, it's his native tongue. He claims to be gifted in languages and studied English throughout his schooling. The radio has been part of the church for years, and last year it was updated to a newer model. He was probably making a point with his wife and reverted back to German."

"He's never spoken harshly to me before, it stunned me."

"You might have surprised him." Rolf patted his grandson on the shoulder. "You did the right thing, David. America had severed ties with Germany when the church called Pastor Novak. The elders had no way to check references. We'll talk with Chief Dunsmore."

~ ~ ~

In spite of his troubles last night, Martz made it to work on time. He could feel a knot in his stomach while boarding the boat. It had been much easier to play the role of a drunk than being drunk. His head ached something awful after consuming a pint of gin yesterday. He spent his time at the stern working the nets, while his shipmates avoided contact.

At nine he was throwing up from an empty stomach. By ten, Martz was on his knees trying to cope with the discomfort. When help came, he was spitting up blood. Captain Larsen fetched a bottle of brandy from his pocket and offered Martz a drink. "I'm sick, Captain, very sick."

With a good catch on board, Captain Larsen decided to head for shore and take Martz to the Biddeford clinic. Martz passed out before the boat reached the docks forty minutes later. Captain Larsen needed help to put Raymond in the back of the pickup. The man helping frowned when Larsen asked him to ride in the truck bed with Martz.

"The fresh air will help, it's a short ride."

The nurse working the front desk asked for name and address, the usual information. "I don't know his age," Larsen answered.

"His name is Raymond Martz. He's the guy who wanders around town drunk. The man needs to be washed before he's treated for anything."

"Do you know what's wrong with him?"

"He came to work sober, but probably drank last night. He started to throw up and an hour ago he spit blood. Only God knows what's wrong with him. You can't help him in his present condition without bathing him first."

"Where is he now?"

"He's passed out in the back of my truck. Send an orderly out with a gurney and we'll get him to the clinic."

"Are you responsible for his bill?"

"I have no idea if he has any money, but I'm not responsible for his debts." Larsen stopped to think. "As irresponsible as he lets on, the man pays cash for everything. I haven't heard anyone say he didn't pay his bills."

"We'll take good care of him. I didn't get your name."

"Captain Larsen, I live in Saco. Here's my phone number, don't hesitate to call."

The nurse said, "I'll have the orderly there in a few minutes."

~ ~ ~

Before leaving the office, Andrews and Dunsmore were reviewing what they had discovered. Martz didn't have a car, and Dunsmore had never seen him drive one.

"Whatever value he has would be limited to recruiting and possibly hiding agents in a remote cabin. Though limited, he would be playing an important role. If not by phone, how would Martz and his contact stay in touch?"

Dunsmore smiled. "As a boy, I read a mystery that had two lovers leaving notes in a park. This time of year, there are few visitors other than those taking morning walks? The lovers placed notes in the crevice of a large maple tree, their parents never learned of their correspondence."

Andrews said, "I remember a movie where two burglars placed notes under a rock in the park. I think they wrapped them in wax paper. Does your park have a rock in an out of the way place?"

"There's a large rock in the center area where two paths cross." Dunsmore laughed, "Could it really be that easy? A note placed under a rock."

"Before the park, let's get warrants to search Martz's cabin and Fritz's shack."

Dunsmore said, "I prefer not to. Can't you use your authority under the War Powers Act to conduct searches under reasonable suspicion?"

"I can, but we prefer to follow the local laws. The bureau doesn't like bad publicity."

"We've had a fire and a murder in Biddeford. There won't be any bad publicity coming from here. We'll take the Martz cabin first." Dunsmore laughed. "You have more resources than Biddeford; we'll use your car and gas."

Martz wasn't at the cabin, but the bunk was made and the dishes washed. For a bachelor living in the woods, he had day-to-day living under control. The mattress on the bunk was of good quality and the pots and pans were a top brand.

Dunsmore went through the desk drawer finding writing paper on top of an old address book. Martz had lived in Rhode Island at one time and most of the addresses and phone numbers were from there. He removed the drawer to look for items hidden behind the drawer, there were none. Replacing the drawer, something didn't seem right. "Take a look at this drawer, it looks strange to me."

"It's a false back, Chief. There must be a way to open it." Andrews took the drawer and played with the handle with no success before accidentally dropping it. The false back opened revealing a wallet, some pictures and a wad of bills. "I hit the jackpot; the guy isn't broke." He handed the wallet to Dunsmore while sitting down to count the money.

An expired German driver's license showed his age to be forty-seven. He also had a German Social Security card.

"There's three hundred sixty-six dollars here. If you live off the land, like Martz, and work a steady job you can save money. That's more than I have in my savings account."

"Put it back as you found it, we don't want to arouse suspicion. If he's a traitor, there's no evidence to prove it." Dunsmore straightened up the desk and wiped footprints from the floor on the way out. "I see no reason to search the outhouse and storage building. If he's hiding something, two men won't find it in an hour."

Andrews agreed. "Let's head back to town."

On the way back, a passing truck blew the horn. "I'll pull over and see what he wants."

"Larsen took Martz to the clinic. He was throwing up and spitting blood."

"Thanks, Ollie, we'll check to see how he's doing." Dunsmore frowned, "He didn't stir last night after he fell, and it troubles me that I didn't take him home."

Andrews said, "He probably spent the night sleeping on the sidewalk. Your lack of consideration didn't do him in, the booze did. Drink a bottle of gin on an empty stomach before boarding a boat is a recipe for disaster."

"Let's stop at the clinic before we visit Fritz. I'm sure they need more information than Larsen could provide."

Andrews reminded, "I want to check with the post office to see if Martz has a box. Without a phone and no mailing address, most people have a PO Box. Before we visit the clinic, we should know as much about him as possible."

"I hadn't thought of that."

The local supervisor cooperated when Andrews showed his identification. "The rent on the box is paid monthly and due ten days in advance. Most pay quarterly, including Martz. I don't see everyone that comes in and I seldom work on Saturday. Last week, he was here when I opened the door on Saturday. Sorry, Chief, I'll need a search warrant to open the box."

Dunsmore smiled. "Thanks, Jerry, you've been helpful."

On the way out, Andrews said, "I'll have Hurley do the paperwork. I want to open that box on Thursday before Martz gets there."

"I agree. Martz would need the mail to communicate with others."

At the clinic, Dunsmore gave the receptionist Martz's age and financial condition. "He may look like a bum, but he has money to cover the bill."

"I'll take your word for it, Chief. He's in room 140, down the hall on the right."

Martz lay sleeping with an IV in his arm. He looked like a sick man in his forties with his hair combed. The doctor walked in. "We've taken care of him, but the nurse is concerned about who pays the bill."

"I can assure you, he'll pay the bill."

"A patient without a medical history is always a challenge."

Dunsmore said, "I know he drank a pint of gin yesterday and passed out. I doubt he had breakfast before work."

"Captain Larsen said he was throwing up on the boat and started spitting blood, that's all we know. When he wakes up, the nurse will give him soft food and milk to calm his stomach.

The man appears to be in good physical condition with normal vital signs.

"The Orderly said he's the man that smells bad and wanders about town at night. I've observed him since coming here two years ago." The doctor paused. "We have medicine to coat the stomach before eating. If he continues to bleed, I'll send him to Portland."

"Please call the station before you leave this afternoon to update us on his condition. Give the information to Joyce if I'm not there."

The doctor assured, "With proper rest he should feel better soon."

~ ~ ~

Tuesday morning Schroeder woke at five. He wanted an early start, needing to make a payphone call to Brown on the way. When Brown heard the news, he terminated the call and headed to work. With both Martz and Schroeder compromised, he needed to change plans. Canceling the landing wasn't an option, it could take a month or longer to get another team of agents to America.

~ ~ ~

Later that afternoon in the woods of northern New Hampshire, Schroeder decided to turn onto an old logging road. After a short distance, the road ended in heavy brush surrounding the car. *This is a good spot to hide the car.* The trunk had the necessary tools to finish the job. Thirty minutes later, the car was completely covered with brush.

Satisfied with his effort, he cut several branches to brush away the tire tracks, working his way back to the main road.

Before starting the trip, Schroeder checked the route with a compass to make sure he would head in the right direction. After three or four hours in the woods, one could easily become disoriented, walking in circles. His food supply consisted of beef jerky and hard biscuits, not enough to sustain him for more than a week. A hungry man could snare a rabbit or catch a trout. Tying his tent and bedroll to the back pack, he slipped his arms through the straps and settled it on his back. He used the twenty-two rifle as a walking stick.

With two hours of daylight left, he'd cover as much ground as possible before making camp for the night.

~ ~ ~

Gestapo Headquarters, Nazi Germany

At Gestapo Headquarters, Colonel Kurt Falk had the latest transmission from *Kapitan* Hruby. The Atlantic had taken its toll on the agents and crew. U-boat 74 needed to spend more time on the surface to reach its destination. Falk sat sipping tea when his secretary rang, "Herr Himmler is on the line."

"Good morning, Herr Himmler."

"Good morning, Falk. Are you busy?"

"Nothing important, we can talk in ten minutes."

Falk hung up and headed to Himmler's office.

Himmler greeted him, "Would you like something to drink?"

"No thank you."

"Is there anything new from Hruby?"

"As I reported two days ago, it's been a rough crossing. The crew was doing better and they were spending more time on the surface. Ruling out something unexpected, he'll be there

241

by midnight. The agents are doing better and should be able to make the trip to Boston."

"What's the status of the other agents? Have they contacted Brown?"

"We should know tomorrow. Brown's radio will be able to reach the U-boat."

"The Fuehrer wants daily reports, keep me informed."

"When we hear from Brown, I'll prepare an updated report."

"Heil Hitler!"

CHAPTER 32

U-boat 74 – Plying the Atlantic

Tuesday Afternoon, April 28, 1942

At 4:00 p.m. Eastern Standard Time, *Kapitan* Hruby was talking with *Korvettenkapitan* Merkel. "What's the condition of the crew?"

"Better than yesterday, but there are eight more that should go in the water, they can't keep food down."

"Make arrangements to put them in the water at six. I want to surface early to gain time. If we're detected, so be it."

"I support your decision. Finding a U-boat in the middle of the Atlantic is next to impossible this time of year. The exercise shouldn't take more than an hour. I'm going to pray that God will protect us."

"Make it a good prayer, the crew first, the mission second."

"I serve the Reich and trust my *Kapitan.*"

After Merkel left, Hruby bowed his head to pray for several minutes. He ended his prayer with, "Please, God, watch over us. If our time has come, let it be in combat serving our country."

~ ~ ~

Biddeford, Maine

Andrews said, "Let's get sandwiches we can take to the office."

"The restaurant has ham and cheese, and egg salad wrapped and ready."

"I like ham and cheese, Warner favors egg salad with potato chips."

Warner sat talking on the phone when Andrews and Dunsmore showed up. "My ear is worn out, I've been on the phone all morning. Did you get me egg salad?"

Andrews grinned. "Yes, with potato chips."

Dunsmore placed lunch on the table and fetched three cokes from the refrigerator. "There's an extra half sandwich for the young guys, I'm watching my weight. What did you learn about our mystery man?"

Warner checked his notes. "Let's take one thing at a time. Records had a stolen Maine plate, 60-748, reported the same time Schroeder arrived at the cabin. Max Schroeder, alias John Becker, is a known Nazi sympathizer and an organizer for the Klu Klux Klan. From what I've learned, his only source of income is from the Klan.

"Manchester, New Hampshire has two black Ford sedans reported stolen, one the last week of March. There's a good chance the 1937 Ford Schroeder's driving is one of them. We know he has the stolen plate. The man has no prison record or work history the bureau could find, and we can't check the Klan. He had access to a radio and was here when the spies landed. The code book you found is simple codes used by amateurs."

Andrews wondered, "The guy is a suspect, but there is one thing that troubles me, if he's involved, where did he get a key? He arrives on Tuesday needing the key on Thursday to use the Stiles' home. If Rolf Radke and Hans Klinger had keys, getting one to Schroeder wouldn't be difficult, but communicating their plans would be difficult if there are three or four working together."

"We'll never find the key," Warner averred. "Let's change the subject. Mary Shiffman has never been married and she's worked for the State of New York for seventeen years. She has no political party affiliations, keeps to herself, and has few friends at work. She isn't churched, but she's devoted to her two collies. Her parents live in New York City and there are no siblings. Mary met Schroeder last year; they have been as thick as fleas since then. He moved into her home in January under the guise of a boarder. The end of March, Schroeder came to Biddeford alone."

Dunsmore said, "That's the oldest plot known to man. Unattractive woman in her late thirties is seduced by handsome man and before she knows it, he's involved in a crime. Unless we find new evidence, there's no reason to involve Mary Shiffman."

Warner agreed, "We don't need to damage her reputation for falling in love with the wrong guy." He stopped to finish his sandwich. "The bureau prioritized my request to match the phone numbers. Here are names of the people Martz called … do you know them, Chief?"

Dunsmore checked the names. "The first name goes to my church, they aren't involved. The second one runs a mill out of town, he's not involved. Martz confessed to making random calls around midnight, he was probably doing that Monday night."

Andrews said, "We need to eliminate Fritz or treat him as a serious suspect. Right now, the picture is muddier than it was last week. From the evidence, I'm not sure about Fritz. He wouldn't need a radio to pass a key to the contact."

Dunsmore explained, "Many of these German sympathizers have friends and relatives serving in our military. They also have friends and relatives serving in Germany. To say the least, they are conflicted. At this time, I'm not sure what part the Amsels and Martz play, but that's why we look under every stone, no pun intended."

Warner directed, "You two can continue the ground game. There are more calls to make, I'll man the phone."

Dunsmore suggested, "We'll start at Fritz's shack and then the rock. We can stop at the Amsels and check on Schroeder on the way to the clinic. Martz should be up by then. Warner can clean up here and we'll get the hamburgers and fries when we've finished our ground work. All of these burgers and sandwiches— I'm going home for dinner tomorrow night."

"You're living the life of an FBI agent with a time frame to solve the case. Hamburgers and cokes are part of it. I'm ready if you are."

~ ~ ~

Heidi Klinger welcomed Dunsmore when he knocked. "Hi, Chief, ready for some lobster cakes, they're as good as the crab."

"Regrettably, I have to say no. We're here to search Fritz's shack. Please don't get upset, we're in the process of eliminating suspects, we're not going to arrest anyone."

Heidi wiped her brow. "If you're concerned about the radio, it's been broken all week. Fritz said he couldn't find the tubes he needs to fix it."

"That's too bad, but the radio isn't the only reason we're here. We have authority under the War Powers Act to search the shack. We'll wait for Fritz and Hans to get back from fishing."

Fritz lagged behind Martz in housekeeping. The shack was a mess. The back of the radio had been removed and tubes lay on the table. Unless Fritz confessed to providing the key, the shack offered no evidence of any value.

As they were leaving, Fritz and Hans drove up in his pickup. Dunsmore smiled. "We're here to see if you have any information we can use."

A troubled Fritz said, "Nothing new." He stopped to gather his thoughts. "I hate Russians and Jews, and wish America would stop shipping supplies to England. I miss Aldrich, he was a good man. I told you the key to the Stiles' house is at the bottom of the bay." He stopped again. "My parents are Nazis, that's why Heidi and I left Germany; her parents are Nazis too. America is our home, my home, and I love living on the water and fishing. I would never do anything to hurt this country." He shrugged his shoulders. "America is my country. What can I say?"

"Do you know a Max Schroeder?"

"Not by name. Where does he live?"

Dunsmore looked to Hans. "Have you heard the name, Hans?"

"I don't know Schroeder."

"You have no reason to know the man. That's all for now, have a good afternoon."

"I believe him, Chief. What he said was from the heart, it brought tears to my eyes. We should remove him from the suspect list and move on."

"I agree. It's close to three, let's check the rock."

Andrews parked close to the walk. "If we're lucky enough to find a guy looking under the rock, we may need the car."

"Give me the keys. I'll follow in the car while you're chasing him."

Andrews grinned. "That's teamwork. Does this path go to the intersection?"

"The rock is over the rise."

Dunsmore thought things looked different, but he hadn't been in the park for years. Too early for flowers and the large rock has smaller stones surrounding the base. From a first appearance they sealed the base, making it difficult to dig under the rock.

"It's been three or four years since I've been here. I don't remember those stones surrounding the base. Working on my knees isn't my strong suit."

Andrews went into his jacket pocket and unfolded a piece of silk with a protective coating large enough to kneel on. "The bureau thinks of everything, this will only take a few minutes."

On his hands and knees, he crept around the rock finding stones that looked out of place. Andrews removed several stones revealing a pocket large enough to hold an envelope and the dirt had been disturbed. "Someone is leaving notes under this rock, but we can't be sure it's Martz, or two teenagers in love. The only way we'll know is to stake it out."

Dunsmore determined, "This time of year, an envelope could be left day or night. The rock isn't visible from the parking lot so we have another maybe that challenges our limited resources. Let's pay a visit to the Amsels. We can check on Schroeder later to see if he flew the coop."

~ ~ ~

The Amsels were home when Andrews and Dunsmore knocked on the door. Marlene Amsel greeted them. "Good day, gentlemen."

"I'm Police Chief Dunsmore and this is Agent Andrews from the FBI. We have a few questions, may we come in?"

"Who is it, Marlene?" Karl Amsel shouted from the bedroom.

"It is nothing I cannot handle."

Andrews said, "We would prefer to talk with both of you at the same time."

"You better come, Karl, I need you. Sit down, please. Would you like a drink?"

Dunsmore replied, "No thank you, Mrs. Amsel."

Karl Amsel came into the room freshly bathed. Dunsmore rose from his chair. "I'm Biddeford Police Chief Dunsmore and this is Agent Andrews from the FBI."

A shaken Karl turned to gather himself. Looking back he replied, "Pleased meet you. We are working on English, I get words mixed up."

"We understand that Raymond Martz is a close friend."

Marlene said, "He helps with English. Martz is smart man and looks good cleaned up. We let him wash here."

Andrews asked, "How long have you known him?"

"About two years. We found Martz on roadside and took him home. Like Karl say, he nice man and English is good." Marlene looked at Andrews as she spoke. Karl wouldn't establish eye contact with his adversaries.

Dunsmore asked, "Does he drink when he's here?"

"He drinks much, not at my house. I make Martz take clothes off at laundry tub. He wraps towel round waist for bathroom. I not know what he does rest of time."

"You're saying he comes here a couple times a week to use your bathroom? Does he bring a change of clothes?"

"He put on clean clothes to eat and dirty go in new washing machine. Men who fish smell like fish or lobster end of day."

"He has no place to bathe?"

"That right! Without help, where would he go? Karl tells him to drink less and talks with Martz."

Andrews asked, "Does he have any friends, other than you two and the men he works with?"

"I know none. We found Martz on street one night. No one came to help. Marlene wakes him, he asks for help."

Dunsmore asked, "You brought him home and let him bathe?"

"Brought, that is new word. Martz is hard worker and good comrade."

"Does he have any relatives?"

Marlene shrugged. "I know none. He tells of relatives in Germany. He comes here, I not know if has other friends."

"Most people dislike him, is that what you are trying to say?"

"I think so. No one wants him near, Chief."

"Do you know Max Schroeder?"

Marlene looked to Karl who was shaking his head no. "No, we stick to our neighborhood." Marlene smiled. "I just learned neighborhood."

Dunsmore looked to Andrews who nodded his head. "I should have mentioned this earlier. Martz was taken to the Biddeford Clinic this morning. Captain Larsen said he passed out after spitting up blood."

Marlene said, "The gin gets him in trouble. Can we see him?"

Andrews observed the Amsels learning of Martz's hospitalization on short notice. Karl seemed upset, and Marlene showed no reaction.

"You can see him today." Dunsmore smiled. "Take good care of Mr. Martz, he needs friends. Thank you for inviting us into your home."

In the car, Andrews sat absorbing what they learned. "Are you going to swing by the cabin where Schroeder should be?"

"There's nothing we can do about it if he's gone."

"I'll bet the place is empty and the code book is gone. If he's the contact, he'll find places to lie low and surface in the fall. There's no reason to risk being caught."

The black Ford was gone and the cabin looked deserted. "I have a warrant and I've already keyed the lock. Let's take a look."

The notebook sat next to the radio. The dresser drawers were empty as well as the closet. With a spotless kitchen sink, the cabin stood ready for inspection. "Probably the way Schroeder found it," Dunsmore said. "You were right, he's flown the coop."

"To me he has the mannerisms of an outdoor guy who could disappear in the woods. If the car is found, the State Patrol could start a search in that area."

"You guys think ahead; it might take me a week to figure that out. If what you're saying is right, the window for catching him is today or tomorrow."

"The car will be the key. Schroeder knows where he's going, big advantage. I'll place the listening device when we visit Martz." Andrews looked at Dunsmore, shaking his head. "Let's think this through based on what we learned today."

Dunsmore agrees. "Schroeder shows up in April with access to a secluded cabin, the perfect safe house. If there's a Plan B, he might be part of it."

Andrews adds, "Then by chance, or divine intervention, Griffiths spots a stranger in town and tails him to a wilderness cabin. Schroeder tells us the rent is paid through April, and then leaves the morning after we question him, the middle of April."

Dunsmore adds, "The evidence says he's running from the law, a normal response if you're driving a stolen car. The Germans still need information on convoys sooner than later. There must be a Plan B. I think the Germans will send agents every month for the balance of the year. Their lives are insignificant when compared to the loss of life fighting well-supplied troops armed with new equipment arriving every week."

Andrews said, "Time to visit Martz, he might be a player."

They arrived at the clinic as the nurse was leaving. "Mr. Martz is still sleeping. We'll feed him soup and jello when he wakes up."

"We'll talk with Mr. Martz if he's awake. His friends, the Amsel family, will be visiting later." Dunsmore took Andrews aside. "We can plant the listening device if he's sleeping."

A tranquil looking Martz lay sleeping. The picture over the bed offered the best place to plant a listening device. Andrews put it there with a thumb-up gesture.

They left the room and went outdoors to listen in. The curtain surrounding the bed blocked their view, but the nurse checking her patient came through loud and clear. The Amsels walked in twenty minutes later. Martz held his finger to his lips pointing to the window with the other hand.

He blinked several times before speaking and pressed the call button before addressing his friends. "I'm so sleepy and very hungry."

Marlene said, "You need to treat body better."

"I know, Marlene. I'm going to cut back on the drinking."

The nurse returned. "If you're hungry, Mr. Martz, I can offer you some cream of chicken soup and cherry jello."

"Thank you, both sound good."

"You can stay until I return; Mr. Martz needs his sleep."

"If all goes well, I can leave tomorrow afternoon. Would it trouble you to give me a ride home?"

Karl blurted out, "We do better, dinner and ride home. We come at four."

"Thank you so much! Good friends like you are hard to find."

"Stay until get better, do not rush home, Raymond."

"I feel much better, Marlene, leaving tomorrow is reasonable."

The nurse walked in smiling. "I'm going to help with the soup; you're welcome to come back later."

"Suppertime for you, Raymond, see you tomorrow."

"Thanks again, Marlene and Karl."

Outside the window, Dunsmore shook his head. "He suspected we were listening, the conversation was too pedestrian, like he was acting."

"If he and the Amsels aren't involved, Martz has no reason to think we're monitoring his behavior. There's no evidence the Germans plan to land agents this week. The radio at the cabin is harmless unless Martz or someone else we haven't uncovered monitors it. Maybe Warner has information on Mary Shiffman that would be helpful. We've done all the damage we can do today, time for dinner."

Back at the office, Warner had fallen asleep on the sofa. "Wake up, Little Red Riding Hood; the big bad wolf has dinner. I know better than to ask, beer or coke?"

"Beer please, a day on the phone can wear a girl out. I have more information to share, but let's have dinner before the food gets cold."

Dunsmore said, "I'll have a beer, but I'm having dinner with my wife."

As they were eating, Rolf and David Radke walked in. "Good evening, Chief, David has something to report."

"Go ahead, David, you can tell us while we're eating."

He explained what had happened Monday night.

Dunsmore replied, "The church had a new radio when Pastor Alex came, he moved it to the cottage. If he was speaking with his wife, his explanation makes sense."

Rolf added, "The elders had no way of vetting Pastor Alex, we only had his resume and a short letter from the pastor of his church. The letter said he was qualified, nothing else. We know his wife is caring for her mother in Boston, but no one has met her. He visits her, but we don't have an address."

Dunsmore said, "Thanks, David, keep your eyes open when you deliver papers, we need leads. Please don't discuss this with anyone beyond these doors."

Andrews smiled. "The church pastor, the bureau won't believe it." He turned to Warner, "Tell us what you learned today."

Warner looked at his notebook. "Mary Shiffman rented the cabin for three months. She and Schroeder intended to use it in April and couples from her office planned to use it in May and June. Her promised vacation was canceled when a worker became ill. Schroeder claims a bad back prevents him from holding down a regular job. If Miss Shiffman knew anything about his past before getting serious, she didn't share it. Schroeder doesn't exist in government records. He uses several aliases, but they don't exist. Did you find any clues at the cabin?"

Andrews said, "He's gone. I'll bet he disappears into the woods."

Joyce rushed into the room. "A hunter training his dog found a 1937 black Ford sedan without plates in northern New Hampshire. The report says the car was locked and covered with brush."

Dunsmore said, "That could be Schroeder, how do we contact the man?"

"He's home waiting for your call."

Warner said, "I'll call the New Hampshire State Patrol. They have access to a dog and can be at the scene tomorrow morning."

Dunsmore considered. "The guy looks like an outdoorsman and has a substantial head start, but tracking him is worth the effort."

Andrews said, "On second thought, Pastor Novak might be the local contact. Rolf said he didn't offer any references they could check. Martz doesn't fit the model of a sophisticated contact, but he fits the mold of a sympathizer. Being the town drunk is a ploy to deceive us. We have three hard suspects, two that require our attention."

Dunsmore scratched his chin. "It's difficult for me to believe Pastor Novak is part of this. I'll leave you two to figure out the next move. I'm going home to spend time with my wife."

CHAPTER 33

New Hampshire

Wednesday, April 29, 1942

Wednesday morning, veteran guide Hugh Ward and his dog accompanied New Hampshire State Trooper Donovan and his dog to the abandoned car location to set out on a search for Schroeder.

The guide commented, "Please forgive me if this sounds negative, but a well-conditioned man could be ten to twenty miles ahead of us. If the dogs lose the scent, it could take ten minutes to find it. One man moves faster than two men with dogs."

"I know, but the FBI wants it done. We could determine where he's headed so they can search from two directions. We're chasing a suspect involved in the Biddeford fire." The trooper sighed, "Who knows, we may get lucky."

"Let's have at it, I get paid either way."

~ ~ ~

Wednesday morning found Chief Dunsmore in the office at 7:30 to make coffee. Joyce walked in minutes later and poured two cups before she greeted her boss. "Good morning, Emmit, you're up bright and early."

"Sorting through paperwork left from last week, council meeting Monday night."

"I'm getting the folders ready. All this activity is wreaking havoc with the budget. You better catch the guy by June or I'll never get my raise."

"Patience, Joyce, have patience, my dear. Have you considered the guy might be a woman?"

"Women don't think like a spy, spying is a male endeavor."

Jones walked in as Joyce sat down for a day's work. "Smile, Joyce, I'm back."

"So is my dandruff, some things are hard to get rid of."

"Please announce me to Sherlock Holmes."

"Stand still and I'll draw you a map so you can navigate the space on your own."

Dunsmore broke up the friendly conservation. "Welcome back, Charlie." He crossed the room and shook his friend's hand. "Sit down and have a cup of coffee."

"Thanks, Emmit, but I can get my own." Coffee in hand, he asked, "It's after eight, where are Andrews and Warner?"

"Good question, they're generally here by this time. Take a look at my notes, I'm writing a report for the council." He could hear the phone ring in the outer office and Joyce punching line one. "Good morning, Chief Dunsmore here."

"Good morning, this is Hurley. I'm sorry, but the bureau has requested Andrews and Warner work out of the Boston Office for the rest of the week. I haven't received a report from them, but Andrews said you had three solid leads and may have discovered their drop location."

"We've taken some small steps this week, but nothing definitive. Chief Jones is back and Chief Robinson should be able to help. Don't be too optimistic, we might end the week where we began."

"Please send me a report at the end of the week."

"We've connected the Amsels with Raymond Martz. They're picking him up this afternoon from the clinic. Andrews placed a microphone behind the picture over the bed and left with the listening device. We could be the fly in the room if we had one."

"That's more important then pushing a pencil in Portland, I'll be there in an hour."

"We'll be waiting."

Jones smiled. "With Hurley, you won't need me. I'll catch up on my paperwork and meet you for lunch about one."

Dunsmore busied himself preparing a report for the council. An hour later, Joyce walked in. "I made a fresh pot of coffee. Chief Robinson is on his way."

Hurley and Robinson arrived at the same time. After their hellos, Dunsmore brought them up-to-date. "*That* pretty much does it. Right now we've connected the Amsels with Martz, but I doubt either one is the contact. The rock bears watching."

Hurley poured more coffee. "We better check the rock for messages before heading to the clinic. You might want to check it daily for the next month."

"If Martz is involved, he and his contact are both using the rock. We have a large cadre of volunteers to protect the city. Using them to monitor the rock for the next month would help. If it were me, I would select a new spot. The park has too much activity after May."

Robinson said, "Jones has a list of volunteers. He could set up a watch for the next month."

"Good idea," said Hurley. "Whatever makes their communication more difficult makes sense. Let's head for the rock, then the clinic."

Robinson said, "You fellas have things under control. A small home on the edge of town burned down last night. The family was in Boston attending a wedding; they're due back this morning. Charlie will help me sort through the ashes."

~ ~ ~

Dunsmore said, "We need to know if Martz has an account, let's stop at the bank first. He has a PO Box, but I can't inspect it without a federal warrant."

Hurley set his cup down. "From what I've read about Martz, his normal behavior seems abnormal. If he were any other suspect, checking bank accounts are standard procedure."

Dunsmore nodded. "You can do that without a warrant, I can't. Getting a warrant without a good case is difficult; the local judge is strict when it comes to privacy issues. Let's take your car, mine draws attention."

The park was deserted when they checked the rock. Hurley pondered. "The overnight rains have destroyed footprints or any signs of activity. We've drawn a blank for now. When can you start monitoring the rock?"

"No later than Saturday. Jones will be itching to be in the hunt by tomorrow morning. Let's go, we have a good chance to talk with the postmaster if we get there before noon."

Jerry, the day shift supervisor, said, "Martz has a box, but he doesn't empty it on a regular basis. He works on fishing boats, so he comes Friday afternoon or Saturday. Here's the box number."

The box was empty and a check of the clerks didn't help. Dunsmore said, "Thanks for your cooperation, Jerry. We'll both forget this ever happened."

Hurley and Dunsmore headed to the bank. Dunsmore and the manager were good friends. "Good morning, Connor. Meet Special Agent Hurley from the FBI."

"Good morning, gentlemen, what can I do for you?"

Hurley showed his badge. "We're interested in Raymond Martz, the guy who appears drunk most of the time."

"What makes you think he has an account?"

"He's not suspected of a crime, we're making a routine check."

"Martz does have an account, but you'll need to sign a form to view it."

"His savings account has over one hundred dollars with a deposit made last week, and he withdrew a hundred in March."

Dunsmore looked toward Hurley. Other than being drunk or acting drunk, Martz's routine was no different than many others that lived in the woods. "Have you ever talked with him or handled his affairs?"

"Other than seeing him on the streets, or having my tellers hold their nose when he's in the bank, no one talks with him. He was sober when he opened the account years ago."

Emmit said, "I have one more request. Does Pastor Novak have an account?"

"You'll need to sign another form." The manager handed Hurley the paperwork. Viewing the pastor's account, the bank manager said, "He has an active checking account with a seventy-dollar balance. The record shows a fifty-dollar deposit on Monday. Pastor Novak writes a fifty-dollar check to the church each month."

"Thanks, Connor, we'll be on our way."

Hurley said, "There's nothing unusual about their finances. We have some time. Let's stop at Martz's cabin."

"In that case, I'll drive." Ten minutes later, Dunsmore parked a block from the cabin. "In the woods, you never know what you'll find. Best we walk from here."

"All these wilderness cabins look similar. These guys must know what works here in the winter." Hurley opened the door. "I've been in a half dozen of these; this one by far is the cleanest. Check the drawer where he keeps his stash."

Dunsmore opened the drawer to check the hidden compartment. He held up the stack of bills, "The money is here." He replaced the drawer, while thinking out loud. "He must plan to pay his hospital bill on Monday."

"We can check at the clinic. Does the cabin look the same as it did earlier in the week?"

"Nothing has changed."

"That's what I thought. If he's involved, they don't meet here to make plans."

CHAPTER 34

Biddeford Clinic

Wednesday, April 29, 1942

Martz, feeling better after a good sleep, ordered a large breakfast. After finishing the meal, he sat down on a folding chair to do his daily stretching. When the nurse came for the tray, he was bright-eyed and bushy-tailed. "I'm going to shower and read the paper. My friends are bringing fresh clothes. They'll be here after four to pick me up."

"We tried to wash the clothes you came in, but they fell apart. Betsy saved your boots."

"Don't worry about it, I'll go to the Goodwill store to replace them. I remember being dressed in rain gear when I passed out on the boat."

"You have a good memory, Mr. Martz; the rain gear is in your closet."

"That's good news. Rain gear is expensive and I can't always buy it at Goodwill."

While Martz was in the shower, Pastor Novak stopped at the desk. He alternated with a Catholic priest to visit patients on Wednesday mornings. As Novak entered the clinic, Dunsmore and Hurley were taking positions under the window.

The nurse greeted Pastor Novak. "Good morning, Pastor."

"Good morning. I know the folks in three rooms, but I haven't met Mr. Martz."

"Captain Larsen brought him in Monday afternoon, he was spitting up blood. The doctor thinks its alcohol related. Mr. Martz is the drunk that wanders around town with a strong fish smell."

"He must be the man I found lying on the sidewalk. When I offered to help, he swore and told me to mind my own business."

"He's taking a shower. You might want to visit the other patients first."

"Good idea!"

Thirty minutes later, Pastor Novak, found Martz sitting in the armchair reading a book. "Good morning, Mr. Martz, looks like you're feeling better."

"Good morning, Pastor. What brings you to visit a sinner?"

"We're all sinners, Mr. Martz, in an imperfect world. Christ died for our salvation. If we confess our sins and accept Christ into our hearts, we're forgiven."

Dunsmore recognized Pastor Novak's voice. "Pastor Novak is with him. I forgot that he makes visits on Wednesdays."

The conversation revealed nothing unusual about either man.

At one o'clock the nurse came to the room. "You had a late breakfast, Mr. Martz. We have tuna sandwiches and tomato soup for lunch with a glass of milk."

"Thank you, that sounds like the perfect lunch. I don't eat this well at the cabin."

"I'll be right back."

"Thank you for your concern, Pastor, but I'm an agnostic. If I change my mind you'll see me in church."

"Good to meet you, Mr. Martz. Stop the drinking and take care of yourself."

Hurley wrapped up the listening device. "Time for lunch, a tuna sandwich with soup are whetting my appetite."

"That's the luncheon special on Wednesday, but I like the meatloaf. My department is way over budget this month, it's your treat. I want to stop at the phone company to check on something before lunch. If I'm right, it could be important."

"Sounds like a hunch."

"Hunches have solved many cases."

The operator smiled when Dunsmore walked in. "Gladys said you're the real Dick Tracy."

"Be nice or I'll spank you."

"You'll need Dorothy's permission. Who's your sidekick?"

"FBI Special Agent Hurley, meet Ruth Goldberg."

"Good to meet you, Mrs. Goldberg. We need some information." He showed his badge.

Dunsmore said, "I know the Biddeford Church has several extensions, are there any other lines?"

She looked in the phonebook before going to the file cabinet. "There's a separate line the church pays for, but it's not listed."

"Thank you, Ruth; I thought the additional phone was in the cottage."

Dunsmore was quiet on the trip to the diner. Hurley remained silent allowing Emmit to think. As they were eating, Dunsmore said, "I have a farfetched idea to bounce off you. If I'm right, a lot of people will be affected."

"I see you're troubled, please share."

"We know Pastor Novak speaks fluent German. The cottage has a ship to shore radio and a separate phone line. He lives in the cottage, and to my knowledge no one goes there. When the church called him to serve, he was living in Boston with his wife's family. No one has met the wife and he visits Boston once a month, or as needed. He claims to be from Czechoslovakia, but other than his resume that's all we know about him."

"David Radke was late with the paper and delivered it to the cottage instead of the church. He heard Novak speaking German. He seemed angry when he opened the door, but quickly changed when he recognized David. If you were rounding up suspects, he would be the one with an alibi that made sense but couldn't be checked."

Hurley said, "This must be hard on you as a parishioner. I doubt if we'll catch Schroeder tomorrow or any time soon. If the contact is Novak, we can check phone records, but my gut tells me he would use the radio to contact Boston."

"Martz is acting, he's not a drunk." Dunsmore stopped to think. "Maybe Martz has never met the contact face-to-face. He could call the cottage for instructions and use the rock for messages to minimize use of the phone. My gut tells me the Germans sent him here to be ready if we entered the war. Knowing less about other agents is better if you're caught."

"Suppose you're right. How do we catch Novak without constant surveillance?"

"You can't follow Novak for weeks in a small town. Our best chance is a lead from someone he trusts. He wouldn't be in the picture if David's bike hadn't broken down. Well, so much for hunches. We best investigate the Martz–Amsel connection. If Martz suspects something, they'll talk in the car."

Dunsmore added, "We can check with Clay Graycheck, he works for Maine Outdoors. I'll call before he leaves for work."

Thirty minutes later, Graycheck called back. "Their personnel folders contain nothing of interest. Marlene Amsel is taking Friday off to attend a funeral in Boston. Karl Amsel is working, and she's expected back on Monday."

"Thanks, Clay, take care of yourself."

Hurley asked, "Why is she going to Boston unescorted? It's a three-hour drive at night."

"We think alike. She may leave Friday morning for a Saturday funeral. At Maine Outdoors, you have to work to get paid. An employee needs five years' service to receive time off with pay and a week's vacation. Could be that Karl needs to work on Friday to pay the bills."

Hurley reasoned, "If she travels Friday and Sunday, it makes sense. If she leaves Thursday after work, it's a different story. One car maintaining contact would draw attention, you'll need help."

"We could find out this afternoon if we're lucky. It's not uncommon for locals to attend funerals in Boston and Portsmouth. If Martz goes with her, it's a different story."

"Can Jones drive the second car, if she leaves Thursday night?"

"He plays bingo at church on Thursdays. Let's go next door and ask if he'll give up bingo for something exciting."

Jones agreed to help. "Thanks, Charlie, you're back in the game."

Hurley thought for a minute. "The fishing boats should be docking before three, I want to talk with Larsen."

Dunsmore replied, "We know Martz is having dinner with the Amsels. Nothing was said about spending the night."

Larsen docked before three. "Good afternoon, Captain, how's the fishing?"

"Pretty good, we limited. I have a couple lobsters you can have for dinner." He turned to the crew. "Pack the one claw lobsters in ice for the chief."

"Thank you, but that's not why we're here. This is Special Agent Hurley from the FBI. Have you talked with Raymond Martz since he was hospitalized?"

"Me and the missus paid a visit last night. Martz said he was going home today. He wouldn't accept our offer to take him to dinner Thursday night."

Hurley asked, "Is he returning to work on Friday?"

"He said he would work on Monday. I thought it a good idea, one needs to rest after the ordeal he put himself through. He'll be back, no work, no pay."

Hurley said, "Thank you, we'll be on our way."

"I'll drop you at the office, Chief. Sorry I can't stay, but a promise to have dinner with the family needs to be kept."

Emmit agreed. "It doesn't take two to listen at the window."

Dunsmore arrived at the window outside Martz's room fifteen minutes before the Amsels showed up. The conversation confirmed he was having dinner with them and planned to spend the night. Martz, dressed in the clothes Marlene Amsel had purchased at the Goodwill store.

Dunsmore moved to the front of the clinic as they drove off. After checking with the nurse, he went to the room to remove the microphone.

~ ~ ~

Martz knew Karl Amsel would try to cancel the trip. After listening to his reasons, Martz replied, "I have a good reason to miss work on Friday. No one in town, other than the two of you, cares if I'm alive or dead. Dunsmore and the FBI are questioning German families in the community, not just the three of us."

Marlene said, "I agree, Raymond. We have done nothing to make them suspect us. I have more clothes from Goodwill store and underwear I got at Sears. You have boots, but I got shoes and socks, is ten all right?"

"Ten is right. Stop at the post office, I need to check my box." Martz smiled when he found an envelope. The obituary listed the funeral parlor where the deceased was laid out, and the church for the memorial service.

Martz left the post office with a smile. "We have all the details for a successful mission. The man is your uncle on your mother's side of the family."

Marlene said, "We have Riesling to celebrate good fortune. You have one glass, Raymond."

"No thank you. I won't be doing any drinking from now on. When we get back from Hampton Beach, I'm going to become an outstanding citizen and attend the Lutheran church."

~ ~ ~

Hurley phoned FBI Headquarters requesting information on Pastor Novak. The bureau would have a preliminary report by noon.

Jones greeted Dunsmore at the office. "What's next, Emmit?"

"When we hear from the FBI, we'll know if Pastor Novak is a suspect. I'll ask Sam Griffiths to watch the Martz cabin tomorrow."

Jones said, "Martz will need clothes and other personal needs."

"I checked at the Goodwill store. Marlene Amsel bought pants, shirts, belt, shoes, and a warm jacket. It appears he'll be with them for three or four days. He has personal items used at the clinic."

Dunsmore looked toward his friend. "This isn't suspicious behavior. The Bible has references regarding 'Be your brother's keeper,' and most of us know the 'Golden Rule.' If he accompanies Marlene Amsel to Boston for a funeral and memorial service, that's not unusual if her husband needs to work." Dunsmore paused.

"Captain Larsen gave me two lobsters for dinner and Dorothy is expecting me."

CHAPTER 35

Biddeford, Maine

Thursday Morning, April 30, 1942

When the alarm sounded at six, Dunsmore jumped out of bed shaking his head to wake up from his nightmare. In the dream, an American merchant ship was listing to one side. The crew was jumping ship into the icy waters of the Atlantic Ocean to avoid the roaring fires on board. His wife, Dorothy, awakened by the activity asked, "Are you all right, dear?"

"It's the dream, that damn dream."

"Dreams originate in your subconscious. Come back to bed and hug me, things will get better if we share the good with the bad."

"I'll reset the alarm. Rushing to the office to wait for phone calls makes little sense."

~ ~ ~

At the office, Dunsmore found Jones and Joyce enjoying chocolate chip cookies she had baked. "Good morning, Emmit, you better have a couple cookies, only God knows when the stores will get more chocolate chips."

After Emmit poured a cup of coffee, Charlie said, "I wired the weather station in Nova Scotia. A severe storm is headed our way, heavy rainfall with winds up to thirty miles per hour."

"The Germans might like bad weather, no one walking on the beach and poor visibility." Joyce held the cookies toward Emmit. "I'll have a cookie, they look delicious."

Following a bite of cookie, "Time to go to work, Charlie, it could be a long day."

Jones followed Dunsmore into the conference room. "I put myself in a German uniform. The guy running this operation needs information from the local contact before he sends more agents. The Germans need information on the convoys *now*; they can't wait three or four months. Their plans could use a different site for agents landing tonight or tomorrow night, I would use Hampton Beach."

Jones continued, "Martz and Marlene Amsel would pick up the agents and drive them to Boston, with adequate time to catch the morning trains to NYC. They would spend Friday night in Boston, attend a memorial service on Saturday and return Saturday afternoon. No one knows everyone at a memorial service and both sign the guest book. Obituaries list the funeral parlor, cemetery, and church for the memorial service. The information is available in newspapers."

"What you're saying makes sense. The German timeline is sooner than later. Hampton Beach is a good spot to land, but there's activity on the weekend. If their plans are for this week, they'll land tonight."

Charlie said, "My gut tells me it's tonight. I checked the local map for the best way to Hampton Beach using back roads. I've marked the map where the pursuit car leaves the road and another car replaces it. Robinson has a pickup and we have cars. It makes no difference whether it rains or snows;

the cool air gives us an advantage with the rear window fogged over."

Dunsmore said, "So far, so good, you call Robinson, I doubt if Hurley will come on short notice. Tonight might be the first in several fruitless searches. I'll monitor Highway One if Martz decides to use a direct course. If they follow your route, I'll be the last car in the chase. Griffiths first, Robinson second, you third, and I'll bat cleanup."

Hurley said he couldn't be with them at Hampton Beach but would call Dunsmore after the bureau finished checking Novak's activity in Boston. "We have three agents on the case. I'll get back to you after lunch."

Robinson walked in as Dunsmore hung up the phone. "What's up, Emmit?"

"We think the Germans plan to land agents tonight at Hampton Beach."

"You'll get no help from the town or the surrounding area."

"I know, are you available?"

"I wouldn't miss it. Have you finalized plans?"

"Not yet, we wanted your input. There's a bad storm heading our way, heavy rainfall with winds to thirty miles per hour."

While Dunsmore was at the front desk, Robinson paced the room. If Dunsmore's wrong, this could be the first of many calls asking for help. If he's right, they'd be contributing toward the war effort. *This could be an exciting night.*

"Charlie will be back in fifteen minutes. We need to finalize plans for the beach."

Robinson said, "Hampton Beach Park has shallow water. The U-boat captain isn't going to ground the boat to get close. In rough seas, the rafts will be in the water thirty minutes to make the beach."

Dunsmore said, "Let's hope the agents aren't carrying weapons. The men accompanying them in the rafts will be ready to tackle any situation."

Robinson recommended, "We should carry side arms and rifles. Our best defense is to separate so our fire isn't concentrated."

"I've never shot anyone in thirty-five years, and I know the same goes for Charlie. If the Germans feel threatened, they'll open fire. We'll have to kill them or they'll kill us."

Robinson stayed silent for several seconds. "Unfortunately for us, you're right. Deputize Griffiths and take him along."

"Sam wouldn't miss it, he's already deputized. I haven't been to Hampton Beach in years, we need a reconnaissance."

Robinson said, "I served in the Spanish/American war, I'll go. I should be back before three to finalize plans. When Charlie returns, send him to watch the Amsel home. If Martz leaves, we want to know where he goes."

Dunsmore replied, "Griffiths is watching Martz's cabin. Charlie has developed a plan to follow the car if Martz uses the back roads. If it were me, I would take the main road; the back roads with deer can be chancy. I'll monitor Highway One and call if they show up. They need to cross the bridge to take either route. Griffiths will follow either way."

Robinson said, "You both can't be right. We'll plan accordingly. I think they'll leave about eight to allow for a flat tire or the car breaking down. I checked with a friend in Rhode Island. Martz had a driver's license when he lived there. Driving without a license is a traffic ticket, but we want Martz meeting the Germans when we arrest him."

Dunsmore had a map the park offered to visitors. A small beach a mile north of the park was accessible by boat. *It offered an ideal spot for a picnic on a warm summer day.* The map showed a dead-end dirt road that stopped short of the beach. This was the trail for well-conditioned hikers.

He showed the beach to Robinson, "On the way back, check this beach, it could be a safe spot for a rendezvous."

"I've seen that beach from the water. Other than the rugged terrain; it's a good landing place. The beach must be a half mile from the road. I'm betting on the service drive at the south end of the park, it's not visible to the surrounding homes."

~ ~ ~

Thursday morning, Schroeder woke to a scratching sound on the tent. It took thirty seconds before the impatient bear tore a hole in the tent searching for food. Schroeder crawled from the tent with his rifle. He had selected a site with a tree that looked easy to climb. He shouldered the rifle and was on the fourth branch when tree bark flew in all directions. Wanting to climb faster, he shouldered the rifle. The bear, in hot pursuit, was keeping up as he neared the halfway point to the top.

He climbed faster, wanting separation from the bear to get a first-rate shot at his eyes. Out of breath, he secured a position on a limb to watch the bear work his way through the branches. As the animal drew near, Schroeder released the safety, took aim and shot the bear on the bridge of its nose. The large male roared with pain, almost losing his grip.

With only four bullets left, he reloaded taking careful aim at the bear's left eye. The bullet hit above the first shot causing the bear to fall backwards, hitting a branch before rolling sideways to continue a downward spiral. With a resounding thud the bear hit the ground remaining there for several minutes before showing any signs of life. Five minutes passed before the bear got to its feet, wishing it had searched somewhere else for a free meal as it walked away.

Schroeder had encountered bears in the past but none had chased him up a tree. With the adrenalin rush disappearing, the morning chill caused shivers as he worked his way down the tree. The campsite and belongings remained intact, but having slept longer than intended and dealing with the bear had disrupted his schedule. After putting his boots on, he wolfed down beef jerky with hard biscuits for breakfast, keeping his eyes on the path the bear took. Twenty minutes later he headed northwest.

~ ~ ~

After the Amsels left for work, Martz sat with a cup of coffee pondering the options. His pistol was buried behind the cabin, but going to the cabin was out of the question.

He went to the Amsels' bedroom to search the closet for a rifle. Not finding one, he looked in the guest room with no luck. The closet shelf was too deep to see objects at the back. Standing on a kitchen chair, he found a blanket wrapped around something heavy. To his surprise, the blanket was wrapped around a .38mm revolver and a box of shells.

The gun was oiled and ready to fire. After loading the weapon, he put six extra bullets and the pistol in a coat pocket. Wrapped in a separate towel, he found a hunting knife that could be useful. The knife went in the other coat pocket. Facing a long day and satisfied with his find, he slept until the Amsels returned from work.

~ ~ ~

Standing at the window after lunch, Dunsmore watched the weather change. Dark clouds appeared to the northeast followed by gusts of wind and rain. He was second-guessing the decision for an all-out effort to apprehend the Germans. One could do this two or three times before those helping would lose interest.

The bad weather wouldn't scuttle the Germans plans if tonight was the night. Griffiths would be the first car following the Amsel car, then Jones, followed by Robinson in the pickup, and he would be last. He sat down to study the locations Jones had marked where a car could leave the road and be replaced by another car. Driving the last vehicle, he could use the radio to notify Jones and Robinson on the next move. Satisfied the plan would work, he went to the conference room to have lunch with Joyce.

She said, "I took a coke from the fridge, are they free to the staff?"

"You're part of the team, help yourself."

"I heard the conversation about Pastor Novak. I think you're barking at the wrong tree."

"Pastor Novak fits the profile. He lives in a secluded cottage, speaks German, with access to a radio. The FBI is checking his activity in Boston before we called him. Church history is cluttered with false prophets."

Joyce sighed, "Do your plans change in bad weather?"

"The bad weather favors us. We'll be hard to see dug in on the beach."

"Call the State Patrol, Emmit. No offense, but you're a little old to be fighting Germans on the beach. I fear for your lives."

"The State Patrol won't send troopers unless there's clear evidence. Other than a hunch, we have no evidence the Germans plan to land tonight. If they come, we'll be ready. Midnight is witching hour."

"What about Chief Smith in Hampton, can he help?"

"Twisted his knee, he's home on crutches. The station is being manned by volunteers, mostly women. They're always short-handed until park security arrives in June. Kennebunk and Kennebunkport are in the same dilemma, all the young men have joined the army and the older men are working in the cities. We're the last line of defense."

"I'll pray for you."

CHAPTER 36

New Hampshire

Thursday Afternoon, April 30, 1942

Wanting to distance himself from a posse, Schroeder ran and quickstepped through the woods. The rugged terrain and weight of the backpack caused him to sweat profusely. He removed his jacket to find his flannel shirt and undershirt soaked. He needed them dry by nightfall when temperatures dropped fifteen degrees.

He checked the compass frequently to make sure he was traveling west. On the trail for four hours, Schroeder wasn't sure of the distance traveled. He ran the time frame through his mind, *I'm at least five to six hours ahead of a posse.* A fire would warm the body while drying the wet shirts. After placing a drying rack downwind, Schroeder stripped off the wet clothes and sat down to watch the crackling flames throw sparks to the ground. Whatever the problem, one felt better sitting next to a warm fire.

Bracing his back against an oak tree, a hungry Schroeder wolfed down hard biscuits with beef jerky for lunch. When he finished eating, it didn't take long before the heat of the fire put him to sleep. A curious squirrel and the rain pelting down woke him. Shivering in the colder air, Schroeder reached for the damp warm shirts. Needing dry fuel, he threw the drying rack on the fire. The branches burned quickly, but the wind-swept rain reduced the fire to smoldering ashes minutes later. Schroeder pulled on the damp clothes knowing they wouldn't dry on his body. The rain jacket protected his upper body, but his pants were soaked through. After several deep breaths, he shouldered the backpack to resume his trek. "I need to find shelter for the night."

~ ~ ~

Sitting on a stump to rest his legs, Griffiths fell off banging his shoulder after dozing off. *That didn't work; I need to be walking to stay awake.*

~ ~ ~

Try as he may, Jones couldn't stay awake sitting in his car at the Amsel home. He had consumed several cups of coffee with little help from the caffeine. A passing car woke him the first time and a barking dog the second. *So be it, I'm doing my best,* he thought. At four, he returned to town.

~ ~ ~

Chief Robinson stopped at the diner to pick up a sandwich. On the drive to Hampton Beach, he mulled over what he already knew. A frequent visitor to the park, he knew the layout well. The park and the Town of Hampton were under a blackout. The main building hosted Saturday afternoon bingo. The off-season maintenance was performed by men in their sixties. The war had changed the way the park operated.

The beach was almost a mile of soft sand that offered little cover for men trying to defend it. The Biddeford team wearing dark rain gear would be hard to spot in a driving rain lying on wet sand. The team had no reason to challenge the Germans on the beach when they landed. The Marines accompanying the agents would be armed with machine pistols. German agents were trained to bite on a cyanide capsule if challenged, they wouldn't be taken alive. An asphalt road at the south end of the park offered access to the beach. Martz could back the car to the end of the road and be a short block from the water. At the park entrance he could see the bad weather moving in from the northeast. By nightfall it could be a full-blown storm. It's time to check the other beach.

A muddy road full of puddles led to the North beach. Needing both hands on the wheel to steer the car, Robinson stopped alongside the road to eat. The map showed sand stretching one hundred yards with steep banks fifty feet from the water at normal tides. At roads end, he walked half a mile to find a poorly maintained trail overlooking the beach. Climbing the steep bank at night in the rain with suitcases was out of the question. If the Germans landed here, they would be sitting ducks.

~ ~ ~

Waiting for the FBI to call, Dunsmore checked and rechecked the plan to follow the Amsel car. Andrews called at two; he'd been working in Boston all week. When they finished greetings, he went over the report on Pastor Novak.

"Novak spent two years or longer in Boston, working as a mechanic in a German neighborhood. He attended the Lutheran church where he served as a deacon, not an ordained minister. If there's a wife, no one has met her. The name he used to migrate to the states in October 1938 was Janacek Kardos. He came from Czechoslovakia, not Germany. The man enhanced his resume to receive the calling. It's common practice for others to fudge their resume, but they're not answering a call to serve God. The minister at the Lutheran church Novak attended took a vacation after Easter. The head elder said Novak was a good man, but had little contact with him other then church business."

Dunsmore said, "Pastor Novak is well liked by the congregation, he's done a good job at replacing Pastor Mitchell. To think he could be helping the Germans is incomprehensible for some parishioners. Did you find anything on Schroeder?"

"The man doesn't exist under Schroeder or Becker. He probably has more aliases. We haven't given up, but nothing so far."

Dunsmore said, "He fits the profile of a man trying to save his skin by taking up residence in another state. If he can get to a Midwestern state, jobs are available in defense plants."

Andrews replied, "He doesn't need to go to the Midwest. There are defense jobs in Pennsylvania. Do you have any evidence the Germans are coming tonight?"

"We both know the Germans are coming sooner than later. There's the Martz–Amsel connection and Schroeder leaving abruptly. Something is going on, but there's no concrete evidence. I'm sure Martz and the Biddeford contact are on the same team." Dunsmore paused, "Marlene Amsel is taking Friday off and her husband is working. We're convinced Martz and Marlene Amsel are headed to Hampton Beach to pick up a team of agents. We'll know for sure if they head south tonight. Robinson is doing reconnaissance at Hampton Beach to develop a plan to defend the beach. If the Germans show we'll be ready."

"Sorry I'm not there to go with you. Down deep, I hope the Germans stay home. You and the others have done enough without risking your lives."

"A merchant seaman risks his life on every crossing, we're no different. Thanks for the report, Andrews."

"Take care, Chief."

I need to break the news to the church elders that Novak could be a phony. Dunsmore drove to the docks to speak with Rolf Radke, a church elder. He met Rolf at his boat to share the information. Rolf listened intently shaking his head.

"Lying on your resume isn't a crime, he hasn't broken any laws."

Rolf looked at Emmit with tears in his eyes. "I told you we couldn't vet him; the elders believed his story. Knowing what we know now, the church wouldn't have called him. On the surface he's been a good pastor and popular with the congregation. We'll meet with Pastor Novak tonight. I'll contact the other elders."

"This will be difficult for the congregation, but we'll survive, we always do. Got to go, Rolf, duty calls."

~ ~ ~

Robinson sat down with Dunsmore in his office. "I have good news. The beach north of the park has steep banks and would be extremely difficult to climb at night in a storm. At the south end of the park buildings there's an access road leading to the beach. It's a secluded area surrounded by swamp grass and tidal-pools for blocks. The alternative is the main entrance next to the bandstand. Common sense would have Martz using the access road. The weather at the park is worsening by the hour; the storm will be full-blown by tonight."

"I think you're right, we'll plan accordingly."

"Normal protocol would have one raft with the agents and two sailors. If the agents have suitcases and a radio, they'll need two rafts and four sailors. We've been ordered to take the agents alive; that's a problem. The German agent at Yankee Stadium chewed on a cyanide capsule, he wouldn't be taken alive. The agents won't carry machine pistols to NYC, but they could have them on the way to the car. We need a plan that avoids confronting the Germans on the beach."

Dunsmore replied, "Is that possible?"

"Consider this plan. The Germans don't know what Martz looks like. I can take Martz out on his way to the water and signal the U-boat. You arrest the Amsel woman and replace her with Jones. Charlie will offer spiked coffee while he warms up the car. When the agents fall asleep we'll arrest them on the way to Boston. Once the landing party is in the rafts, you and Sam can open fire with the M-1's."

Dunsmore said, "It sounds good if things go as planned. What happens if the Germans send three rafts and ten marines? We could be in a fight with trained military carrying machine pistols if something unexpected happens. That plan won't work, Ralph."

Robinson said, "Let the Germans carry out their plans. The fight with them doesn't take place until the landing party is in the rafts. When the rafts are fifty feet from the beach, you open fire. You and Sam will either shoot them in the rafts, or they'll drown or get shot getting back to the beach. Machine pistols are worthless in a bobbing raft."

"We'll be killing defenseless men."

Robinson responded, "You'll be killing enemy combatants, we can't let German submariners return to their boat to sink our convoys."

Dunsmore took his time to respond. "If Germans land on our shores, we'll have to kill them." He paused, "Spies use international cities or colors for code names. You're Green, I'm Black, and Jones is White. I could be Paris, you're Montreal, and Jones is Chicago. You'll need his code name to replace Martz."

A dejected Robinson replied, "You debunked in minutes what took me an hour to plan."

"I debunked one part of it, your plan will work. It makes little sense to risk our lives capturing German agents alive if they're trained to use cyanide. Let the agents leave the park in the Amsel car. We can arrest them on the road to Boston with a road block. If Martz or the agents refuse to get out of the car with hands raised, we'll open fire." Dunsmore raised his eyebrows. "Your Thompson machine gun won't help you on the beach, but it's the perfect weapon for a road block."

"I'll be on the beach with Griffiths."

"Your plan to shoot the Germans in the rafts works well, but it doesn't require two men. You're deadly with an M-1, Ralph, you don't need help. Like you said, the number of rafts isn't an issue; they're not built for combat. Half of the sailors will have their backs turned manning paddles, and the other half will be rowing. Their machine pistols will be in storage compartments under the seats."

"I like the plan, Emmit, good results with little risk. It looks like I'll be the one shooting defenseless men in the water."

"German U-boats refuse to pick up survivors when they sink our ships. You'll be a good distance from the Germans; they won't hear an order to surrender. There will be Germans in the water, some wounded, and others trying to get to the beach, they won't be carrying machine pistols."

"I'd feel better if Sam were with me on the beach. If the Germans send ten, there's bound to be survivors from the first volley. If they don't return fire, there won't be a second volley. I'll need Sam to help with the wounded and guard the others. You and Charlie can handle the agents."

"You're right, it's better to work in teams. If you're dealing with two sailors, you can challenge them on the beach, they might speak English. If there are four or more you'll use the original plan. With the Thompson and a shotgun, Charlie and I can handle Martz and the agents. Wait for us at the access road; we could be gone for thirty minutes or longer."

Robinson folded his hands. "Some agents will not have the courage to take their life—every Nazi is not a zealot. I'm not sure what I would do under the same circumstance."

"That final step party loyalty requires could be the reason every German isn't a Nazi. Many Christians couldn't leave Germany after Hitler annexed Austria and some were serving in the military."

Robinson shook Dunsmore's hand. "We can't go through this exercise more than a couple of times without losing our edge. I hope the Germans come tonight."

Dunsmore replied, "We'll be ready if they show up."

"Jones and Griffiths will be back after four. We'll meet at six to finalize plans. If Jones or Griffiths say no, I'll understand."

"So will I. It's a personal decision. See you at six, Emmit."

~ ~ ~

A tired and wet Schroeder changed direction hoping to find a cabin. As night closed in he had his back to a tree looking at the remains of a cabin. There were two partial walls forming a corner, part of a door, and a collapsing fireplace that wasn't usable. No longer walking, he started to shiver knowing hypothermia would overtake him in an hour. A gust of wind reminded him the temperature would drop another ten degrees by midnight. He needed to walk to stay warm, but the storm could last all night. He moved to the corner sitting with his back to the wall. An hour passed before hypothermia set in, taking his life before daylight. His final thoughts drifted back to his childhood in upstate New York, *Celebrating his sixth birthday with friends and family.*

~ ~ ~

Early Thursday afternoon, Ward and Donovan ended their chase heading east to find shelter. Before dark they found an occupied cabin. Wilderness cabins were twelve by fifteen with little room for visitors. The owner had a bunk bed and insisted his guests use it. After a meal of venison stew and rutabaga, the men fed the dogs that were sheltered in the shed. The owner wanted to play bid whisk, a popular card game. With nothing to do, Donovan and Ward were content to spend the evening playing cards. Try as they may, neither one won a game.

When they finished playing cards their host said. "There are only a couple of cabins west from here. If the guy you're chasing doesn't find one, he won't survive. In this storm you can't build a fire under a tree. Hypothermia is a tough way to go, but he'll fall asleep before he dies." The man hesitated, "There are coyotes wandering the woods and the usual male bear protecting his territory. I doubt if either are looking for food in this weather."

Ward replied, "That's why we looked for a cabin. We're headed back to civilization tomorrow; the storm will destroy his tracks."

Donovan said, "We haven't the manpower to search the woods, let's hope someone finds the body and buries it."

~ ~ ~

Pastor Novak met with the elders at the church. The senior elder asked Rolf to bring forth the charges as Pastor Novak sat expressionless. At the end of the charges, Rolf asked, "What saith you regarding the charges?"

"On the surface, it looks like I lied. My wife didn't want children and I divorced her in NYC. She moved to Boston to be with her family and I followed six months later. I worked hard as a mechanic and served the Lord as a deacon during my time in Boston. You didn't check with the Theology School. I earned the required credits to become a minister, but I'm not ordained." Novak paused. "I helped with incoming mail at the church and read the letter requesting a pastor for the Biddeford church. With the war and the shortage of Lutheran ministers, I knew God was calling me to Biddeford. I enhanced my resume and you called me. After three months of serving the Lord in Biddeford, I think I made the right decision to answer God's calling."

Rolf said, "You studied to become a minister and completed the courses but didn't get ordained? What did you tell the pastor in Boston when you left?"

"I told him the Biddeford Lutheran church had called me. He said I was ready and should take the position. If you remember, he wrote a letter summarizing my work in Boston. He's ready to retire, but there's no one to replace him."

An elder rose to address the others. "I think Pastor Novak's explanation makes sense. The war has changed many lives and will change many more. He's met all the requirements of his calling, we should continue his employment. When God calls, we are obligated to answer. Many leaders of the early church had no training, they wanted to serve and God let them."

A second elder agreed and the vote to retain Pastor Novak had no opposition. Rolf Radke voted yea as a nay vote would divide the congregation.

CHAPTER 37

Biddeford, Maine

Thursday Evening, April 30, 1942

Chief Robinson placed two M-1 rifles and a Thompson machine gun with ammunition in his truck. Small town police chiefs and their deputies weren't expected to fight trained military, but he readied for the worst. Pleased with his preparation, he left to join Dunsmore after kissing his wife goodbye. She watched the truck disappear, wondering if she had kissed her husband for the last time. He prayed for God's help on the drive to Biddeford.

Sam Griffith's wife tended to expect the worst, so he didn't mention where he was going, only that he would be home late. "Chief Dunsmore needs help and I'm deputized." Telling his wife not to worry, he kissed her goodbye. When she turned to leave, he grabbed the deer rifle from the wall on the way to the car.

Dunsmore kissed and hugged Dorothy who knew the danger her husband faced. "It looks like you're ready, your hands aren't shaking."

"I hope they're steady enough to fire a gun. If there's shooting, we'll shoot first, Robinson has a good plan. Pray for us about midnight, I know sleep is out of the question. I love you as much now as the first day we met."

"That's the nicest thing you could say. Take care of yourself, Emmit."

Jones kissed his wife goodbye. "I love you. Pray for us about midnight."

"I'm proud of you. When duty calls, you answer. I'll pray for you and the others."

"Pancakes and bacon would be nice for breakfast."

At seven, the group gathered in the conference room at City Hall.

Robinson spoke first. "We've developed a plan to capture the agents and deal with the landing party. We're not fighting Germans on the beach, they'll land without incident. The agents will say their goodbyes and leave the park in the Amsel car. On the road to Boston, Charlie and Emmit will capture the agents at a road block. If they refuse to be taken prisoner, they'll be shot as enemy combatants. When the sailors are in the rafts, Sam and I will open fire with M-1's. It makes no difference if there are ten men or two men, in a bobbing raft they can't return accurate fire."

Dunsmore said, "Charlie and I will have the Thompson machine gun to defend the road block. German agents won't be taken alive; they'll use cyanide capsules when confronted. Ralph and Sam will take positions on either side of the beach to fire at the rafts. The number of survivors depends on how many are sent. Landing agents on an enemy beach is a stealth operation. Once they're discovered the manhunt begins."

Robinson reviewed their plan. "We're not concerned about capturing agents alive or taking prisoners. Our job is killing enemy combatants without putting our lives at risk. However, if the Germans surrender, we'll lock them up."

Dunsmore said, "It sounds easy until you have to pull the trigger. The main entrance to the park is exposed and farther from the water. We think Martz will use the access road at the south end of the park. Are there any questions?"

Sam said, "Good plan, defending Hampton Beach when the Germans landed made me nervous."

Dunsmore concurred, "It made all of us nervous."

Dunsmore went to the wall map. "The wind and rain will help while following the Amsel car to the park. With a wet rear window they can't distinguish between headlights, but we need to follow the routine. If you lose the group, go to the meeting place.

"Lying on the beach in black rain gear, we'll be hard to spot. The same goes for the Germans. The agents will be in dark rain gear, and the crew will be wearing black wet suits. Ralph and Sam will park in the North parking lot. Charlie and I will set up a road block here, using the wall map for reference. This old logging road is halfway, Martz will probably stop here."

Sam said, "Sounds exciting, Emmit, much better than listening to Fibber McGee and Molly."

~ ~ ~

Karl Amsel couldn't control his emotions and paced the floor while his wife and Martz prepared for the trip. "I don't feel good with thing you doing. We all in prison if catch you. Government torture spies and shoot them."

Martz said, "Calm yourself, Karl, the plan is sound and we'll be back by Saturday night."

"I know you sleep in same room."

"We're serving the Reich, not running off as lovers."

A nervous Marlene walked over to give her husband a hug. "We come back. Martz promised me one hundred dollars. Things are fine."

"Worth two hundred, agents have money."

"All right, Karl, two hundred when we return."

"Go, I stay home and worry."

Martz put Marlene's suitcase in the trunk and a suitcase with clothing and essentials for the agents in the back seat. He had packed a duffel bag for himself.

Martz turned to Marlene. "I'm ready if you are. We just drove to Hampton Beach and know it doesn't take three hours. At the halfway mark, we are going to stop and rest and see if anyone is following. We meet the U-boat after midnight."

"Like good plan. Car follows, have plan? Thank you, not be in prison."

"It is time to go." Marlene pulled out of the driveway and drove to the bridge that connects Saco with Biddeford. The rain increased as they left Biddeford and headed to the back road.

~ ~ ~

Sam Griffiths sat in his car at the Biddeford-Saco Bridge waiting for the Amsel car. *If the car shows, I could be fighting the war at sixty-two.* With the exception of Robinson, no one else in the group had shot a man. He prayed for a minute and ended the prayer with "Father, I pray you're on our side."

When he finished praying, he poured coffee from his thermos, trying to relax. At 8:15 he began to think they weren't coming and by 8:30 he was sure. Twenty minutes passed before two cars crossed the bridge with Martz in the first car. Not in any hurry, Griffiths followed both cars on the road south to Hampton Beach. *Martz is going to pick up the Germans, Dunsmore was right.*

~ ~ ~

On board U-boat 74

One hundred kilometers from Portland, Maine, *Kapitan* Hruby and *Korvettenkapitan* Merkel opened the envelope containing their orders. Hruby frowned as he read Plan A that delivered the agents to Hampton Beach to meet code name yellow. "Someone forgot to check the tides. At midnight, we need to stay a kilometer or more from shore. That translates into sixty minutes or more on the surface without something going amiss."

He explained to Merkel, "There are six rafts on board and I plan to use three of them. The first raft will have the agents and two marines. The second raft will be fifteen meters to the left, and fifteen meters to the rear with two sailors, the crew chief and radio operator. The third raft will be ten meters to the right of the first raft with four sailors."

"I want two marines to accompany the agents to the car. Yellow and the agents can carry the luggage; the marines are there to protect them. In this weather, the rafts could be on the surface for two hours. We'll both pray in our own way for a successful mission."

"Prayer is good if God hasn't chosen sides, the Americans are also praying. Please bear with me, *Kapitan*. We have orders to deliver agents to Hampton Beach. Once the agents are on the beach, our mission is complete. A better plan has a raft with two marines an agent and suitcases. A second raft will have two marines, an agent, and radio. The rafts should be twenty meters apart. If the police are waiting, there's nothing we can do. Your plan has ten men on the beach with two of the four marines accompanying the agents to the car. With the car gone, local police and volunteers could open fire on the rafts returning to the boat from concealed positions. Rubber rafts aren't built for combat, our men will be easy targets. The

Americans will capture the agents on the road to Boston and we'll lose ten men.

"From what I've read, men from Maine and New Hampshire have high-powered rifles and know how to use them. *Mainahs'*, as they're called, will fight, they won't retreat. With an unknown number of men on the beach, if something unexpected happens on the way to the car, it could trigger a battle with heavy losses for both sides."

"You've done your research, Merkel. The park and surrounding area are blacked out for miles with no security this time of year. In this weather, no one will be on the beach. Falk wants ten men and three rafts."

"Falk has no combat experience. We're transporting two agents, not invading America. I'm concerned for their safety, *Kapitan*, they're our shipmates."

"Calm down, Merkel. We're delivering two agents to Hampton Beach as ordered. If the mission is hopeless, getting our men back to the boat is the mission. You and I aren't Nazis, but we serve the Reich and follow orders."

Merkel shook his head, "I have discussed this with the agents and crew, they're aware of the risk."

"We should reach our destination with a couple of hours to spare. The agents we're delivering could provide valuable information on American convoys that could shorten the war. Once Russia is defeated, the British and Americans will enter into peace talks and we can go home."

Merkel responded, "The landing party is prepared to handle any challenge."

Hruby said, "Please bring the agents to the bridge."

Engel asked, "You wanted to talk with us, *Kapitan*?"

"I know you're not carrying weapons. That's good strategy for the trip to Boston, but tonight you may need to defend yourself."

Hruby waived the envelope. "The order comes from Colonel Falk. If they know you're coming, you'll be fighting men who have handled weapons all their lives. You'll need to kill them to get back to the boat. The marines will give their lives to protect you, but they'll need your help."

Engel replied, "We know how to handle weapons, sir. I prefer a machine pistol."

Tesoro answered, "I'll take a Luger and a machine pistol, sir."

"I'm required to say this. If you're captured, you have the cyanide capsules."

Engel nodded, "Thank you, *Kapitan*, for reminding us."

As Merkel was leaving, the radio operator handed Hruby a message.

CHAPTER 38

On Road to Hampton Beach

Thursday Night, April 30, 1942

Martz checked the rearview mirror, there were two cars following, but he couldn't distinguish one set of headlights from the other through a fogged rear window. Five miles out of town, the car directly behind them turned into a private drive and the other car turned at the next intersection. A short distance passed before a pickup entered the road falling in behind them. *So far, so good, let's see how far this guy goes.*

Marlene drove to an old logging road where she parked. Martz wanted to arrive at Hampton Beach before midnight. Visibility was less than one hundred meters in the driving rain.

"No one will be walking on the beach in this weather, much better for us, Marlene."

"I not put dog out in this weather."

The Biddeford team knew of the logging road and expected Martz to park there. They continued the trip and turned onto a logging road ten miles from the beach. Convinced Hampton Beach was Martz's destination, Jones, Griffiths, and Robinson joined Dunsmore.

Jones inhaled a deep breath. "Everything is going as planned, what's next?"

"This is where we split. Ralph and Sam head to the park and Charlie and I will check out a good location for a road block."

~ ~ ~

Robinson parked in the north parking lot a mile from the access road. He and Griffiths walked to a defensive position north of the access road.

"Go as far south of the road as you can, Sam. I'll set up here."

"We have no way of communicating. I'll wait for you to fire the first shot. It could be over after the first volley, neither one of us misses many shots."

Robinson replied, "Once they're in the rafts, move closer to the water, I don't want to use a flare."

"I was planning to do that."

"If they send ten, there'll be wounded sailors in the water and others swimming for their lives. The survivors will need to help the wounded. If there's six or less we'll probably kill them with the first volley."

"It'll be like shooting decoys. Good luck, Ralph."

"Good luck, Sam. I'll pray for us."

"I'm praying for God to be on our side."

With time to spare, Robinson used a small spade to dig a foxhole, piling loose sand around the hole facing the beach. Satisfied with his work, he snuggled down to wait for Martz.

Griffiths found a good place to hide in swamp grass bordering the beach.

Dunsmore and Jones studied a curve in the road with ditches on both sides filled with water. In an hour the ditches would overflow forcing cars to slow down. Dunsmore placed a warning sign north and south of the water. A gravel drive to a cabin offered a good view with easy access to the road. With few cars on the road, the Amsel car would be easy to spot.

Jones said, "The Amsel car will have to stop or go in the water to get around an angled road block."

"My thinking too; this looks like the perfect spot."Dunsmore paused, "The agents will be in the back seat hoping to catch some sleep. Martz is the wild card if he's armed. Shoot him if he's brandishing a pistol, he'll be on your side of the road."

"I'll shoot him in the legs with the rifle. Martz can reveal the contact, we want him alive. I brought a shotgun for close fire if they try to escape in the car, I won't miss."

"I think the agents will bite the capsule after the first shot. Time will tell."

~ ~ ~

At 11:30, Marlene Amsel continued the drive. Shortly after, a car gained on them, blinking the lights wanting to pass. Marlene returned the blink and the car went around them and sped away. Marlene entered the park with headlights off using the trolley tracks to find the access road.

Martz said, "Back the car to the end of the road."

Marlene replied, "I can't see road in the dark."

Martz left the car saying, "Move over, I can back the car in. Open your door a crack and help me stay on the road."

After several tries, Martz reached the end of the road. He wiped his brow, saying, "I would like to check the area, but the weather won't permit it. Fifteen minutes from now, I'll go to the water and signal. You'll be warm and dry in the car."

~ ~ ~

At 12:15 a.m. Martz flashed the signal light with no response. *I'll signal every fifteen minutes. In this weather they could be running late.* He adjusted his hood and turned to put the wind at his back. *Just be patient, they're coming.*

Robinson saw Martz signal to no avail. He was ready for a landing party. He dried the scope of his rifle to look for rafts. After several minutes he mumbled, "Where in the hell are they?"

Martz continued to signal for the next hour at regular intervals with no answer.

Martz signaled at 1:30 a. m. with no response. At 1:45 a. m. Robinson, Griffiths, and Martz had reached the same conclusion, the Germans weren't coming.

"Son-of-a-bitch, all our planning down the drain," Martz screamed as he walked to the car.

Marlene Amsel asked, "Where are the Germans?"

"They're not coming. Start the car, I'm cold and tired."

"We go back to Biddeford?"

"That's the plan."

Robinson watched Martz walk slowly back to the car with head down, the heavy light swinging at his side. From a practical standpoint, the only thing accomplished was to identify Martz and the Amsels as accomplices. Did the Germans abort the mission or was Martz a decoy to lead them astray? Other than ignoring the blackout, Martz and Marlene Amsel hadn't broken the law.

Robinson said to an approaching Griffiths, "The Germans could have aborted the mission because of the weather."

A stiff Griffiths responded, "It's better for us, but I was ready to fight."

As they walked to the access road Dunsmore and Jones met them.

Dunsmore said, "We figured they didn't show. The storm could be the reason."

Jones added, "On second thought, Martz and the Amsel woman aren't important, they could be unknowing decoys to mislead us."

A frustrated Robinson looked at Dunsmore, "What Charlie says makes sense. When the Germans didn't show up, I could hear Martz scream, 'Son-of-a-bitch, a week's work down the drain.'"

Dunsmore shook his head. "I'll call the Navy, they might send a destroyer to look for the sub."

When Dunsmore returned, he said, "We're on our own until eight, that's when the decision makers start. There's no guarantee the Navy will send a destroyer."

Griffiths asked, "What about Novak, maybe we should check on him before morning?"

Dunsmore answered, "If Novak runs, we'll know he's the contact. We can wait on him."

Jones said, "The contact might have picked up the German agents while we were babysitting Martz."

~ ~ ~

On the ride back to the cars, Griffiths said, "From what I've learned, crossing the Atlantic takes twelve to fourteen days. Rough seas will take a toll on the boat and crew and be difficult for civilians. The U-boat might be a hundred miles off shore if they sailed with a tight schedule. Bad weather could have cost them a day."

Dunsmore said, "There are good reasons why we witnessed a no show. By ten we should hear from the FBI, and we'll plan accordingly."

Griffiths shook his head. "If weather wasn't the problem, I'm not comfortable waiting until ten. We'll be back in Biddeford before four. I think we should check the Martz cabin, the cabin Schroeder left, and the church. One of the three could be hiding German agents. We need to know if we've been spoofed."

Dunsmore noted, "Martz will be at his cabin by the time we get there, and the other cabin makes no sense. We could have it under surveillance. Same goes for the church, and Pastor Novak has Friday off, why wake him early?"

Jones pointed out several facts. "There's a fine line that separates acting and overreacting. We can only speculate why the U-boat didn't show. We learned that Marlene Amsel and Martz are German sympathizers and bear watching. We also know that Novak falsified his resume to receive the calling, but he hasn't committed a crime and there is no evidence that connects him with tonight's aborted landing. Schroeder is being tracked by a posse for stealing a car and license plates. Other than the color of the stolen car, we have no evidence connecting Schroeder to the fire and the first landing. Plus, most would not use a stolen car to meet a landing party. And the guy is a philanderer who'll do anything for a buck or free meal."

Dunsmore agreed. "Charlie is right. We'll probably solve the case with a tip from a local resident. Get some sleep, Sam; I may need you again this weekend."

Frustrated, Sam said, "Maybe I'm overreacting, but my imagination is running wild and so are my emotions. I want to hang the bastards who helped the spies on the first landing. Heads up, Emmit! Don't miss the logging road, it's coming up after this curve."

"I got it, Sam."

On the ride back to Biddeford, Dunsmore considered what would happen to the Amsels and Martz. *Pennsylvania has a large German population and the government is building internment camps. I'll let Andrews and Warner arrest them, the government can determine their fate.*

CHAPTER 39

On Board U-boat 74

Late Thursday Night, April 30, 1942

Aboard U-boat 74 *Kapitan* Hruby was handed a message. Scanning the note, he said to *Korvettenkapitan* Merkel, "Message from Brown, we're using Plan B."

He opened the second envelope reading aloud:

"Plan B – New landing site, Fortune Rocks, Maine
"Repeat – New landing site, Fortune Rocks, Maine
"Set course – Fortune Rocks, Maine.
"Load raft – 2 Marines, Agents, luggage, radio.
"Launch raft – 11:15 p.m. EST.
"Brown will signal – 2 flashes. 11:30 p.m. EST.
"Acknowledge signal – 2 flashes.
"Recover raft – Await new orders."

Merkel took a deep breath and exhaled slowly. "Fortune Rocks is south of Biddeford. Likely the same beach used on first landing. Much better for us *Kapitan*, it's a secluded area."

"I've located Fortune Rocks on the chart, the water is deeper. There's time to travel submerged and be ready by eleven. Weather is coming from northeast; we'll surface north of the beach."

With new coordinates, *Kapitan* Hruby surfaced U-boat 74 a kilometer from the beach. The crew prepared a raft as Engel and Tesoro joined Hruby on deck.

Hruby spoke in German. "A lot of weight for one raft, you'll need to paddle hard." He switched to English. "Speak English only, and remember the cyanide capsules if you run into trouble. The boat is rocking, if you're not sure of your footing, I suggest you crawl to the raft on your hands and knees. You're meeting a man, code name Brown. Good luck!"

Engel said, "Thank you, *Kapitan*, hands and knees works for me."

As the submarine submerged, freeing the raft from the deck, Hruby turned to his executive officer. "This miserable weather is better than a clear night. I'm anxious, Merkel, awaiting the landing outcome."

"Whatever happens, *Kapitan*, we are helpless to change things. The first landing was successful."

When U-boat 74 surfaced fifteen minutes later, the raft was out of sight.

In the raft, the crew chief said to Tesoro, "Take my oar. I need to face the beach."

It seemed an eternity in the rough sea before a light flashed from the beach. The crew chief flashed twice to acknowledge. "We're on the right course, let the wind take us to the beach."

The road to Fortune Rocks had little traffic this time of year and no cars this night. Still nervous from a lightning strike near his car, an anxious Brown looked to the sky when he signaled the raft. "Thank you, Lord, for this bad weather, but a little less lightning, please."

He signaled once with no response. Minutes passed before he signaled again. His heart raced when two flashes of light appeared from the water. "Please, God, keep them safe."

Earlier that night, Brown observed Griffiths following the Amsel car and was sure Dunsmore and Jones would join the pursuit. Schroeder running from authorities and Martz carrying out a failed mission at Hampton Beach were perfect ruses. Plans made for the first landing were sound, but Aldrich and David Radke had showed up unexpectedly. In this weather, no one was walking their dog or visiting friends. He flashed the light again to assist the raft. Ten minutes later, the raft came into view on the right course to reach the shore.

The crew chief said, "I see a figure on the beach, we're on the right track."

Engel replied, "The sooner I'm on dry land, the better."

As the raft approached the beach, Brown tossed a rope to the crew chief. "Welcome to America, it's all downhill from here. I'm Brown, the local contact."

Engel leaned over the side of the raft to throw up. A minute later he spoke. "Sorry to greet you this way, but I'm no match for the Atlantic Ocean. Help me out, please; I don't want to end up in the water."

Brown moved quickly to Engel's side. "I'm not surprised you're sick, a U-boat isn't first-class passage. I'll help Herr Engel, the rest of you can carry luggage, the trunk is open."

Tesoro asked, "Is the weather always this bad?"

Brown laughed. "Yesterday was a fair day, but this is typical weather for this time of year."

~ ~ ~

On the ride to the cabin, Brown said, "Take off your shoes when we get to the cabin. It's heated by oil, no fires. The bedrooms are upstairs where you'll find clothes worn in this part of the country. You can use the bathroom and kitchen, but the place must be spotless when you leave. Put your old clothes and anything else in the suitcase provided. I'll dispose of them. There are egg salad sandwiches for tonight and you can prepare hot soup for tomorrow. I'll be back Saturday morning, at two a.m. Eastern Standard Time. You'll be in Boston by six for morning trains to New York City."

Engel said, "We'll sleep most of today. Where's Langer?"

"There'll be time to discuss Langer and other details on the trip to Boston. Get some rest and regain your strength, Saturday will be a busy day. Remember, English only, no German."

After Brown left, Engel and Tesoro washed down their sandwiches with beer.

Tesoro smacked his lips. "I like the potato chips and sweet pickle; they go well with the sandwiches. I read someplace we should try the southern fried chicken with sweet potatoes."

Engel replied, "Southern fried chicken is very good but a little greasy for me. The sweet potatoes with butter are delicious. Let's get out of these clothes and get some sleep. For dinner we'll have sandwiches, soup, and more potato chips."

Yawning, Tesoro said, "Don't wake me before noon, I can sleep for hours."

"I won't wake you, I'll be sleeping."

Lying in bed, Engel pondered the change in plans. The first briefing had them landing at Hampton Beach and being met by a man named Yellow. Hampton Beach was closer to Boston, their planned destination. Landing at Fortune Rocks meant Hampton Beach wasn't a safe landing site. Had the Americans discovered their plan, or was he kept in the dark on purpose? If the plans were changed in the past week, Boston was out of the question, the FBI would have agents on every corner. If not Boston or Portland, how would they get to NYC?

While teaching at Columbia University, he had taken a train to Albany, New York, to attend a conference. Albany has frequent trains to NYC, but it's a four to five-hour drive from Biddeford. If the FBI is watching Boston they'll also cover Grand Central Station.

Whatever the reason for changing the plans, it meant they would have to wait to travel to NYC. If we're going to wait, I prefer Chicago. After a month in Chicago, they could take a train to Philadelphia and drive to NYC. On second thought, he and Tesoro will have to split; traveling together they fit a profile. The thought of reaching Chicago and defecting entered his mind. That's a choice I can make after Brown explains the plan to get us to NYC.

~ ~ ~

The two Marines were back in the raft and well on their way when U-boat 74 signaled its position, having moved south for a better course.

The crew chief said, "We'll make better time if we turn around; I can check our course with the compass."

Thirty minutes later, the Marines were on deck with crew handling the raft.

Kapitan Hruby asked, "All went well on the beach?"

"Yes sir, the agents were picked up, no surprises. We made good time coming back with the lighter raft."

Greeting Merkel, Hruby smiled. "Take the boat to deeper water so we can get some well-earned sleep."

~ ~ ~

Biddeford, Maine

Joyce worked late Thursday night, hoping to hear from Dunsmore. She left the office at nine knowing if Martz showed up at the bridge, Dunsmore, Jones and Griffiths were headed to Hampton Beach to confront armed Germans.

She maintained and lived in a winterized vacation home located on the road leading to Fortune Rocks. The owner spent summer months with her daughter and grandchildren in Biddeford while her banker-husband stayed in Boston.

After a late dinner Joyce settled down on the couch to read *War and Peace*. As the rain and wind increased, she couldn't help thinking of her friends waiting for a German landing party. Around eleven, Joyce went to the window as thunder roared and lightning struck rocks on the beach. The lightning flashes revealed a car driving slowly south with lights out. Joyce jumped back from the window.

After several deep breaths, she regained composure as her heart rate dropped. *Whew, that was too close for comfort.* The beach road had vacation homes not used in April and little if any traffic this time of year. Not sure what she witnessed and unable to sleep, Joyce returned to the couch, but three pages later, she had no interest in *War and Peace*. At 11:30 she went back to the window to observe the storm. The icy wind from the ocean and rain beating on the storm windows fogged the glass making it difficult to see the road. Ten minutes passed before she turned to go to bed. Unobserved, the car made a return trip to town.

~ ~ ~

When Pastor Novak returned to his cottage, he backed the car up to the first step of the porch. He toweled his face dry before opening a beer to wash down a bowl of potato chips. He couldn't wait until Saturday to move the agents, it had to be tonight. *My best chance is to head west, Boston is out of the question.* He had today off and use of a '36 Ford sedan through the weekend. Leaving

Biddeford in two hours, he could reach Albany by eleven. From Albany they could catch trains to Buffalo, New York, Cleveland, Ohio, or Chicago, Illinois. In a new city, the agents could lay low for several weeks before traveling to NYC. The drive would give him time to determine his own fate.

Novak brewed a fresh pot of coffee before studying a road map of northeastern states. He used a red pencil to mark the best route to Albany. Satisfied with his work, he poured a second cup of coffee and shaved before making sandwiches for the trip. An empty box was filled with food from the refrigerator and the cupboard was emptied into a paper sack. He placed his tool box and suitcase in the trunk. The food was placed behind the driver's seat and the map and notes went in the glove box.

Satisfied with his plans, Novak turned on the radio and sat down to write a message. 'Must leave Biddeford immediately ... under surveillance. Will transport agents to Albany, NY, to board trains to major cities. It could take weeks to make new arrangements ... end of message.' He wrote a second message to place on the front door of the church.

EMERGENCY CALL FROM NON-PARISHIONER

Son ill, needs prayer.

Transporting son to Portland hospital, be back after lunch.

Novak transmitted the message and checked the cottage a final time before leaving.

After taping the note to the church front door, he said a prayer thanking God for the calling and asking forgiveness for his sins.

~ ~ ~

Novak used back roads to the cabin, not passing any cars or homes. The trip tested his driving skills as he dodged mud holes caused by melting frost. He breathed a sigh of relief once the car turned down the road to the cabin. Knowing Dunsmore was at Hampton Beach, he entered the cabin with a flashlight to locate a lantern. Upstairs, he found Engel and Tesoro sound asleep. It took several shakes to wake Engel.

"Wh … what are you doing here? Is it two a.m. already?"

"There's been a change in plans, we need to travel tonight. Wake your partner and be ready to leave in thirty minutes. I'll leave the lantern and start cleaning up downstairs."

After cleaning the kitchen, Novak went to the front door to wipe up footprints and move Engel's and Tesoro's shoes to the rear door.

Upstairs, Engel and Tesoro had finished dressing and were making beds. Engel said, "Good work, we'll leave through the back door. Is everything the way we found it?"

Tesoro yawned. "Exactly, I have a photographic mind. You have our shoes?"

"They're at the back door. Let's go, we'll make a final check before leaving."

CHAPTER 40

Biddeford, Maine

Early Friday Morning, May 1, 1942

Novak said, "I need one of you to ride in the front seat to help with the map."

Tesoro answered, "That would be me, Engel is still under the weather."

Settled in the car, Engel said, "When I left Germany, Langer and Bernhard were in New York City. Have they established contact?"

A pause followed before Novak responded. "We have six hours to reach Albany, New York, and be there by ten. I've marked the map using back roads, if we fall behind schedule we'll have to chance the main road."

"Following the map will not be a problem. That's why I'm here and not on the front lines. I joined the SS to fight the Russians, not to spy on America. If you're bright and speak good English, you end up in Covert Operations."

Brown took a deep breath before speaking. "You need to know the current circumstances and why I changed plans. My name is Alex Novak—I'm pastor of the Biddeford Lutheran Church since January of this year. I developed the safe house concept to deliver agents to NYC. The first landing went well until the caretaker and a twelve-year-old boy wandered in. Our agents killed the caretaker and burned the house to cover the crime, the boy escaped. Langer used the caretaker's car for the trip to Boston and took the train to NYC. Two weeks ago, Langer and Wellenhofer were caught by the New York Police and FBI at Yankee Stadium. Langer was knocked cold and didn't recover, Wellenhofer used the cyanide capsule."

Engel almost cried when he heard of Langer's death. Down deep he knew the terror device had played a part in his demise. In a shaky voice, he said, "I'm sorry to hear that, Otto and Bernhard were good comrades."

"When I learned of their death, I developed a plan to land you at Hampton Beach and use local sympathizers to meet the raft and take you to Boston. Last week the local police started tracking my helpers and followed them last night to Hampton Beach. They also discovered I lied on my resume to receive the calling. By afternoon, they'll be at the church ready to arrest me. If we're caught, we'll be interrogated and sentenced to the electric chair. I need a couple of cyanide capsules, I won't be taken alive."

Tesoro quipped, "As they say in America, 'The jig is up.' My grandfather taught me that as a small boy. His brother migrated to America and ended up in Utica, New York. I read a book on New York. Albany is the state capital and a major railroad hub. From Albany, we can take trains west to avoid being captured. Do the authorities know we landed?"

Novak continued, "I'm a part-time mechanic at Biddeford's Ford dealership. The owner is a deacon at my church and lets me use a car on my Friday day off and weekends. I changed the license plates Thursday afternoon. Once authorities sort things out, they'll be looking for this car. That could be today or surely by tomorrow.

"I sent a car last night to Hampton Beach to meet you at midnight. The local police followed the car. The man I sent signaled from the beach, but the submarine didn't show. The Biddeford police would have forwarded that information to the FBI. At this time, the FBI thinks the Germans aborted the landing." Novak shook his head. "There's a saying in this country, 'You're a day late and a dollar short.' It would have been better if you had landed yesterday while things were normal."

Tesoro whistled, "No one knows we're here. We're free to travel today and tomorrow before they figure things out."

"All the rail and bus stations in the northeast will be under surveillance, they're looking for me. They'll release a sketch of me by afternoon. I need to steal a car, to get away. Taking a train or bus is out of the question."

Tesoro asked, "What about Buffalo? It's a good-sized city that borders Canada. Niagara Falls, Canada, has trains to Toronto and Montreal."

Engel quipped, "We'll split in Albany and meet at Yankee Stadium in front of the ticket windows the first Saturday home game in June."

Novak said, "If you can get to NYC tonight, I have the address of a radio operator willing to help. The man is crippled and needs to be contacted in person. Langer had his name, I'm sure he contacted him."

Sounding dubious, Engel said, "You want me to take a train from Albany to NYC today?"

"The sooner you're operational, the better. Tesoro could take the bus tonight, or tomorrow morning. I've been told we need convoy information sooner than later. Our effort could save thousands of lives and bring an end to the war. If German U-boats sink half the American convoys, the British and Russians will be forced to sue for peace by year-end. Every month we delay is another month the Americans help our enemies."

Tesoro argued, "You said authorities will be watching Grand Central Station. If we wait our chances decrease."

Engel said, "I taught German in NYC for a year. In two days my face could be all over New York. My time is now, not next week. When the FBI pieces together all the information, they'll look for the three of us. If we make it, I suggest we meet at Ebbets Field. Yankee Stadium hasn't been kind to our cause."

"You go today, Engel, I'll go tomorrow."

"Good choice, Tesoro, we'll meet next Saturday for lunch at the Sandwich Shoppe in Manhattan. You'll need a week to get familiar with the city. In the meantime, I'll contact the radio operator and set up a get acquainted meeting."

Novak interrupted. "I already know too much, no more details. On the run, I'm of little value to the party. Protecting me isn't a priority."

Tesoro suggested, "We are close to Vermont. I would use the main road for the rest of the trip. Being in traffic won't hurt us. Take the next right; it's less than a mile."

~ ~ ~

Zeke Zypt was on his way to pick up his nephew in Albany. The nephew had torn a meniscus in boot camp and was having the cast removed at the Veterans Affairs Hospital. He had a weekend pass to spend time with his uncle. When John Jenkins returned home from the first war in 1919, the love of his life had run off with a married man. Bitter and confused, he spent six months drunk and fighting in bars. After losing a tooth in a Saturday night brawl, he decided to change his name to Zeke Zypt, the last name in the phone book or in any public record.

Zeke lived with a friend for a year learning how to survive in the wilderness before building a cabin with his friend's help. Now a legendary trapper, Zeke works as a game warden during summer months when Vermont's pristine lakes and streams attract many fishermen. Last year he bought a new 1941 blue Chevrolet pickup truck with a signal light on the roof and a two-way radio. The state purchased a new boat and trailer and paid Zeke $250 a month when he worked. The violations Zeke issued and fines collected more than covered his salary. Every two weeks, Zeke mailed paperwork and a money order to the state.

The blue pickup, traveling at forty-five mph, closed on the 1936 Ford. Zeke had listened to the radio before leaving and remembered something about a black Ford sedan with Maine plates. He slowed down to count the occupants; there were two men in the front seat. Deputized, he turned on the signal light and blew the horn.

Tesoro turned to see a blue truck gaining on them. "There's a truck with a light on the roof. He's signaling for you to pull over."

Novak replied, "A routine traffic stop, I'll handle it."

Novak pulled to the side of the road as a car slowed down from the opposite direction. Zeke fetched his shotgun from the rack and waved the car on as he approached the Ford sedan. From the rear of the car he shouted, "Get out of the car driver, and bring the registration."

Novak looked out the window saying, "I have my driver's license; the registration is in the glove box." Holding out the driver's license, "You can check them, please."

Novak rolled up the window as Zeke approached the driver's side. When he was parallel to the car Novak shoved the door open knocking Zypt to the ground. Trained in martial arts he was out of the car before Zypt could react. With knees on Zeke's chest and arm, Novak broke his neck with one twist. Tesoro rushed to the scene throwing the shotgun into the brush.

Tesoro said, "Help me move the body to the woods."

Novak said, "There are no keys in his pockets, take the truck, you can ditch it in Albany. This is where we split, Engel will travel with me."

Tesoro handed Novak half the money he was carrying and two cyanide capsules, "You may need these. Open the trunk, I need my suitcase." Walking toward the truck Tesoro turned, "Good luck, Novak, hope to see you at Ebbets Field."

As he started the truck Tesoro thought, *Thank God no one saw what happened.* Still miles from Albany, Novak had sufficient time to distance the pickup from the Ford.

Back on the road, Engel reasoned, "The man would have reported us, you had to kill him. Tesoro gave you money, was it enough?"

"It looked like half. He also gave me two cyanide capsules."

"That's enough money to get to the city next month. If all goes well you won't need the capsules."

"The money is sufficient, your facial appearance is fine, but the clothes, not so good. Friday afternoon there are four, five, and six o'clock trains to NYC full of politicians and businessmen going home for the weekend. You need to wear a suit and carry a briefcase to blend in."

Engel replied, "A little girl said, 'Businessmen look the same.' She couldn't tell one from the other. I know where you're coming from."

"The four and five o'clock trains are express service, they're your best choice." Novak paused, "In your shoes, I would buy a ticket first and get something to eat then shop for a suit with all the accessories, including two ties. Get a hotel room close to the station. Shower, shave and change clothes before boarding the train. Being clean and well-dressed gives one a sense of self-confidence. If you can get in the bar car, buy a drink and mix with fellow travelers. Half the people in the bar car will be consultants; you could be an education consultant."

"An education consultant with a home in the Queens makes sense. You're a smart man, Novak, I hope we survive to meet at Ebbets Field."

"Don't forget your suitcase; you'll need it for traveling."

Novak didn't expect a road block at the bridge entrance and there wasn't one as he exited into downtown traffic. He turned onto a less traveled street to open the trunk. "Good luck, Engel, and God speed."

Engel gave him an inquisitive look. "You think God is on our side?"

"If God is on our side, I want him to know help is needed. You can eat too much, but you can't pray too much."

"Good luck Novak."

Novak put on sun glasses and a mustache for the trip to the airport.

The parking attendant asked, "How many days will you be parked?"

"Five, could be more."

"Place the ticket on the dashboard and park in lot B, please."

Novak parked toward the rear of lot B across from a vacant space. He was looking for a driver walking to the airport with a suitcase or two. Ten minutes passed before a late model Buick pulled into the spot. Running behind schedule, the driver hurried to the trunk for his suitcase. He slammed the trunk shut and ran toward the airport.

Not wanting to be taken alive, Novak placed a cyanide capsule in his mouth. Stealing a car from a parking lot required a lookout, but he didn't have one. He fetched the toolbox from the trunk, took several deep breaths and headed to the Buick. The doors were locked and the car looked inaccessible. He tried his master key ring to no avail. Five minutes passed and there was no one on the entryway. He went to work on the window and failed to see a large man emerge between two cars to his rear.

Lieutenant Mark Jeffries from the state patrol was on his way home from a meeting in Buffalo. Hurrying home to have lunch with his wife and watch his son compete in a track meet, Jeffries cut across the grass and scurried up a small hill to Parking Lot B. He jumped over a railing and went between two cars to the main entryway. Jeffries looked to his left and saw a man trying to get into the car parked next to his car. Fifty feet from the man he asked, "Did you lock your keys in the car?"

Seconds before Jeffries appeared, Novak had checked the main entryway and it was clear. In a state of shock, he answered, "It's none of your business," then turned and saw a large man in a trooper uniform drawing his pistol.

"Put your hands behind your back."

Out of options and wanting to protect Tesoro and Engel, Novak bit down on the cyanide capsule, falling to the pavement face down."

Jeffries said, "If you move again, I'll be forced to fire." There was no response, the man seemed unconscious.

Jeffries moved with caution toward the prone man. When he rolled him over, the smell of cyanide filled the air. The training class he attended in Buffalo dealt with cyanide capsules and German agents. *I'll be damned; the guy must be a spy.*

As he closed Novak's eyes, the first thing that entered his mind, *Another broken promise to my family.* Then reality set in. *I'm an eye-witness, there's no way for me not to be involved.* He went to the trunk of his car for flares to mark the area and cones to block traffic. Five minutes later, he called the FBI for backup.

FBI agent John Bowers arrived fifteen minutes later. "Are you sure it was cyanide?"

"The guy looked shocked when I challenged him and fell face down. There are scrapes on his forehead and blood. When I rolled his body over, there was a strong cyanide odor and the mustache was on the ground. I checked his ID; he's either Pastor Novak from the Biddeford Lutheran Church, or Gregg Hawkins, a teacher from New Hampshire. There are two sets of identification."

"We have a 'be on the lookout' for a 1936 black Ford sedan with Maine plates, driven by a Pastor Novak."

"The car is across from here on the far side of the main entryway. I didn't search it."

"We'll take charge of the body and the investigation; this is a National Security issue. Did you call for an ambulance?"

"Not yet. When I discovered cyanide, I suspected the man was a spy. The state patrol has enough to do. Consider me a witness; it's your case. At this point, no one else is involved."

"In the final report, you and the state patrol will receive credit, I'll see to that."

"We both know the FBI will take credit. Hoover will see to that. I've already missed lunch with my wife and my son's track meet."

"Stay here while I make arrangements to have the body moved. The FBI will notify the other offices and the Biddeford police. I learned in training that German agents work in pairs."

Jeffries said, "If he's pastor of the Biddeford Lutheran Church, he's not a German agent. However, we both know German agents burned a house in Biddeford last month, maybe he helped them."

"Get on the phone, John, the office geniuses will figure it out."

CHAPTER 41

Albany, New York

Friday Morning, May 1, 1942

Twenty minutes later, Tesoro crossed the bridge and headed to the bus station. He purchased a ticket to Utica, New York, on the Saturday morning train. His attire matched the others in the bus station. A few men looked out of place dressed in outdated suits with old ties and shoes, probably older men and farmers attending funerals.

He circled the downtown area looking for a men's store on a side street. He purchased a gray suit, white shirt, belt, tie, shoes, socks, matching kerchiefs and four sets of underwear. He said to the clerk, "I need a hotel room for the night, wedding tomorrow. Is there one close to the Catholic Church on the Westside?"

"The Milano Hotel is two blocks from the church."

"While you're doing the alterations, I'll get something to eat."

"Your suit will be ready in an hour."

Tesoro left the truck on the street with keys in the ignition. He glanced over his shoulder before entering an Italian restaurant to see two teenagers admiring the truck. Quite hungry, he ordered spaghetti with meatballs and a slice of chocolate cake and coffee.

Albany was no different than Berlin, everyone smoked but him. He picked up a newspaper and sat at a sidewalk table to enjoy his lunch in the sunshine and cool air.

He had been out of touch with the outside world for a month. The newspaper reported bad news with the good news. The Japanese had kicked the Americans out of the Philippines and Corregidor was under siege. The Americans had lost every naval battle in the Pacific and their navy was on the run. Suddenly it struck him; there were no posters of Roosevelt, only different-sized American flags hanging in every shop. Some were new, others looked worn. The people must buy their flags. The bank had a picture of Uncle Sam advertising war bonds.

He turned to the editorial page to find a story criticizing Roosevelt for not being ready when Japan bombed Pearl Harbor. The Yankees had beaten the Tigers and were playing at one o'clock. Major league baseball players were joining the military to fight for their country. German newspapers never criticized Hitler. *I have much to learn about America, much to learn.*

He watched the boys steal the truck as he ate the cake. *Let them explain where they got the truck and why the owner is dead.* As he left the restaurant, he noticed police officers on street corners that weren't there an hour ago. After picking up the suit, he purchased personal items and makeup at a drugstore before taking a bus to the hotel. An hour later, dressed in the new suit, Tesoro left the hotel to take a cab to the train station. He put on horn-rimmed glasses and purchased a one-way ticket on the four o'clock train to NYC. The clerk at the ticket window advised, "For a few dollars more, you can buy a round trip ticket."

"I'm not coming back to this hick town. Does the train have a bar car and dining car?"

"Of course!"

"What track does the train depart from?"

320

"Check the departure board. Next!"

"You are not deaf and dumb, why can't you tell me?"

"Look at the departure board, you're holding up the line."

Not appreciating the delay, the man behind him said, "Move it buddy, the departure board is over there," and shoved Tesoro from the window.

Not used to being pushed around, Tesoro bristled.

The next man in line was a burly fellow who stepped between Tesoro and the roughneck. "Let's not have a scene, friend. I'm headed to NYC to wrestle Saturday night. If either one of you hits me first, it's self-defense."

Tesoro knew he had met his match and went to the departure board. Satisfied with his effort to create a scene, he searched the train station on the way out for likely suspects that would be searching for him. The man in a tan raincoat was still watching the ticket windows. With a dining car and bar car to accommodate the passengers, the conductors were never sure how many passengers were on the train; they wouldn't notice an empty seat.

After Tesoro left, the man in the raincoat questioned the clerk at the window Tesoro used.

"He bought a ticket on this afternoon's four o'clock train to the city."

Returning to the hotel, he had the cabby pull over four blocks away. Stepping from the cab, Tesoro handed the driver a two-dollar bill, saying, "Keep the change. My sister lives in the next block. Can't wait to see her, been away three years."

"Thanks for the tip."

On the walk to the hotel, Tesoro decided to take a nap and have dinner in his room.

~ ~ ~

Biddeford – Friday Morning

Dorothy Dunsmore phoned Joyce Friday morning. "Emmit and Charlie will be in late, they're sleeping in. The Germans didn't show last night, they'll give you the details."

Joyce breathed a sigh of relief and shared the information with Sheila Graycheck. "Please handle the phone, Sheila, I have work to do."

Joyce knew the church had volunteers answering the phone. Marge said, "Pastor Novak has the day off. The note he left on the door said he was driving a boy to the Portland hospital, and he'd be back after lunch."

Joyce called the Portland hospital. Pastor Novak wasn't there. The woman in admitting asked, "Would you like Pastor Novak to call when he comes in?"

"No thank you, we'll make other arrangements."

Sheila shouted, "Call on line one."

On answering, Warner greeted her. "Is the chief there?"

"Got home in the wee hours this morning from Hampton Beach and slept in. You aware the Germans didn't show?"

"Yeah, Chief Dunsmore called the office. Do you know the whereabouts of Pastor Novak?"

Joyce said, "He has the day off and he's not where he said he would be. The owner of the Ford dealership is an elder at the church and provides him with a car on weekends. The service manager keeps track of the borrowed cars."

When Warner called the service manager, he checked the file box for loaned cars. "Pastor Novak has a 1936 black Ford sedan with license plate 61-111. Is he in trouble?"

"I don't think so, routine check."

Warner turned to Andrews. "Novak has the day off and use of a '36 black Ford sedan, license plate 61-111."

Andrews smiled, "Car dealers have many cars on their lots. Novak works there part-time as a mechanic and has access to all the cars. Call back and ask the service manager to check all the cars on the lot for that plate. If he complains, use National Security, it always works."

Warner met with resistance. "We're short-handed; I haven't time to check license plates."

"It's a matter of National Security."

"You said Pastor Novak wasn't in any trouble."

"You're wasting valuable time, check the plates. I'll call back in twenty minutes."

After checking five cars, the service manager found license plate 61-111 on a car being scrapped. *I'll be damned; Novak switched plates.*

He went to the owner's office. "He switched plates, Dick, the FBI is after him."

"Only people on the run switch plates. This will be a shock to the community."

The service manager heard his name on the speaker. "Call on line two."

"You were right, agent Warner, the '36 black Ford sedan Novak is driving has license plate 61-209. He switched plates Thursday afternoon."

"Please don't mention this to anyone, and if you have to, use my National Security warning. Thanks for your assistance."

Warner hung up the phone. "Good instinct, partner, Novak switched plates. We're looking for 61-209. I'll have the bureau update the alert."

Andrews said, "Joyce had it right, it was her idea to call the Ford dealer. We can be certain Novak is on the run. Let's assume he figured things out early in the game and left Biddeford between three and four this morning. He knew the roads going south would be covered, and going north or northwest makes no sense. That leaves Albany as the best choice. He could be in Albany as we speak, it's after eleven. I'll update the bureau and they can alert the state patrol and Albany office. Call Joyce, Dunsmore and Jones should be in the office around noon."

~ ~ ~

Martz woke at eleven Friday morning, still exhausted from the previous night. Marlene Amsel couldn't handle driving in the storm and he drove back to Biddeford. The conditions were less than ideal for a man who hadn't driven in three years. As he finished breakfast, his mind turned to his contact. Novak found him on the street in February and addressed him in German. Over cups of coffee at Novak's cottage, both realized they were on the same page, wanting to help Germany. Novak asked Martz to continue his charade as the town drunk while they waited for an opportunity to help the Reich. Last night was his chance, and the Germans didn't show. *Wait a minute, Raymond, you can't control the outcome. Do your part and hope for the best. If landing agents was easy, NYC would be full of them. Take the weekend to do things you've been putting off waiting for warmer weather. Novak will let you know when you're needed. Just be patient.*

~ ~ ~

As Andrews and Warner were piecing together the evidence, they received a call from the Albany office.

Andrews hung up the phone and smiled at his partner. "Approaching noon, a lieutenant from the state patrol caught Novak breaking into a car at the Albany Airport. When he challenged Novak, he bit a cyanide capsule and died immediately.

For the record, Novak died Friday, May 1, 1942 at 11:52 a.m. in Albany, New York. The black Ford sedan with the Maine license plate 61-209 was parked on the opposite side of the main entryway."

"We got our man." Warner took time to reflect. "Did Novak get the cyanide from Langer, or did he get it from an agent he just picked up?"

"Langer had no reason to give Novak a cyanide capsule. The landing was flawless and he expected Novak to return Saturday morning for the trip to Boston. They had no contact on Friday before Aldrich ruined their plans. Chances are he got it from an agent that just landed."

"The agents and Novak would have discussed their options on the trip to Albany, take the train or take the bus. With that information and knowing their physical characteristics, Novak couldn't risk being captured alive." Warner shook his head. "The guy at Yankee Stadium bit a cyanide capsule and now Novak. These guys won't be taken alive."

Andrews said, "Let's see if headquarters reaches the same conclusion." After calling DC, he said, "Albany is on full alert with every available police officer on the street. The state patrol and FBI are covering the bus and train stations. I'll call Biddeford."

~ ~ ~

FBI Headquarters, DC – Friday Morning

Two staff investigators at FBI headquarters were calling colleges in NYC and Boston, looking for German students that had studied in the United States between 1935 and 1940. The list had over a hundred names, far too many for a meaningful investigation. At 3 p.m., Columbia University in NYC called back. "We have two professors that taught the German language in the past ten years. Gunther Engel, an outspoken German nationalist, was here in 1931–32. The professor that replaced Engel left in 1933.when the university cancelled the class, he was fifty-six. I'm sending Engel's records and a photo to the NYPD, Lawrence can do an updated sketch."

~ ~ ~

Biddeford, Maine – Friday Noon

Jones and Dunsmore arrived at the office to learn Pastor Novak had committed suicide in Albany. Sam Griffiths wasn't surprised; he'd wanted to check on Novak before they went to bed in the wee hours this morning.

Griffiths said, "I'll watch Martz. If he leaves the cabin, I'll arrest him."

Dunsmore smiled, "Thanks, Sam, Charlie and I will clean up the details."

After Sam left, Joyce said, "Hoping you guys would call, I didn't leave here till nine last night. With the wild storm, I couldn't sleep so did some reading. About eleven or later, I went to the window to check on the storm. Lightning struck across the road and scared the daylights out of me. When lightning flashed again, thought I saw a black car going south with the lights off. Read a few more pages and went to the window again, but they were fogged from the rain and cold weather, could barely make out the road so I went to bed. I checked this morning and no cars were parked on the road."

Jones said, "That car could have been Novak meeting more German agents. He used Fortune Rocks two weeks ago. Did you mention the car to Warner?"

"Since I wasn't sure what I saw, I didn't mention it."

Jones urged Dunsmore. "Call him, Emmit. If Novak was found in Albany, the spies are there, too."

"I'll call Warner first then we'll check the pastor's cottage and the cabin Schroeder was using."

~ ~ ~

Albany, NY – Train Station

Early afternoon in the busy Albany train station, Engel bought a ticket for the five o'clock train to NYC. The clerk said, "You are lucky, there are only five coach tickets left. The five o'clock has a dining car and a bar car, enjoy your trip."

Planning to eat dinner on the train, Engel ordered a tuna sandwich and milk shake at the coffee shop. After lunching, he purchased a suit and accessories at a downtown men's store and agreed to pay five dollars extra to have alterations finished in an hour. As he walked to a hotel, there was a noticeable police presence on the streets that wasn't there an hour ago. *They could be looking for Novak.*

Early evening Engel left the hotel to board the crowded five o'clock train to NYC. Dressed in a new blue suit, red tie, and carrying a soft-sided briefcase he looked like one of thirty or forty passengers that boarded with him. Standing next to the conductor was a state trooper checking IDs. The identification he used at the hotel read Charles Miller with an address in the Queens. The trooper eyed the driver's license and said, "Have a good trip, Mr. Miller."

A conductor directed him to his seat. "Is the bar car serving?"

"Yes sir, but it's crowded. If you're planning to eat, I would go to the dining car and make a reservation. They always run out of food on Friday nights and you'll end up with a peanut butter sandwich. They never run out of peanut butter."

He handed the conductor a dollar. "Sounds like good advice. Thank you."

The dining car had a line with a waiter taking reservations. "I'll see you at seven, Mr. Miller. Please be on time, there's lots of folks needing to eat."

Engel joined a line at the bar car.

A waiter asked, "Would you like a drink while you're waiting, sir?"

"Yes, please. A glass of beer would be fine."

"We only serve cocktails in this line, sir. Cocktails are a dollar with a quarter tip, and you need to pay in advance."

"I'll have an old-fashioned, please."

The man behind him said, "First timer on the Friday night train to NYC, you must be a lobbyist. I'll have a Manhattan, waiter."

"We like to say we're consultants. I'm involved in education."

"The last time I asked that question, the guy said he worked in religion. Regardless of what you call it, we're all lobbyists."

"Where did that expression originate?"

"At the end of a busy day, President Grant would walk to the hotel and sit in the lobby with a glass of whiskey while smoking a cigar. When the power brokers found out, they lined up to buy Grant a drink so they could sit in the lobby, pushing their cause. Some newspaper reporter called them lobbyists and the name's been in use ever since."

~ ~ ~

After a drink in the bar car, Engel and his new friend, Brent Knowles, had the same time reserved for dinner and decided to dine together.

Knowles represented the Association of Bicycle Manufacturers. "Working with the states to have uniform safety laws is my job. There are many accidents and injuries taking place that are preventable. I want bike safety taught in the fourth grade and one assembly a year on the subject."

"I've been in Europe several times. Some kids wear helmets while riding bikes."

"Helmets would save hundreds of lives every year, but that's not going to happen in the states for some time. You're an education consultant, make it part of the curriculum, and some states will use it. If bike safety laws reduce injuries and deaths, states will adopt them."

They both ordered prime rib with mashed potatoes, green beans and tossed salad.

The waiter asked, "Would you like something to drink with your meal?"

Knowles responded, "My friend bought the last round, it's my turn. A bottle of Taylor Cabernet Sauvignon, please."

Engel held up his half empty glass of beer. "Cheers, Brent. Cabernet will be perfect with prime rib, but I've had my limit."

"The man knows his limit. Make that a glass of wine."

Engel wolfed down dinner and followed it with cherry pie a la mode and coffee. It was his first solid meal in two weeks. He leaned back in his chair and sighed. "I was up early and missed breakfast to attend a meeting."

The waiter said, "I don't want to rush you, gentlemen, but there are folks waiting to eat. Please pay now, and thank you for choosing the New York Central."

Knowles smiled and handed the waiter a ten. "Keep the change."

Engel read the bill upside-down; it was less than eight dollars. His bill was slightly more, and he handed the waiter another ten. "That's good, waiter, thank you for the excellent service."

"Thank you, gentlemen, enjoy the rest of your trip."

Knowles said on the way out, "I've been in the last seating a couple times, limited menu. Do you have a business card, Charles?"

"I'm sorry, I don't. We moved the middle of the month and the secretary missed my name when the new cards were printed. Give me your card and we'll have lunch later this month."

"Good idea. I'll be back in Albany next week. Perhaps the week after will work. Good night, Charles."

As Engel walked away, Trooper Reynolds tapped a passenger on the shoulder. "Follow Miller when he leaves the train."

Bob Justice rode the five o'clock train on a regular basis, tracking politicians making frequent contact with the mafia. Today, the trooper checking passengers suggested he follow Miller. The man spoke good English, but he seemed to be hiding something. Suddenly it dawned on him, Miller looked brand new, suit, shirt, tie, and shoes. Most guys on the Friday night train had a disheveled look, wrinkled suit, scuffed shoes and a five o'clock shadow. Miller should have taken a nap in his suit to blend in.

CHAPTER 42

New York City

Friday Night, May 1, 1942

Engel waited several minutes before detraining. Men working in intelligence had a certain aura about them. Try as they may, the look traveled with them. The man he suspected of being an FBI agent hadn't left the train yet. *He's probably behind me. Act normal and I can lose him.*

Twenty minutes passed before Engel stepped off the train, claimed his bag and headed to the ticket windows to purchase a one-way ticket on the midnight train to Atlanta, Georgia. The terminal was packed shoulder-to-shoulder with hundreds of men in uniform. The ticket windows were on the other side of the terminal which helped him make an important decision. Following anyone in this crowd would be difficult so there was no need to purchase another ticket as part of a ruse to escape detection. He sensed there were FBI agents searching the crowd, but none had asked for his ID.

Engel went to the restroom to change into something more comfortable. He replaced the suit with slacks and a cardigan sweater to wear under a dark raincoat. He added a mustache, glasses, and a flat hat for a new look.

FBI Agent Bob Justice observed Engel from a safe distance. On the job since eight in the morning, fatigue was setting in. The crowd moved him away from the restroom and there was nothing he could do to stop it. Looking for another agent was senseless. Tracking a suspect in these conditions was nearly impossible, and Engel probably changed clothes in the restroom.

A soldier asked, "Where can I buy a ticket?"

Justice answered, "Move with the flow, they're going in the right direction."

Engel didn't see his tail. *Now's my chance to get away.* He placed a cyanide capsule in his mouth and headed to the subway for a train to Manhattan. From experience, he knew expensive hotels in Manhattan had vacant rooms on Friday nights.

~ ~ ~

Special agent Larry Pennoyer, in charge of the FBI office in NYC, needed the NYPD artist to create a current likeness of Engel. He called Detective Richard Tracy to explain the information Columbia University had provided and what FBI headquarters had learned.

Pennoyer said, "The Biddeford Police identified Pastor Novak as the local contact. He fled Biddeford and when caught by a state trooper, committed suicide by biting cyanide capsule at the Albany airport. Chief Dunsmore thinks Novak picked up another team of German agents last night and drove them to Albany."

Pennoyer continued, "A professor named Engel taught the German language at Columbia in 1932. He was an outspoken Hitler supporter now in his mid-forties. Columbia provided a ten-year-old photo of Engel. We need a current likeness to cover the bus terminals and Grand Central Station. If your artist can perform his magic, we might get Engel today. There's no information on his partner."

"Meet me at the office in forty-five minutes. I'll brief the commissioner and police chief if they haven't left for the weekend." Tracy's voice sank. "God help us if this team is equipped with the same terror devices. The thought of another Harlem or Latin dance hall getting terrorized sends shivers up and down my spine."

Pennoyer responded, "Our press didn't report the terror attacks. The Germans had no way of knowing if the devices were used or their effectiveness. We need to prepare for more terror attacks."

Tracy agreed. "Unfortunately, you're right. I'll ask the commissioner to go 24/7 on Saturday. He'll want definitive proof the spies are here, and we don't have it."

"The man charged with helping the agents is dead. The car Novak drove is going through forensics with no clear evidence of other passengers. The commissioner will just have to trust us on this one."

"The artist may be gone. He's worked long hours this month. We can clean up the old photo and have copies on the street for the night shift."

"Having sketches at the terminals will help. Albany has three afternoon trains to the city. Engel could be on one of them. I'll see you later, Rich."

Tracy didn't reply. *If Pennoyer thinks we're going to find Engel on Friday night in Grand Central Station, we'll need an army.* Rich checked his watch on the way to headquarters, muttering, "Fat chance of meeting with the commissioner at five o'clock on Friday afternoon."

The city relaxed after the spies were eliminated two weeks ago. Without concrete evidence, the powers-to-be won't listen.

The commissioner was due back at noon on Monday, and without his blessing, Tracy was helpless. The May training class for new recruits had been cancelled and retirees were complaining when asked to work consecutive days. The NYPD was short-handed, and there was nothing they could do about it.

At headquarters, the regular artist had the weekend off. Featured in magazines for years, Guy Murray, a seventy-year-old cartoonist, had volunteered his time.

"If you have a good photo, Lieutenant Tracy, I can draw a current likeness."

"The photo came from Columbia, it's ten years old."

"That's all I need," Murray stated as Pennoyer walked in. He couldn't help notice the respect the two men had for one another.

"You have the picture?"

Pennoyer handed him the picture, saying, "Aren't you Guy Murray?"

"None other," Murray said, studying the picture with a magnifying glass. "The man in this picture is starting to bald. He might be partially bald ten years later; I have no way of knowing. With a toupee, mustache, and glasses, he would look considerably different."

Pennoyer looked to Tracy. "That's the only picture we have, but I have the form he filled out for Columbia with age and physical characteristics."

Murray pointed out, "People change in ten years, hairline and weight for most men. I'll add ten pounds and pattern baldness, that's the best I can do."

Tracy said, "That will help our detectives and the FBI, but not the cop on the street. We'll take any help we can get."

"You two go for dinner. I'll be finished in an hour."

After they ordered, Tracy said, "The city let its guard down, we're not ready for terror attacks. Nothing will happen until the spies explode another device. We haven't the manpower to cover the city night and day."

"We wouldn't be talking if Dunsmore and Jones hadn't followed their instincts." Pennoyer continued, "They were sure the Germans would land at Hampton Beach Thursday night, and they were there to greet them. Dunsmore thinks Hampton Beach was a ruse, and Novak picked up the agents at Fortune Rocks. The gal that works for Dunsmore couldn't locate Novak Friday morning and suggested we contact the Ford dealer. Novak changed plates Thursday afternoon and was caught Friday stealing a car to make his getaway."

Tracy noted, "Dunsmore has good instincts, but the powers in NYC wouldn't listen to him. The NYPD will do our best to cover the city. The FBI can cover the major subway stations and terminals."

"I'll have additional agents by noon." Pennoyer shook his head. "What if Engel decides to use a device tonight. He didn't spend as much time as Langer in the city, but he lived here for a year. He might have a target for tonight and there's nothing we can do if he gets out of Grand Central Station."

Their meals arrived and Tracy said the grace. "Please, Lord, give us the wisdom to stay a step ahead of the German agents, and the strength to catch them before they hurt others. Amen."

Pennoyer raised his head. "Well said, Rich, we're going to need help."

~ ~ ~

Standing on the subway train to Manhattan, Engel looked like the other men, anxious to get home. He remembered a Bronx swing club he frequented ten years ago. The place would be packed with servicemen and plenty of young women chasing

them. *Check into the hotel first and set the device around midnight.*
A subway station three blocks from the club offered a secure
getaway. Getting back to the hotel after two a.m. would be typical
behavior on Friday night. Better to use the device without the
smallpox virus. A hotel close to 42nd Street has clean rooms
with a reasonable rate for NYC.

~ ~ ~

When Pennoyer and Tracy returned from dinner, Guy Murray
had taken his work to the reproduction room to have copies
made.

Returning to the office, Murray smiled. "I understand
Lawrence drew updated sketches of the spies captured two weeks
ago, he's an exceptional talent. There are three likenesses. I dressed
him in a navy-blue suit with red tie in likeness one. He's wearing
a jacket with a Yankee cap and mustache in likeness two. Likeness
three has him wearing a raincoat with wire frame glasses, mustache
and old Giants cap. If he's out at night, I'm betting on the raincoat
with the collar turned up. No cartoonist would draw a spy with the
collar flat. The copies will be here shortly."

The man doing the reproductions came in with three boxes
of copies. "It's a good thing I ran fifty of each before the big run.
I'll have the rest in a couple of hours, the press is down. Nothing
serious, the repairman has the part. I'll be operational by ten and
the copies will be available for the early shift."

Pennoyer eyed a copy. The man in the blue suit looked to
be forty-five to fifty with graying sideburns and medium build,
it looked just like Engel. The other copies with mustache and
glasses were not as distinguishable. He took twenty-five of each,
saying, "There's a car waiting for me with three agents to cover
Grand Central. Maybe we can catch Engel tonight."

"Good luck, Larry, I need to complete a report for the precinct captains."

At Grand Central, Pennoyer directed two agents, "Cover the ticket windows until eleven. The rest of us will take the cab stand and exit doors. If you see Bob Justice from Albany, give him copies. There are two agents from Boston, Lowell and McCann, circulating in the crowd. They're new, we've never met them. If Engel is smart, he'll stay in the terminal and grab a subway train going north. Park the car, Joe, and meet me at the front doors."

CHAPTER 43

New York City

Friday Night, May 1, 1942

Engel carried his own luggage after checking into the hotel. Much better for him, a bellhop could identify him. As he sat on the bed handling a terror device, anxiety began to set in. *I'm putting myself at risk by terrorizing civilians, and for what?* The servicemen dancing at the club will be wearing winter uniforms the darts can't penetrate. Even if successful, his effort wouldn't sink a single American ship delivering munitions to Germany's enemies. An elitist Nazi, he often spoke of cowardice displayed by French troops in the battle for France. Staring at the device on the bed, he paced the floor for several minutes to regain his courage. "Follow your plan, Gunther, sinking convoys can wait till tomorrow."

Engel placed the device and trigger in his coat pockets before checking the subway schedule. Wanting to arrive at the swing club about 11:30, he decided to take a bus and walk two blocks to the club. A restaurant close to the hotel had espresso coffee and a large display case of pastries, a treat he enjoyed several times when he lived in the city.

At the swing club, Engel walked into a party atmosphere. The floor was packed with young couples doing the jitterbug, a dance he hadn't seen or heard of. Many of the scantily clad girls were trying to teach their partners (mostly servicemen) the jitterbug with little success. The girls whirled and twirled with little help from their partners.

An older waitress approached him, "The tables are full, are you alone?"

"I'm meeting my daughter and her boyfriend at midnight; they sent me to get a table."

"People come and go, first come, first served. There are three parties waiting, so you could have a table by midnight. What's your pleasure?"

"A glass of beer would do. Can I stand here, the bar looks crowded?"

"A bottle of beer is fifty cents on Saturday, with a dime tip. Please pay in advance."

Engel sorted through his change, handing the waitress sixty-five cents."

"I'll be right back."

Engel asked the waitress, "I would like to see the dancer's footwork, can I sit at a table near the dance floor while they're dancing?"

"Not a problem if you promise to leave when the couples return. The band will take a break after this song. The first song after the break will be a slow one, cheek to cheek dancing."

Before the song concluded, several girls left their date to don an apron. Engel spotted a table on the dance floor with a clear path to the door. Sipping his beer, Engel was unaware of the people coming and going.

After midnight the orchestra leader announced, "We've had several requests for *Sentimental Journey*, snuggle up kids."

The empty table Engel wanted seemed okay as he sat down. He had brought a wash cloth from the hotel to wipe the surface dry. Glancing right and left, no one was watching. He removed the adhesive strips from the device before securing it to the table. *I should have brought two; the risk of getting caught is the same.* He rose from the table not noticing a soldier and his girlfriend come through the door.

Army Medic Star Booth was tired after a day of pleasing his newly met date. They had met her sister for lunch, attended a birthday party for a cousin, and he was ready to call it a night, but his new girlfriend wanted to dance. Standing in line for a table, he surveyed the room noticing an older man sitting at a table bordering the dance floor. The man looked out of place as he rose and headed to the door, almost walking backwards. The scene seemed identical to the one he witnessed at the *Dime a Dance* hall in Bayridge. The man glanced at the front door before turning to point something at the table followed by a flash fire and girls screaming from being hit by flying darts.

Engel froze as young girls tore at their blouses and dresses to fight the sudden pain while others beat their heads to put out flames burning their hair and scalps.

"Son-of-a-bitch, he's done it again." Booth charged a statue-like Engel who was horrified by what he had caused. Booth lowered his shoulder hitting Engel in the middle back, smashing his head into a table edge. Engel, knocked cold, never knew what hit him as an enraged Booth banged his face on the floor several times before realizing the man was unconscious. Regaining his composure, Booth headed to the door shouting to no avail, "THERE IS NO FIRE—NO FIRE, stay in the building, there is no fire."

The panicked crowd struggling to get out were stumbling over several girls pushed to the floor in the mad rush to escape the building.

Booth grabbed several servicemen. "Help the girls on the floor, I'll get others to help move the crowd away from the door."

He stood on a chair shouting, "THERE IS NO FIRE—NO FIRE! Stay inside the building, help is on the way."

The orchestra leader shouted on the microphone, "There's no fire, get away from the door, help is on the way. Clear the entrance please, help is on the way."

The bartender called the police and ordered the waitresses to help the people on the floor. Booth approached a screaming girl to remove a dart from her arm tearing the flesh. The injured girl slapped at his hand, "You're hurting me."

"Stay still, help is on the way."

He shouted to others, "Don't remove the metal darts; wait for the doctors to help. Please stay still, please stay still; doctors will be here shortly."

NYPD Detective Steve Stafford was less than a mile from the call and responded in five minutes with a second patrol car close behind.

An officer rushed to the front door with a first-aid kit saying, "I'll help the people on the sidewalk, Sergeant. My partner will call for doctors and ambulances. This looks like another terror attack."

Stafford shouted, "Clear the door, doctors are on the way."

A second patrol car arrived and Stafford instructed, "Clear the street, ambulances will be here in minutes. When help arrives, keep the sidewalk and door clear. I'll go inside to check on the others."

Booth's girlfriend said, "The injured girls need to be sedated before they're treated. They've been struck by metal darts that tear the flesh when removed. My friend tackled the man who did this; he's out cold over there."

"Is he alive?"

"I've been busy helping others, you can check him."

"You're the trained one, you better check him."

When he rolled Engel over, his face was a bloody mess. She shuddered before taking his pulse. "The man is barely breathing, he needs oxygen."

Stafford replied, "Stay with him until help arrives."

Booth approached his girlfriend to get a look at Engel, he had destroyed the man. He took Stafford's arm, "I didn't mean to kill him. He's the man that did this in Bayridge, I was there." Shaking his head, Booth said, "Couldn't control my anger, the son-of-a-bitch has hurt hundreds of innocent people."

Stafford looked into Booth's eyes to see a troubled soul. "You acted in self-defense, good work, Corporal. The doctors are here!"

"Look around officer, the device that did this looks like a clam shell."

"We'll do a thorough search."

"You and your friend have done enough. Have a drink, son, they're on the house."

~ ~ ~

Leaving Grand Central, Pennoyer received a call. The Germans had terrorized a dance hall in the Bronx. The streets surrounding the club were blocked off and medics were carrying young women from the club to waiting ambulances. He found Stafford talking to a soldier who sat wiping tears from his eyes.

After introductions, Pennoyer asked, "Aren't you the same medic that helped in Bayridge?"

"Yes sir. At Bayridge, I saw the man leaving with the others. Tonight, I was standing at the door when he fired the device." Booth broke down. "I don't like hurting people, that's why I joined the medics. There wasn't time to stop him from firing the device, but I charged the man in a fit of rage, couldn't control my anger." Booth started to sob. "May God forgive me, I've taken a life."

Pennoyer looked to Stafford; both had tears in their eyes.

Stafford put his hand on Booth's arm, "My son is a Marine training to fight in the Pacific. Like you, he's serving his country to preserve freedom for others. You didn't kill the man. You reacted to his crime defending your country."

Pennoyer said, "The man is a German spy sent to terrorize our city. He committed an act of war. You're trained to retaliate in the defense of others. He used the terror device, but you had no way of knowing if he had other weapons. You eliminated the threat before Engel could hurt more people."

Booth lifted his head to wipe his face.

Stafford said, "If an enemy soldier charges your position with fixed bayonet while you're treating a comrade, you pick up a nearby rifle and shoot the enemy. If the rifle is empty you use it in self-defense. If necessary to protect your wounded, you kill the enemy."

His girlfriend leaned over to kiss Booth on the cheek. "I'm very proud of you risking your life to protect me and others. You're a good man."

Stafford addressed Pennoyer. "You're free to make the necessary calls and start a preliminary report. I have enough men for the statements. Is there anything happening tomorrow that I need to know?"

"Lieutenant Tracy wanted to go 24/7 until we caught Engel. No need for that now, thanks to Corporal Booth. I'll notify the bureau and state police."

Pennoyer reached for Stafford's hand, "It would have been better to meet under different circumstances. Make sure Booth and the NYPD get proper credit before Hoover gets involved, your men did all the work."

"Thanks, Pennoyer. German agents work in pairs, we're only halfway there."

"We have no idea what the other agent looks like or where he's at. For security reasons, they probably split in Albany and planned to meet in a week or two. Did you know we caught the first team of agents at Yankee Stadium two weeks ago?"

"I heard rumors, never saw the report, not in the loop."

"You're in the loop now. Tracy needs help, and you're up to speed. Don't be surprised if you become one of the team."

~ ~ ~

After Pennoyer made the necessary calls, he dictated a report for his secretary. At four in the morning, he sat back to reflect. The good news and the bad news were the same. With Engel and Novak dead, they had no way of capturing Engel's partner. He could show up at the Polo Grounds with no one meeting him. Marlene Dietrich became famous playing spy roles in European movies. If he or she gets out of Albany and makes it to the city, they could have more devices. Langer might have triggered three devices and Earl one, or Wellenhofer could have triggered one or two. In the previous attacks, no one at the scene had a good look at the terrorist.

As he stretched out on the sofa in his office for some well-earned sleep, wondering, *Where will the lead come from, and how long will it take to narrow the search? Only time will tell.*

CHAPTER 44

Albany, New York

Saturday Morning, May 2, 1942

With ten hours sleep, a refreshed Tesoro dressed in the gray suit he purchased Friday. He wanted to leave the hotel dressed for the wedding he had mentioned to every person working at the hotel. Planning to change clothes in the restroom, Tesoro arrived at seven to catch the eight o'clock bus to Utica, New York. He followed a mother accompanied by three young dark-haired children into the terminal, a perfect family. He turned and smiled at the woman before entering the restroom. Ten minutes later, he walked into the restaurant with a mustache, graying sideburns, and wire-framed glasses looking like his fellow travelers dressed in work pants with flannel shirts and work jackets.

At the newsstand, he saw a book titled *Sin City USA, Utica, New York*. He read the preface, Utica, with a population 101,000, was run by the Mafia and corrupt politicians. It looked like a smaller version of Rome. He purchased a paper to read while enjoying the Saturday breakfast special. The bus originated in Albany had baggage service. As they were checking their bags, the woman and the children didn't recognize him. She spoke Italian to the children and lived in Utica. Tesoro considered changing his ticket to Syracuse, but that could cause unneeded attention.

The baggage handler handed him a stub, saying, "The trip takes three to four hours on Saturday with a bathroom stop."

Tesoro thanked the man and handed him a quarter. Then he waited for the woman and children to be seated before going to the back of the bus.

The trip offered a scenic view of the steep hills and valleys that never seemed to end. The driver used the brakes going downhill and the lower gears to climb the next hill. *German buses with diesel engines are more powerful and better built.*

Utica is situated at the base of the Adirondack Mountains in Mohawk Valley. The old textile mills kept busy making needed cloth to clothe the military. Tesoro planned to use the afternoon studying the city, with dinner and a movie to occupy the evening. A theater near the bus station featured *Yankee Doodle Dandy*.

The clerk at the hotel provided a map of Oneida County. "There's a phone book in your room and four payphones down the hall. Long distance rates change at eleven if you're planning to call home."

"I'm visiting my uncle. Unfortunately, I misplaced his address. Is there a bus going north where he can pick me up?"

"There are two buses a day, one at seven in the morning and the other at 1:30 in the afternoon, the buses are seldom full. Is your uncle a farmer?"

"He's a retired electrical engineer living alone. The last I heard, he was writing a book about the early days of radio."

"The bus uses Route 8. Most of the retirees live in these towns."

"You have been very helpful. I'm looking forward to seeing my uncle tomorrow."

The clerk watched Tesoro walk toward the elevators. An out of work actor, he recognized the clear wire-framed glasses, false mustache, and graying temples as makeup. He looked at the "be on the lookout" alert for suspicious activity. *Why is a guy in his thirties trying to look like a forty-five-year-old local?*

With little trust in the Utica Police Department, he decided to call the state patrol in Albany. The operator suggested he talk with Lieutenant Jeffries.

"My name is Dan Richards. I'm the desk clerk at the Sorrento Hotel in Utica. A man off the Albany bus checked in five minutes ago. He's in his thirties, using makeup to look ten years older. The man registered as Peter Angotti from New York City."

"Strange behavior, what was he wearing?"

"Work pants with a heavy flannel shirt. The guy is trying to look local, but he's too sophisticated to play the part. He plans to visit his uncle tomorrow and spend the night there. At present, he's in his room."

"Don't call the Utica police; I'll be there in two hours. Keep this conversation private, don't confide in others."

"I'll be off duty at eight. Angotti may have plans that run late."

"Can you change shifts with the night clerk?"

"He's a good friend, I can arrange that. I'll offer to buy dinner for him and his girlfriend if the state picks up the tab."

"The state will reimburse you. If he leaves before I get there, note what he's wearing. He might change his disguise hoping to slip by the front desk."

"The hotel has parking in the rear with a doorman on Saturday nights. He could use the stairs and go out through the rear door; his room key fits the lock. There is no way to track his coming and going without covering the rear door."

"I'm on my way with another trooper."

Tesoro took a shower and stretched out on the bed for a nap. Twenty minutes later, sleep hadn't come. Living like a monk wasn't easy, he needed female companionship. In Germany, easy women were part of life for Gestapo agents, and he hadn't been with one for over a month. Certainly, he could score in sin city. Dinner at six, followed by a night of bliss is better than a movie. He set the alarm for five and had no trouble going to sleep.

~ ~ ~

Albany, New York

Jeffries walked into his boss's office knowing he would be rebuked. He explained the situation never moving his eyes from Captain Quinn's face.

"We're short-handed, Jeffries, the troopers assigned to Utica are working in Syracuse, call the FBI."

"Like it or not, Captain, I'm involved in this case. The desk clerk knows I'm coming and arrangements have been made. I'd prefer to take Trooper Graham with me. We'll be back tomorrow."

"If the guy gets away and you pursue him to NYC you won't be back tomorrow. If what you're saying is correct, this is a National Security issue, that's why we have the FBI. Call Bowers, he handled the Novak case."

"His sister is getting married, he's not working today. By the time I explain things to the FBI and they find two men to work the case, the suspect could be in NYC or Erie, Pennsylvania, by tonight. We're wasting time, Captain; time is not on our side."

Captain Quinn shuffled papers before looking up. "All right, Jeffries, I understand your concern. The people upstairs are still mad that you didn't take full credit for catching Novak, they like getting their picture taken." Quinn pulled a report from a pile of papers on his desk. "The Germans hit a club in the Bronx last night. Their hurting New Yorkers, Mark, catch the bastards."

"If he's a German agent, we'll bring him back. I'll have a full report Monday morning."

Jeffries nodded to Trooper Graham. "Do you have your essentials? We're leaving in fifteen minutes."

"Just like you, Lieutenant, I keep a suitcase in my locker. Let's go."

~ ~ ~

After one o'clock at the hotel in Utica, Richards needed to answer the phone and work the front desk until three. Before Jeffries arrived, he had a busy stretch where he couldn't watch the elevators. At three, his friend showed up and Richards went to the office to sit and rest. Shortly after Jeffries and Graham showed up to handle surveillance.

Richards explained, "I was busy for fifteen minutes a while ago and couldn't watch the elevators."

"I'm sure you did your best. If this is the suspect we're looking for he hasn't had much sleep in the past three weeks. I'd say he's in his room making plans to take advantage of the night life in sin city. Please don't ask why he's a suspect."

"My friend will handle the desk until six, then I'll take over."

"Trooper Graham does caricatures. Tell him what Angotti looks like and he can create a likeness."

Twenty minutes later Graham had a likeness, "Does this look like the man?"

"Yeah, that's good, but I forgot to tell you he was a wearing an English tweed flat cap. The cap looked newer than the rest of his clothes."

Graham replied, "I don't draw caps or hats."

Jeffries praised his effort. "You did a good job, Graham, at least we have an idea what he looks like." Then to Richards, "Do you have a bellhop uniform that fits either of us? I wear a 42 long suit coat."

"They come small, medium, and large. The large should work."

Jeffries said, "Take the back door, Graham; I want to watch the front door."

Richards added, "By the way, Angotti has room 402."

~ ~ ~

When Tesoro woke at five that afternoon, he took ten minutes to stretch his aching muscles. After a short break, he did two sets of thirty pushups followed by a series of exercises using his own muscles for resistance. In the shower, he doused his head and washed his hair, then showered and washed his hair a second time to get rid of the makeup. He selected a white shirt with a black pinstripe and burgundy tie to wear with the gray suit. He combed his hair straight back after slicking it down with a hair dressing. The suit accented his youthful build; he looked like a thirty-year-old Italian gangster on the way up to the top. *Perfect, absolutely perfect!*

Tesoro felt safe in Utica, but his training dictated a cyanide capsule be in the mouth at all times. He took it out at the front desk when checking into the hotel. He placed a cyanide capsule in his suit coat pocket. After checking the lock on his door, Tesoro turned to see a man having difficulty with his key.

He smiled, "Let me help you, these locks can be tricky."

"Thank you, I cut my hand yesterday."

Tesoro opened the door and accidentally handed the man his key. 'There you go, have a good evening."

"Having a good evening is why I came to Utica, Thanks for the help."

Tesoro rode down with another couple. As he left the elevator, the bellhop asked the couple, "May I see your key please?" Then to Tesoro, "Please wait, sir; I need to check all keys."

"It's right here." He handed the key to the bellhop.

"Sorry to trouble you sir, there's been a mix-up in keys. Handing the key back to Tesoro, the bellhop wished him a good night.

Trained to notice differences in protocol, Tesoro crossed the lobby to watch the bellhop. He was asking everyone riding the elevators for their key. He looked at his key, room 405. *I must have given the guy across the hall my key when I helped him open the door, I'm in room 402.* The last thing he wanted was a scene of any kind. He placed a cyanide capsule in his mouth.

Working the front desk, Richards had his eye on the elevators. He noticed Angotti crossing the lobby and observing Jeffries. When Angotti looked at his key, his face registered a surprised look. He sat still for several minutes with a perplexed expression, not knowing how to handle a change of events. Richards waved to his friend to handle the desk and went to the elevators with a key in his hand.

He addressed Jeffries, "Take this key from me, the man in the gray suit could be your man, and he's sitting behind you. For some reason he has the wrong key, this is the second key to room 402."

"He didn't have 402. The man looks much younger than the guy you described."

"Makeup, Lieutenant. He can't overpower you from a sitting position, but he could outrun you. I can defend myself, I'll go with you for backup and hand him the key."

Tesoro watched the desk clerk address the bellhop holding a key. *Makes sense*, he thought, *the keys are mixed up.* As the smiling desk clerk approached, he felt uneasy. He rose to greet them, *Act normal, this is no big deal.*

Richards spoke, "I didn't check you in, may I see your key please?"

Tesoro handed him the key to room 405.

"Mr. Bradley is in room 405, you have his key."

Tesoro needed to answer quickly, "I helped the man in 405 open his door, I must have given him my key. I'm in room 402."

Jeffries stepped forward, "You're under arrest, Mr. Angotti, hands over your head."

Richards moved to his left, making it difficult for Tesoro to run or attack one of his accusers before the other would respond. "What am I charged with?"

"Put your hands over your head or I'll use force. You're under arrest."

Tesoro placed his hands over his head. *The war is over for me.* "Have it your way." He bit the cyanide capsule.

Richards watched his expression change as he slumped to the floor.

Jeffries responded, "The bastard bit the cyanide capsule, he'll be dead when I check his pulse." He turned to Richards. "Get my partner and notify the Utica police."

When Jeffries rolled the body over, the stench of cyanide filled the air. *These guys won't be taken alive.* "Please stand back, folks, the man had too much to drink."

A man asked, "What's that smell?"

Before Jeffries could answer the question, Graham showed up with badge in hand. "State police, please clear the lobby."

Richards asked, "Why did he commit suicide?"

"Our friend was headed to the electric chair, he's wanted for murder in Vermont. Who he is and why he committed suicide isn't important. The man took his own life; that's your story for reporters until you here from me next week. If people pressure you, tell them the case is under investigation and a full report will be available when the case is closed. Can you handle that?"

"I'm an actor, Lieutenant; I can play any part with a straight face." Richards sighed. "The military doesn't want me, I'm near-sighted. Catching a German spy is my way of serving my country."

"You were on the front lines, young man. What you did tonight saved lives and prevented the Germans from harming civilians. In the last month, German agents have killed two men and injured hundreds more in NYC."

"I'd swear he's Italian."

"Maybe a thorough investigation will reveal why an Italian was in German intelligence."

"You could find his name when you search the room."

"Not my job. The FBI will search the room. The Utica police will guard the door until they get here."

"I'll go back to the desk, my friend's girl just walked in."

"Have him send the bill to me, here's my card."

"Do you want rooms for tonight?"

"No thank you, we're going home. I want to attend church tomorrow with my family; this has been a hectic week."

CHAPTER 45

Biddeford, Maine

Monday Morning, May 4, 1942

Andrews and Warner arrived at the police station before noon on Monday.

Joyce greeted them. "We have two-thirds of the three musketeers, Emmit. There really is an FBI."

"Still the same sweet Joyce I fondly remember," Andrews quipped.

"Other women may desert you, but I'll be here to the end."

Dunsmore came out of his office. "You must be headed to Portland. Take the Amsels and Martz with you. Biddeford is overcrowded with Nazi sympathizers."

Warner said, "We're taking them back to Boston, Chief. Martz could wind up in the slammer. The Amsels are headed to an internment camp in Pennsylvania. We'll be here overnight to help the Amsels pack and make plans to close their home. Same goes for Martz if he cooperates."

"Sam Griffiths said Martz went to work this morning, the boat should be docking between two and three."

Dunsmore added, "Karl Amsel isn't the kind of man to take chances. He may have objected to his wife getting involved."

Andrews replied, "Makes no difference," Chief, "he didn't report her."

Dunsmore frowned. "It will take months for our town to heal. Aldrich and Novak will be sorely missed. Hopefully, we'll go back to business as usual when the summer people start showing up in six weeks."

Warner asked, "Did you find anything in Novak's cottage?"

Dunsmore replied. "Whatever he used went with him when he left town."

"Our forensics team searched the car with the same results. At this point, it appears the Germans sent four agents with nothing to show for their effort. The terror attacks were a diversion while they set up shop to spy on convoys." Andrews looked to Dunsmore. "We have time to kill, Chief, join us for lunch?"

"If you promise not to discuss spies, I'll have lunch with you."

Warner chuckled, "Our interest is catching striped bass. Can you get that Willie fellow to take us fishing this fall?"

~ ~ ~

Monday Morning – Aboard U-boat 74

When the crew reported a plane circling the area and a destroyer bearing down fast, *Korvettenkapitan* Merkel knew their boat could be in serious trouble. He quickly changed course to NE and sent for *Kapitan* Hruby.

"*Kapitan*, there's a plane overhead and a destroyer closing quickly. I've set a northeast course to reach deeper water in fifteen minutes."

Hruby ordered, "Man battle stations! I'll take over."

Merkel added, "Ship following is faster than normal, our crew suspects it's a new warship."

The new destroyer, recently commissioned in Philadelphia, was wrapping up a week of sea trials when the call came to confront a German U-boat.

The new destroyer traveled at 21 knots. A U-boat made seven knots submerged.

The veteran captain's inexperienced crew had shown improvement since sailing, but they had a long way to go. With help from a PBY (pontoon surveillance plane), the captain was certain they could sink the enemy ship. The PBY radioed, 'Your course is correct; we have the target on our radar. Follow us and we'll sink the bastards.'

The destroyer in fast pursuit, Hruby ordered, "DIVE! ... DIVE! The *Kapitan* next ordered, "All engines stop!" U-boat 74 settled softly on the ocean floor.

Five minutes later, they heard the destroyer pass directly overhead. The ship dropped depth charges set to explode at 100 feet. The multiple explosions unnerved the crew.

Several minutes passed before the destroyer dropped a second set of charges set to explode at 150 feet. The crew of the submarine wiped their brows as charges exploded all around shaking their *boot* mightily.

Kapitan Hruby put a finger to his lips to indicate silence while waving his other hand up and down trying to calm young crew members new to combat.

The destroyer again passed over their position before unloading a third set of depth charges set to explode ten feet above the ocean floor.

Exploding drums punished their boat mercilessly, creating havoc. Merkel and other officers quickly lit lanterns and went to work temporarily securing leaking pipes. Minutes later, U-boat 74 sent an oil slick to the surface with the usual worn-out clothes and items a submarine carries.

The destroyer didn't fall for their ruse and fired another barrage of depth charges with two direct hits on the German target. The submarine lurched sideways when a charge hit the stern. Before the crew could recover, a charge exploded aft of the conning tower, instantly killing *Kapitan* Hruby and most of his crew.

On board the destroyer, the crew saw the huge explosion and knew U-boat 74 would forever remain on the ocean floor.

Prepared to rescue survivors, the new warship waited twenty minutes as debris floated to the surface.

The executive officer said, "No survivors, Captain, time to head for home."

The captain shook hands with his executive officer, saying, "You congratulate the men, I never get close to the crew."

CHAPTER 46

When Pennoyer and Tracy searched Engel's hotel room, they found three terror devices and a code book. The FBI reported the capture of two German agents by the New York State Patrol, the NYPD, and the FBI. The federal government, knowing Engel carried a weapon capable of delivering the smallpox virus, didn't want the public to panic. Newspapers played down the terror attacks to focus on the spies and the Biddeford contact being captured.

Author's Notes:

German U-boat VII had a crew of fifty men. The boat made 14 knots on the surface using diesel engines. Submerged, it made 7 knots with battery-powered engines. In 1944, newly designed German submarines were equipped with diesel engines that increased the surface speed to 21 knots. Germany lost its submarine port when the Allies invaded France in April 1944 and few of the newer boats saw service.

The PBY was named by the company that designed it. The plane was used extensively in the Pacific Theater and the Atlantic to scout for submarines, rescue downed pilots, and deliver Special Forces to enemy territory. For those interested in World War II movies, the plane is featured in *Midway* and *In Harm's Way*.

Review Requested:

If you loved this book, would you please provide a review at Amazon.com?